Ways to Improve Bailey

CORI COOPER

© 2026 Cori Cooper

www.coristories.com

Cover Art by Cori Cooper

All rights reserved, including the right to reproduce this book or portions thereof in any form whatsoever.

This book is a work of fiction. Names, characters, businesses, organizations, places, events and incidents either are the product of the author's imagination or are used fictitiously. Any resemblance to actual persons, living or dead, events, or locales is entirely coincidental.

ISBN 978-1-953491-53-4 (Paperback)

ASIN B0BYWQS15R (Kindle Edition)

To Jackee and Melissa
Inklettes Forever

Ways to Improve Bailey #11

Tell the truth

I really need to tell a lie right now.

When I made that stupid promise to my stupid brother, Dayton, last week, I didn't realize how hard it was going to be to tell the truth all the time.

"Bailey?" Marnie's big brown eyes reminded me of Bambi. "I asked you what you think about Todd."

Exactly the problem. If she had asked me what I thought about the new Ryan Reynolds movie or Dove moisturizer cream, I could give her a pretty awesome monologue. Asking me about Todd was just mean.

"Oh, shoot, Marnie! Would you look at that gummy bear bin? It's totally empty. I should refill those right now."

I went to work as if gummy bears were the most important thing in the whole world. Right up there with keeping your Netflix subscription current.

Marnie eyeballed the half empty bin for just a moment before her eyes lit up. "Did you notice who's buying all the gummy bears?"

"I didn't, sorry." I stuck my bottom lip out in gross exaggeration.

Gross exaggeration is not lying.

Well, probably not.

"Oh, too bad!" Marnie mimicked my pouty face, except hers was totally sincere. "That's okay, though. I'll try to pay attention while I'm here. Gummy bears are *so* tricky to match. They go with gummy worms, of course, and chocolate, and any of the fruit toppings, but that's pretty much it."

"Um hm." I pulled a new package out from under the counter and looked around for the scissors. "Wait, what do you mean gummy bears are tricky to match?"

Most likely this was another one of Marnie's Pinterest-inspired projects, but it didn't really matter. What mattered was that she gave me the perfect opportunity to change the subject. The more we talked about something else, the less we talked about Todd. And the less we talked about Todd, the better.

Marnie licked her spoon and dipped it back into her frozen yogurt cup. "Didn't I tell you? I thought I did."

I shook my head.

"Bailey, it's the most amazing thing! I can totally match people together, like as couples, based on their favorite frozen yogurt or ice cream and what they choose to put on top."

I paused with the scissors poised in the air. "Are you for real?"

"Yes!" Marnie nodded so enthusiastically that her brown curls bounced around her head like manic springs. "I had the idea when Ricky and I broke up. I can't believe I didn't tell you about this!"

"You told me about Ricky." I sliced open the top of the gummy bear bag. "I remember cause that's when you decided you were giving up on love forever."

Marnie leaned her cheek into her hand, making her lips pooch out. "Oh, yeah. That's right. For a little while there, I thought love was *impossible*! It looks so easy in the movies. Meet the perfect person, fall in love, have a three-quarters-through-the-movie falling out, make up, get married. Simple, right?"

"Sure," I nodded. "Easy peasy."

"But then," Marnie straightened and laid her spoon on the counter, so she could emphasize all her words with hand gestures, "I watched a documentary about penguins. Penguins mate for life; did you know that? And the male sits on the egg. It's crazy! I was eating a huge bowl of chocolate ice cream with fudge on top, and I had this flash of inspiration: Ricky always ate sherbet with zero toppings, and I always choose chocolate ice cream with chocolate toppings. Sherbet and chocolate do not go together. That's why we didn't work."

There was no doubt that Marnie was completely serious. She fully believed that what she said was true. It was lucky she didn't ask my opinion about it because lying would be necessary to preserve our friendship.

"I tested it out with some of our friends," Marnie said.

"Who?" Now I was interested. It was like getting sucked into the tabloids at the grocery store. The more ridiculous, the better.

"Darek likes banana-flavored everything, and Hazel is obsessed with peanut butter, so they are meant to be together. Also, Randy and Zuri. He likes coconut, and she's crazy about pineapple. See?"

Marnie spread her hands to the sides like that was all the proof I would ever need. "It really works! Well, actually it only works if the flavors and toppings are the person's very favorite, not just a craving or a whim. That's why I need to know what you think about Todd. He always chooses peanut butter, so he might be the one for me."

Wait, how did she circle back around to Todd so fast? I didn't even get a chance to head her off.

Diabolical.

I looked down at the bag of gummy bears that was still sitting on the counter in front of me, then remembered that I was supposed to be restocking the toppings. I tugged the gummy bear bin out of place and set it next to the bag. "Why do you need to know what I think about Todd? It sounds like a match made at Reese's."

"Yeah," Marnie picked up her spoon and swirled tight figure eights through her yogurt. "It does sound perfect, but it doesn't feel right."

"Why not?" I tipped the bag into the bin and watched the gummy bears fall in an avalanche.

So satisfying.

Marnie shrugged one shoulder. "I don't know."

Well, that was ridiculous. I could give her a thirty-minute lecture on why it didn't feel right entitled "Dating Todd Is a Horrible Idea." Instead, I pretended to drop the gummy bear bag and ducked under the counter to hide my grimace.

Grimacing is not the same as lying, either.

When I stood back up, my face was as smooth as soft serve. "Chocolate can go with a lot of things, Marnie, not just peanut butter. Even if your matchmaking thing works, it doesn't have to mean Todd is the *only* guy you can be happy with."

There was a long silence as Marnie stared into space, tapping her spoon against her cheek.

"Okay, Marnie. Spill your guts." I shoved the bin aside and leaned towards her, my elbows pressing into the countertop. "Why doesn't it feel right?"

"I don't know. That's the problem. He's nice to everyone, and hard-working, and loves kids, and has a dreamy smile."

"*So* dreamy," I mimicked with a wicked grin.

Marnie didn't even notice. She just kept staring somewhere beyond my left ear. "He seems perfect. But then he sometimes does something that just really irks me. I don't know. Maybe it's just me. I'm a bad person."

"Give me a break." I rolled my eyes, but Marnie didn't notice.

"Help me out here, Bailey. What do you think about Todd? Tell me honestly."

And we were back.

I *hated* that we were back.

"I think Todd is…" I turned away to plop the gummy bear bin into place on the toppings bar. A few spilled onto the counter with the momentum. I tossed some to Marnie and the others into my mouth. The chewing didn't help me find a word to fill in the blank.

Todd is what?

A buffoon?

A cretin?

Annoying? Conceited? Absurd? How could I be in my second semester of college and not be able to find a word that described Todd without offending Marnie? Suddenly, I questioned my university choice. Maybe I should have lived at home and gone to ASU instead of NAU.

"…swell," I blurted.

"Swell?" Marnie narrowed her eyes slightly, but not because she was upset. The scrunched-up face she gave me was just her thinking face. She was trying to figure out what I meant by "swell".

I chose the word because Todd was so full of himself that, at the rate he was going, his head was going to *swell* to epic proportions. Soon, there would not be a single doorway left in Northern Arizona that Todd and his bloated ego could fit through. Marnie would never in a million years put the words "bloated" and "ego" next to each other in a sentence so, basically, I chose the perfect word. Marnie could go on her merry way, thinking I meant "swell" as some kind of retro throwback compliment, and I could rest easy that I kept my promise to Dayton without crushing Marnie's soul. Last time I told her what I really thought about the guy she was dating, the scarred look in her eyes gave me nightmares for a week.

She really needs to start asking my advice *before* she goes out with a guy. We'll both be so much happier that way.

"Yes, Todd is just swell." I smiled with confidence—pretend confidence, but it worked the same way as the real thing. Pretending wasn't lying, either; it's acting. People in California get paid millions of dollars every day to do what I'm doing.

"Yeah?" Marnie chewed on her lower lip.

"Yeah, sure. Of course. Super swell." I tossed the half-full bag of gummy bears back under the counter without looking where it landed. "Anyways, what time are you working at the aqua center tonight?"

Marnie glanced at her watch. "I need to be there in about a half hour. What about you?"

"My first lesson is at six forty-five. Will you still be around?"

"Yes! So, I'll see you tonight. Yay!" She slipped off the bar stool and pulled her purse on her shoulder. "Oh, hi, Keith!"

My manager grunted as he stepped out of the stockroom. The doors swung behind him, swaying back and forth before they finally closed. "You don't have to leave," he said to Marnie. "It's slow today. You girls can keep yakking."

I scoffed. "We were not, and never have been, yakking."

Keith gazed around the empty store and indulged himself with a sigh before he peered at the inventory clipboard in his hands.

"It will pick up," Marnie said brightly. "It's always busier on the weekends."

Ah-ha!

Where was Dayton when I needed him? Everybody, even *Marnie*, tells lies to make people feel better.

Keith jerked a thumb at Marnie but looked at me. "Have I told you how much I like this girl?"

I rolled my eyes all the way to the ceiling and back again. Of course he liked Marnie. Everybody liked Marnie. Marnie was the nicest person on the planet. She was also the most oblivious. She didn't even notice that Keith gave her a compliment; she was too busy thinking of the next thoughtful thing to say.

She should have realized that a compliment from Keith was like finding a one-hundred-dollar bill stuffed between the couch cushions.

"How's your new grandbaby?" Marnie asked.

The girl was good. If there was one thing to take Keith's mind off inventory woes and an empty frozen yogurt store, his new grandbaby was it.

Keith stopped moving as if one of us had hit the pause button. He pulled his phone out of his back pocket and let his glasses slide to the tip of his nose so that he could peer over them.

"My grandbaby," Keith smiled. All the tension leaked out of his shoulders like he was a balloon with a pinhole. "She is an angel. Lookee here." He flicked his thumb at the screen a few times and handed the phone to Marnie.

"Oh!" Marnie cooed and turned the phone so I could see, too.

It was a baby. "Cute."

"No!" Marnie shook her head, her long curls sweeping across her back. "Not just cute, Bailey! Oh. My. Goodness! She is the cutest thing I have ever seen! Look at her tiny little fingers. Keith! She is perfect!" Marnie scrolled through more pictures, her face just inches from the screen. "What's her name?"

Keith leaned over with a creaky groan. "Emmie." He looked so relaxed that I almost didn't recognize him. His face was suddenly void of stress wrinkles. He never looked that way when he was talking to me. "She's something else, huh?"

"Absolutely darling." Marnie pulled her eyes from the screen and pushed the phone back to Keith with the air of a person performing the ultimate sacrifice.

Keith turned to me with a stern look on his face. "It's refreshing to see a girl still go ga-ga for babies. Gives me hope for the rising generation."

"Ga-ga? Really?" I smirked. "Please don't start your next sentence with the words 'back in my day'." I lowered my voice during that last part to sound like an ancient grandpa.

Keith opened his mouth, then closed it again. "Have I fired you yet today?"

"Yep, about an hour ago."

"What for?"

I squinted at the ceiling, trying to remember the specifics. "I squirted whipped cream into my mouth."

"Hm." Keith pushed his glasses back up his nose and shuffled the inventory papers, as though he were reminding himself of how much work he had to do. "You're just lucky I love your parents, Bailey Hendrix."

"I know."

Keith glared at me, trying to hide the smile that was totally obvious, and went back to the stockroom.

I grinned cheekily, waggling my fingers.

Marnie's eyes shifted from the swinging stockroom door to my face. "You really are lucky. This is a great job."

"Yeah?" I tipped my head back to drop a handful of peanut butter chips into my mouth.

"Yes!" Marnie gave me a stern look—well, as stern as Marnie could be—and then leaned over and spoke in a whisper. "Bailey, I really think you hurt Keith's feelings about the baby. You could have been a little more excited."

I shrugged. "I don't see the big deal. It's just a baby. Now, if you want to show me a picture of a Rome cathedral or a pastry in Paris or a Scottish castle, I promise to get all dreamy-eyed and sappy like you just did."

"Oh, Bailey." Marnie smiled at me all indulgently, like I was a toddler playing in the middle of a huge mess. "Don't you ever want to settle down? I mean, I know you want to travel the world and see all the things, but don't you want a family and a home and a handsome husband?"

"Don't you have to get to work?"

"Not quite yet!" She pointed her finger at me. "You are avoiding my question! Come on. Just this once, answer me."

The bell over the door rang, signaling that a new customer had just come into Froyo. I prepared myself for a greeting because Froyo is a place for friendly people or whatever, and because I was super grateful for the interruption. Then, I saw who it was.

"Oh, hey, Tanner." I tried to muster a wave, but my hand flopped down to my side without any real substance to keep it up.

Tanner's eyes darted around the empty store, resting on my face for the barest second before moving on to something else. He let the corner of his mouth quiver into a smile—or a smile-ish thing. To me, it looked more akin to the face people make when they are standing in line at the MVD.

He focused on the corner booth and made his way there, working his way through the maze of tables and chairs as if someone were reeling him in on a line.

"Does he come here every day?" Marnie leaned forward to whisper. "I mean, I feel like I'm here a lot, and he is always here when I am."

I turned on the scale so it would be ready when Tanner was, then went back to Marnie. I waved my hands in front of my face, used my creepiest voice, and slowed the words to build suspense. "Every single day. Like clockwork. At the stroke of two. In he walks. He sets his laptop on the corner table, turns it on, and while the computer loads, he swirls a medium vanilla cup with..."

"Strawberries, please." Tanner dropped a cup onto the scale next to me.

I gave Marnie a knowing look as I reached for the spoon that rested in the container of strawberries. I scooped one spoonful on top of his plain vanilla yogurt.

"Ten ounces on the dot," I said. "That will be..."

Tanner set a ten-dollar bill on the counter and scooted it toward me.

"Keep the change," he said as he took his cup. His total was always the same. Every day he swirled precisely ten ounces, which rang up to exactly five dollars.

Then he gave me a five-dollar tip.

That's the only reason I put up with him.

I exchanged the ten for a five, and then closed the cash register drawer with a slam. Tanner jumped slightly but didn't look at me. Instead, he chose a spoon and a napkin, then made his way back to the corner table and his beloved screen.

I shook my head as I stuffed the five-dollar bill into the empty tip jar. Marnie let out a slow breath. "Wow."

"Right?" I reached for a rag to wipe the counter, even though nothing had spilled. I only did it so I could tell Keith the truth when he asked me later if I'd cleaned up between customers.

"So, does Tanner just sit there like that every day?" Marnie asked. Her neck craned at a strange angle as she tried to stare at Tanner without being obvious.

I nodded. "Every single day, for hours and hours. I keep rotating the chairs at that table, so his booty doesn't mold into the plastic."

Marnie covered her mouth to muffle the giggles, but she didn't need to. The frozen yogurt machine could have unplugged itself from the wall and started salsa dancing across the tile in a bright pink bikini, and Tanner wouldn't have budged. Once he got in the zone of whatever it was he did over there all day, he was like a piece of furniture. In fact, I think I accidentally dusted him a few times.

"I wonder what his story is," Marnie's eyes danced.

"His what now?"

"His story!" Marnie wiggled closer to me. "Everyone has one. Do you think he might be an underworld spy?"

I opened my mouth but stopped myself just in time. I always forgot that Marnie didn't have a sarcastic streak, like, at all. She literally meant everything she said. So, in all seriousness, she sat there imagining Tanner in a James Bond suit and dangling from a helicopter.

"He looks lonely." She tapped her finger on the counter. "Do you think he's lonely? I'm going to match him. What goes with strawberries?"

I didn't even want to know. The thought of someone hooking up with Tanner really did make me want to do some yakking, but not the kind Keith was talking about.

I bit back an extremely not-nice response. This honesty thing was making my brain hurt. From now on, our conversation needed to stay on neutral subjects, like candy and swimming.

Tanner scooted his chair, making it screech obnoxiously in the silent room. "Sorry," he mumbled.

I assumed he was talking to his computer screen since that's what his eyes were glued to.

A smile toyed along Marnie's lips. "I wonder why he comes here all the time."

"Don't know."

Also, don't care.

"Hmmm," Marnie turned to me with bright eyes. "What do you like on *your* frozen yogurt?"

Oh no.

Nonononononononono. She was so not about to match me with Tanner! That was seriously the most offensive thing anyone had ever said to me, and I lived with a brother who made it his mission in life to make my life miserable. He even had a list on his bedroom wall of things I needed to change entitled "Ways to Improve Bailey."

Marnie appraised Tanner discreetly for a couple seconds. "He's cute," she offered.

"Sure, he is, Marnie. The two of us can get married in The Shire and raise our family on the trek to Mordor."

"What?" Marnie's face went blank.

I lowered my voice even more and leaned forward. "Don't you think he looks like a hobbit?"

"He's not short or fat, and I've never seen a hobbit with a beard," she said finally.

I waved her words away with my hand. "Look at his hair. It's all curly and longish. He's like Frodo's twin."

Marnie shifted in her chair. "Maybe."

I let the subject drop. It's not necessary to convince someone of something when you already know you're right. "It doesn't matter. Even if he looked like Zac Efron under all that facial hair, it's still not happening."

Marnie nodded. "Okay, not Tanner. But let me find you someone else. I really think you need a guy."

"Whatever, Marnie. I go out with guys all the time."

"Just on lunch and dinner dates. You need something consistent, a relationship."

She said the "ship" word. I was so done with this conversation.

"Hey, aren't you going to be late for work?" I stuck my watch in her face and tapped it with my finger.

"Yikes! I better run," Marnie said. "But, before I go, I need you to tell me what you like on your frozen yogurt."

"If you don't leave right now, you're going to be really late and Jordan will be super mad." I wiggled my watch to make it look more urgent.

"Fine," she sighed. "Hey, Todd's meeting me after work for dinner. You should come."

I didn't trust myself to say something nice, so I didn't say anything at all.

"Oh, you probably have plans, huh? Where is your date taking you tonight?" Marnie rummaged through her purse for her keys.

My date?

Hopping Milk Duds, my date! I slept in this morning and missed my morning classes, which means I didn't have a chance to convince one of the guys to take me to dinner tonight!

"Are you alright?" Marnie pursed her lips.

I slapped my palms on the counter. "I have to find a date!"

"Does that mean you're free?" Marnie's face lit up. "You could come with Todd and me!"

So not happening. I needed a plan, and I needed one, like, now. Tapping my fingernails on the counter made a spastic clicking noise that helped me think.

Marnie waited.

"Where are you guys going?" I asked, as though I was considering it.

"I don't know. Maybe Wildflower."

"I was just there. Thanks, though." That was not a lie. I'd gone for lunch two days ago with some guy from my biology class. Traeger or something manly like that.

Actually, I think Traeger was his last name.

Didn't matter.

He was not a repeat date.

Marnie's phone chimed.

"It's Todd!" She literally sparkled when she said his name. I would be cleaning glitter off the floor for days.

"Yay," I said with just the teeniest, tiniest hint of sarcasm.

Sarcasm wasn't lying, either.

Her eyes were glued to her phone screen as she asked, "Are you sure about dinner?"

"Yeah, yeah, go." I waved her out the door. "I'll see you at the pool."

Marnie nodded and put her phone to her ear. "Hey, Todd!" She floated out the door to her car. As I watched, I was glad I hadn't burst her bubble by telling her what I really thought about him.

But enough about that.

I had another problem, a bigger problem. A problem which would become urgent in about three hours. Since I didn't go to my morning classes, the only male humanoids I'd seen since saying good-bye to Dayton that morning were Keith, who was married, and Tanner, who was...Tanner. I needed to find a real guy pronto and flirt my way to a dinner date. There was no way I was going to get stuck eating leftovers at home by myself.

It was time to pull out the sample tray.

Ways to Improve Bailey #7

Don't use potty words

"Honey, I'm home," I called as I walked through the front door and kicked it shut behind me. Dayton left it unlocked, as usual, even though it was almost nine o'clock at night.

Despite his high-and-mighty ideals about how I should live my life, Dayton did the dumbest things.

Examples?

He never locked the house, whether he was home or gone for the day.

He put jam in the cupboard instead of in the fridge, even when it consistently grew mold.

And his cell phone battery was always below twenty-four percent, despite the chargers we had plugged in all over the house. There was literally one in every room.

That's just the start of all my evidence that Dayton is a world class nincompoop.

Dayton padded down the hall and met me in the kitchen. He was wearing knee socks, boxers, and an old NAU shirt that used to belong to Dad. "Hey, sweet cheeks. How was your day?"

I glared at him. "Did you get my message?"

He hadn't answered his phone when I called him from work to tell him how his stupid no-lying incentive was complicating my life, so I'd left him a lengthy voicemail.

I yelled a lot.

And disowned him for the thirty billionth time. Not that it made a difference. He never listened to anything I said.

Ever.

Dayton ran his hand through his already messy brown hair and looked around the room with pursed lips. "Uh…no. Have you seen my phone?"

Ten to one it was under his bed, the battery completely drained.

I sighed and opened the fridge. "Is there any leftover pizza?"

"Are you hungry?" Dayton walked over to me, mock concern all over his face. He placed a hand on my shoulder. "Do you mean to tell me you couldn't find a poor sucker to take you out to dinner tonight?"

I shrugged him off. "I had dinner. But then I swam for an hour and taught three rigorous swim lessons to tweens with water issues and helicopter parents. So, I'm hungry again, okay?"

Dayton leaned against the counter and folded his arms. "So, who was the winner winner chicken dinner who took you out tonight?"

I leaned into the fridge so I could talk without getting walloped by Dayton's judgy expression. "You mean who was the lucky guy who got to take your cutest sister on a date?"

"Yeah, that," Dayton said dryly.

"His name was Guy."

Dayton coughed hard into his fist. "That's not his name. No one would do that to their kid. Guy must be a nickname."

"Maybe," I shrugged, pushing aside a half-empty milk carton.

Or was it half full?

"You didn't ask?" Dayton folded his arms. "You went out with some random guy without finding out his entire name?"

"Of course not, Dayton. That would be so irresponsible. Before we went to dinner, I made sure to scrutinize his birth certificate and immunization records. We also stopped by the Urgent Care on the way to the restaurant to leave a sample for drug testing. We should get the results back in forty-eight hours." I pulled out a plastic carton of spring mix and grimaced. "Whose turn is it to clean out the fridge? This is not good."

"Let me see." Dayton took the carton from me and sniffed, then made a face and handed it back to me. "You are so snarky, Bailey. Remind me to add that to the list."

I threw away the slimy salad and ignored my idiot brother. Like I would ever in a million years remind him to add anything to that stupid list. It was already way longer than I wanted it to be.

"Really, I don't like you going out with these random guys we don't know anything about."

I opened the vegetable tray with more force than it needed and had to work to wiggle it back into place. All that work was for nothing, it was completely empty.

"Gruyere."

"Grew what?" I glanced over my shoulder, lifting my eyebrow.

Dayton resumed his lean on the counter. "I bet Guy is short for Gruyere. You know, the cheese?"

"Right." I shook my head. "Because someone would totally name their kid after fancy cheese. Where's the pizza?"

"I finished it, and don't you have a friend named Brie?"

I shot him a double-sided stink-face. One side for talking about cheese and the other for finishing the pizza. I whined to myself as I shoved aside an empty water bottle. I really wanted that pizza.

Though, I guess leftover Thai food didn't sound awful. I reached for the takeout container.

"Yeah, don't eat that. It smells funky." Dayton pulled himself up on the counter and began kicking his legs against the lower cabinets like he was five years old.

"Why didn't you throw it away then?" I opened the lid and jerked back. "Oh, ew! How old is that?"

"Dunno. So, are you going out with this Guy again?"

I gave Dayton a look. "He took me out for fast food, Dayton. What do you think?" I arched the Thai container into the trash. The swish of a perfect shot did not make me feel better. There was nothing left in the fridge except curdled milk and limp lettuce leaves. This was no time to celebrate something as insignificant as a lucky shot. I slumped against the wall and stared at the empty fridge all dejected.

Dayton stopped kicking. "You know, this might be a good teaching moment. Maybe there is no food in this house for a reason. I just read an article somewhere that said it isn't good for you to eat after seven at night."

He looked at the microwave clock. "And it is definitely after seven." His voice turned stern, like it did whenever he decided it was time to improve Bailey.

Fabulous.

I slammed the fridge and pointed a finger at him. "Don't you even start with me, Buck-o."

"Bailey," he said again with the voice, the voice I hate. He drew my name out until it sounded like the words "bay leaf". "I made a promise to Mom and Dad." He placed his hand over his heart, covering the U and part of the Lumberjack's head on his shirt. "I swore I would take care of you, and I take that promise very, very seriously."

I rolled my eyes and opened the freezer while he went on and on about his promise to our parents. He'd delivered this speech so many times that I could say it along with him. And I did, mouthing the most enthusiastic parts with great feeling—just the opposite feelings from those Dayton expressed. Like, instead of Dayton's dogged determination, I felt increasing irritation bubbling up inside of me.

Like a Bailey volcano.

I pulled a half-eaten carton of ice cream out of the freezer and eyeballed it. I should totally have that for dinner, just to bug Dayton. It was super tempting, but I couldn't bring myself to do it. Mediocre, freezer-burned ice cream was so not delicious.

I shoved the carton back inside and closed the freezer. I leaned against it while Dayton wrapped up.

"...And so, I do everything in my power to make sure you are living your life in the very best way possible."

He ended with a look of self-satisfaction that made me want to retrieve the moldy Thai food and throw it at his stupid head. I restrained myself. It was easier to let him bask in his own awesomeness without interruption, so we could move on to something else.

Dayton reached across the sink to the fruit bowl and tossed me a wrinkly apple.

"Thai food and pizza are too heavy for this time of night. You'll get indigestion or something. Let this be a lesson to you: eat a healthy, appropriate-sized dinner at the regularly scheduled dinner time."

I caught the apple with one hand. "Yeah? When did you eat dinner?"

Dayton shook his head. "We aren't talking about me."

"Dayton," I said, fully exasperated, "you realize you are only, like, eighteen months older than me?"

His eyes widened. "That is not the point. I made a promise to Mom and Dad." He jabbed his index finger onto the counter thirteen times to accentuate each one of the words he said.

I set the apple on the counter. I was not going to eat it, strictly on principle. Dayton was being ridiculous.

"Yeah, about that. Stop with this 'promise to Mom and Dad' garbage. You make it sound like a touching deathbed scene where our parents use their last breath to beg you to watch over me."

Dayton opened his mouth to protest, but I showed him the palm of my hand.

"They are alive and happy as clams. I just talked to Mom this morning. Dad's living the dream at that golf course in Phoenix while Mom lounges by the pool. When, or should I say if, they ever asked you to watch out for me, it was probably a passing thought when I first moved here. Like, make sure Bailey takes her vitamins. But that was months ago, Dayton! I don't need you to tell me how to live my life. Especially since you can't even keep track of your cell phone."

A long moment of silence followed. I knew Dayton too well to think that he was affected by what I had said. He probably spent the whole time I was talking devising more idiotic things to add to his list of ways to torture me.

I turned away and opened the cupboard where we kept the snacks—when we bought snacks, which apparently hadn't been in a while. Behind the stale saltine crackers and half a bag of tortilla chips, there was an unopened bag of pistachios. I pulled it out and took the whole thing to the kitchen table, where I plopped into a chair and started cracking.

Dayton slid from the countertop to sit across from me. "My cell phone is in the bathroom. I just remembered." He took a handful of pistachios from the bag and made his own pile. "And for dinner, I ate a burrito from Juanicitas's when I got out of class at five-thirty."

I stopped cracking and stared at Dayton, rage bubbling up my throat. Juanicita's had the best pork carnitas burrito on the planet. It wasn't fair that Dayton got Juanicita's while I got drive-through chicken nuggets from the dollar menu with Guy.

I had to make a concerted effort to keep my arm from sweeping across the table. My muscles actually shook from the effort it took to remain still. Maybe I should just let go. It would be so satisfying to watch all the nuts scatter across the kitchen. For sure it would have soothed my irritation.

Life was so unfair.

I cracked the next pistachio with a vengeance, tossing the shells into one pile and the nut into another. There was no point in eating any of the pistachios until I liberated the full amount that I wanted. Once I started eating, I didn't want to have to stop to open more.

"You're so weird," Dayton said, nodding at my piles.

I snorted. This coming from the guy who sucked on pistachios shells until the salt was gone, then cracked the shells with his teeth and spit them out on the table before he ate the nut.

"Aw, come on Bailey." Dayton leaned forward with his hands out. "Love me, okay? You know I just want to help you."

I did know that. But Dayton's idea of helping was not helpful. He was constantly complicating my life.

And he ate fantastic Mexican food without me.

Dayton raised an eyebrow. "Oh, I get it. You're not really mad at me. You're just mad that hunka-hunka-burning-love Guy didn't take you somewhere awesome."

I sighed heavily. It was just my luck that Dayton was taking a psychology class this semester. It made him think he was smarter than he was. For weeks I'd watched him transform from a misguided know-it-all to a self-justified know-it-all.

He went on despite my death glare. "It's not like we're destitute, Bay. You can go out to eat without a date."

"Or you could go with me." I curled my lip into a smirk.

Dayton grimaced. "You know I don't like trying new places."

"Whatever!" I tossed a shell into my growing pile. "If we never tried new places, we would never have found Juanicita's."

"Yeah, that was lucky, but you can't argue that trying new restaurants is risky. What about that Vietnamese place in Glendale?" Dayton shuddered. "The grilled octopus? It had eyes, Bailey. Eyes."

I swatted his words away like the pesky flies they were.

"Never again," he continued. "There's no way. Give me meat from an animal I can identify with fried potatoes on the side. That's all I want out of life."

"Then you are going to live a very lame life," I said, inspecting one of the nuts I just shelled. Yeah, it was definitely furry.

Into the trash pile it went.

"Depends on how you define 'lame'. I, for one, think it is extremely lame to pretend to be interested in someone to get a meal out of them." Dayton examined a pistachio like it was a nugget of gold, purposely not looking at me.

There was no way in spandex I was going to admit to Dayton that he might have a point. I was getting weary of random guys with lame taste buds. I almost always ended up at a fast-food place these days.

In fact, the only good dating experience I could think of from the past year was a guy from my Spanish class who took me to a place that made English pasties. Now that was fantastic; they were all savory and flaky. Just thinking about it made my stomach rumble. It was too bad he moved somewhere back east for graduate school. I would have dated him forever if he'd stuck around.

"Besides," Dayton said with that dumb voice of his again, "I'm pretty sure flirting for dinner counts as lying. All you're interested in is the food, but you act like you like the guy. A little deceitful, maybe?"

"It is not!" I totally disagreed. "Flirting is not lying!"

"It might be." He pursed his lips. "Tell me how you get a guy to ask you out."

I stared at him. "Are you serious? How does any girl get a guy to ask her out?"

"Stop answering my questions with questions! You're stalling your butt off. It's dishonest, and you know it!" Dayton clamped down on a shell so hard it made my jaw twinge.

"No," I shook my head until my hair swung over my eyes. "No way. I'm not doing anything wrong. Unless you think flirting in general is lying."

"Prove it." Dayton spit shells onto the table with a grin.

I wrinkled my nose. "Prove what?

"Prove you aren't lying. Show me what you do right before a guy asks you out."

I looked around. "Now? With all the hot guys in our kitchen waiting for me to flirt with them. How exactly should I do that, Dayton?"

"Well, there's at least one hot guy in here." He turned his body to flex from the side.

"Ew," I said, looking away. "Just ew."

Dayton smirked. "Come on, Bailey. Just describe to me what you do and say to get a date. You worked your magic with Guy a few hours ago; it shouldn't be too hard to regurgitate what you did."

I dug my nails into a particularly stubborn shell, pretending to really concentrate on it so that I had more time to consider my options. I knew my brother wasn't going to let this go. The more I protested, the more he would insist.

"Fine," I said, throwing the stupid, unyielding pistachio shell on the table. "I filled the sample tray at work—"

"Classic," Dayton nodded.

"Then I stood outside the store until Guy came by. Then I—"

"Guy, or a guy?"

"Dayton!" I picked up an empty shell and flung it at him. "Quit interrupting. You made me lose my train of thought!"

"Choo choo." He opened his mouth to reveal a mash of chewed up nuts and then slapped the table with is hands. "Get it? Choo choo? Train of thought?"

Super mature.

"Anyway, Guy walked by. I dazzled him with my smile, and he asked me out. I said dinner tonight works for me, and he came by after my shift ended at five. See, no lying."

Dayton shook his head. "Unsatisfactory. How did it get from samples to a date?"

"Ugh! Seriously? I asked him if he wanted a sample of yogurt, he said sure. I asked him if he went to NAU, he said yes. I asked him how the sample was, he said good. Then he asked me out."

More head shaking. "No, you're leaving stuff out. What did you do?"

"What do you mean? I held the sample tray."

"Come on, Bailey. Don't pretend like you don't know what I'm talking about. What did you *do*?"

I shifted in my seat, unable to find a comfortable spot. Dayton was making a big, hairy deal out of nothing. I narrowed my eyes at him as he sat draped across his chair with that cocky head tilt like he was so sure I was hiding something—which I wasn't. I hadn't done anything wrong. He needed to stop looking at me like he could read my thoughts. Despite what he thought, he did not know everything about me.

I traced the kitchen table's wood grain pattern with my finger.

"Come on!" Dayton wiggled his finger at my arm. "Don't hold out on me. I know there's more."

"I don't know." I flopped my hands onto the table. "I smiled, I blinked, I breathed. What are you looking for exactly? Just tell me what you want me to say, so I can go to bed."

Dayton swept aside his gooey shells to rest his elbows on the table. Mom would have had a fit. "Did you twirl your hair?"

"I don't know."

"Did you do this?" He opened his eyes really wide and batted his long eyelashes so quickly I felt a breeze.

"Stop. Gross. That's so weird." I waved my hands until he quit.

"Did you?"

"I don't know, maybe. Why does it matter?"

"It matters!" Dayton slapped his hand down. "Because using your feminine wiles is not honest unless your intentions are genuine. You wiled. Admit it! You batted and smiled and touched his bicep and giggled. You giggled, didn't you?"

I pushed my chair back a fraction. This was getting way too specific. "Maybe I did. I don't know! Do you pay attention to every little thing you do when you're talking to someone?"

"Talking, no. Flirting, yes. Come on. Out with it."

"Okay, yes. Maybe I twirled and smiled and possibly batted."

"Ha!"

"Give me a break! It's just flirting!"

"Right!" Dayton stuck a finger into the air. "Right! But people flirt when they are interested in someone, like, they want to get to know that person and spend more time with them. Flirting like that, that's honest. Flirting with a person to get something from them is *not* an honest use of flirting. It's just plain manipulative."

What?

Was Dayton also contemplating law school this semester? Because that was just not fair.

Dayton leaned back in his chair. His smug face drained all my remaining energy. I limply flicked at a couple of shells. It would probably be easier to give in about the flirting thing. If I purposely lost this battle, maybe I could eventually win the war.

I sighed and pushed the bag of pistachios to the side. "Fine, Dayton. You win. I won't flirt my way to dinner anymore. Happy?"

"Ecstatic!" he beamed, showing all his teeth in case I had any doubts about his feelings.

"Good. So…" I hesitated. I wasn't sure if now was a good time, but if I didn't bring this up now, I may not get another chance for days. "Since you brought up the lying thing, Marnie asked me today what I think about Todd."

Dayton made an impressive puke face, complete with bulging eyes and protruding tongue.

"Yeah." I nodded emphatically, opening my eyes super huge, but Dayton was totally oblivious to the subliminal messages I was trying to send him. Messages like: *the promise you forced me to make is a stupid promise, and you should let me out of it, you ding-dong.*

He flipped another pistachio into his mouth. "What did you say? You didn't lie, did you?" His dorky face went all stern.

I narrowed my eyes. "No, I didn't lie. I keep my promises."

"So, what did you say?" He spit another set of empty shells onto the table. "Even I think Todd is a dufus, and I'm his friend."

I ignored that comment. If I thought about it too much, I might rage throw myself across the table and pull out all of Dayton's hair. "I said something generic and changed the subject. But that's not the point, Dayton. Stuff like this is going to happen all the time; that's, like, part of life. I think you need to let me out of this no-lying promise."

Dayton was shaking his head before I even finished speaking. "No way."

Heat rose to my cheeks, a telltale sign that I was on the verge of a temper tantrum. "This is ridiculous! Everybody tells lies."

Dayton swished his head in a way that looked alarmingly like something Mom would do. "You are not everyone."

I put a handful of shelled pistachios into my mouth and chewed while I spoke, just because I knew that was one of his pet peeves, and I needed to do something that would make him feel as annoyed as I did. "Today at the pool, Sawyer told Miranda that she loves her new suit, but then, when we were changing in the locker room, she started trashing Miranda's taste. Mrs. Faulkner asked Camille how her daughter is doing with diving, and Camille raved about the girl's swan-like grace but spent the whole lesson yelling at the kid and telling her that her legs look like a frog when she dives."

I could tell that Dayton was about to interrupt me, so I raised my voice, spraying little bits of pistachio onto the table. I was too distraught to be embarrassed about it.

"Marnie told Keith things would pick up at Froyo, even though we all know frozen yogurt stores are dropping like flies. If Marnie tells fibs, it can't be that bad. And Keith does it too! When one of the customers asked how business is going, he said it couldn't be better. What the heck!"

"I think you're confused. That sounds like optimism, not lying."

I swallowed hard and shoved another handful of pistachios in my mouth so I could finish my rant. "Did you know that we had a grand total of five customers my entire shift today? Five." I held up one hand and wiggled my fingers in case he needed a visual. "And one of them was Marnie!"

"I like Marnie," Dayton said.

I drummed my fingers on the table. "Everybody likes Marnie."

"Hm." Dayton pressed his lips together as though he might be considering what I had said.

I chewed quickly, swallowed, then cleared my throat. Was it possible something actually got through Dayton's titanium skull?

"You know, Bailey, you're right. We might need to rethink some things."

I felt a flicker of hope. "Yeah?"

"Yeah," Dayton nodded. "We need to rethink who you spend time with. With all these dishonest people, no wonder you have a problem."

I slammed my hand on the table, knocking over the bag of pistachios and making the shells scatter like beetles. "I do not have a problem!"

Dayton raised his eyebrows. "But you do have a temper, apparently."

I swallowed hard. "Please, Dayton. It was a stupid promise. I only made it because you ate beans and sat on my head until I gave in. It wasn't a fair fight."

Dayton grinned, sweeping the empty shells back into a pile with the side of his hand. "I know."

"You know?" I gasped. "Did you plan that whole thing?"

Dayton nodded happily. "For, like, a week."

"That is so totally unfair!" I flung my arms onto the table and buried my head in them, wishing the darkness was a portal to another world where I could disappear, a world where my brother wasn't my misguided, self-imposed guardian.

"Bailey?"

I refused to look up.

Dayton patted my head a couple of times. "This is for your own good."

I shook my head back and forth, because I seriously doubted it.

"You'll see. Twenty years from now, when you are a successful, upstanding citizen, you will call me in tears, thanking me for setting you on the right road."

That was just too much.

"Dayton," I said, lifting my head to look at him.

He snapped back from his far-off, completely unrealistic daydream. "Yes?"

"You are a butthead."

"Such language," he laughed. "That's on the list from a few weeks ago, Bay. No more potty names."

I groaned and lowered my head until one of my cheeks rested in the palm of my hand. I traced a pattern through the pile of shells. "This totally stinks."

"I know." This time Dayton sounded almost sympathetic. If I wasn't so mad at him, it might have been comforting. "But, Bailey, in all seriousness, you needed an intervention."

I pooched my lips and blew air until my cheeks deflated.

"No, really. Think about what brought this on. You weren't just telling fibs to spare people's feelings, and you know it."

"What? I—"

"Like when you padded your resume?"

"Why do you always bring that up?" I said, flinging my hands in the air. "It was just for that one interview where they wanted someone who could speak fluent Spanish."

"Right." Dayton opened his hands on the table in front of us. "Doesn't that seem like a problem, telling a business you can speak Spanish when you can't?"

"I can speak Spanish."

"You can get by in Spanish, this is Arizona, we all can get by in Spanish. You aren't fluent, Bailey, and your accent is atrocious."

I scowled and shifted in my seat. "Eres un idiota."

"If that makes you feel better, go ahead and believe it." Dayton shook his head. "And anyway, the Spanish thing is just one tiny little example of what I'm talking about. You also told a telemarketer that you had to hang up so you could save a child from a runaway moving van."

"Everybody says stuff like that to get rid of telemarketers," I protested.

"And there's the big kahuna. Don't look at me all innocent; you know what you did. Two weeks ago, you turned down a date with Tanner."

"What?" My confusion morphed into surprise. "How did you even know about that?"

"He told me." Dayton looked at me with his dumb, disappointed face. "Seriously, Bailey? How do you think I felt when he stopped me in the library to tell me I have the most thoughtful, caring sister in the world? An angelic Mother-Theresa-like sister who sacrifices her Friday night every week to volunteer at the soup kitchen. Apparently, he has an uncle who was homeless for a while, and the soup kitchen saved the family from starvation."

"Well, that's an interesting coincidence," I said in a small voice like I totally didn't know, even though I totally did. That's why I used that particular excuse with Tanner. I knew it would let me off the hook in the best possible way.

I couldn't go out with him; he was such a nerd! When he asked me out, he was wearing suspenders.

Suspenders!

Only super old men, little boys, and babies can pull off suspenders. Everyone else looks like they missed their exit to the circus.

I think I deserve some credit. At least I didn't go all medieval on him for daring to ask me out in the first place. I could have done and said so many things, but I didn't.

That was something.

Dayton took both of my hands in his. "Bailey, you are my only sister. I love you too much to let you be this girl anymore. You are so much better than this."

I flipped my hands over and flung Dayton away from me, blustering for words that didn't come.

"This is for your own good." Dayton stood up and swept bits of pistachio crumbles from his hands. They rained down on the tabletop, making it look like a much bigger mess than it was. "I'm going to go charge my phone and listen to my messages. Something tells me I missed a call or two. I believe in you, kid. You got this."

I glared at his back as he walked away. I couldn't even feel satisfied that one of those messages—mine—would probably damage his ear drums for life.

I sighed and went to the kitchen for a rag to wipe off the table.

Ways to Improve Bailey #12

No more flirting for dinner

"Strawberries, please," Tanner said.

I lifted the spoon so that he could see it, already scooped and waiting for his command. Then I turned it over and dumped the strawberries onto his vanilla yogurt. Before I could announce the weight and total, Tanner held up a ten-dollar bill between two fingers.

I snatched the money out of Tanner's hand, slammed it into the cash register, pulled out a five, and shoved that into the tip jar. Then I resumed the position I'd been perfecting since I got to work: slumped forward, curled shoulders, elbows on the counter with my chin in my hands, and staring into space as I obsessed about my life problems.

I let out a long sigh.

And then I realized I was not alone at the counter.

Instead of taking his yogurt to the corner table like a good robot, Tanner continued to stand in front of me with his cup resting in the palm of one hand. He hadn't even grabbed a spoon or a napkin yet.

I stared at him in wonder. What was happening?

"Hey." He cleared his throat.

I straightened. Keith would be impressed at how well I was playing my part as a caring employee, despite how tragic and full of endless woe my life had suddenly become. "Did you forget something?" I asked.

"No, I have what I need. You, however, seem upset."

I didn't answer. I couldn't. I had never heard that many words come out of Tanner's mouth before. It completely threw me off. I didn't realize he could speak in actual full sentences. Even when he asked me out, it was in mumbled half sentences. I gaped at him like a wide-mouth tree frog while he turned beet red, running his fingers through his curly hobbit hair until it stood straight up.

"Sorry, what?" Not only was I surprised and borderline shocked, but I didn't actually hear what he said to me. I was too stuck on the *number* of words he'd used to pay attention to the *actual* words.

Tanner coughed and shifted from one foot to the other. "I asked if you are well. I noticed you seem sad or..."

Now I was surprised for a different reason.

I didn't know that Tanner noticed anything outside of his laptop screen and yogurt cup.

I impersonated a guppy for a few long seconds while I tried to think of how I should respond. I could have said I was just fine. People did that all the time when they didn't want to answer a question truthfully, or when they knew the person asking didn't really care. If I said fine, then the whole awkward exchange would be over just like that.

But I didn't feel fine, so I couldn't say that I was. It would be an obvious lie. Even a space cadet like Tanner had to notice by the not-so-subtle way I sulked on Keith's polished countertops that everything was not fine.

Plus, I didn't feel like pretending.

I slapped my palms onto the counter and leaned forward. "Do you have a brother?"

Tanner leaned away from me and shook his head.

"No? Okay. Well, feel lucky, buddy, because brothers are the worst! The *worst*! Especially my brother. Do you know what? I'm pretty sure his whole purpose on this planet is to ruin my life. I could tell you stories," I waved my hand in the air, "but I won't because we don't have that kind of time.

"He's such a nimrod! Completely unreasonable! He makes one dumb promise to my parents and—" I stopped for air, feeling years' worth of frustration throbbing in the space between my eyes. And then, a lightbulb. "Wait a second, I just thought of something. I never actually heard my mom, or my dad, ask Dayton to promise to watch out for me. I bet Dayton made the whole thing up, so he could justify torturing me. I can't believe he did that! Evil genius." I tapped the counter. "I should put ex-lax in his protein shake."

I slapped the counter again. My palms stung, but I didn't care. "And it's not like I *need* someone to watch out for me, you know?" I narrowed my eyes at Tanner in case he was thinking about disagreeing with me. "I'm fine. I have this great job at Froyo, where I can snack on junk all day long. See?" I reached over and grabbed a handful of mini chocolate chips directly from the container—yep, without using the spoon. Then I shoved them all in my mouth.

I yanked a napkin from the dispenser and wiped my hands with a vengeance. "I am a really good person. I teach swim lessons to little kids for such a small amount of money that I might as well be volunteering. I am a great friend. I always have my phone charged and the ringer on. I give veterans a discount whenever they come in. If I haven't picked a major yet, so what? I'm just starting college. No one knows what they want to do when they first start college. Did you?"

Tanner blinked.

"See! My point exactly. That's why they have general requirements, so you can work on them for two years while you figure out what you want to do for the rest of your life. So, it's not like I'm wasting my time here." I stuffed the dirty napkins into the overflowing trash. Someone forgot to take it out yesterday.

Seriously? Do I have to do everything around here?

"I totally don't get it! What is his deal?" I crossed my arms and finally looked at Tanner.

There were no words to describe the expression on his face. A sad drip of frozen yogurt slid down the side of his cup and plopped onto his worn tennis shoe. He was going to have to drink his froyo now.

I sighed and pushed the button to open the cash register. "That one is on the house." I nodded to his melting yogurt as I pushed a ten-dollar bill across the counter. After another awkward moment of silence in which Tanner still didn't move or say anything, I grabbed some napkins and a spoon and added those to his growing pile.

"Thanks for listening, pal. Enjoy your yogurt and have a nice day." I pasted a smile on my face and waved him off with both of my hands.

Tanner nodded and slowly backed away. I might have traumatized the poor guy. Oh, well. I was sure he would be as good as new after a couple of hours with his nose just a few inches from his laptop screen.

I waited until Tanner was sitting in his designated seat before I went back to moping. I had barely settled into my mental self-pity monologue when the chime rang over the door.

Great.

Just great.

I stood up mechanically and stretched my face into a smile so wide it made my cheeks hurt. My tragedy melted to the back of my mind as three potential dinner dates walked towards me. All three guys were fairly clean cut. They didn't have any weird piercings or shirts with graphics that should be in a rated R movie, and, best of all, there were no gold bands on that one incriminating finger.

I flipped my hair over my shoulder, grateful that even in the depths of despair, I had the presence of mind to shower and do my makeup that morning.

Then I remembered that I promised Dayton I wouldn't use my wiles to get a guy to ask me to dinner anymore.

That was crappy timing.

Um, okay. So, I just had to be sincere while I flirted. I could do that.

"Hey! Welcome to Froyo!" I smiled just enough to make them want more.

Smiling is sincere.

One of the guys, tall and built like a swimmer with broad shoulders, stepped in front of his bros and ran his fingers through his hair in a way that made his biceps pop.

So original.

I refrained from rolling my eyes and chose to bat my eyelashes instead.

Oh wait, I wasn't supposed to do that anymore. I stopped and rubbed at my eyes like I had a piece of dust in them and had to blink it away.

"Have you been here before?" I asked when I was done rubbing.

Swimmer boy leaned an elbow on the counter. He was so close to me that I had to take a step back or breathe in his exhales. "I haven't. I'd remember you."

I giggled and was about to twirl a piece of hair around my finger when I remembered that I wasn't allowed to do that anymore, either. I didn't realize how automatic it was for me to do these things.

"How about you two?" I talked over swimmer boy's head to his friends, just in case he didn't work out. The way he was responding made me think that the chances of him asking me out were pretty high, but it was always a good idea to keep my options open.

Sometimes the guys who express this level of interest this quickly try to take things further than I was willing to go. It wasn't anything I couldn't handle. I had years' worth of arsenal ready—tried and proven—to turn even the most enthusiastic octopus into a harmless sea slug.

Like a black belt in Tae Kwon Do, for example.

Usually, just the word "no" was enough to keep a guy in check. It had been years since I had to twist anyone's arm and flip them over my head.

"I've been to yogurt places like this, but not here," one of the other guys answered. He wouldn't look me in the eyes. Ten to one he had a girlfriend or someone he wished was his girlfriend. Waste of my time. My eyes slid over to the third guy.

"Nope. How does this work?" He held my gaze, a slow smile spreading while he worked his charm. He wasn't bad looking, but if his stubble had even one more day to grow, that would have been too much for me. Hopefully he would shave that scruff before he took me out.

And since I was hoping, maybe he could take me somewhere without a drive through.

I waited for all three boys to look at me—or in Girlfriend Guy's case, look in my general direction. When I knew at least two pairs of eyes were watching my every move, I started the frozen yogurt spiel: choose your cup, fill it up, weigh, and pay. Yada, yada, yada.

While I talked, I assessed. Based solely on their appearances and my intuition, which one would be the best dinner date? Swimmer or Stubble? Who would be the most likely to take me to an amazing restaurant? It was a tough call. Both of them looked like they could afford to eat somewhere other than fast food chains. Based on the way he nodded at everything I said and complimented my swirling technique, Swimmer was definitely eager to please. I'd bet money he would take me to dinner wherever I told him to go, and there was this new German restaurant I was itching to try. It had currywurst on the menu. You can't get more authentic than that.

But then, Swimmer was just eager beaver enough to expect a return investment, which was so not happening.

Stubble it was, then.

Now, how was I supposed to get him to ask me out without being all feminine and wily?

I waited at the register while the guys swirled their cups on their own. I leaned on the counter to show them I was there if they needed me to answer any questions. I was as sweet as a gumdrop, but if I didn't ramp it up, I was pretty sure they would leave, and I would be dateless. It was my experience that most guys don't make the first move without some pretty hardcore convincing.

I weighed each cup in the order received: Girlfriend Guy, Swimmer, and finally Stubble. I stopped myself from brushing Stubble's hand when I took his cup and didn't do anything to draw attention to my lips—which meant, my efforts to get him to ask me out went nowhere. Stubble kept giving me furtive glances, but nothing else.

"You guys go ahead. I'll pay," he said, waving Swimmer and Girlfriend Guy out the door. Swimmer hesitated, glancing between the two of us so rapidly that it gave me a headache watching his eyeballs bounce. It was like he was trying to follow a hyperactive tennis match.

After a very manly stare-down, Swimmer left with his bruised ego and slouched on the passenger door of a red lifted truck.

I turned encouraging eyes to Stubble and waited.

And waited.

And waited.

He hemmed. He hawed. He discussed the weather. He introduced himself, again.

Oh my goodness. This was ridiculous.

"Do you want to take me out to dinner tonight?" I interrupted.

Stubble, also known as Preston, blinked. Then he smiled. It was a huge smile that stretched all the way across his face, and it was about as relieved as any smile I'd ever seen.

"Yes, I would. Where do you want to go?"

I paused to think, counting his change from the register. Oh, what the hay. I'd already asked the guy to take me out; there was no reason to be demure now. "There's an interesting-looking German restaurant that just opened downtown. Are you game?"

A brief look of discomfort flashed across his face, but my challenge swept it away. "Sure, I'm game. I'll eat anything."

"Perfect!" I held out a hand full of coins for him. "You can pick me up here at five."

"All right, Bailey. I will see you in a couple hours." He winked. "Keep the change." Then he strolled out of Froyo like he'd just saved the world from aliens.

I leaned against the counter, completely drained. Whew. That was hard work, but it felt kind of good to just say what I was thinking instead of all the roundabout coercion it usually took to get a dinner date with someone I barely knew.

"Impressive."

I startled and put my hand on my chest—very cliché—as I turned around. "What is it you always tell me, Keith? Eavesdroppers are never rewarded?"

"Wrong. It's that they never hear good of themselves." Keith grunted and dropped his clipboard on the counter. "You know that show on the TV, the one where they play videos of people doing wild things? Ramp jumping a bicycle into a swimming pool and all. You think it's going to work, but it never does. The bike slips, the person hits the pavement, they go in upside down, or what not."

I stared at him like he had a gummy worm crawling out of his left nostril. "What?"

Keith nodded to the parking lot where Preston and the boys were backing out. "What just happened here is like that television show. It's painful to watch, but you can't look away."

"Whatever." I glared at him. "It worked, didn't it?"

"Sure, it worked, but that isn't the point. Why do you waste your time on those fellows, sis? They're all marshmallow fluff and whipped topping, no substance."

"So help me, Keith, if you say anything that starts with 'back in my day', I will throw caramel syrup in your face."

Keith held up his hands in defense. "I hear you. I'm not saying anything. I'm just saying."

"Sure," I said, shaking my head. "Besides, I don't want substance. You know that. Substance takes time and energy."

"I know, Bailey." Keith took off his glasses and squinted at them through the light, then rubbed them on his t-shirt. "I know you. Your daddy is the best friend I ever had. I was there when you were born; I held you before your grandparents got a chance. You are like the daughter I never had."

I sniffed loudly and wiped away a nonexistent tear with exaggerated motions. Keith clicked his tongue, his eyebrows furrowing just a notch. "Someday, little miss, you are going to see yourself the way I do, and then you will stop all this nonsense."

"Okay," I nodded, crossing my arms. "And someday you will start saying things that actually make sense."

Keith put his glasses back on and wagged his finger at me. Without another word, he kissed the top of my head and went back to the stock room.

I put my hands on my hips and surveyed Froyo for something to do. It was immaculate, as always—oh yeah, except for that trash. I had better take that out before I forgot again. My eyes caught movement as Tanner's head snapped back down to his computer screen.

Had he been watching me?

With a toss of my head, I turned away to wrestle with the overstuffed trash bag. It was right at that moment, of course, that my phone vibrated in my back pocket. I balanced the tipsy bag on my hip and pulled out my phone.

"Hey, Daddy."

"Bailey! How's my girl?"

"Good, Daddy. I'm at work."

"Are you now? I can't keep up on these schedules you kids have."

I smiled as I tied the top of the bag closed and leaned it against the cabinets, where I would trip over it until I got annoyed enough to take it out.

"How is Keith doing these days? Is he hanging in there?"

"Oh, you know. Same as always." A thought suddenly flitted through my mind. Keith was my dad's oldest friend. I think they wrangled herds of Brontosauruses together back in the day. If my dad asked anyone to lookout for me, it would have been Keith, not Dayton!

I felt a thrill of excitement. I was so glad my dad chose that moment to call. This was the perfect opportunity to find out just how full of baloney Dayton really was. Then, I could throw it back in his face and maybe, finally, get him to stop bugging me all the time!

This was so good!

"Hey, Daddy, I have a quick question for you."

"Sure, precious. Shoot."

"Did you make Dayton promise that he would take care of me while I'm at college?"

There was a long, long silence. I leaned against the counter, wondering if there was something wrong with our connection, but not wanting to pull the phone away from my ear to check. I didn't want to miss the moment when my dad answered my question.

"Daddy?" I said finally.

"I'm here, pumpkin." My dad's voice always made me think of sunshine and acres of green grass.

"Did you hear what I asked you?"

"I sure did, sweetheart, but here's the thing. When you moved to Flagstaff to live with Dayton, your mom and I made a pact of sorts."

"Yes?" I prompted. I didn't like the direction this was going.

"We decided that since the two of you are adults now, your mom and I are going to stay out of your squabbles."

"Dad!" I gripped the phone. "This is not a squabble; it's a question. Did you or didn't you make Dayton promise to look out for me? Did you tell him to act like he's my dad or something? Did you ask him to be all up in my business all the time? To be an all-around pain in the patootie? You don't understand, Daddy. He is ruining my life, and I want to know if you put him up to it!"

My dad's laugh was full, from the belly. "That's a great question, hon, but here's the thing. I talked to Dayton this morning, and he told me about your spat last night. I don't want to say anything to fuel that fire. Understand?"

Too late. The fire was raging and wiping out all the underbrush.

"You there, Bay?"

I unclenched my jaw. "Yep."

"Aw, Baybee." His wheedling tone and childish nickname were not going to get him anywhere this time. "Don't be mad. I love you more than my gold-plated putter. You know that, right?"

"Yep," I said.

And that was all I said or was planning on saying for the rest of the phone call. Maybe for the rest of forever. The desire to never speak to my dad again was not a passing whim this time, it was real as Rome. For sure, there was no way in Wimbledon that I was going to tell him I loved him more than my subscription to *Travel* magazine.

Today I loved my magazine way more.

Stinking Dayton. I should have known he would call Dad first thing. He was such a cheater!

"Well, I'm on the green, so I'm going to skedaddle. I love you, girlie. Make sure you call your mama soon, okay? She misses you."

"Yep."

I jabbed the button to end our call. In a burst of rage, I reeled my arm back and launched my phone into the air as hard as I could.

Ways to Improve Bailey #9

Stop throwing tantrums (and other things)

I should have thought that one through a little better.

As I watched my very expensive smartphone fly through the air, it was like time slowed down, the way people talk about near-death experiences where their life flashes before their eyes. I could see the perfect arc of my throw tracing through the air, making me think that I should have taken up a sport that utilized my fantastic pitching arm.

I tried to take a step forward to somehow stop the imminent disaster from striking, but I was frozen to the spot, watching my phone hurl itself like a freight train toward Froyo's glass storefront. It was aimed to crash right between the eyes of the dancing yogurt swirl on the window mural.

I closed my eyes and covered my face, waiting for the horrible sound of shattered technology resulting in a mangled phone. But it didn't come. Slowly, I peeked out of my splayed fingers.

Tanner was once again standing in front of me on the other side of the counter. This time, however, he was breathing hard and holding my phone in his hand.

My arms dropped to my sides. For just one tiny moment, I was completely speechless. It was like Tanner had ridden up to the counter wearing chainmail on a gleaming white steed.

He saved the day.

"Oh my goodness! You just saved my life!" I leaped forward, grabbed my phone from his hand, and cradled it next to my heart.

It was kind of impossible to function in the world without a phone, and this was my third phone in two years. Last time I called my dad to tell him I'd wrecked my phone, he'd said if anything happened to this one, I'd have to replace it myself.

I checked every inch of my phone to make sure it was unscathed. It looked perfect. I was so relieved that I kissed it with a smack and placed it in my back pocket where it would be safe.

I was so grateful that I didn't have to call and wheedle my dad for a new phone, especially since I was determined to never ever talk to him again. Well, at least not until he dissolved his alliance with Dayton.

I reached for Tanner and grabbed the edge of his flannel sleeve. I pulled it until I could get a grip on his arm, and then I squeezed out all my gratitude like I was a human anaconda.

"If my phone had smashed against that window..." I trailed off, savoring the drama of the moment. "Seriously, Tanner. You just saved my life."

"It's really not a big deal." Tanner slowly eased himself out of my kung fu grip and flexed his hand to check mobility. I didn't know what he was all worried about; his fingers worked just fine. "I stood up to throw something away. I was standing there anyway, and...I'm happy to help." He started to back away.

I felt totally let down. It was kind of the same feeling I had when I was a little girl and decided to follow Santa out of the mall so that I could catch a glimpse of his sleigh. Instead of the reindeer and jingle bells I was hoping for, I saw him yank off his beard and climb into a rust-colored minivan full of screaming kids with a lady who was so not Mrs. Claus.

This, too, was so anti-climactic. I had to do something. I couldn't just let Tanner walk away. I couldn't go back to staring into space and pouting.

That was super boring.

"You're wrong!" I climbed over the counter and dodged chairs as I followed him back to his corner table. "This is a *huge* deal! You don't get it!" My mind, in trying to figure out how to make him understand, came across the perfect solution. I slid across a table and landed on my feet right in front of Tanner. "You have to let me repay you! What can I do? You saved my life and my job."

That was the truth. Even Keith's great love for my family would not have kept me employed if I damaged anymore of his property. Especially if my phone had cracked his beloved window display. He'd thrown a big enough hissy when I dented the stockroom door.

It wasn't a big deal; you couldn't even see the dent anymore—as long as you squinted and looked out of the corner of your eye.

Tanner sat down at his table so that I now stood above him. His big brown eyes took me in thoughtfully. I had my hands on my hips Peter Pan style, waiting with for his response.

Tanner's eyes shifted to his laptop, lingering there for a hundred and fifty years before he finally brought them to my face. "Actually, there is something you could do for me."

"Oh good. What is it?"

Tanner lifted a hand with his palm facing upwards. "You could go on a date...with me."

A what?

Did he just say "date"?

All desire to return the favor evaporated in an instant, and in its place, I found myself filled to the brim with irritation. For reals? Did he really just ask me out?

Again?

I'm pretty sure those were the words I heard, but they were not making logical sense. I mean, each word on its own was perfectly clear, but when he arranged them in that order, they became a mess of mashed bananas.

I narrowed my eyes and took a long look at Tanner. From shaggy hair to worn tennis shoes, there was not much to inspire a yes to his question. The gray t-shirt he was wearing under a long-sleeved flannel jacket had definitely seen better days. Actually, both shirts had seen better days. His jeans were over-sized and ill-fitted, meaning they were held up by a canvas belt that was cinched so tightly there were wavy creases around his waistline. The whole vibe was like he went shopping at a thrift store.

In the dark.

With his eyes closed.

And don't get me started on the facial hair. His face was completely hidden by brown curls, and frankly, I didn't want to know what was under there. Seriously, why didn't he just shave? It looked like a small animal clinging to his face for dear life.

He saved my phone. Yes, that was awesome, but I was thinking about payment along the lines of a week's worth of free yogurt, not a date. What kind of guy asked a girl out when she had already turned him down once?

I opened my mouth and was about to tell him exactly what he could do with his date request when my eyes drifted to the table next to us.

It was completely empty.

In fact, the whole store was completely empty. Tanner was Froyo's best customer. Most days, he was our only customer. If I unleashed all my honest thoughts about going on a date with him, I would surely offend him. Tanner may not be totally with it all the time, but even he wouldn't be able to mistake my meaning if I really let my thoughts fly.

He would never come back to Froyo, and then what? I couldn't offend Tanner and risk him setting up residence at the corner table of a coffee shop.

Okay, so, what was I supposed to do now that calling him creative adjectives, throwing him out on his backside, and lying about being busy were not options?

Tanner shifted, drawing my attention to his rigid shoulders, which were hunched closer to his ears than they were a few minutes ago. I smoothed my curled lip into a smile and unwrinkled my nose as I tried to achieve a more neutral expression.

"Um..." I stalled, trying to give myself some more time to think. There was nothing in my brain. Not even the dimmest, flickering light to draw moths.

"...Here's the thing."

Tanner shook out his shoulders and crossed his arms. His brown eyes blinked at me through the frames of his hideous black glasses.

"...I don't really..."

Tanner waited.

"I can't— I mean, I don't think..."

"Yes?"

I needed more oxygen in my brain. I took a big breath and suddenly knew exactly what to say to Tanner. "Unfortunately, I can't go on a date with you. I'm already dating someone."

"Really?" Tanner said, one eyebrow arching.

Why did he sound all skeptical and junk? Going on a date was the beginning of dating, and I was going on a date with Preston in just a couple hours. I wasn't lying. Plus, since Preston agreed to take me to that German restaurant and not fast food, I knew I'd go out with him again. Technically, I was dating Preston. He just didn't know it yet.

"Really," I nodded.

Tanner's eyes moved to the front window. "That guy who was just here?"

"Yep." I flipped my hair over my shoulder. "Preston."

"Preston..." He raised his eyebrows expectantly.

I considered making up a last name for Preston. There was a chance I'd stumble upon the right one, so it might not be a lie, but I drew a blank and couldn't remember any last name except my own.

And that obviously wasn't going to work.

Tanner leaned forward. "Would that be Preston Wallace?"

Oh, I guess I didn't consider that Tanner would know Preston. Now that I thought about it, it made perfect sense. Flagstaff isn't super big.

"Yeah, sure."

He pushed his glasses up on the bridge of his nose. "I didn't realize you were dating. Though, I suppose that explains why you asked him out the way you did, if you're already together."

Some people are more observant than they should be.

"Were you eavesdropping?" I said the words slowly to give them extra indignation.

"This is a small store." Tanner leaned against the back of his chair, stretching his arms behind his head. There was a hole in one of the elbows of his flannel shirt. I averted my eyes like I'd seen something indecent. "It echoes."

"Hm." I made a mental note to remember that even though Tanner might look like a plastic chair all bunched in the corner, he still had ears.

Tanner raised an eyebrow. "Then, you're dating Preston?"

"Mm hmm," I said, studying my watch to get away from the way he looked at me.

"I find it interesting that you're in a relationship without really knowing anything about Preston *Walton*."

Crap.

I waved my hand in the air between us. "Yeah, well, you know, anyway, I can't go on a date with you. How about a week of free yogurt instead?"

"Well..." Tanner squinted as if considering. My hopes rose like helium balloons. With how much he loved frozen yogurt, this was only the most unrefusable offer ever. "That is generous."

I nodded. Of course it was. It was good to know he recognized that, even if it raised my opinion of him by less than one percent.

"I wouldn't want to get you in trouble with the guy you're *dating*."

"Right-o."

"How about we just go to dinner together? A casual dinner, not a date."

Wait, what? That was not what he was supposed to say. Didn't he know how this worked? I make excuses, he says he understands, and we are done.

Maybe it was time for a more direct approach.

"So, okay." My brain stalled, trying to think of a nice way to tell him to forget it. It was just too bad that offering free yogurt didn't work. I thought that was foolproof.

"Okay?" Tanner stood up. "Great. I'll pick you up here after work tomorrow."

And then he gathered all his things and left.

I stared at his retreating back, my mouth drying out as it hung open.

What the heck just happened?

I didn't mean 'Okay, I'll go with you'. I meant 'Okay, that didn't work. Let me think of a different excuse'. Couldn't he tell the difference?

I stared at the empty corner where Tanner had just been, and I had the most violent urge to throw my phone again.

Determination filled my soul from my tippy toes to the crown on my head. As soon as my dinner with Preston was over, I was going to track down my brother. I had to get out of this promise once and for all. There was no way in flannel town that I was going to go on that date with Tanner.

As soon as I got out of Dayton's stupid honesty thing, I was going to call Tanner with a big, fat, old-fashioned falsehood explaining why I couldn't go anywhere with him, now or ever, and then I was going to go back to my normal, happy life.

That's what I was going to do. And this time it would work.

It had to.

Ways to Improve Bailey #13

Seriously, the pouting has to go

Less than two hours later, I sat in the passenger seat of Preston's car, staring at my phone as we idled in the parking lot of the NAU Skydome. If I stared at it long enough, Dayton had to call me back, right? I was so sick of driving around aimlessly searching for my brother. I'd tried calling him at least six times, and it always went straight to voicemail. I couldn't think of anywhere else he would be, and Preston kept sighing heavily. It was getting harder and harder to ignore him.

"Any luck?" Preston added a jolt of peppiness to the question, but it was all an act, and a pretty poor one, too. The way his eyebrows furrowed into a straight line on his forehead contrasted drastically with his voice.

He'd been grumbling to himself for the last twenty minutes, ever since we left The German Restaurant.

Where in the world was Dayton?

We already looped around campus three or four times. I'd checked all of his usual places: Jamba Juice, the engineering building, and now the dome. He wasn't anywhere.

My phone chimed. I swiped the screen so fast I could have qualified for some kind of medal.

It wasn't Dayton.

Do you have lessons tonight?

Marnie.

> No, on a date.

I stared out the car window, trying to think. Where else would my dumb bunny brother be on a Thursday night?

"Was that him?" Preston tapped the sides of the steering wheel with his thumbs. I bet he wished he had an ejector seat. That was the only way I was getting out of this car without having my brother in line of sight.

It really was too bad about Preston. Under different circumstances, I might have ended up saving him in my contacts. He was a lot of fun at the restaurant, but ever since I refused to make out with him and made him drive all over campus to find my brother, his patience had been slowly leaking out. Sad, because there was a Korean place on San Francisco Street that I was dying to try.

Okay, it had been three minutes. Time to try calling Dayton again.

"Pick up, pick up," I muttered, tapping my feet with each ring of the phone.

"What?" Preston looked at me.

I ignored him.

"Hey, Bay! How's my favorite little sister?" Dayton's voice was loud, but just barely louder than the background.

"Dayton," I said, almost dropping my phone. I was relieved and super irritated at the same time.

"The one and only."

I shuddered to think what life would be like if Dayton was a twin.

"Where are you?" I asked.

"What?"

"Where. Are. You?"

"B-dubs, watching the game. Where are you?"

I pushed the End button and tossed my phone back into my purse. "Let's go. Buffalo Wild Wings." I smacked Preston's arm to get him in gear. He'd been staring out the windshield at nothing.

He put the car in drive and pushed the speed limit as much as he could without going over. The sooner we got there, the better.

When Preston pulled into the parking lot, there were no spaces near the entrance. Preston pulled in front of the restaurant and grumbled while I gathered my things.

"Thanks for dinner." I double checked that I had my phone in my purse, then tugged on my jacket and eased out of the car.

Preston pulled away before I closed the door. It slammed shut with the momentum of his squealing tires.

Whatever.

I didn't need that kind of drama. Especially now. When I talked to Dayton, I had to be at my best. I needed him to take me seriously because I seriously needed out of that dumb promise.

I felt a heavy weight as I paused to take a deep, cleansing breath. I could do this. I could make Dayton see reason for once in his life. With my head high in the air, I walked through the door of Buffalo Wild Wings.

And almost turned right back around. It was atrociously loud inside, and every table was full. I couldn't imagine a more horrible place to have this conversation. The whole scene was barbaric. Sports and sweat, ugh.

I paused at the entrance to get my bearings.

"Table for one?" The hostess smiled at me, showing her gleaming, white teeth. Dental hygiene major. I'd bet money on it.

"No!" I said, maybe a little too vehemently. The hostess stepped back with a concerned look on her face. "I mean, no thank you. I'm just trying to find someone."

"Oh, okay." She waved her arm out in a sweeping motion. "Feel free to look around. I'll be right here if you need any help."

"Thanks," I said, already dismissing her. I spotted Dayton at a rowdy table in the back corner, flipping pretzels into his mouth.

I squared my shoulders and plunged in. My timing was terrible. About three seconds after I stepped into the room, one of the teams on the big screen scored, and everyone around me erupted. I almost got beaned in the head with a plastic container full of ranch dressing. But I totally got off easy. I squeezed by a poor girl with root beer dripping down the front of her shirt. It took some maneuvering to get to where Dayton was, and by the time I did, I was so not happy.

"Dayton." I spread my hand around the top of his head so that my fingers splayed across his forehead. I slowly turned his head until he faced me.

"Bailey?" Dayton choked. "What are you doing here?"

"I need to talk to you."

"Okay."

"Not here!" I hissed, leaning closer to his face.

Obviously Dayton. Come on, use your melon. We could barely hear each other's words and we were only a few inches apart.

But, as always, what was so obvious to me was not so obvious to my brother. He just sat there, staring at me. Was he seriously waiting for me to bear my soul in front of his wing buddies and the rest of the random people in the restaurant? Had he lost his mind?

I sighed heavily and pulled on his arm. "Outside."

He slowly got to his feet, shrugging at his friends. I waited for him to walk in front of me. While he took his sweet time, I half glanced at the rest of the guys at Dayton's table.

And then I looked again.

Tanner?

He didn't notice me staring; he was too absorbed in whatever was going on with his cell phone screen. But that was no surprise. I'd never seen Tanner without his face glued to a screen.

Maybe Marnie was right. Only an underworld spy or an FBI agent would be on the internet that much. Unless he was just trying to maintain status as top scorer on *Plants vs. Zombies*.

I found it hard to believe that Tanner would hang out with Dayton and his boys. They had absolutely nothing in common, but there was no mistaking that flannel shirt. It made Tanner stand out like a big, black fly in the middle of plain vanilla ice cream.

An unsettled feeling came over me as I followed Dayton out of the restaurant. I didn't know Dayton and Tanner knew each other well enough to hang out. But really, I should have figured it was a possibility. Somehow, despite his many shortcomings, Dayton was friends with everyone.

This was a super big problem for my epic conversation with Dayton. If he and Tanner were close enough friends to hang out together, he wouldn't listen to a thing I said. He was fiercely loyal to his bros.

That was another line on my own list of things I thought were messed up about Dayton. I was his sister; he should be fiercely loyal to me. Sisters before misters. Isn't that how it was supposed to go?

It took a minute for my eyes and ears to adjust when I stepped outside the restaurant. It was warm for the end of February, and I was beginning to feel uncomfortably hot in my long-sleeved cardigan and boots.

"What's up?" Dayton asked, a little too loudly.

I fingered the strap of my purse. Now that I finally had his full attention, I wished I'd spent more time devising the perfect argument. All the things I'd planned on saying were starting to sound super lame in my head. "I need to talk to you," I stammered out.

"Yeah, I caught that." He grinned and scratched his neck.

"Right." I clasped my hands to get them to stop fidgeting. "Right. So, about that honesty promise..." As soon as the words left my mouth, I knew this conversation was doomed. Dayton's eyebrows instantly furrowed.

"Bailey." His voice was low and full of warning, like thunder before the clouds rolled in during monsoon season. But it was way too late to back out now. Like it or not, doomed or not, I was committed.

"You have to let me off," I said, wishing the words, or maybe the tone, were more confident and less pleading.

Dayton's head was shaking before I finished my sentence, but I held up a hand to stop him. I had to make him listen to me. He had to hear what I was saying.

"How about we strike a deal? Strict honesty days Monday, Wednesday, Friday, and Sunday. Stretch the truth Tuesday and Thursdays. Or how about truth during the week and wiggle room on weekends? Think of it like that soup diet you made us do last year. Remember how important cheat days are for your mental health?" My voice was not cooperating. I sounded like a whiny toddler.

"Bailey." Dayton linked his fingers behind his head, his elbows sticking out to the sides.

"Please, Dayton?" I made my eyes as wide as they could go, hoping I looked like a Disney princess or a cute woodland creature. "Please?"

Dayton rested his hands on both my shoulders, pushing his forehead gently into mine.

I went cross-eyed trying to keep him in focus.

"You're completely missing the point, Bailey. You only care about getting what you want. That promise was supposed to help you care more about other people."

"I care about other people!" I said, squirming away from him. The more I squirmed, the tighter his grip got. I should have clued in, but I was starting to feel trapped in more ways than one, so I just kept squirming. "That's why I lie, dim bulb! To protect people."

Dayton shook his head, "You know, that right there is what worries me the most. You really believe that's true." He finally let go of my shoulders. I reeled back and smacked him as hard as I could in the arm, but he didn't even flinch.

The jerk.

"There is hope for you, though. Like, the fact that you keep asking me to let you off your promise. There's lots of people who would make that promise and then do what they want. You might be a liar, but you have some integrity. There's potential for greatness, Bay. I want to see you rise to it."

How was I supposed to respond to that? It was like he had memorized a paragraph from *The Dad Manual*. Or he was impersonating Yoda, Gandalf, Dumbledore, and Obi-Wan all at once. My hands dropped to my sides, and my shoulders drooped.

I was truly doomed.

Dayton laughed and patted my head. "You're going to be okay, kid."

I pouted.

Unabashedly.

It only made Dayton laugh more.

"Pouting is not super attractive, Baybee. We probably need to work on that. I'll add it to the list."

That was just too much.

I folded my arms and turned my back on him. I would have left in a huff, but my ride was gone.

"Come on," he stifled a laugh. "I'll drive you home."

"I can walk," I said, tossing my head.

Dayton's voice lowered. "No, you can't, not in this weather with that flimsy jacket. I wouldn't even let you walk to the bus stop dressed like that."

"I'll call Marnie, then."

Dayton grabbed my arm with a Superman grip and pulled me towards the car. I stumbled as I tried to get my feet under me. Dayton tightened his grip, which helped me get my balance, but honestly, I would have rather eaten concrete.

While he unlocked the passenger door, I yanked my arm out of his grip.

"In you go." He pulled the door open for me and stepped out of the way.

I got in, but I didn't have to like it. I buckled my seat belt because I knew Dayton wouldn't drive until I did. Then I scrunched as far away from him as I could, even though it meant having the door handle dig into my ribs.

Dayton started the car and slowly backed out of the parking spot. It gave me a great deal of satisfaction to know he was going to lose his spot right in front of the restaurant and have to park in Timbuktu when he came back.

"Wanna tell me why the sudden need to break your promise? Did Marnie ask you about Todd again?" Dayton laughed.

I scowled, not appreciating his sense of humor.

"Come on. Tell me, please." Dayton batted his long, thick eyelashes at me. That didn't make me like him more. He only succeeded in emphasizing the unfairness of life by doing that. I had to order eyelash serum online that cost a bazillion dollars to make my lashes look like his.

Beast.

"Baybee," Dayton wheedled, "don't be mad at me. Please?" He twisted his face into the dorkiest expression imaginable when he glanced at me. "I wub you so much!"

I tried not to smile, but my lips quivered in the corners. Traitors! I pulled them down hard and scooted further away from Dayton. "I hate you so much."

"You wish you did," he grinned, wagging a finger at my mouth where that dang smile had threatened to show. "Now, be a pal and tell me why you want to break your promise again in less than twenty-four hours."

"No." I stuck my tongue out at him. "You can't make me."

"Real mature, Bay."

I took a deep breath through my nose, the kind a toddler might try before throwing a rip-roaring tantrum. But I wasn't throwing tantrums anymore. I learned my lesson. That was why I was in this mess in the first place—because of that whole debacle with my phone and Tanner.

"Fine!" I huffed. "I got asked out on a date. I said yes, but I don't want to go, and I need to make up an excuse to get out of it. Happy?"

No, he was not happy. That was obvious by the distinct droop in every single one of his facial muscles. His forehead settled into crevasses that would have made the Grand Canyon jealous.

Crevasses that meant he was seriously disappointed in me.

Crevasses I hated.

"Bailey, do you know how hard it is for a guy to ask out a girl he likes?" Dayton's lips were stretched into a thin line. "It's hard. Just go out with the poor guy. You go out with guys all the time that you have no interest in. This isn't exactly new for you."

I waved one hand in the air. "It's not like that." As quickly as possible, I explained what happened at Froyo. I was extremely proud of myself for being one-hundred percent honest, no embellishments. I mean, I even admitted I threw my phone at a glass window in a fit of rage. That's how honest I was. I could have sugarcoated that. In fact, maybe I should have. After hearing that little tidbit, Dayton rubbed his forehead and sighed.

"See?" I finished. "He didn't, like, work up his courage for weeks to ask me out. It was some kind of random, fluky thing. I don't wanna go, Dayton. This guy is weird." I tried, but I couldn't stop the whine from invading my vocal cords this time.

Dayton pinched the bridge of his nose with one hand.

"Who's the guy?" Dayton asked as he pulled into the driveway at home. He turned the car off but made no move to get out.

"Huh?"

"The guy that asked you out. Who is he? Do I know him?"

I picked at a torn piece of the seat, careful to stare at Dayton's right earlobe instead of meeting his eyes. "You know a lot of people."

"Name?"

Dayton was running out of patience with me, which irritated me a super ton. I should be running out of patience with *him*! Him and his dumb 'Improve Bailey' kicks. This was all his fault.

"Uh, Tanner," I mumbled.

"Come again?" Dayton turned his ear to me.

"Tanner," I said, clearly this time.

Dayton's hand dropped. He peered at me with a look I couldn't define. "Tanner who?"

"I don't know his last name."

"Was he in B-dubs?" Dayton's voice was low and steady.

"There's lots of guys in there."

"Yeah," Dayton said with a short laugh. "Let's try this again. Was. He. In. B-dubs?"

"Yes..." I sounded like I had a slow leak.

"Bailey!"

"What?" I widened my eyes. What was the big deal?

"If that Tanner, the one that was sitting at the same table as me, asked you out and you agreed, then you are going, sister. I would say that same thing if it was any guy, not just one of my friends, by the way. But especially Tanner. You already turned him down once. I am not going to let you do it again. You. Are. Going." He jabbed his finger at me three times. "Request denied."

And without another word, Dayton faced forward and pulled the gear shift into reverse so hard that I'm surprised it didn't break off in his hand. He didn't look at me while I got out and, for the second time that night, I got an earful of squealing tires.

Well, that went well.

I let out a burst of air, and I stared at Dayton's retreating headlights, thinking thoughts I would never say out loud—or at least never admit to saying, since potty words weren't allowed anymore.

What was I going to do now?

The obvious solution would be to break my promise anyway, since Dayton was completely unreasonable. He wasn't being fair at all. I could just call Tanner with my made-up excuse, and that would be that.

Except, I really couldn't do that. As much as I wanted to throw Dayton in the garbage most of the time, he was my brother, and I never broke my promises to him. I really did love Dayton, even though I hated his guts at the moment.

So, okay. Whatever. I didn't need Dayton's help. I was super smart and resourceful. All I had to do was figure out a way to get out of the date without telling a fib.

No big deal.

Yeah.

Or, if that failed, I could always just think of a way to keep tomorrow from coming.

Ways to Improve Bailey #5

Don't blame others for her problems

Tomorrow dawned bright and early, despite my best efforts, making it officially today.

Time is relentless.

No wonder there were so many sayings about it. Time marches on. Time flies. Time stops for no man. I thought that since I wasn't a man, I might squeeze by that last one, but no dice.

I laid in my bed and stared at the ceiling, bleary-eyed and annoyed. I was still half asleep from trying to stay up all night to keep today from coming, so it took me a few minutes to remember why I felt so annoyed. Then I punched my pillow.

Dayton.

Everything was his fault.

Logically, I knew it was pretty ridiculous to try and make time stop by staying up all night, but I was desperate. No matter how I tried—and believe me, I tried hard—I couldn't think of a single honest excuse to get out of going on that date with Tanner. All of my ideas ended with Dayton duct taping himself to my side to keep me with Tanner the whole night.

That's not horrifying at all.

I might possibly be scarred for life just thinking about it.

So, basically, I had to go on that date.

And to top it all off with a big juicy cherry, I was sleep-deprived and super, duper cranky. Not even the smell of blueberry pancakes and bacon made me feel better. In fact, it made me feel worse because having breakfast ready for me was what my suck-up brother did whenever he was trying to be the peacemaker.

Well, I was having none of it. I still wanted to be mad.

Maybe until I was eighty.

With a growl that could be heard around the world, my stomach turned traitorous villain, and all I could think about was pancakes. Dripping with butter. And warm, real maple syrup. Sizzling bacon...

Argh!

Not fair!

I rolled out of bed and hit the floor with a scowl. Dayton was playing dirty. That shouldn't have surprised me a bit; he always played dirty. The dude had no soul. Or too much. I couldn't decide which one it was.

With squinty, red eyes I dragged myself to the kitchen and slumped into a chair.

"Morning, sunshine," Dayton said without turning around.

I rested my chin on my arms, watching him flip pancakes high into the air.

Show off.

"Hungry?" He held a plate behind his back and expertly tossed two pancakes onto it. He set the plate in front of me with flourish, nudging the glass pitcher of syrup and plate of butter closer. "Bacon needs another minute or two. Extra crispy, just the way you like it."

I sighed in total resignation and started slathering butter onto my pancakes. "Why are you so mean?" I asked.

Dayton just chuckled.

After I ate five huge pancakes and two pieces of bacon, I felt much better. Better enough to look Dayton in the face for the first time that morning.

"Thanks for breakfast."

Dayton sipped his milk daintily, so he wouldn't get a mustache. "You are super lucky I don't tell the guys how much food you put away. Girls are supposed to have no appetite."

"Says who?" I snitched a small piece of bacon and popped it in my mouth.

"Use the tongs, you neanderthal," Dayton said as he slapped my hand. "Says everyone. It's unwritten girl code to pretend you're a rabbit when a guy takes you out to eat. You know this."

I did know, and I thought it was incredibly stupid. What was the point of dating if you didn't get an awesome dinner out of it?

"Well, you have killed that for me," Dayton went on. "If I take a girl out and she orders a salad and only eats half of it, I'm out. I know she's a fake and a liar, and I'll never ask her out again."

"Speaking of lying..." I began. Perhaps I was pushing it a little, but I didn't have much time left to get out of my date with Tanner. And at this point, I had nothing to lose.

"Nuh-uh." Dayton held up a hand. "We are done with that conversation. We wrapped it in duct tape, stuck it in a trunk, and there is a huge, fat guy sitting on top. You are committed."

I ran my finger through leftover syrup on my plate and sucked it off noisily, earning a furrowed brow from Dayton for my efforts. I smiled and wrinkled my nose to look my most adorable, and I did it again. This time he just shook his head. I could almost see him adding 'no more slurping' to the list of things to improve about me.

I traced a smiley face into the syrup while I considered my next move. Time to switch tactics.

I widened my eyes, all vulnerable and misunderstood. "You didn't let me finish. You don't know what I was going to say."

"Don't be so sure," Dayton grunted.

I stood up, taking his plate and mine to the sink. "You don't know everything going on inside my head, buddy," I tossed the words over my shoulder.

Dayton shifted so that he could see me while I rinsed plates and stacked them in the dishwasher. "Fine. What were you going to say?"

I wiped my hands on a towel. "I meant to say dating. Speaking of dating, I was just wondering how well you know Tanner. I should know a little about the dude since I have to go on a date with him, right?" It was so clever of me to throw that in. Whenever I regurgitated his words back to him, it put Dayton in a super good mood.

Sure enough, he brightened up and pulled out the chair next to him. "Have a seat, little sister."

I smoothed the damp hand towel over the oven handle, then sat down with my hands clasped together.

"Here's what I know." Dayton sipped his milk again. "Tanner moved to Flagstaff about a year ago from somewhere on the coast. Not sure where, though. He has two sisters. One younger, who is newly married with a baby, and one older, who is a biologist or something. She lives in Hawaii."

"Rough," I quipped.

"Snarky." Dayton flipped my hair.

"How did you meet?" I asked. This was what I was most curious about. Tanner was so not like the other guys my brother hung out with. It was a shame, really. If Tanner was more like my brother's usual good-looking, preppy friends, this date might not be the most unbearable thing ever.

"I had a class with him last semester." Dayton shifted in his seat.

"Which class?"

"Uh, calculus."

I remembered when Dayton took calculus. It was a dark time for us both. "Is that why you did so well? Did he tutor you or something?"

Dayton shifted again. "Okay, Bailey. Don't freak out."

Well, I wasn't going to until he said that, but now I reserved the right to throw a certified hissy if I chose to. "What?" I narrowed my eyes.

"Tanner was my calc professor."

"What?" I couldn't help it. I leapt to my feet and lunged for Dayton, gripping his face between my hands until his lips puffed out like some new species of demented tropical fish. "Are you crazy? I can't go on a date with a professor! That's got to be illegal!"

Dayton wrenched my hands apart so that he could shake out his face. "Geez, woman." He used my arms as leverage to make me sit back down. I had the tiniest twinge of satisfaction as I watched the color return to Dayton's pale lips, but it didn't last nearly long enough to make me feel better about the situation.

"Dayton," I pummeled him with my most pathetic face, "think about this. I can't date a professor! Why are you doing this to me?"

Dayton raised an eyebrow. "Tanner asked you on a date, and you agreed to go. I am merely making sure you keep your word."

I looked at my hands. "If he's a professor, he's got to be like a hundred years old. Is that why he has so much facial hair? To cover up the wrinkles and liver spots?"

Dayton rolled his eyes. "I told you not to freak out for a reason. He's my age. Ish. He's twenty-one."

"How is that even possible?"

"He graduated from high school with his associate degree. He did a dual enrollment thing. Then, he got his bachelor's degree in one year and his graduate degree in two. Twenty-one."

I hugged my arms around my body tightly. "So, he has a masters? Or is it a PhD? Do I need to call him Dr.? Is he, like, some kind of whiz kid genius?"

Dayton ignored my rising hysteria. "The point is that you will never find a better guy than Tanner. I could give you so many examples of how awesome he is."

"Go," I said without smiling.

"Nope." Dayton shook his head. "I want you to find out on your own. I am just telling you this much to reassure you that I am not letting you go out with some old creeper."

"Well, yay. That's just...swell." I choked on the word.

Dayton punched my shoulder. "Buck up, little soldier. Who knows? You might have fun."

"Dayton!" I swatted at his arm. "You are super stupid and completely delusional. How am I supposed to have fun? I was pretty sure this date was a bad idea when I thought Tanner was just a hobbit hobo. But now, I find out that he's an ancient, brilliant one. This is just the worst."

"He is brilliant." Dayton pursed his lips. "Totally genius levels, but you would never know it talking to him. He's really great, Bailey. Give the guy a chance."

I flung my arms onto the table and hid in them, getting déjà vu. I could smell pistachios from the other night. "I don't wanna. Why did he have to ask me out, anyway?"

Dayton poked me. "Maybe he likes you."

I refused to respond to that.

"Or maybe he's lonely. It can't be easy being such a young professor. He doesn't really relate to either group entirely, you know?"

I snorted.

"He goes out with me and the guys sometimes," Dayton continued, "but I haven't seen him do much with anyone else, and I've never heard him talk about girls. He's not shy, exactly, but he is super reserved. It was probably really hard for him to ask you out, but he did it. You should think about that, Bailey."

"Yeah?" I popped up and glared at Dayton. "I am so sorry this is so incredibly hard for *him*. Poor, poor brilliant hobbitses." I stood and stomped out of the room, but it wasn't nearly as satisfying as I thought it would be. My bare feet made zero noise on the vinyl and even less noise on the carpet, and even if they had made noise, it would have been drowned out by Dayton's belly laughs.

"You are the *worst!*" I yelled and slammed my bedroom door shut with all my might so that his stupid snickering would come to an end.

I dove back into my bed and pulled the covers up over my head. I didn't have to go anywhere until my Froyo shift at noon; I was totally going back to sleep.

Ways to Improve Bailey #14

Get over herself

"What are you doing?"

I wasn't sure how long Keith had been standing there, watching me stare at the corner table. I hadn't heard him come out of the back room.

"Um," I said as I looked around and spotted a washrag, "I was just thinking about wiping all the tables down again before I leave. Just in case I missed a dribble or something the first time." Not that wiping anything was necessary today. No one had come into Froyo at all during my whole shift.

Not one single person.

I glanced at the corner table again.

"Okay," Keith said, waving his hands. "Get on with it, then."

I wrung out the rag and swept it across the tops as I made my way to the corner of the store. I was drawn there as though the table, or myself, was magnetized. As I moved the rag in wide circles, I wondered what this could mean.

Today was the first day in all the time I'd worked at Froyo that Tanner hadn't occupied this spot all afternoon. Was it a coincidence that this was also the day we were going on a date? According to the clock right above the cash register, my shift was over in five minutes.

Was he going to stand me up?

Maybe he wasn't going to show up at all. Maybe this whole thing was payback for turning him down that one time.

I couldn't decide if that made me feel relieved or annoyed. Thinking about it was driving me bonkers. I wanted to call him to find out. But I couldn't do that. I didn't have Tanner's phone number. I didn't even know his last name.

I scrubbed hard at a nonexistent spot on the next table to relieve the tension I felt. This whole thing was a big, fat disaster. I slapped the rag against a chair and then, for good measure, wiped around the toppings bar, even though it was still immaculate. Keith grunted in approval. He loved it when I did extra stuff like that.

I triple-checked the clock, my watch, and my phone. Each one said five-o-clock on the money. Where was Tanner? On autopilot, I went into the employee bathroom to touch up my makeup and brush through my hair. I couldn't decide whether to leave it up or down, so I compromised and pulled it half up with a clip. Five minutes later, I stood behind the counter, wondering what to do with myself next.

"All right, girlie. Out with it." Keith removed his glasses and rubbed his eyes.

"Out with what?"

He gestured at me. "I can't remember the last time you stuck around here after your shift was over. You usually fly out the door without a backward glance and leave me to do all the wiping up."

"I do not."

Keith put his glasses back on and peered over the top, making me squirm.

I started for the door. "Nothing's going on. Everything is normal. See, I'm leaving. Byeeeeeee." I waved as I pulled the door closed behind me.

Keith shook his head and started refilling the toppings, even though nothing had been used the whole day.

Not even the strawberries.

I watched him until he caught my eye, then I waved again and hurried out of sight. I walked to the corner of the strip mall, then I leaned against a brick pillar and crossed my arms.

I couldn't believe Tanner was standing me up. That was so wrong on so many levels. If anything, I should be the one standing him up.

And that wasn't even the worst part. If Tanner didn't show, it would be too late to try to get another dinner date. I would have to go home and eat pistachios again since neither Dayton nor I had done any grocery shopping. That thought alone kept me loitering at the edge of the building instead of heading to the bus stop.

Also, I didn't know how this worked. I'd never had a date be late before. How long was I supposed to wait for him before I called it? I tugged the ends of my hair and decided I would give him, like, ten more minutes, then I would call Dayton to come get me and make him take me somewhere awesome. It was only fair; I did my part. Tanner was the one who flaked on the date.

What time was it, anyway?

I dug through my bag to look for my phone and wondered why I had thought it was a fabulous idea to buy a mammoth-sized purse.

Okay, seriously. Where was my phone?

I went back through each compartment more carefully. My phone was not in there. With a huff, I looked at the sky. When did I use it last? I know I had my phone at work today. I remembered checking the time in Froyo. Did I leave it in the bathroom?

Ugh.

I was going to have to go back and look. Keith would think I was a lost cause, but I guess that wasn't much different than what he usually thought about me, so, whatever. I squared my shoulders and strolled back to Froyo, trying to look chill and breezy.

"Hey, Keith, have you seen my—"

He held my phone up with one hand.

"Thanks." I took it and stashed it in my purse, then zipped it up for good measure. I for sure wasn't going to check my messages here, not with Keith staring at me with his X-ray vision. I would wait until I was outside. Hopefully one of those messages was from Tanner.

Canceling.

"Okay, see ya." I turned to leave, just as Tanner swung the door open. "Oh...hey."

"Hey." He ran his hand through his hair, making it look even wilder and more hobbit-like. "I'm so sorry. I got stuck on a phone call. I feel terrible that I kept you waiting."

"Yeah, well, whatever. Are you ready now?"

He stepped to the side and held the door open for me. I walked out without glancing back at Keith. I didn't even want to know what his expression was saying. Surely, I would get an earful at work the next day.

When we were outside in the cool, evening air, Tanner took a deep breath and let it out slowly. "Thanks for waiting for me. I know you like to get out of there right at five."

I felt squirmy. I didn't like that Tanner had noticed my schedule. In fact, it made me feel weird to think that he noticed me at all. Is that why we were on a date? Was Dayton right, and Tanner was secretly crushing on me from behind his computer screen for all these months?

Cause...ew.

That was just what I needed: Tanner obsessing over me, following me around all the time, and calling me his precious.

I arranged my face into the most understanding expression I could imagine. "Oh, don't you worry about it. Really. If this is a bad night for you, we can cancel."

Oh please, oh please.

Yes, I crossed my fingers behind my back. I'm allowed to be immature and superstitious if I want to. It's a free country.

"No, no. I have everything resolved. We can go to dinner."

I dropped my hands to my sides.

Boo.

"I would have texted you to tell you I was going to be late, but I don't have your number. And with the time it would have taken to track down Dayton or call Froyo, it seemed like the better choice was to finish my call and get here as soon as I could. I really am sorry. I hate to keep people waiting."

"It's fine." I waved his words away with my hands. "So, what's the plan?"

Tanner cleared his throat. "I thought we could go out to dinner, and then take it from there."

I wasn't sure what "taking it from there" meant, but dinner sounded fantastic. I was starving. "Where to?"

If he needed some suggestions, I had a whole Google doc of restaurants that I wanted to try.

"Have you been to Basil's?"

"Have I been to Basil's?" I mimicked, wagging my head with each word.

Tanner blinked multiple times.

I leveled my tone and put a hand on my hip. "Basil's is only my favorite restaurant in this entire town."

A tiny smile cleared the wrinkles in Tanner's forehead. "Well, that's fortuitous."

Basil's was located across the parking lot from Froyo. We walked the short distance in silence, listening to the wind howl and the distant sounds of rush-hour traffic. Once we were inside, I smiled.

A genuine smile this time.

I really did love Basil's. The vibe was jazzy, and the food was fantastic. My stomach rumbled at the scent of garlic and roasting tomatoes. I'd tried everything they served at least once and hadn't come across anything that I didn't love. Right now, I was so hungry I felt like I could eat the whole left side of the menu.

Oh my goodness!

I just had the most amazing idea!

And I had Dayton to thank for it, ironically enough.

This morning, he made that lame comment about my enormous appetite, and I knew for a fact that my brother was in the minority when he said he wanted a girl to order something other than a salad. Most guys didn't want that at all. Most guys liked a girl who didn't eat much. Not only did it save them money now, but it also gave him a false sense of security that her teeny appetite meant she wouldn't be super fatty when she got old.

It was all coming together in my mind. Thanks to Dayton, I now knew exactly what to do to make sure this date didn't have a sequel. With a spring in my step, I followed the hostess to a booth near the fireplace. It was all cozy and almost romantic. But trust me, there would be nothing romantic about our dinner tonight.

I took my seat and instantly picked up the menu, even though I had it memorized. I was just using it to hide my scheming face while I formulated a plan.

"I haven't been here before. What do you like?" Tanner asked, leaning over the menu in front of him.

"Oh, everything is good." I waved his question away. He was distracting me from the details of my nefarious plot.

The waitress approached our table. "Welcome to Basil's. My name is Gena. Can I get you started with some drinks?" Her unenthusiastic monotone matched the theme of our date perfectly.

Tanner looked at me.

"Strawberry lemonade," I said.

"Just water for me, thank you."

Gena made a note on her pad and trudged away. It felt like an eternity of silence before she returned with our drinks.

"Are you ready to order?" Gena asked, her pen at the ready.

Tanner looked at me again. Was he really that much of a gentleman, or was it just that he didn't know what to order yet? I'd place money that he just couldn't decide. The menu was huge.

"I'm ready when you are," I smiled, sweetly.

Tanner glanced at the menu, still lying there on the table. Was that sweat building up on his brow? I smirked, wondering what he would do next.

"I haven't eaten here before. What would you order if you were me?" He tilted his chin to smile at Gena.

There was a brief moment of blessed silence before Gena's face erupted into a smile and the dam broke. Gena began peppering Tanner with questions. She asked if he had any allergies or food dislikes, and what he normally ate at Italian restaurants. Then she went on about the awesome food. He couldn't go wrong with anything on the menu.

Blah, blah, blah.

Well, duh. I could have told him that. About halfway through her discourse on the desserts, I interrupted. I had to, otherwise we were going to be there all night talking about food and never eating anything.

"Just get the chicken parmesan. Everybody likes chicken parmesan."

"Yes!" Gena beamed. "Best on the planet!"

Tanner's smile eased into place. "That sounds great. I'll have the chicken parmesan."

Then Gena had to gush about his excellent taste, how fabulous the marinara was, and the intricacies of tomato roasting. I interrupted again, this time with a super loud "ah-*hem*" to get her attention back on me. Seriously, if the girl loved the menu that much, she should marry it.

"Yeah, so, along with his chicken parm, I'd like to start with some boneless wings with honey BBQ and garlic bread. Just bring them out whenever they are ready," I said.

Tanner's eyebrows drew together, making lines on his forehead. I almost felt sorry for him. A storm was coming because I was just getting started.

I bit my lip, pretending to be in deep consideration. "Do you think we should get the spinach-artichoke dip, too?"

"Um," Tanner flipped his menu over, scanning for the appetizer section.

"Oh, never mind. I'm not in the mood for artichokes. We'll get the fried zucchini instead."

Gena raised her eyebrows as she scribbled on her notepad. She started to tuck her notepad into her pocket.

"And then," I raised my voice and waited for her to get out her handy dandy notebook, "I'll take the rigatoni with chicken. Extra sauce. And the house salad with ranch dressing."

"Oh, the salad is a main dish, not a side." Gena gestured to the menu with the eraser of her pencil.

"I know."

"Okay," Gena hesitated, then went back to scribbling. "Anything else?"

Tanner stared at me with his eyebrows raised.

"For sure a pizza cookie with macadamia nuts, but don't bring that out until the end." I looked at Tanner with serious eyes. "The ice cream will melt."

Gena waited. She was catching on, so I looked at her. "That should be good for now."

She tucked her notebook away and collected our menus. "Coming right up."

I'd bet my atlas she couldn't wait to show that list to the cooks. My order would be a kitchen joke for years to come.

Perfect!

Tanner and I sat in silence after that. I kept waiting for him to say something about the fact that I'd just ordered enough food to feed a small country.

He must have a few thoughts about it.

Like, was he embarrassed by me? Or maybe he was embarrassed for me. He kept toying with the dumb straw wrapper. Straw wrappers were not meant to hold anyone's attention for that long.

I straightened and smiled. I think we are right on track for a one-date wonder.

Tanner crumpled the wrapper into a ball and began twirling his straw in his water glass. I didn't worry about the silence anymore. My mission was clear. I was just going to sit back and wait for my delicious food to hit the table so that I could stuff my face.

"How was your date with Preston?" Tanner obviously didn't have the same mission as me. His question took me off guard.

"My what?"

"Your date last night. How was it?"

I paused for a minute to remember. "It was good. We went to The German Restaurant that just opened downtown. It was super yummy. The sauerkraut rocked, the currywurst was to die for, and so was the schnitzel, actually."

Tanner waited, but that's all I had to say about that. After a moment, he cleared his throat again. "And what did you think of Preston? Are you two *still* dating?"

His emphasis on the word "still" made me remember the dirty trick he played to get me on this date. I don't care what Dayton said. Tanner was the worst.

"Probably." I pulled my lemonade closer and tried to suck a strawberry through the straw.

It didn't work.

"Probably?" he prompted.

Why was he asking me about Preston? It was Dating 101 not to talk about other dates when you are on one. Didn't he know that?

I glanced at his faded blue plaid shirt. I think the answer to that is a no. He probably didn't go on dates often enough to realize there were rules. I should take pity on him.

Except, I didn't want to talk about Preston. So, I let out a breath and looked at the ceiling. "Where's the food? I'm starving."

Tanner traced the lines on the table with his finger, letting the subject drop. Maybe I should have suggested we go for Louisiana BBQ. Then we could at least color on the tables while we waited for our food.

A slow movement caught my eye. Tanner was checking his phone under the table. He was smooth. If I wasn't such an expert at covertly checking my own phone, I wouldn't have had a clue what he was doing.

My admiration was short-lived, however, and quickly replaced with indignation. He was checking his phone on a date. Was I *boring* him? Seriously? Tanner set his phone on the table and looked at me, concern etched in every line of his face. "I'm sorry, Bailey. I'm being rude. It's work. There's this-. Anyway, it can wait. I turned my phone off."

"Wait." I remembered some things Dayton said when he filled me in on Tanner's story. "What do you have to do for work after classes are over for the day?" All those super important papers to grade? Life and death stuff there.

"You really don't want to hear about the life of a college professor," Tanner shifted. "Now you have my full attention. You don't want to talk about Preston, so, tell me about you. Dayton says you love to travel the world. Where have you been?"

My leg twitched against the table leg. I used both hands to steady the table so that our drinks wouldn't topple. Did Dayton fill Tanner in on my story? I did not like that idea at all. "I haven't been anywhere yet. I mean, I'm still in the planning stages."

"Then tell me about your plans." This was super confusing. The way Tanner said those words sounded like he was really interested to know my plans.

The same words from Dayton always had a teasing glint. From Marnie, they were accompanied by a confused head tilt. My dad got a V-shaped wrinkle between the eyebrows, and my mom was the master of the disappointed sigh.

Tanner, on the other hand, looked at me and waited like he really cared to know. That look, free from mocking, and his judgment-free tone was completely irresistible.

"I want to graduate from college and become fluent in all the languages. I want to travel the entire world, taking pictures and blogging about all the amazing things I see. And eat! Especially eat. I am passionate," I pressed my hand to my heart, "about good, authentic food from interesting places. After I'm done with all that, I want to start a business." I shrugged. "I haven't decided what kind yet, but it will be amazing!"

Tanner opened his mouth to respond, but I wasn't done yet. I gulped some air.

"The business and stuff, that's later. The thing that I want to do most right now is try different foods from all over the world. That will be the main point of my blog. I want to inspire people to travel and immerse themselves completely into a new culture. I think food is the best way to do that, don't you? It's like the universal language."

"I think you are absolutely right," Tanner said. "That is quite the plan. Where are you headed first?"

Before I could answer, there was a screech and a jolt against the table. Everything went down so quickly that I didn't realize what had happened until Tanner was completely covered in ranch dressing, lettuce, and spaghetti with that fabulous marinara sauce.

"Oh my gosh, oh my gosh." A server other than Gena lurched at Tanner with a handful of napkins. "I'm so sorry. I tripped."

I slid my purse underneath the table with my foot.

Tanner removed his glasses because they were useless now. They left two perfectly clean circles among the streaks of red and white all over his face. The server dabbed Tanner's face and shirt, then dropped the rest of the napkins into his lap.

"I'll go get some more. I'm so sorry!" She dashed away, almost plowing over a waiter. He steadied his tray above his shoulder and waited for the girl to pass before continuing to the table behind us.

Tanner opened a napkin like he was a ridiculously patient child opening a Christmas present one fold at a time. Then his face disappeared. He rubbed a few circles before pulling the napkin away. It was a soggy mess. He picked up another napkin and started the process all over again.

At this rate, I would be fifty when he finished unwrapping all those napkins. Not to mention the time it would take to actually wipe the ranch and marinara off his face and the gross hairs of his beard.

"Gimme." I reached across the table and grabbed a stack of napkins. Much less carefully, I unfolded them and made a pile near Tanner's elbow. I wrinkled my nose at the growing pile of soggy napkins on his other side.

Tanner worked steadily, cleaning his face, his hair, his neck. It might have been more effective to hose him down out back. He pulled out the hem of his flannel shirt and surveyed it with pursed lips. Marinara was a beast to get out of clothes. He was going to have to throw that thing out.

The thought made me wonder if Karma hated plaid flannel as much as I did.

A tall man in a nice suit stepped up to our table. His face wrinkled with every flick of his eyes. A wrinkle for the mess on the floor, a wrinkle for the pile of napkins, a wrinkle for the state of Tanner's clothes.

"Pardon me. I'm the manager of this restaurant. I wanted to offer my sincere apologies." He spoke in clipped sentences and braced himself like he was expecting a barroom brawl.

I leaned back and folded my hands over my belly. This was super entertaining.

"It's no trouble." Tanner stopped cleaning his glasses long enough to smile at the man. "Accidents happen."

"Yes, well," he sniffed, "be that as it may, I'd like to comp your meal, and I assure you this will never happen again."

Tanner stopped cleaning and set his glasses down. "How?"

"Excuse me?"

"How," Tanner cleared his throat, "will you assure me this will never happen again?"

The man bristled. "What are you implying?"

My head swung back and forth between the two men. This was getting good.

"You misunderstand me." Tanner held his hands out. "I merely wondered if you meant that you're going to fire that waitress."

The man looked down his nose. "Not that it's your concern, but no. I am not going to fire her."

"Oh, goo—"

"I fired her already. Such behavior is unacceptable in a restaurant such as this."

Blah, blah, blah. Insert snooty, self-promotion talk that goes on for way too long.

I watched Tanner's face instead of listening.

"I don't mean to interrupt," Tanner said when the man drew a breath, "but I wish you would give that girl her job back."

"Excuse me?"

"It was just an accident. People aren't machines; they make mistakes. I think it's a shame that she is fired for such a minor thing."

"Do you?" The man lifted his chin. "Would you feel the same if she'd spilled scalding coffee on you? Or broke a glass that cut you?"

"But she didn't." Tanner gave a half smile. "I wish that you wouldn't punish her for something that could happen to anyone."

My eyes flipped to the man. The silence had gone on for far too long. His mouth opened and closed and opened again.

Tanner leaned forward. "How about I pay for the meal, and you give that poor girl another chance?"

Considering how much food I ordered, this was not a light bargain. Indecision and indignation were at war on the manager's face. I couldn't guess what he was going to do next.

Finally, he looked away. "Well, right then. I'll give Trisha her job back." He stepped aside so that Gena could set garlic bread on the table and gritted his teeth. "And never mind about paying. Please, enjoy your meal."

"Thank you," Tanner smiled. "We will."

The manager walked away without saying anything more.

The scent of deliciousness known as garlic bread wafted under my nose, but I didn't reach for the basket. My gaze stayed on Tanner, trying to figure him out. The list of things I knew about him was growing rapidly. In addition to "great tipper" and "screen obsessed", there was now "treats waiters like humans", "is interested in others' opinions", and "champions unfortunate females who got fired because I left my purse sticking too far into the walkway".

I stared at him while he pulled a napkin into his lap—even though he couldn't possibly get messier—and chose the smallest piece of garlic bread. It didn't seem to bother him that his clothes were drying cardboard stiff, and his hair stuck up in weird angles.

Was this nice-guy thing just an act? He didn't look like he *wasn't* a nice guy, but that didn't always mean anything. Marnie's question from the day before came into my mind and made me wonder. What *was* his story?

"Where would you like to travel?" Tanner asked as if nothing had happened to break up our conversation.

I waved my hand to swish his words down the drain. "Let's talk about something else."

"Sure. What else would you like to talk about?"

"You," I said.

"What?" Tanner made a face. "Me? Why?"

"Because you are a big mystery, and I don't like mysteries. I trashed all my Nancy Drew books when I was ten years old."

Tanner laughed. I'd never heard anything like it before. The sound bubbled from his toes and couldn't wait to burst out of his mouth. It had such an amazing sound that several people turned to smile at him.

"I'm not mysterious," Tanner shook his head. "Not in the slightest. You, on the other hand, are extremely mysterious. At the risk of sounding cliché, I have to say that I don't think I've ever met someone like you before."

"I'm not sure that's a compliment."

"I'm not sure, either." Tanner's eyes glinted.

Wait.

Was he teasing me?

I was filled with a sudden determination to figure him out. "Where are you from?"

"The, um, coast."

I stared at him. "Yeah, okay. Where exactly? West coast? East coast? Are you from a actual state or just live on the coastline?"

"I live in a state." A small smile quirked the side of his mouth.

"Which one?" I pressed.

The throat clearing was back along with some fidgeting. "California."

"Where in California?"

"Uh, what? Sorry?"

I leaned forward. "Where. Are. You. From. In. California?"

Tanner chuckled uneasily and reached for his water. "Southern."

"Like that narrows it down. Don't they call everything south of LA 'southern California'?" I tapped my fingernail on the table and waited.

Tanner swallowed hard. "Uh, San Diego area."

"Oh!" I exclaimed. "Really?"

He narrowed his eyes slightly. "Why?"

"What do you mean, why?" I asked.

There was a long moment of silence before Tanner twitched and shook himself. "Sorry, I...I was just—. Have you been to San Diego, then?"

I decided to just let him be weird. I already knew he was; I was just going to stop expecting him to act normal.

"No." I worked hard to keep my voice light. "I mean, I've seen pictures. I love the ocean. Once I see it in real life, I'm pretty sure the ocean will become my happy place."

"It is beautiful," Tanner said in a distant way.

I was about to ask him why he had suddenly gone all zombie-eyed when Gena reappeared with her arms full of wings and zucchini. That thoroughly distracted me from Tanner. It was time to put my master plan into effect.

"Thank you so much," Tanner said.

"Enjoy." Gena winked and disappeared again.

Tanner's eyes widened. "That's a lot of food. I didn't know the portions were so big."

I reached for the wings. "The only thing small here is the parking lot." I used my fork to slide four wings onto the little plate Gena had set in front of me. I followed up with three pieces of zucchini and a boatload of ranch, all the while waiting for Tanner to say something about the amount of food on my plate.

He totally didn't.

He just chose one of each appetizer, ate slowly, and didn't seem to care that I was heaping food onto my plate like it was my last meal. Didn't he think it was so disgusting how I ate like a guy?

Maybe he didn't notice. Most guys I knew weren't super observant. Dayton for sure wasn't. I once cut six inches off the end of my hair, and two weeks later Dayton asked me if something was different.

Whatever.

I was on this date for the food, and I was totally going to enjoy every bite of it.

Ways to Improve Bailey #15

Come on, girl. Be real

Oh my goodness.

I felt disgusting.

I was so stuffed. Like, *so* stuffed. Thanksgiving dinner wished it could make people feel this stuffed.

I couldn't even think about how much I ate without all the food in my stomach churning back up my esophagus. It was delicious while I was chewing, but now I was thinking it totally wasn't worth it.

Tanner didn't seem to be fazed a bit by the fact that there was only one take-home container coming out of the restaurant with us, and all it had in it were two chicken wings and about half of the spaghetti that came with his chicken parmesan.

So, basically, the only person seriously grossed out by how much I ate was me.

I could barely walk. Everything hurt.

I pasted a sickly smile on my face and strolled passed Tanner into the cool night air. I wrapped my arms around myself to keep from shivering, or to keep my stomach from up-heaving, one of the two.

"Are you cold?" Tanner asked, jogging to catch up to me. He had stayed behind to hold the door for a couple that was coming in as we left. Of course he did that because that was the kind of guy he was. A door-holding, waitress-humanizing, big-tipping, job-saving, paying-even-though-the manager-said-not-to, refusing-to-be-disgusted-when-his-date-ate-a-ridiculous-amount-of-food kind of guy.

"I'm good," I said through chattering teeth.

Tanner shot me a sideways look. "Uh-huh. Well, in that case, I thought we could take a walk around campus."

His expression and voice remained neutral no matter how long I stared at him.

He better be joking.

As good as I was at pretending, I could no longer hide the fact that every step I took made my stomach think it needed to brush up on its projectile vomiting skills. There was no way I could go for a walk.

I opened my mouth to croak out an excuse to end the night so that I could go home and roll around the living room carpet in abject misery, but when I did, no words came out. I opened and closed my mouth at least three times, trying to get something to happen, and I was disappointed every time. Maybe there was so much food backed up in my system that the words couldn't get through.

"Are you okay?" Tanner asked, his face softening into genuine concern.

Because Tanner was a sincerely nice guy. I got that now. I couldn't help but notice that one simple fact despite my plan to make this a one date wonder. That was part of the reason I felt so uncomfortable, besides how full I was.

I've heard Dayton say that everyone has a moment in their life, maybe more than one, when they get the rare and valuable opportunity to step back and see themselves from a different perspective. It would probably be described as an awakening or some other hoo-hoo thing like that.

Maybe it was because of all the carbs rolling around in my system, all that evil gluten, but for some reason, the universe chose that moment to reveal something to me.

About me.

I was not a very good date.

And maybe not a very nice person.

The exact words that went through my mind were "self-centered brat." But for the sake of my ego, I decided to choose a different sentence that meant almost the same thing.

Here was Tanner being all considerate, generous, and gentlemanly throughout the whole night. He looked me in the eye, responded to what I said, and he was super nice to the strangers we passed.

And then there was me.

Being a rotten date was my whole plan from the beginning. I didn't want any second dates, and I was right on track. Everything worked out the way I wanted it too.

Except, I couldn't muster any satisfaction. My full belly seemed to have broken my filter. Kind of like that time Dayton got the stomach bug and crawled down the hall to my room to confess he used my toothbrush to clean his toenails.

I couldn't deny what a stinker I was, both on dates and otherwise. The truth was that my brilliant plans had only ever gotten me fast food, indigestion, and now nausea.

Maybe Dayton was right about me.

Ugh. I felt terrible.

This was not the best moment to have a life changing epiphany. Walking through a parking lot in the dark and cold with a stomach so full that it was a miracle nothing was leaking out of my ears. This was more of an alone-time-on-an-early-morning-walk kind of thing.

"So," Tanner said, clearing his throat, "do you want to go for that walk?"

I stopped and tugged Tanner's arm to stop him, too. I stepped in front of him so that I could see his face fully in the streetlight.

"Do you really want to go on a walk?" I asked.

Tanner seemed a little unsteady on his feet. It took him a moment to even out his stance. "I'm good for whatever. It was just an idea I had, but then, I'm a So-Cal boy. I forget how cold it gets when the sun goes down."

I bit my bottom lip. "Can I be honest?"

"Please." One corner of Tanner's mouth lifted slightly higher. The expression did wonders for his face: his beard looked more groomed, and his hair was less clown wig-ish.

I tried to smile back, but I was in too much pain to pull it off completely. "I am so seriously full, like, past the point of stuffed, that I don't think there is a real word in the English language that covers how my stomach feels right now. If you want to keep hanging out, can we go for a drive instead of a walk?"

Tanner shuffled his feet. "Do you want to keep hanging out?"

"I—." I paused. Did I? I didn't know anymore. Part of me wanted to go home and fall into a food coma, and the other part wanted to find out more about Tanner, which was really hard to admit, considering how I felt about him only a couple of hours ago. Strangely, hanging out longer didn't sound like the worst thing in the world. "Yeah, sure. Let's go for a drive."

"Okay." Tanner grinned, his teeth gleaming white through all the facial hair. I noticed that his eyes crinkled up in the corners when he smiled. My favorite grandpa used to do that, too. It made me feel suddenly as though I'd known Tanner for a really long time.

"Do you have your car here?" he looked around.

"No," I shook my head and then stopped because it was making me feel worse. "I don't have a car. Dayton dropped me off."

"How do you get to swim lessons from work?"

I stared at him. How did he know I taught swimming lessons? I hadn't told him that, had I?

"I just walk. It's not far." I gestured across the highway towards campus.

"What about when it snows?"

"Sometimes Marnie picks me up, sometimes Dayton does. Sometimes I walk. Again, it's not that far away."

"It doesn't seem safe to walk across that road." His keys jingled in his hand. "People drive like maniacs on Milton."

I just shrugged. "A lot of students cross there. Drivers are used to watching for people."

"Never assume that." Tanner narrowed his eyes. "Let me know when you don't have a ride, okay? I can take you to the Aquatic Center."

"What? No, it's-"

"I insist. Now, let's get you in the car. You're shivering." He started walking again.

I tried to keep up, I really did. After a minute, he slowed down to my super snail pace.

"Do you need me to carry you?" he asked.

Was he being serious? I glanced from the corner of my eye to check his facial expression and still didn't know. It was too dark without the glow from the streetlight. Whose idea was it to make Flagstaff a dark-sky city? The stars were not enough to read expressions.

"I can walk." But I had to know. "Would you really carry me?"

"What would you do if I did?" He turned his head in the opposite direction to see if cars were coming.

I decided to ignore that question. The answer was I would bust out with my Tae Kwon Do skills and flatten him. I didn't want him to know I could do something like that in case he was a well-disguised creeper and I needed to neutralize him later on. "Where the heck did you park? Outer Mongolia?"

Tanner laughed. "It's a good habit to park far away, so you have to walk more."

Whoever came up with that idea had not stuffed themselves silly at Basil's. We stopped walking when we reached a small, dented, old, blue Dodge pickup truck. I'd once overheard Dayton and some of his dumber friends talking about how people resemble their vehicles. I thought it was hogwash at the time, but seriously, Tanner kind of looked like his truck.

Except it didn't have a beard.

"Where to?" Tanner asked as he opened the passenger side door for me. The truck was low enough that I could slide right in without too much bending, which was good. I waved Tanner away while I slowly got settled. He walked around to his side, then started the truck and adjusted the heaters to blow on me.

I buckled the seatbelt and then stretched the strap out, to keep it from touching my stomach. I gave an audible sigh and leaned back into the seat.

Tanner started laughing.

"Shush. Not funny." I wiggled around to find a more comfortable position. "I should have worn my stretchy pants."

"Help me out here, Bailey." He dropped his laugh as quick as he'd picked it up.

"With what?"

"Since you don't weigh three hundred pounds, I'm assuming you don't always eat like that. So, did you do it to impress me, or to get rid of me?"

"What do you think?" I rolled my head to face him. It took way too much effort to lift it off the headrest.

He went on, almost thinking out loud. "I also can't figure out where, on your tiny person, you fit all of that food."

I was too sluggish to be indignant about his comment on my size. Dayton was always rubbing it in that he was over six feet and built while I was just over five feet and...not built. I spent my whole sophomore year of high school doing yoga, drinking protein shakes, and lifting weights, thinking it would help my body stretch and bulk up so that people would stop asking me which elementary school I went to.

It didn't work.

Being small paid off on the swim teams, though. I literally put the speed in speedo. But I was too full to point any of this out. Every time I opened my mouth, I felt like I was taking a huge risk.

"If I had to make a guess, I'd say you were trying to scare me off." Tanner tapped the steering wheel without looking at me.

I raised my eyebrows.

Well, well, well.

"It's a great strategy. That was epic eating back there. I bet that works on most guys."

"Um, yeah." I lowered one eyebrow slightly, surprise and shame played tug-of-war with my insides.

"I didn't mean to upset you." Tanner said in a sympathetic voice.

"I'm not upset." I lifted my chin. "I ordered a butt ton of food. It's about time you commented on it."

Tanner chuckled, "I had many thoughts, if that makes you feel better."

"It does." I picked up my purse and hugged it against my belly. At first, I wanted nothing touching me, but now it felt way better to hug something. Though, I would have preferred a fluffy pillow.

"Indulge me for a moment." Tanner continued. "I am quite curious about you."

"Are you, quite?" I said in a snooty voice, then sniffed to make my point even more clear.

Tanner peered at me. "That was pompous?"

"Quite."

His face relaxed into a smile. "You're teasing me, I see. I apologize for sounding like a college professor."

"I'll blame the day job." I said. "What are you curious about?"

"You, mostly. Your intentions, specifically. You went to great lengths of epic eating to get rid of me. I would initially take that as proof that you don't care to go on a date with me, personally, ever again. But I have also noticed that you don't *ever* date the same guy for more than a couple of weeks. Do you do something drastic to get rid of all of them?"

"No, you're just special," I smirked. Like I was really going to divulge that kind of information on a first date.

Actually, this wasn't even a date. It was two people catching dinner together. I wasn't obligated to explain myself at all.

"I see," he stared out the window. "Your flippancy indicates that you don't want to answer that question. I'm sorry if I crossed a line."

"You didn't. It's fine." I shifted, trying to find a comfortable way to sit. Every position so far resulted in thirty pounds of delicious food cutting off my air supply.

"I am very curious about you and, obviously, interested in the workings of the female mind."

Okay, that also sounded like something a college professor would say. A different field, though. Psychology, not math.

"Why is that obvious?" I wondered out loud. I couldn't fathom why anyone would want to know what went on inside other people's minds.

That sounded terrifying.

Tanner gave me an amused look. "Isn't it the quest of all men? To understand what women think?"

"I don't know, is it?"

"It is," Tanner nodded. "Though, I suppose you can't speak for all the female minds, can you? Just yours." He sounded disappointed, like he really thought I could teach him the key to understanding all women by telling him my techniques for getting rid of guys.

"So then, Bailey Hendrix, if you would be so kind as to explain yourself to me. You consistently date but never long term. Are you afraid of commitment? Are you avoiding relationships, so you can focus on your life plan? If it is one of those, why do you date at all?"

Wow.

Just, wow. First prize goes to Tanner for the most penetrating question I'd ever been asked. Probably in my entire life.

I opened my mouth no less than five times, but nothing came out, which was a good thing. My stomach gurgled uncomfortably as I clamped my teeth together. I wanted everything to stay put a lot more than my stomach did.

"You can be honest. I'm just curious." He kneaded his hands on the steering wheel and glanced at me. "Actually, you'd do me a huge favor if you'd explain. I'll be up all night trying to figure you out. Occupational hazard of this mathematical brain." He tapped the side of his head and laughed like it was all a joke, like he was trying to convince himself it was no big deal. His voice lowered enough that his words were hard to hear. "I just can't let it go until I solve it."

"Lake Mary," I said.

"What?" He gave me a strange look.

"You asked me where to go. Let's drive out to Lake Mary. It's my favorite place. Have you been?"

Tanner shook his head as he picked up his phone. Of course he was the type that has to map things before he did them. "It's about twenty minutes from here to the lookout," he said, almost to himself. He turned the screen so that I could see the map.

I shrugged. "We don't have to go that far. Really, the drive is the whole point. You can turn around whenever."

"I was just working out logistics. I think it sounds great." He took one more look at the screen and then put his truck into drive.

We were barely out of the parking lot when it became impossible to ignore the old ladies passing us in tiny sedans. I leaned over to glance at the speedometer. We were going the speed limit, exactly. It never varied. Tanner was the first person I'd ever met that saw the speed limit as an actual limit. I couldn't believe it.

Especially considering he was from California.

That was just one more thing to add to the list of a gazillion things *I* couldn't figure out about *him*.

We drove in silence while we turned onto Lake Mary Road and started to leave civilization behind. But unlike the restaurant, it was not an awkward silence; it was peaceful. I loved this drive so very much. There was something so soothing about being in the trees. It looked especially breathtaking in the moonlight.

And then, we rounded a curve, and the moon was sparkling on the water. Lake Mary was truly at its best at night, mostly because it was too dark to see how brown and murky the water was.

Tanner whistled a low note. "I didn't think Arizona had water."

"Okay, ocean boy." I felt good enough to sit up all the way. "It's not the Pacific, but it's pretty beautiful. You have to admit."

"Absolutely," he said without hesitation.

This warmed my insides as if I was the one responsible for the scenery. I turned slightly towards him. Words billowed up my throat and came out before I could stop them.

"I love this place so much. I was born here. In Flagstaff. So was Dayton. I am addicted to the mountains and the pines. My dad retired early, and my parents moved to Phoenix. I thought I was so sick of Flagstaff, so I went with them for my senior year. It was miserable." I paused, searching the floor of Tanner's truck to see if my defenses or my pride were lying somewhere at my feet. I couldn't see them so I gave myself permission to stop pretending. I was going to be as sentimental and ridiculous as I wanted. It wasn't like I really cared what Tanner thought about me, anyway.

"And, for the record, I don't try to get rid of all the guys I date, just those that..." It sounded bad no matter how I put it. "I mean, I just like to try new restaurants, but I don't want to go alone, so I go on dates." Dayton's words worked through my mind, starting a shame spiral. "I guess I am sort of using some of them. But the good news is that I don't go out a second time with the guys that don't measure up. I'm not leading them on. I'm being honest. That's a good thing, right?"

"That's an interesting theory." Tanner's voice wasn't judgy, but I felt a twinge of shame nonetheless.

"It's terrible, isn't it?" I took a deep breath. Now I felt uncomfortable for a different reason.

"Don't be too hard on yourself. The truth of it is, Bailey, people are abominably selfish. It's not just you; it's human nature. It's mind-boggling that anyone gets beyond it long enough to marry and propagate the species."

I tried to process his words, but he'd switched to some professor or lecture tone, which my brain was conditioned to tune out completely. "It just feels so pathetic to do things alone," I said.

Tanner nodded. "Such as sitting at a corner table at your local Froyo all day?"

I pointed at him. "That's what I mean! Totally pathetic!"

"Thanks a lot." Tanner shook his head, but I saw a dimple deepen in the cheek closest to me.

I chewed my lip, still ruminating on the way I dated. There had to be a way to make it sound better than using guys to try new restaurants. "It's just that relationships are a lot of work and a lot of...what's the word? Compromise. I like to do stuff with people, but I also want to do what I want to do without someone forcing me."

"And you think a relationship forces you to do things?"

"Or not do things. My mom was an amazing dancer before she got married, but she never did anything with it because they had Dayton right away."

"So, you don't think Dayton is worth giving up your dreams?"

I snorted.

"In all seriousness," Tanner swallowed a chuckle, "I'm curious if you think marriage and family are enough to compensate for giving up something you love?"

"Absolutely not," I shook my head. "Nothing is worth giving up your dreams."

"Can dreams change?"

I squinted at the road ahead. "I don't think so. I think that's called quitting."

"I see. That explains why you date the way you do. If the end isn't something you want, then the means wouldn't be justified."

My brain rolled, trying to understand what he meant. "I don't know about all that. I just don't want to be stuck in a relationship."

"Understandable. But, what about the other person?"

"What do you mean? Like, the guy I date? What about him?"

"Yes, him." Tanner adjusted the heat to a lower level; it was really cranking. "What about what he wants?"

"I don't know what he wants," I said before I thought it through. Then I realized that was exactly what Tanner was getting at. I didn't take the time to find out what the guy wanted.

I peered at him in the gloomy darkness. I didn't like what he was hinting at all. It was one thing for me to think I'm a terrible person. It was another thing entirely for someone else to think it.

"What about you?" I asked. There was a note of challenge in my voice.

"What about me?"

"What are your thoughts on dating? If you think everyone is naturally selfish anyway, what's the point of trying?"

"That is a very good question." He shifted in his seat and stared at the road. "A few years ago, I would have answered you very differently than now. Ultimately, I think the goal is to find someone you choose to love more than yourself. That's the clencher, though, isn't it? That someone would then need to choose to love you more than themselves. And we have no control over that, do we?"

"Uh, no?" I answered even though it was beyond obvious that Tanner wasn't talking to me anymore. My words jolted him upright, like he'd really forgotten I was there.

"Maybe that's the problem, Bailey. Maybe you haven't found someone you love enough to compromise for."

I liked it better when he was lost in his own whatever. This conversation was venturing into places I did not want to go.

"Anyway," I raised my voice and tried to sound perky, "I really love Flagstaff."

Tanner pressed his lips together. For a second, I didn't think he was going to let me get away with the subject change, but then he said, "I know exactly what you mean. I feel that way about home. I miss the water." His head moved back and forth as he tried to divide his gaze between the road and the lake.

I pointed out the windshield. "There's a turn off right up there. Not a real parking lot, but if you pull over, we can look at the lake and not die in a car accident."

Tanner laughed as he followed the direction of my finger. He turned the truck off and laid his keys on the dashboard.

"If you love the ocean so much, why are you here?" I asked as soon as Tanner settled.

"That's complicated." Tanner looked at his hands, then up at me. His mouth tried to turn up at the corners. "You really don't want to hear about it. Trust me."

I pursed my lips and then decided to let him get away with not spilling his guts. He let me get away with a subject change.

Now we were even.

After several silent moments of staring at the water, Tanner's eyes shifted to me. "If I didn't know better, I would think you lured me out here with an agenda. This would be a great make out spot."

I sat straight up with a gasp that locked my seatbelt. I unbuckled and edged towards the door. "Excuse me?"

"Hey, don't look at me. You're the predator here. I had no idea where we were going."

"What?" I choked.

Tanner laughed that great laugh again, all the way from his belly. "You should see your face."

Without a seatbelt to restrain me, I punched him as hard as I could in the arm. "You were messing with me?"

Tanner clutched his arm and laughed so hard he had to gulp for air.

It was totally contagious. I started laughing, too, and before I knew it, I was wiping tears off my cheeks. "I can't believe you just said that. Who are you, anyway?"

Tanner's face drooped suddenly. "Isn't that the question?" he stared ahead, his eyes drinking in the lake. "Who is anyone?"

"What kind of a question is that?"

He didn't respond. He just stared out the windshield with the side of his head resting on the side window. I didn't like the weight that his question brought into the truck, and my stomach was still rolling from that make-out accusation. Part of me wanted to change the subject to something lighter; the other part wanted to make sure he was absolutely clear that we were not about to make out right now.

For multiple reasons.

I smacked his arm with the back of my hand. "You're super broody. What the heck are you thinking now?"

Tanner blinked and looked down at his arm. "Sorry. It's nothing."

I narrowed my eyes. "That is a lie."

"Is it, though?" Tanner pursed his lips to the side. "How do you know?"

"Oh, I know." I held up my hands. "I am the master of lie detecting. You know the saying, 'it takes one to know one'?"

"Yes."

I waved my hands in front of me. "Liar. I can spot one a mile away."

"You admit you lie?"

I narrowed my eyes, daring him to disagree. "Everybody lies."

"Yes, they do." Tanner let loose with a sigh that totally tugged at my heart. I've heard people use that phrase before; it is a particular favorite of my mom. I thought it was a load of baloney before, I mean, seriously? How does something tug at your heart? But inside my chest it felt like someone wrapped a string around my heart and was trying to pull it out.

Not that I knew what to do about any of these profound realizations I was having. I sort of hoped they would all go away when I woke up in the morning, and I would be the same as always.

"Hey, Tanner?" I ran my fingers along the bottom of the passenger's side window. "I, um, I lied to you."

"I know."

I whipped my head around. "What do you know?"

"I know you lied to me."

"When?"

Tanner smiled. "Was there more than one time?"

"No!" I paused. "Well, maybe. But what are you thinking about specifically?"

Tanner leaned back on the headrest, so he was looking at the ceiling. "When I asked you out a few weeks ago. You told me you had to volunteer at the soup kitchen, remember?"

Oh, I remembered. "Did Dayton tell you I lied?"

Tanner shook his head. "I just knew."

My stomach rolled. I thought I was starting to feel better, but everything was all curdled again. "Why did you ask me out?"

"Which time?"

"Either time." I flung a hand and almost smacked the window.

"I was curious."

I waited for him to elaborate, but he didn't. "About what?"

"You."

It was like I had to fight to pull out every word he said. I slumped into the seat. "What about me?"

Tanner turned to look at me. "I was curious if you would say yes."

"Why?"

His smile was mocking, but it wasn't directed at me. "You don't go out with guys that look like me."

"So, I was, like, an experiment?"

Tanner rubbed his hands back and forth over his jeans. "I wouldn't call it that. I guess I was trying to prove something to myself."

I should have known better than to think he would just tell me. I let out a gust of air. "What were you trying to prove?"

"It's not important. You said yes. So, what I thought doesn't matter."

It blew me away that he could be so honest about himself. It made me want to try it out, too.

"I *was* trying to get rid of you," I said.

"Excuse me?" Tanner blinked.

"Earlier you asked why I ate the way I did. I was trying to get rid of you. I didn't want to come on this date, and I didn't want you to ask me out again. Dayton is always threatening to tell his friends how much I eat, like it's a bad thing. I had the brilliant idea to eat a ton in front of you and send you running."

"How'd that go for you?" Tanner raised his eyebrows.

I groaned and rubbed my belly. It was not as bad as it was forty minutes ago, but it was still not okay. "Don't ask. It's not funny yet."

"Thank you, Bailey." I could hear Tanner's smile in his voice. "Thanks for being honest with me."

"Yeah, well," I shifted to find a more comfortable spot, "I'm just saving myself from the phone call at three in the morning, the one where you beg me to solve the puzzle, so you can finally go to sleep."

"I don't have your phone number, so you're safe."

I flopped my hand out onto the console between us. Tanner looked at it and then at me. I rolled my eyes. "I'm not asking you to hold my hand, dummy. Gimme your phone," I said, wiggling my fingers.

He set his phone into my palm. I looked at it and sighed, handing it back. "Unlock it, goofus."

He did, his eyes darting from me to the screen. "What are you going to do, exactly?"

Did he think I was going to crank call China or have Sam's Club deliver twenty boxes of diapers to his office?

I'm not twelve.

"Putting my number in, duh." I pushed the button to add a contact and typed "Bailey" into the name line. I would have taken a dorky picture to go along with it, but it was way too dark now. I saved my info and handed the phone back.

"I wasn't hinting to get your number when I said that."

"Whatever."

"I really wasn't. I had no ulterior motives."

"Do you want me to delete it?" I held my palm out again.

Tanner twirled his phone through his fingers, then tucked it into his back pocket. "No, I think I'll keep it. Thank you."

"You don't have to give me your number. I'll just save it when you call me."

"*When* I call you? I thought you were trying to get rid of me."

"I changed my mind," I said, sitting up. "Girls are allowed to do that, you know."

There was a long silence after my words faded.

"Oh, I know," Tanner whispered.

Ways to Improve Bailey #16

No more sleeping in

At the crackiest crack of dawn, my idiot brother pounced on me like a lion in the Serengeti. I shrieked and tried to push him off, but he was taller and much stronger, so he stayed.

"I was sleeping! Go away, you monster."

"No way! Tell me about your date. Tell me everything. You got home super late last night, so it must have been good, right?" He tried to twirl a lock of his hair, but it was too short. "O-M goodness. Was he sooooo dreamy?"

I reached for my alarm clock and slammed it onto the end table. "Dayton Bernard Hendrix! Did you even look at the clock before you galloped in here?"

He shook his head. "Why?"

I shoved the clock in his face.

"Dang, it's early," he said.

I wanted to smack him so much. Like, so much! Instead, I sighed and wiggled out from under his bony knee to curl up more comfortably with my pillow. There was no point in prolonging the inevitable.

"So?" he prompted.

"I didn't get home late. It was only ten." But then I stayed up way later watching a sappy chick flick because I was still too sick to sleep—which was why I felt like there was a herd of elephants sitting on my eyelids.

"It went well? You had fun?"

I nodded without thinking. Dayton didn't need encouragement to be a know-it-all booger, and there I was, giving him fuel. I should have told him it was just okay. Then maybe he would let me sleep instead of bouncing around my bed like a nincompoop, singing, "I told you so, I told you so".

The only good news was that his bouncing threw him off balance, so it made it easier to push him onto the floor with my foot. He hardly hit the carpet before he was crawling back onto my bed.

"Say the words, Baybee. Say them. Tell me Tanner is a nice guy. Do it now."

I did my best robot impression. "Tanner is a nice guy."

"And..." Dayton rolled his hand, waiting for more. He was relentless.

"And he has terrible taste in friends."

"And..." Dayton said, as if I hadn't said anything at all.

I sighed again. "And what? It wasn't the worst date ever. The end."

Dayton pursed his lips. "Okay, girl. Keep your little secrets."

The suggestive look in his eyes pushed my buttons. He was totally insinuating that something had happened between Tanner and me, like I was covering something up. His smug little face made me want to scream.

Now I was going to have to tell him everything so that his weird brain didn't contort my date with Tanner into something it wasn't.

For the next forty-five minutes, I methodically told him every last, insignificant detail about my date with Tanner.

He asked for it.

"I can't believe you ate that much!" Dayton said when I finally finished my story. He could hardly talk he was laughing so hard. "I wish I'd been there to see it."

I shook my head. "No, you don't. It wasn't good."

"I'm surprised you didn't throw up or have, like, explosive diarrhea!"

I clamped my mouth closed. Okay, so maybe I hadn't told him every last detail.

Dayton stopped laughing and surveyed my face. "Bailey, did you have explosive diarrhea?"

"No!"

"Did you throw up?"

"Yes, all right? It wasn't that big of a deal. We were driving back into town, and the truck was hopping over that dumb, bumpy road."

"You threw up in his truck?" Dayton snorted.

"More like out the window."

Dayton's look of horror was strangely satisfying.

"It was really dark. It's not like anyone saw me."

"What did Tanner do?" Dayton sucked his breath in sharply, like he just realized the same thing could happen to him someday and he had no idea how to handle it.

"He pulled over so I could finish up in the bushes, and when I was done, he brought me wet wipes from the glove compartment."

"Okay," Dayton said, nodding like he could totally do that. He was fooling himself; he totally couldn't. Besides his terror of vomit, I was pretty sure Dayton didn't even know what wet wipes were.

I should have told him that Tanner held my hair back and made sure the puke didn't get on my shoes. I wondered what he would have said to that.

"Go on," Dayton poked me. "Then what happened?"

"Then, we drove through the carwash by Culvers and went to Safeway because I was super thirsty, and my mouth tasted like barf. I couldn't decide what sounded good, so Tanner got a bottle of water, chocolate milk, apple juice, Sprite, and pomegranate juice for me to choose from. We sat in the truck and talked. Then he brought me home."

"What did you talk about?"

I squinted, trying to remember. "Lots of stuff. Sea turtles, aspen trees, the State of the Union."

"Come on!" Dayton punched my shoulder.

"I don't know, Dayton. We talked for a long time about a ton of stuff." I paused. "Though, actually, we really did talk about sea turtles and aspen trees."

"Why would you do that?" He looked both bored and intrigued at the same time.

"Sea turtles are his favorite animal, and aspens are my favorite tree."

"That is probably the weirdest date I have ever heard of."

"Yeah," I agreed because it totally was.

"So, what are you making for breakfast?" Dayton asked, switching the subject with a literal twinkle in his eye. "It's your turn. I'm starving."

That was too much! My pillow and I beat his backside out of my room.

Once he was gone, I locked my door and looked around with my hands on my hips. My bed was so adorable and comfortable that I debated if it would be worth it to try to fall back asleep. Probably not. I was wide awake after talking to Dayton for so long. I might as well get moving.

I wanted to go for a walk, but not alone. And not with Dayton. I needed some space.

And maybe some girl time.

I picked up my phone and called Marnie. She was the typical early bird, so I knew she would be awake.

Sure enough, Marnie answered midway through the second ring. "Bailey!"

"Hey, are you up for a walk this morning?"

"Absolutely! I'll meet you at the mailbox in five."

"Perfect."

I tossed my phone on my bed and rifled through my closet for a sweatshirt. A big fluffy one. I pulled it over my long-sleeve pajama shirt. It would be cold outside. At least, it would be at first, depending on how long we stayed out. It would warm up fast. That was one of the loveable quirks about Flagstaff winters: freezing in the morning, sweltering in the afternoon.

I slipped on tennis shoes and jogged down the hall. Dayton was in the kitchen, sitting on the counter and looking at his phone.

"Gross, Dayton. We put food where your booty is right now."

He looked up sort of glassy eyed and lifted one side of his behind to check the counter underneath him.

"Never mind." I pulled on a stripped beanie. "I'm going for a walk with Marnie. I'll be back in about an hour."

"Marnie?" Dayton blinked.

I sighed. Whatever he'd been doing on his phone had fried his brains. "Yes, Marnie."

"You're going on a walk with Marnie right now?"

Sheesh, he was moving way slower than usual. "That's what I said."

Dayton scratched his ear. "But, it's dark and cold, and there's dark and cold people out there. Where are you walking? Not in the forest, right? You know that's off limits without me or pepper spray."

"I know." I dragged the word out until it was whiney and ridiculous.

"Maybe I should come with you, Bay. I don't like it."

I tucked my phone in my pocket with a sigh. "We will stick to the sidewalks, look both ways when we cross, and go to the park where there's a bazillion street lights. You can hear us if we scream."

Dayton's forehead furrowed.

I probably should have left off that last sentence. Dayton was not getting the joke.

"I walk to the park all the time," I said in a softer voice. "It will be fine, okay?"

He studied me for a minute, then nodded. "On three conditions: one, you keep your phone handy and the ringer on the highest volume."

I nodded.

"Two, you come back in thirty minutes."

Whatever, that wasn't a big deal. "Okay, what's three?" I shrugged a jacket over my sweatshirt.

He hopped off the counter. "You show me that Tae Kwon Do spinning jump kick, so I know you can still do it."

I rolled my eyes, but I did what he asked.

"She's still got it!" Dayton snapped his fingers three times. "Okay, have fun. I'll see you in thirty minutes."

"Yep, see ya." I waved and closed the door behind me.

It was still dark when I stepped outside. And it was cold. Thank goodness for layers. I pulled out my phone to make sure it was still there after that kick demonstration, and to check that the ringer was on highest volume. Then I jumped off the porch to propel myself into the morning.

By the time I reached the mailboxes on the corner of our street, Marnie was waiting for me, hopping from foot to foot, her curls bouncing. When she saw me, she threw her hands in the air and shrieked, "Bailey!"

I shook my head. "You are such a goof."

"I know." She put her arm around my shoulder, pulling me into her side. I put up with it for approximately three seconds before I pulled away and started walking. Five minutes later, when we passed the downtown library, I had to shed my jacket layer. It was heating up fast at the pace we were walking.

"So, what's new?" Marnie waited for me to tie the arms of my jacket around my waist. I peeked at her while pretending to give the knot my full attention. Did she know about my date last night? I couldn't remember if I told her Tanner asked me out. It was all kind of a blur now.

"Uh, not much. How about you?"

Marnie looked up as we walked under a row of trees that lined the street. It was like living in Mayberry, I swear.

"Oh, the usual." Her voice stayed light. "Nothing new. No dates to speak of. I did not go out with anyone last night. Did you?"

Okay, I saw what she did there.

"How did you know about that?"

"Dayton told me."

Of course he did.

"Why would you talk to Dayton on purpose?" I grimaced.

Marnie giggled and nudged my arm. "I ran into him at Target. He's really not so bad, you know?"

No, I didn't know that.

"What else did he say?" I asked.

"Nothing, really."

Whatever! Nothing, really. Dayton always had something to say. "Come on!"

She laughed and swung her arms. "Seriously, he didn't really say anything else. I was curious why you went out with Tanner, especially since you don't really hide how you feel about him, and Dayton said I would have to talk to you about it. I'm so glad you called this morning."

I tucked my hands into the front pocket of my sweatshirt, wishing I'd brought gloves, and tried to think of what to say next. It wasn't like I wanted to hide anything from Marnie, but I for sure didn't want her to get the wrong idea and try to frozen yogurt match us or something.

"Bailey?"

"It's not like it's a big deal. He asked me out, and I said yes."

"Yeah, but why? You said no every other time he asked you out."

Every other time?

"It was only one other time."

Marnie made a skeptical noise.

I squinted to help myself think better. I honestly couldn't recall any other time Tanner asked me out.

"You really don't remember?" Marnie glanced at me.

"I really don't."

She tugged at the wristband she used for skiing at Snowbowl. It looked raggedy enough to come apart in her hands.

"He asked you to the Halloween party at McConnell Hall."

Okay, I vaguely remembered that. I think I had measles that night. They were conditional measles though, because I totally went out to dinner at the Oakmont with Dryden from English.

"And he asked you to go to the Christmas tree lighting at Little America."

Okay, yeah, I really couldn't go that time. My parents were in town.

"And he invited you to the Polar Express."

Wait, what? I totally didn't remember that.

"And to the New Year's Gala at Dubois."

I eyeballed the side of her head. Now she was just making things up, I was sure of it. "No, he did not."

"Yes, he did. I remember because I was going with Casey, and I wanted to double, but you said there was no way you'd ring in the new year with a hobbit hobo. It was bad luck or something."

Okay, that sounded like me.

"So, it's curious you agreed this time. Why did you?"

I checked both ways before crossing the street, even though the sun was barely coming up and there were no cars anywhere. Despite what Dayton thought, I was generally responsible.

Maybe it was because it was early, or maybe my brain was still hungover from my Basil's eat-a-thon the night before. I was having a hard time coming up with a good reason why, just a few weeks ago, going out with Tanner seemed like a fate worse than spandex.

"Bailey?"

"Yeah, I guess I sort of got tricked into saying yes and then couldn't get out of it because of Dayton's 'no more lying' improvement."

"Okay," Marnie hopped off the curb. "Well, how was it? Did you have a good time?"

I didn't want to answer that question. I don't know why, but it just made my insides turn into gummy worms.

Live ones.

The only thing I could think of to change the subject was to bring up one of the things I disliked talking about more than anything else in the world.

"Sure, it was fine. So, how are things with Todd?""

Instead of going all sparkly and distracted, Marnie kicked a rock and watched it ricochet, then spin across the street. "Okay."

Uh-oh.

"Just okay?"

Marnie sighed so heavily it lifted her shoulders up to her ears. "He broke it off."

"Your date, or...?"

"Yes, that, and everything else. He broke up with me because he said I'm too nice."

Oh my gosh. Todd was a bigger idiot than I thought.

"So, he wants a mean girlfriend?"

Marnie pursed his lips. "I don't think he knows what he wants. It's fine. I've sworn off romance for reals this time. Maybe the reason I love chocolate on my ice cream is because I'm meant to be friends with everyone, you know? Like, maybe there's no perfect match for chocolate because it just goes well with everything."

While I agreed with the chocolate part of that, I thought the rest of what she was saying was idiotic. "Marnie."

"No, really, I'm fine. I think I knew it wasn't working deep down. I didn't even cry when he told me. I'm just going to concentrate on helping others find their perfect matches. Is it okay if I hang out at Froyo with you? Keith doesn't have to pay me or anything; I just want to observe. That would be fun, huh?"

I bit back my opinion of her yogurt-and-topping matchmaking and focused on the spending-more-time-with-her part. "I'd love that."

"Yay," Marnie smiled a real smile this time and turned us right towards Thorpe Park. "Want to hit the swings?"

"You know it!" I slapped her arm and took off running. I knew she'd pass me; she was in way better shape than I was. Marnie reached my side and matched my pace, so we jogged together to the swing set. They looked irresistible, bobbing haphazardly in the breeze.

Marnie took the swing next to me and was already soaring back and forth. I pumped my legs to catch up, swinging higher and higher into the air. I wanted to laugh out loud. No wonder kids loved swinging so much. It was almost like flying, and it never got old. It was so dang fun; I didn't want to stop.

We swung in silence until the sun came up and the early-morning dog walkers started congregating throughout the park. We would have stayed longer if my cell phone hadn't been ringing its pants off in my back pocket.

"Hang on, someone's calling." I slowed down to a gentle rocking and reached for my phone. I missed the call, so I checked my texts. There were seven, and they were all from Dayton.

> *It's been twenty minutes.*
>
> *Where are you?*
>
> *Are you with Marnie?*
>
> *Are you at the park?*
>
> *You didn't answer your phone.*
>
> *Why isn't Marnie answering her phone?*
>
> *Is your ringer on?*

"Dayton is texting us." I made a face.
"Oh no! I left my phone at home. Is everything alright?"
"He just wants me to come home and make him breakfast. He's fine."

Mom chimed in while I was talking.

> *Good morning, sweetheart. Daddy told me about your conversation. Do you want to talk it out some more? I have some time this morning.*

"We can go back if Dayton needs you," Marnie said.

"Hold on," I said to Marnie. My thumbs took off, rocketing across the phone keyboard. First to Dayton:

> *I'll be home in a sec.*

And then to Mom:

> *Morning, Mommy. I was upset, but it's okay now. You can tell Daddy I love him more than Bermuda. If you want to talk otherwise, I can call you from work. Around ten?*

My swing stopped all the way now, so I stood up. I was barely on my feet when my phone started chiming again. So annoying! This was exactly why I kept my ringer off all the time.

It was Dayton again.

> *Hurry, I'm hungry. Dayton need hash.*

And then Mom.

> *Lovely. Talk to you then!*

I was just about to put my phone back in my pocket when it started ringing. It was a phone call this time.

"Sorry, Marnie! My family is so needy."

"No worries." She jumped off her swing, then stooped to pet a passing Saint Bernard puppy.

"Hello?" I said.

"S'up Baybee cakes?"

"Holy Cow, Dayton. I'm coming already."

"Good," he said. "Is Marnie with you?"

"Yes, Marnie's with me."

"What?" Marnie looked up and missed seeing the huge goober of drool the puppy left on her shoes.

"Do you want to come over for breakfast?" I held the phone away from my ear, so I could hear Marnie's answer instead of Dayton's nonsense.

"It's really all right?"

"Bailey?" Dayton shouted. "Are you even listening to my superb lecture on manners?"

"No."

He let out a long breath. "Well, you missed out. I was telling you to invite Marnie over for breakfast. I think we need to put this on the list; I'm just not sure what to call it."

I shook my head with a smug smile. The fresh air and swinging had lifted my mood so much that Dayton barely even bugged me at the moment. "I already invited her."

"Oh," he said. "Well, good job. Also, I wanted to inform you that in order for you to make me hash this morning, we will need to go to the grocery store. We are out of eggs. And potatoes."

"I—"

"Also broccoli, red peppers, mushrooms, green onions, cheese, and milk."

"Oh my gosh, Dayton! Seriously?" I laughed. "Why don't you go to the store while we walk home? We'd be eating much sooner that way."

Dayton paused. "I'm in boxers, Bailey. The kissy face ones. I don't want to change. I'll drive you to Bashas', but I'm staying in the car."

"You're going to have to change anyway, goofus, if Marnie comes home with me."

There was silence on the line for a long time.

"Oh yeah. I need to take a shower. Can you stall?"

I rolled my eyes so that Marnie could see what I have to put up with. "We'll walk slow."

Ways to Improve Bailey #2

Be more responsible

You know that phenomenon when someone tells you about something, and then suddenly you hear about it all over the place? Example: One day after swimming lessons, Marnie told me about a brand of swimsuits she loves. Then, no joke, I heard two other girls talking about them, saw an advertisement in a magazine, and had a pop-up ad on Facebook about those same swimsuits.

So weird.

Anyways, Marnie, me, and freshly-showered-and-cologned Dayton were walking the aisles of Bashas' looking for snacks to restock our bare cupboards when I stopped. The other two kept walking, totally oblivious, while I backtracked and did a double take.

Was that Tanner?

His back was to me, and he wasn't wearing his usual flannel shirt, this one was blue and gray, but I could have sworn it was him. Then he bumped a can with his elbow and stooped to pick it up.

It was totally him.

I ducked out of sight as fast as I could and scooted down the next aisle.

Then I felt monumentally stupid.

What was I, twelve? Why didn't I just walk up to him and say hi instead of running away? I stared blankly at a box of cereal and shook my head at myself.

"Excuse me, miss."

"Oh, sorry!" I maneuvered my cart out of the way so that an elderly man could step around me. He touched the brim of his cowboy hat and nodded as he passed.

Which was just adorable.

"What are you doing?" Dayton walked up then, shaking his head. "Do I need to add something to the Bailey list about disappearing and blocking the bran cereal?"

I rolled my eyes.

"What list?" Marnie glanced between Dayton and me.

"I told you about this," I said. "You know? Dayton has a list on his bedroom door of ways I need to improve."

"Ways you need to improve?" Confusion wrinkling Marnie's forehead. "What do you need to improve?"

"Ha!" I pointed at Marnie but looked at Dayton.

Dayton pushed my hand away.

"I think Bailey is perfect. What could you possibly put on that list?" Marnie blinked.

Dayton shook his head. "Marnie, you think everyone is perfect."

"They are!" She raised her voice so it could be heard over his snort. "In their own way."

"I know I told you about this," I interrupted. "Remember we talked about the lying thing on our walk?"

"Oh, right!" Marnie nodded. "I got confused because I guess I don't understand why you want to put things like 'blocking the bran aisle' on that list."

"That was a joke," Dayton was quick to say.

I disagreed. He would have totally done it if Marnie hadn't called him out. Blocking the bran aisle wasn't any weirder than wearing mismatched socks and Dayton put that on the list a few months ago.

Now all my socks matched, and it was the worst.

"But blocking the bran aisle isn't a character flaw!" Marnie hesitated, her eyes flicking from me to Dayton. I followed her gaze to Dayton.

Fabulous, he had that look on his face. Apparently blocking the bran aisle was a character flaw. I took a deep breath and prepared myself for a lecture.

Before Dayton could open his mouth, Marnie continued. "Are you trying to change every little, tiny thing about Bailey?"

I quirked an eyebrow. Judging by the stunned look on Dayton's face, he wasn't expecting Marnie to ask that either.

I couldn't resist. "Yes, Dayton, do tell. Are you?"

Dayton shifted and shuffled and looked at something above our heads, then he bumped me away from the cart so he could steer. "Enough dilly-dally, girls. We have to check out before the frozen stuff melts."

I wasn't surprised he didn't answer. Not a bit. I wasn't even disappointed. I didn't need him to say the words to know that he thought I was a disaster. That was super obvious.

Marnie and I trailed behind Dayton, stepping out of the way of a lady and her kids. Was that six? Yes, it was. One lady, one cart, and six kids trying to get around us in the aisle. Every single towhead chattered their opinion about what they wanted to have for dinner that night.

I pulled my eyes away from the chaos and realized that we didn't have eggs yet. That was the one and only ingredient I definitely needed to make a hash.

"We forgot eggs." I tugged Marnie's sleeve. "Tell Dayton I went to get them."

She nodded and skipped to catch up to Dayton. I waded back through the sea of kids to the dairy section. I wasn't watching for Tanner, but part of me prepared myself to run into him without acting like an idiot. It's not like I followed him there. It was a grocery store; people go to those things every day. There was no need to make it all weird.

I snatched a carton of eggs and jogged to the register. Marnie smiled when she saw me and took the eggs to hand to Dayton, who was unloading the cart.

A million dollars' worth of groceries later, Dayton pushed the cart out of the store. He stopped to let a truck go before crossing the street.

My breath caught in my throat. It wasn't just any truck; it was Tanner's truck. I stared until he pulled up to the stoplight and turned out of sight.

I should have thrown a tomato or something to get his attention. Except I didn't buy any. Dayton was allergic—or at least he claims to be, but I was willing to bet money he just didn't like them.

We stashed the groceries in the trunk of our little car and were about to get in when a catcall from a passing Subaru made all three of us pause. It was some of Dayton's friends. He went to talk to them, and I slid into the backseat. Since I had shotgun on the way to the store, it was only fair to let Marnie have it on the way home.

"Who are those guys?" Marnie asked as she buckled her seatbelt and leaned against the window.

I shrugged and then realized her back was towards me. "I don't know. Dayton's friends."

"He sure knows a lot of people."

"Yeah." I tugged the seatbelt too hard, causing it to lock. I had to let it go and then pull gently in order to buckle it.

"He's so friendly."

"Isn't he, though?" I grunted and reached for my purse. I knocked it on the floor when I was wrestling with the seatbelt.

There was a pile of books scattered on the floor at my feet that I didn't notice until that moment. Library books by the looks of them. I hadn't been to the library in ages, so they had to be Dayton's books. Perfect! This was my chance to show Dayton how responsible I was.

I didn't need to improve.

When Dayton slid into the driver's seat, I was waiting for him with the library books on my lap.

"Hey, let's stop by the library really quick and return these books of yours."

"Those are your books, Bailey." Dayton turned with a glare already in place. "They've been sitting there for over a month. At least two weeks overdue."

I turned the top book over and groaned. It was a sushi for beginners book. Since raw fish was not technically a meat or potato, there was no way I could pin this one on Dayton. I slumped into the back of the seat. I should have known I couldn't impress Dayton. I don't know why I keep trying.

"We live five seconds from the library."

"So?" I pushed the books off my lap and crossed my arms.

"So, that should make it impossible to have overdue books."

"And yet," I waved one arm theatrically, "here we are."

Dayton stared at me a minute longer, his mouth working. Then, Marnie reached over and touched his hand. His face went slack, and his eyes swung away from me.

"Bailey is super busy. She works two jobs and goes to school full-time. Not to mention all those dates..."

I appreciated Marnie's defense, but bringing up my dating habits probably wasn't the best way to help me. I opened my mouth, all prepared with an explanation. Then I noticed Dayton wasn't giving me his 'I don't know how you're going to end up an okay human' face anymore. He was too busy staring at Marnie.

So, I wasn't messing with that.

"Give her a break, Dayton. We can swing by the library, right? No problem?"

Dayton finally closed his mouth and nodded.

I was so encouraged by the silence—because it meant a lack of annoying lectures—that I bobbed forward and stuck my head between their seats. "Also, we could go to Biff's. You can get an asiago bagel to go with breakfast."

Dayton started the car and pulled out of the parking spot.

I made him an offer he couldn't refuse. So, I think that means I win.

There was a long line of cars in front of the library book drop. Dayton parked and shooed me out with my armload of books. I was about to protest that Marnie was closer, but then I remembered how she saved my bacon, and I decided to just do it.

When I bumped the car door closed with my hip, Dayton didn't even look up. He and Marnie were too busy talking.

I walked the books to the drop box by the front door. I had to admit it was satisfying to hear the thuds as they landed in the box bin. Maybe I should return books more often.

I turned around to head back to the car and froze.

Was that...?

I think I just saw Tanner's truck pull away from the library.

Okay, that was weird.

Not the part about him at the library. I was sure he read all the time, being a professor and everything. The weird part was seeing him all over town. It was kind of freaking me out. I only ever saw Tanner at Froyo glued to the corner table.

As I walked back to the car, I wondered what books Tanner returned. Did he check out a Regency romance novel and travel guides to Brazil, Canada, and Finland along with that sushi book?

Most likely, he returned books about flannel and growing the perfect beard. I laughed to myself as I flung the car door open.

"Bagels!" I called.

Marnie unbuckled. "It's your turn in front."

"No, no." I was already sitting and almost buckled. "Let's just go. I want bagels."

Marnie clicked herself back into place, and Dayton pulled out of the parking stall before I had my door closed all the way.

Bagels in the morning was the best idea ever. They would be all warm and fresh from the oven. I daydreamed about them the entire drive.

"There's no parking," Dayton said, glancing over his shoulder. "The lot is full."

"Not that one," I pointed.

Dayton shook his head. "You have to pay for that one."

I snorted. "It's, like, a dollar."

"A dollar is a dollar," Dayton said in a high, nasal voice. He dropped back to normal after Marnie was done giggling. "We'll have to park somewhere on the street and walk."

There was no guarantee we'd find a spot anywhere nearby, and I didn't want to wait that long for a bagel. The line was already snaking out of the shop's door. "Just drop me off at the front. I'll go buy the stuff, and you can circle around until a free spot opens up."

"What?" Dayton's head was already shaking.

I glared at the back of his head. "Come on, Dayton. Unlock the door. There are people waiting behind us." I knew I should have turned off the child locks before I got into the back seat.

"I'm happy to go with her," Marnie said as she reached for the door handle, but I stopped her.

"I got this, Dayton. Let me go!" I jiggled the handle of my door to encourage him.

Someone honked behind us.

Dayton narrowed his eyes. "Why are people so dang impatient? I have to think."

Thinking was going to take forever. We'd still be sitting in this car twenty years from now while Dayton hemmed and hawed about whether I was capable of buying bagels without help.

Marnie placed a hand on Dayton's arm. "Bailey can do it. She'll be fine."

Bless Marnie!

Dayton looked at her hand and reached for the button to unlock my door.

"You have money?"

I held up my purse as I slid onto the asphalt. "Go find somewhere to park or circle back around. It will only take ten minutes." I eyeballed the line. "Maybe fifteen."

Then I slammed the door shut and watched the taillights carry away my best friend and my idiot brother.

I took my place at the end of the line and tried not to question myself. Despite what Dayton thought, I was perfectly capable of buying bagels without his help.

I shuffled forward and mentally repeated the bagels I wanted to get.

Plain.

Dayton said he wanted an everything and an asiago cheese, two of each.

Marnie loved blueberry.

The garlic onion looked good and, oh, the maple bacon was a must.

Okay, I was just going to get a dozen. We could eat them or freeze them.

By the time I got all of that sorted, I was in front of the cashier. I placed my order and paid, then remembered I forgot to get cream cheese. There was really no point in eating a warm bagel without cream cheese.

I doubled back to the fridge display and checked what they had available. Honey walnut? Yes, please. And, oh good, there was a chive. I also grabbed a plain because Dayton was a purist, and I got back in line to pay again.

The bag of bagels was heavy and hard to carry. It was seeping steam from the top and heating up my hand from the bottom. I shifted the bag back and forth whenever one side got too hot.

"Bailey?"

"Tanner?" I almost dropped the bag. Luckily, Tanner reached out to steady the bottom while I caught my balance and my breath.

"What are you doing here?" I asked. Heat crept up my neck. That was the stupidest question. What did I think he was doing in a bagel shop?

Tanner chuckled a low manly sound. He pointed to the menu board. "I'm tired of eating cold cereal for breakfast."

"Good choice," I said, feeling like an idiot. "This is our favorite place for bagels."

"That's fortuitous. I did a Google search, and this was the first place that came up. I, uh…" Tanner cleared his throat and looked away. "I was going to call you to ask for your recommendation, but I didn't."

Why was Tanner clearing his throat again? After our epically disastrous dinner the night before, we were, like, friends now. He shouldn't be uncomfortable around me anymore.

"Next time, call me," I said. "I'm full of opinions."

Tanner laughed. "I knew that, actually."

"Yeah. So," I shifted the bagel bag to my other arm, "I saw you at Bashas' earlier and then at the library." I leaned forward and whispered to make it seem like we were co-conspirators in a cool spy movie. "Either I'm stalking you, or you're stalking me. Which one is it?"

Tanner's face reddened.

I nudged him with my shoulder, so he would step up in the line. We were only two people away from the register now. "I'll be the stalker if it will make you feel better."

Tanner said, "Okay," like he was trying to figure out if I was serious.

"Fine!" I said all exasperated. "You can be the stalker. But I'm going to warn you. If you want to steal my identity, you're going to be super disappointed. I have, like, five dollars in my bank account right now."

Tanner just shook his head at me, his eyes crinkling in the corners.

"You think I'm weird, don't you?" I asked.

"Absolutely." Tanner stepped up to the cashier.

I was so taken aback that I burst out laughing. I hadn't expected him to agree so quickly. A young couple with their small, yappy dog glared at me from their table. I didn't care; I think taking a dog out to breakfast is way more embarrassing than laughing out loud.

"What are you buying?" Tanner asked me, glancing over his shoulder.

I awkwardly held out my hand with the three cream cheese containers. "Just these. I forgot them when I bought the bagels."

"And three cream cheese," Tanner said to the cashier.

She'd already pushed buttons and he'd already paid by the time I figured out that Tanner was buying my cream cheese.

Tanner!" I said, following him around the small tables and out the door. "I was just joking about having five dollars in my bank account. I have money. You didn't have to pay for me."

"I know." Tanner held the door as I stepped outside. "I wanted to."

"No really," I squinted at Tanner in the bright sun. "I should have been the one who bought your bagels and stuff, to pay you back for how much food I ordered last night. Also, I don't think I mentioned it was my fault the waitress tripped, so I should also reimburse you for laundry detergent or something."

"How was that your fault?"

"My purse was sort of in the walking area."

Tanner pressed his lips together.

"Let me pay you back?"

"Let me take that bag for you before you drop it?" Tanner gestured to my armful. "I was going to insist on it in the store, but I didn't know what you would do if I tried to take it from you."

"What did you think I would do?" I scooted out of the way of a passing herd of teenagers.

"I imagined you would either say yes nicely or kick me in the shins and steal my wallet."

"Seriously?"

Tanner glanced at me. "I thought it would be best for everyone if I waited until we got outside to offer, just in case."

I heaved my bag of bagels into his arms with a sassy smile. "You way over-thought that one, buddy. Take them."

"Thank you." He shifted his much smaller bag to make room for mine.

"You're welcome," I answered, automatically, although it felt a little backwards.

"Where are we headed?"

I looked around. I had no idea where Dayton and Marnie were. I didn't recognize any of the cars in my line of sight.

"Did you forget where you parked?" A smile played along the side of his lips.

"No!" I squinted into the parking lot behind the bagel shop. I didn't have any expectations, which is the best way to never be disappointed. My phone buzzed in my pocket, so I pulled it out to check it.

There were five texts from Dayton with a picture of the car and parking lot from four different angles, so I could see exactly where they were.

"Right there," I pointed. "Dayton found a spot way on the other side, see?"

"Dayton?"

"Oh, yeah. Dayton dropped me off. Marnie's with us, too."

Tanner followed me into the parking lot. The sun felt deliciously warm on my shoulders while a cool breeze danced across my face, tugging at my hair. I loved Flagstaff so much. Where else in the world could you get a warm, sunny day at the tail end of winter? It felt like May outside.

"Do you ever get used to that?" Tanner asked as I pulled a lock of hair out of my mouth.

"What?"

"Eating your hair."

I looked at him.

"I was kidding. I meant the wind. Do you ever get used to the wind? I've never lived somewhere so windy."

"Huh," I twirled my long hair around itself and tucked it into the back of my sweater so it would stay out of my face. "Is it windy? I totally didn't notice."

"Sure," Tanner smirked as a particularly diligent gust of wind whipped a bunch of my hair out of place and began swirling it in knots around my head. I smoothed it all back into place and tugged the cowl of my sweater up near my ears.

"Me and the wind are best buds. Can't you tell?"

"Yes, of course. What was I thinking?" Tanner paused. "How are you feeling today, by the way?"

How was I feeling? That question seemed out of place until I remembered the night before. Oh, yeah. He's probably referring to that up-chucking situation of mine.

"I'm fine now. I felt great once I puked all that extra food out. Here we are." I banged on the top of Dayton's car and bent to peek inside. "Look who I found."

Tanner bent alongside me. "Hello, Dayton. Hello, Marnie."

Marnie's eyes crinkled at the corners. "Tanner! Hi!"

"Hey, Tanner," Dayton smiled, then switched to a glare just for me. "You almost made me pee."

Marnie coughed.

"I mean it. Don't hit the top of the car like that again. It's irresponsible."

"Well, maybe you need to pay better attention to your surroundings." I took the bagels from Tanner and knelt on the seat to buckle them into the middle of the backseat. I didn't want them sliding onto the floor while we drove home. "What if I was a zombie coming to suck your brains? I would have a full belly before you knew I was there."

"Aw, thanks, Bay. That's the nicest thing you've ever said to me."

"Huh?"

"If you're a full zombie, that means I have *a ton* of brains. Obviously."

I shook my head and backed out of the car. There was no way I was commenting on that one. Sometimes it was better to just let it go.

"Thanks for your help, Jeeves," I said to Tanner. "Where are you parked? Want us to drive you to your truck?"

"Oh, no. I walked here. I just live a block over." He pointed somewhere into the vague distance.

"Okay," I paused.

I just got the weirdest idea. It rolled through my mind like a tumbleweed. I wanted to observe it for a minute to see if it was one of those ideas that you wave to as it rolls on by, or the kind you embrace and roll with.

"I guess I'll see you all later." Tanner started to turn.

I decided to roll with my idea, even though there was a distinct possibility Dayton was going to mock me until the day I died.

"Hey, why don't you come home with us? Dayton and I are making a huge breakfast. Marnie's coming, too. Dayton can bring you home after he drops me off at Froyo in a couple of hours."

Tanner looked stunned, like he didn't know how to formulate sentences anymore.

"You don't have to," I said, giving him an out if he wanted it. "It was just an idea. You're probably busy."

"No, I...I want to." He cleared his throat. "I have a Zoom meeting soon that I can't miss."

"Oh, okay." I shrugged like it was no biggie. Because it wasn't.

Tanner reached out a hand to stop me from getting into the car. "Would it be all right with you if I drive myself to your house? Then I can leave for my meeting after breakfast."

"Sure." I shrugged again. "That works."

"I don't know where you live."

"How about we drive you home to get your truck, then you can follow us to our house?"

A huge smile broke all the creases on Tanner's face. "That sounds great. Thank you."

I shrugged. "There's room behind Dayton."

Tanner took the hint and scooted to the other side of the car. It took him a minute to fold his tall self into the back seat.

No lie, it was amusing to watch.

"Don't smoosh my bagels," Dayton said, peering through the rearview mirror.

Tanner wrapped his arms around his own bag of bagels, trying to make himself smaller.

"The bagels are fine," I said, rolling my eyes. Even though Dayton couldn't see me, it made me feel better. "Where to?"

"I know where he lives," Dayton scoffed as he turned on the blinker and pulled out of the parking lot. "Gimme a break."

"So sorry," I said. "I figured the guy who got lost on his way to the mailbox might need a reminder."

"Did you really?" Marnie asked.

Dayton eased into the street. The turn was sharp, so the back wheels hit the curb and almost upturned the bagels. I caught them just in time. "I have no comment," he sniffed.

"That means yes," I said.

"Really?" Tanner asked. "I need to hear this story."

"Well, it began on a dark night—" I used the spookiest voice I could find.

Dayton interrupted. "Don't listen to her. I'll tell you. I didn't have my contacts in. It was dark, and it was snowing. Did you know everything looks the same when it snows?"

I folded my arms. "Buildings totally look like butterflies in the snow. A carrot looks like a Porsche. The mailbox looks like—"

"So much snark, Bay. You need to work on that."

"It was worth it." I settled into my seat.

"Turn here," Tanner said, pointing.

"I knew that." Dayton flipped his blinker and yanked the steering wheel hard to make the turn.

"Mmm hmm." I wiggled my head to add some sass to the snark.

Dayton shot me a dirty look when Marnie giggled.

I whistled. "That's where you live, Tanner? I didn't know there were houses this size downtown." As Dayton pulled up to the curb, I squished my face into the window to see the house all the way.

"Yeah," Tanner said. "I don't live in the whole thing. Just one room."

"Oh," Dayton nodded. "It's one of those places. Everyone rents a room, and you share the kitchen and bathroom, right?"

"That's right."

I looked at them both in horror.

"It's not so bad," Tanner raised his hands like he was warding off a blow. "I share it with three graduate students and a couple that just got married three weeks ago. Everyone is nice."

Marnie said, "I think it sounds cozy."

"Yeah, but they share a bathroom," I gagged.

Tanner laughed at me. "Have you ever been to a bed and breakfast? It's just like that, only long-term renters instead of weekend guests."

"No," I gulped, shaking my head. "That is inhumane. No one should ever have to share a bathroom with strangers."

"You mean, such as public restrooms?" Dayton raised his left eyebrow. "Ever heard of those?" His confidence was back now that I was the one getting ganged up on.

"Disgusting," I sniffed.

"You want to travel, right?" Tanner said, his voice light. "Some countries offer hotels that are just like this. They're called hostels."

"Out of my car, you, with your crazy ideas. Go on, out!" I used my feet to prod him until he stumbled out of the car. "Hostels," I spit out, like the word tasted bad. Which it did. "You're crazy."

He caught my eye and grinned before he closed the car door. I watched him walk to his truck and then realized Dayton was watching me watch Tanner.

Everything I said and did since I saw Tanner in the bagel shop was suddenly on trial. I could see images of myself, shimmering in the air in front of me.

What had I been thinking, inviting Tanner over? I wanted to bang my head against the back of Marnie's seat. I could only imagine what was going on in Dayton's head.

Whatever. It wasn't a big deal that I invited him over. Dayton could say whatever he wanted about it. I invited people over all the time. This wasn't anything. And besides, Tanner was Dayton's friend, and he was my friend. Like Marnie. Why shouldn't he come over for breakfast? It just made sense.

I opened my mouth to say all of this to Dayton before he had a chance to expound on whatever was brewing behind his closed mouth, but there was a knock on the glass next to me. I screeched and turned to the window with karate hands.

Tanner backed away, his palms up in surrender.

I let out a breath and rolled the window down. "What the heck are you doing?"

"Sorry, I have a slight change of plan. I need to run a quick errand. Can I get your address and meet you at your house?"

I looked around the car for something to write on, my heart still racing. An old receipt was smooshed into the space between the passenger seat and the middle console. I checked to make sure it didn't have anything embarrassing on it, like tampons or zit cream, before I smoothed it out and turned it over to write our address.

All while mumbling about people scaring the pants off people and how not funny it was.

I handed the receipt to him.

Tanner waved. "Thanks. I'll be right over. Sorry, again."

I saluted and rolled the window back up. "What are you waiting for? Let's go home. I'm starving."

Dayton jingled his keys until I looked at him. "So, anything you want to tell me, Baybee?"

I suddenly had an uncontrollable urge to clear my throat. What was that about? I covered it up with a short cough. I rolled my eyes simply to make myself feel better. "The square root of one hundred and forty-four is twelve."

"How nice." He nodded, primly, and waited. The keys mocked me each time they swung into the steering wheel.

"Let's go, nincompoop." I slapped his shoulder as I plopped back into my seat. "It's going to be noon by the time we eat breakfast."

Ways to Improve Bailey #3

No more primping for hours (andhoursandhoursandhours)

In retrospect, I probably shouldn't have tried to carry so many grocery bags. My arms were loaded to the elbows, and the handles of the bags were digging into my arms, leaving deep, red crevasses. When I grabbed the bags from the car, I'd tangled them pretty good. The bag with the eggs dislodged itself somehow and slipped to the very tips of my fingers. It was perfectly poised for a Humpty Dumpty-type fate if I didn't hurry. The door was only a couple steps away. I could totally make it.

Dayton turned around, the keys jangling as he unlocked our front door. With a sigh and a shake of the head, he set his bags inside the house and took two long strides to rescue me.

Not that I needed it.

He took the precarious eggs first, then relieved me of half the other bags. "What are you thinking? Just bring in a few things at a time. You don't gotta be a hero here. Use your melon, kid."

Yeah, where would be the fun in that?

I elbowed around him and walked into the house, unloading what I had on the counter so that I could shake my arms out. Prickles, pins, and needles fired from my elbows to my fingertips. Dayton clicked his tongue as he set his bags next to mine. I ignored him and started unpacking things into piles of what I needed to make breakfast and what we needed to put away.

Dayton watched me in silence for a second, then a sly smile twirled around the corner of his mouth. "So...since we have a second alone, let's talk."

"About what?" I shoved two gallons of milk into the fridge and then opened the freezer to put away the ice cream.

"Oh, I don't know. The weather, politics, you inviting Tanner over for breakfast. So, are you guys like..." He waggled his eyebrows.

"Ew! No!" I shoved him out of my way.

"I don't know," he said, catching himself on the table with a laugh. "You've never invited a guy over before. I really think you might like this one."

"Whatever. I invite guys over all the time."

"No, you don't," Dayton shook his head.

"Yes, I do." I couldn't believe we were arguing about something I was so clearly right about. "Don't you think you should go help Marnie unload the rest of the groceries?"

Dayton kept talking like I hadn't said a word. "Tanner and Bailey Banner. It sounds like a match made in heaven." He clasped his hands together and squealed like a three-year-old girl.

"Wait a second." I turned to Dayton, his words slowly making it into my brain. "Tanner's last name is Banner?"

"Tanner Banner." Dayton puckered his lips to make smooching noises.

"His parents are so mean." I shook my head, setting the frypan on a burner. "Like, so mean."

"Bailey Banner, Bailey Banner." Dayton twirled across the floor until he reached me. He tried to pry my stiff arms away from my sides to dance with him, but I am happy to say he did not succeed.

"The more you bug me, the longer it will be until we eat," I pulled away, opening a cupboard for the olive oil. I swirled it around the pan twice. "Plus, you really should go see what's taking Marnie so long. She might need help."

It was a good reason, but I also wanted him to leave.

"Are you sure you don't want me to start breakfast, so you can go make yourself beautiful for Lover Boy?"

"No need." I yanked a large chef's knife out of the block and started chopping onions. "I already look amazing."

Dayton backed away with his arms up. "I think I'll go help Marnie before you get all violent up in here."

"Good. Go away." I waved the knife at his retreating back.

"Also," he peeked his head back through the front door, "you shouldn't mess around with knives. They are tools, not toys."

I looked around for something nonlethal to throw at him, but he was gone before I found anything that would work.

Who invented brothers, anyway?

The skillet was hot by the time I finished chopping all the vegetables we'd already brought inside. That's also about the time I realized that it had been way too quiet for way too long.

Where was everyone?

I turned the heat down so nothing would burn while I checked. I flung the front door open and almost hit Dayton in the face.

Ah, so close.

"Watch it!" He held up his free hand to protect his face. "Marnie got a call from her roommate. She'll be right back." He dropped the few remaining bags on the table.

"What's going on?"

"She didn't say exactly." Dayton stretched his arms over his head, so his belly peeked out of the bottom of his shirt.

Gross.

"Something about a dog."

"She's coming back though, yeah?"

"I think so." Dayton dropped his arms, finally. "She said she'd be right back. So that gives us plenty of time to talk about Tanner."

"Oh, no. That's alright." I slammed the door and went back to the kitchen. The onions were browned, so I slid them onto a plate and put the peppers in their place. "We don't need to bring that up again."

"Sure, we do. We need to decide what your wedding colors will be and what to name your first baby."

I couldn't decide if the best thing to do would be to ignore Dayton until he went away or beat the crap out of him. For half a second, I waffled, then he got to B-letter names for girls, and I lost it.

Using my super amazing Tae Kwon Do moves, I jabbed my arm into Dayton's chest to throw him off balance, then swept my leg under his feet, making him fall onto his back.

For a second, he stared at me with wide eyes, then he started laughing. "I think I hit a nerve there, Bay."

I rolled my eyes and stepped over him to get the grocery bag on the table that had the rest of the vegetables in it.

He just laid there on the floor, rolling around, laughing.

I wish I was joking.

While I grated cheese, Dayton slithered across the tile and grabbed at my feet. I almost tripped twice. Where was Marnie? She needed to come back so she could see this. It would explain perfectly why I didn't want to get married and have kids.

I nudged him away sort of gently to wash broccoli and break it into bite-size pieces. I wasn't going to cook those ahead of time; they would steam to al dente in the hash. As I searched a drawer for the potato peeler, I felt a tap on my leg.

"Oh, thanks." I took the peeler from Dayton's hand. "Where was it?"

"Next to the cookie sheets."

"What was it doing there?" I wondered out loud. "That's a weird place for it."

"Wanna know what else is weird?" Dayton wiggled his eyebrows.

I stopped working and glared down at my brother. "Dayton, it is not that weird that I invited Tanner over for breakfast. You gotta get a hold of yourself before he gets here."

"Why?" Dayton asked innocently.

"Because you are acting like a toddler, and you need to stop it. Do you want Tanner to know what a freak you are? I'm only thinking of you here."

"Whatever," Dayton mimicked me perfectly as he sat up and leaned against the cupboards across from me. "Guys don't pay a smidgen of attention to how other guys act."

I smirked. "I bet they would if you used the word 'smidgen' in front of them. You sound like Grandma." I peeled the sweet potatoes and diced them up for the fry pan. While they were cooking, I poured all the other cooked vegetables into a bowl next to the pan.

"You should stop being useless and put the rest of the groceries away," I said without looking up from my work.

Dayton didn't get a chance to respond because there was a knock on the door.

"Come in!" Dayton hollered.

I shot him a look and headed to the door like a civilized human being. It wasn't Tanner or Marnie.

It was both of them.

I glanced over my shoulder and saw Dayton on his feet, tucking in his shirt.

"Hey, guys. Glad you could make it." I opened the door wide. "What happened with the dog?"

"Oh," Marnie said, waving her hand. "False alarm. Michelle thought he got out again, but he was in the garage."

"Oh, good."

Dayton took a step forward, batting his eyes. I'd hoped he would act human again when Tanner and Marnie got back, but it looked like I was wrong. When he got in this kind of mood, it didn't matter who was watching.

"Hay-ay, Tah-ah-ner." He wiggled his fingers up by his cheek.

Oh my heck!

Dayton was out of control. The only thing for me to do was leave. I seriously doubted he would keep making dumb insinuations about Tanner and me if I wasn't there to hear them.

"I'm going to go shower while the sweet potatoes cook." I set a timer on the oven and elbowed Dayton in the ribs on my way out of the kitchen. "Keep an eye on them for me?"

"Wait," Dayton stuttered, "you're just going to leave? What if they burn?"

"Turn the heat down." I tossed my hair over my shoulder. "And stir them."

"But, but..." he sputtered. "You take forever to get ready! We'll never eat breakfast at this rate." He reached for a bagel and ripped off a large bite, as though trying to prove to me how starving he was.

"I do not." I paused on my way down the hall. "I'll be out in, like, fifteen minutes."

Dayton covered his mouth and whispered loudly to Tanner and Marnie. "She means an hour, in case you don't understand girl talk. Primp, primp, primp, primp." He shook his hips along with each sing-song word.

"I have sisters." Tanner settled into the couch like it was time to get comfortable.

That was just too much.

I wielded my finger like a sword. "I will be showered, dressed, and have my hair and makeup done before the sweet potatoes finish cooking. Ten minutes, tops. Time me."

Then I turned into a speed demon. I grabbed my clothes out of my room and dashed to the bathroom. With the door locked securely—I triple-checked—I could then start the process of showering in record time. Despite my big talk, ten minutes was usually how long it usually took me to get ready to walk into the shower.

Not today, though. I was determined.

Stupid boys. The only reason girls took so much longer to get ready is because we actually care about not smelling like steamed broccoli and corn chips.

I'm pretty sure I took the fastest shower in recorded history, and I was toweling off when I heard Marnie defending womenkind through the walls. I had no idea our walls were so thin; it sounded like they were all right outside the door, even though I knew they weren't.

At least, I hoped they weren't.

Marnie said, "That's why girls take their time getting ready."

It sounded like the tail end of a super good TED Talk. I wish I'd heard the rest of it.

Tanner pointed out that Marnie made a solid argument and asked Dayton to remind him not to debate with her if he wanted to leave with his ego intact.

Dayton laughed and agreed.

Then Marnie said something was burning. Dayton yelped, and there was a loud clatter before he announced it was fine, everything was fine.

I towel-dried my hair faster. Teaching Dayton a lesson was one thing, but destroying breakfast was another. My stomach rumbled, drowning out their chatter for a minute.

Then, Tanner asked if Dayton was just teasing me about getting ready. He noticed that Dayton gave me a hard time a lot, and he couldn't tell when it was serious or joking. He wondered if I really would be ready in ten minutes.

Dayton said, "No stinking way."

I pulled the zipper on my jeans with more power than I meant to, a deep scowl wrinkling my face. No stinking way? Really? I would show him.

I'd be ready in less than ten minutes.

Eight and a half extremely hectic minutes later, I swaggered down the hall dressed in skinny jeans and a long-sleeve turquoise tunic that I had knotted at my waist. My hair was pulled into a high ponytail, so no one would be able to tell that it was still wet underneath, but my makeup was perfect. I had no idea I could get ready so fast; it was kind of liberating.

"What-what!" I spread my arms as I walked into the kitchen.

Dayton checked his watch and clicked his tongue. "Check again, Bay-bee. That took twelve minutes."

I lifted up a finger. "I started the sweet potatoes." I lifted the next finger. "I walked to the door to let Tanner and Marnie in." I pointed to the timer on the oven. "Three minutes left. I took less than nine."

"She's right," Marnie said, checking her watch.

"Fine," Dayton said, conceding. He was helpless in the face of my logic.

I hip checked Dayton on my way to stir the sweet potatoes. They were perfect: cooked through, but not mushy. I decided not to ask what the burning thing was. Sometimes it was better not to know.

Plus, that would mean admitting I could hear everything they said. I didn't want to reveal that little nugget just yet. It might come in handy later.

I added the peppers and onions to the skillet to warm them back up. When I reached for the olive oil, Dayton flicked a wet dish towel at me.

"Ow!" I screeched, trying to swat him with my free hand. He danced away with a wicked grin.

Marnie shook her head. "You two are so cute. I love how you joke with each other. I wish I had siblings."

"No, you don't." I pushed a stray hair out of my eyes. "You really, really don't."

"Aw, Baybee, you know you love me." Dayton draped his arm over my shoulder.

Tanner waved a finger between the two of us. "I would never act like that with my sisters."

I stirred the hash around. It was time to add the broccoli. "That's probably because you respect your sisters."

Tanner laughed shortly. "More like I'm terrified of them."

"Why?" Dayton sounded appalled. I was sure it never occurred to him to be terrified of me, though it should have. I might be small, but I could still put molasses in his hair gel bottle.

Tanner picked at the corner of the kitchen table where he was sitting. "They are really intimidating."

"What does that even mean?" Dayton asked.

"It's hard to explain," Tanner said.

Dayton grunted.

Marnie's eyebrows came together. "You don't have to tell us if you're not comfortable."

"Yes, he does," I said. "You brought it up; now talk."

This was the first time Tanner had volunteered any personal information at all, and I wanted to hear what he was going to say.

Tanner cleared his throat. I was beginning to notice a pattern here: Tanner cleared his throat when he was uncomfortable. It bothered me that he felt like he needed to choose his words carefully with Dayton, Marnie, and me.

"Tanner," I said, putting my hands on my hips and barely noticing that the spatula dropped broccoli bits to the floor. "This is a safe place. You don't have to think before you speak. Just spit it out already."

Dayton gave a burst of laughter and then tried to cover it up by coughing into his fist. Marnie reached over to whack him gently on the back, even though we all knew he wasn't choking.

"Thanks," Dayton wheezed, reaching for a glass of water.

I cracked four eggs into the vegetable mixture, covered the pan, and turned off the burner. My work there was done; now I could give Tanner my full attention. I leaned toward him, drying my hands with a towel.

Tanner considered the three of us staring at him, then he nodded.

"Very well, then. Picture this: a sterile house with pristine white furniture that nobody wants to sit in. A cook that comes in every Monday and makes all the meals, then leaves them labeled in the fridge in organized containers for the family to heat up whenever they are home—which is never. Most of that food gets thrown out on Saturday. A cleaning lady comes in twice a week and only pretends to clean since there's no one around this multi-million-dollar home to make a mess. The adults work at the office sixty hours a week and spend the rest of their time on phones or computers. The children go to boarding school, and when they are home during the holidays, they spend their time on phones or computers. There's a huge pool with a waterfall in the backyard that never gets used. Imagine a world of unnatural hair color, chiseled cheekbones, acrylic nails, tattooed makeup, and artificial tans. Everyone and everything looks perfect, but it isn't. Nothing is real. No one is what they seem."

Tanner stopped talking abruptly. His mouth worked like he wanted to say more, or maybe he wanted to take back what he had already said. He turned away and stared out the dining room window. I could see his back move as he took deep breaths.

Marnie's eyebrows were scrunched together so tightly that it looked like a tense caterpillar rested above her eyes. Dayton nudged me and mouthed something I couldn't understand. I flicked a glance towards Tanner, back to Dayton, and opened my eyes as wide as they would go.

"Say something," I mouthed.

Dayton pointed at me, but I shook my head. I wasn't putting my foot in this. Dayton had known Tanner the longest. It was his responsibility to break the awkward silence.

"Uh," Dayton the Eloquent began, "that pool sounds awesome."

Tanner answered but didn't turn around. "It is."

There was another long silence that consisted of Marnie blinking rapidly, Dayton examining his shoes, and Tanner staring off into the dramatic mid-distance. I tried to get Dayton to make eye contact with me so that I could tell him with my eyes that I thought he was an idiot, but it didn't work. Finally, I gave up and decided to do the hard work here.

"So, is that your family you're talking about?" I asked.

Tanner turned slowly, like he was recovering from muscle cramps and afraid to move anything. "Technically."

"Meaning?"

Tanner took a deep breath. "Meaning I specifically described my family in this scenario, but technically, the description applies to everyone."

"Excuse me," Dayton said in the same voice as an overly dramatic teenage girl while he waved his finger wildly in the air. "I do not color my hair. This is all natural." He tossed his head.

Tanner laughed, his shoulders un-hunching just a tad.

I took that as a sign that his dark and brooding moment had passed. I checked the eggs, poking them lightly with the spatula. The yolks weren't done all the way, but the whites were.

Perfect.

I lifted a stack of plates and forks, which I passed to Dayton. As he set the table, I divided the hash into four portions inside the pan, then walked it to the table with a potholder.

"Bailey!" Dayton hollered.

I almost dropped the pan. "What?"

He stood in front of the cupboard, his back heaving. "Are we out of El Pato?"

"No way." I set the pan down on a potholder and went to the cupboard to see for myself. I wasn't worried at first; Dayton could never find anything, but after moving things around for a second, my heart sped up.

"Is there any in the fridge?"

Dayton whipped the door open and rattled bottles along the door shelf with shaking hands. "No. How did this happen?"

"Dang it." I swept a piece of loose hair out of my eyes. "We were just at the store."

"I have some at home if you're out," Marnie offered.

"I'm sorry," Tanner said, looking at our stricken faces. "What is El...what you said?"

Dayton clutched his chest. "Do not tell me you don't know what El Pato is."

"Okay, I won't." Tanner said, making it painfully obvious he had no idea what we were talking about.

"It's like taco sauce," I told Tanner as I stooped to check the cupboard with all the pots. If the potato peeler could be with the cookie sheets, the El Pato could be with the pots.

Except it wasn't.

"And, it's good, then?"

"No," Dayton shook his head. "No, no, no, no, no. It is not *good*. It is necessary."

Marnie reached for her coat. "I'll run home and get a can. It will just take a sec."

"Hold on." I raised my hand and then rested it on top of my head to help me think. There had to be a can of El Pato somewhere. We bought it in bulk. There's no way Dayton and I finished it all.

I hopped up and moved around the counter to check the coat closet. Then under the couch. Then the hall closet. There was a case nestled in the back under the beach towels that never got used.

"Found it!" I grabbed a can and held it in front of me for everyone to see.

Dayton fell against the kitchen table with his hand over his heart. "That was too close. Remind me to order some more today."

I handed the El Pato to Dayton, so he could calm down while I went to find the can opener. It was in the vegetable tray in the fridge.

"Let's eat." I gave the can opener to Dayton and sat down at the table. When Marnie and Tanner were also seated, I dished food on everyone's plates, then poured ketchup all over my hash.

Dayton stared at my plate in horror.

"Get over it." I set the ketchup on the table, sidling it closer to Dayton's plate. He yanked his plate out of the way as though the ketchup was going to infect it with a horrible disease.

"That," Dayton said in disgust, looking at Tanner but pointing at my plate, "is sick and wrong."

"It's ketchup on eggs and potatoes," I said, bringing my fork to my mouth. "There is nothing sick or wrong about putting ketchup on eggs or potatoes."

"I love ketchup," Marnie said, taking the El Pato can Dayton passed to her.

"But not on hash." Dayton watched me chew with his lip curled. "No one in their right mind would put ketchup on hash when there is El Pato on the table."

I hid a smile as Tanner took the El Pato Marnie offered him and poured it over half of his hash, then picked up the ketchup to drizzle on the other half.

"Switzerland," Tanner said, when he saw me watching.

Dayton wrinkled his nose. "Disgusting."

"So," I said, now that the El Pato crisis had passed, "your family sounds filthy rich."

Dayton choked for reals this time. He hacked into his elbow for two minutes before he could stop coughing long enough to chug water.

"Take smaller bites," I said.

He chugged another long drink of water, his face slowly losing its tomato-red shade. "You gotta warn a guy before you bust out with stuff like that."

"What did I say?" I speared a piece of broccoli and put it in my mouth. "Was it bad?"

"No," Marnie said, shaking her head.

At the same time, Dayton said, "Yes."

I looked at Tanner to break the tie.

He shrugged. "It was blunt."

"See!" Dayton and I said at the same time. I recovered first and stuck my tongue out at him.

Tanner moved food around his plate. "It's fine. Tell me about your parents. They live in Phoenix?"

And away the conversation went, leaving me far behind. I chewed each bite I took at least nine times and listened to Dayton answer Tanner's questions. Tanner never stopped asking them. The moment Dayton seemed to be lagging, Tanner jumped right in with another question. It's like he knew the perfect question to get Dayton going again.

What was Tanner hiding?

Ways to Improve Bailey #1

Stop giving up without trying

I knew something was wrong the second I walked through the door of Froyo later that afternoon. First of all, it was Saturday, and there was no one in the store except for Keith. Second of all, instead of bustling around or locking himself in his office to do officey things, Keith sat at the bar, slumped on a stool, nursing a root beer float.

And we don't even sell root beer.

"Hey, Keith," I said slowly.

He answered just as slowly. "Hey, kid."

I stepped behind the counter, pulling my apron off the hook and looping it over my head. One eye stayed glued to Keith the entire time.

"Everything okay?"

"What?" Keith looked up, and his eyes darted all around the store like a seriously sus cartoon villain. "Sure, sure, yes. Sure it is."

I leaned on the counter in front of Keith, so he wouldn't avoid looking at me. "What is going on?"

Keith sighed, obviously in a rigorous internal debate. "I guess there's no point in hiding it; you'll find out soon enough. They're raising the rent on this place."

It took me a minute to process, then I got it. Higher rent meant more money we had to pay out every month. I looked around the empty store. Keith didn't share his financial business with me, but I was pretty sure we were barely making ends meet as it was.

"That stinks," I said.

Keith laughed a loud bark that echoed in the empty space. "You sure have a way with words, Ms. Bailey."

"Okay, so, they're raising the rent. What does that mean, exactly? What are we going to do about it? What's the plan?"

Keith slumped further over his float, stirring the spoon so that his drink sloshed over the side.

"I got it," I said, reaching for a napkin.

"I don't know, Bailey." He rubbed his face, pushing his glasses up on his forehead. "This is a tough town. Maybe it's time to call it quits."

"You mean close Froyo?" I stopped wiping, the sopping napkin dripping in my hand as I considered what this meant. Honestly, it didn't sound like the worst idea in the world, especially if it was causing Keith so much headache. He was a smart guy; he had all kinds of businesses all over Arizona. He probably didn't need a dying frozen yogurt shop. I opened my mouth to point all of this out, but something stopped me.

I think it was Keith's face. He looked so much older, like a dimmed light bulb. I don't know where the thought came from, but as soon as I thought it, I knew it was true.

Keith loved this store.

I hadn't picked up on it before. We were always too busy giving each other a super hard time, but now that I recognized what he felt, I couldn't deny it. It would break Keith's heart to close. For some reason or another, he really loved this place.

Determination swelled inside me like a threatened bullfrog. If Keith wanted Froyo to stay in business, then I was going to do everything I could to make sure it did.

Or die trying.

I'm sure it wouldn't come to that.

"Hey," I nudged Keith's arm with a pencil. "We are due for a Sam's Club run. I'll hang out here if you want to go. We for sure need napkins and plastic spoons." I glanced over the toppings bar quickly. "You could probably pick up more chocolate chips, gummy bears, and sprinkles while you're at it."

Keith looked at me with droopy eyes. "Did you hear what I said, sugar? I think it's time to let it go." He picked up his float and chugged it down to the frothy dregs of frozen yogurt, then wiped his mouth with the back of his hand.

I shook my head. "What if we gave it another week? I think we can turn it around. We have to at least try, right? Froyo has hung on when every other frozen yogurt place has failed. That's got to mean something, especially if this town is as tough as you say. Don't give up without trying."

Those were the same words Keith had told me when I first started working at Froyo and was convinced the deep freezer hated my guts. It was electric, and we used a keypad to open it and adjust the temperature. I got super frustrated when it didn't work for me the first couple times. Keith had me try again with him standing there, over and over until it worked.

Don't give up without trying.

Keith stared at me like I'd just decorated my face with jellybeans and put frosting in my hair.

Okay, so maybe I was showing a little more interest in his dumb business than normal. So what? I was allowed to unexpectedly care about random things if I wanted to.

"Or you could just give up, let the business die, and move on with your life," I said, turning to drop the napkin in the trash. "Whatever you want to do."

When I turned back around, Keith was nodding slowly. "You're right about Sam's Club. What did you say we need again? Napkins and what not?"

I reached for a notepad and made him a list with half of my brain. The other half of my brain swirled and whirled with ideas on how we could save Froyo. Not that I cared. I just wanted to be prepared for when we talked about it later.

When I finished the list, I scanned through it to make sure I'd gotten the right parts of my brain in the right place. I was in such a tizzy that it would not have been impossible for me to add 'Advertising Strategies' under 'Evaporated Milk'. I got it right, though. It was good. Every item on the Sam's Club list was an actual thing we could buy there. I ripped the list from the notepad and handed it to Keith.

He gave me a quick peck on the forehead and left, jangling his keys on his way out the door.

As soon as he was out of sight, I started writing the other half of my brain down as quickly as I could.

Advertise: make flyers with coupons.
Update the window display. It stinks.
Have a store mascot that hands out samples.

I was interrupted by a childish voice yelling, "Momomomomomomomom." I reached over and picked up my phone.

"Hey, Mommy!" I said, resting the phone on my shoulder while I tapped the pencil against the pad, trying to think of what else I could add to the list. It looked sadly bare.

"Bailey, darling! How are you today, precious?"

"Good. How about you? What are you doing right now?" I imagined her in a sun hat, clipping flowers from one of the bushes in the front yard.

"I'm fine, sweetums. Just taking a walk around the pond while your daddy finishes his tee."

That was my next guess.

"I'm happy you sound happier than you did the other day," she said. "We were worried about you. You know, I don't know if I told you how much I want you and Dayton to be friends. It was my dearest wish when I was carrying you."

"I know, Mom," I said, trying not to roll my eyes. In my defense, she told that story, like, every time I talked to her. It made me feel guilty on those days when I wanted to throw Dayton out the window. "Dayton and I are friends. Mostly."

"I know, and I'm so glad! Now, what are you up to today? Tell me everything."

And so, I yammered on for, like, thirty minutes about swim lessons, classes, and the girls Dayton was dating. That last part was payback. Dayton hated it when Mom and I talked about his dating habits. Unfortunately, it backfired on me.

"And how about you, Baybee? Have you met anyone?"

Aw, poop.

"Uh..." I stammered. I didn't know how much Dayton had told her about my dating habits. I never told Mom about the guys I dated, mostly because I didn't keep them around long enough for Mom to get attached. She wanted grandkids too much.

"Have you been out with anyone recently?"

Also, I couldn't lie. So, there was that.

"I went out with someone last night," I heard myself saying. My voice sounded too tense. That was no good. Mom would latch onto that instantly, and then she would start thinking Tanner and I were a thing.

We weren't a thing.

We were no-thing.

"Oh! How lovely! What's his name?"

"Tanner," I mumbled.

"I have always loved the name Tanner. I would have named one of my babies Tanner if we'd had more. Tell me about him. Does he have an education? A steady job? Is he a good man? He doesn't live with his momma, does he?"

"Um...uh...um..."

"Can you send me a picture, sweetie? I'd love to see him for myself. I'm picturing him as a young Clark Gable." She actually giggled. "That can't be right though, can it? Where did you meet him?"

That I could answer. "Froyo." Suddenly a light pierced through the dense fog of my mind. Without realizing it, my mom had given me the perfect way out of this awkward conversation.

"Mom!" I interrupted. "Did you know Keith is thinking about closing Froyo?"

"No!" My mom's reply was more of a gasp. "Oh, my dear. That is terrible news. Poor, poor man. Is there anything we can do?"

I didn't stop to congratulate myself. Instead, I read through my list. "Do you have any other ideas?"

"Dear me, this is not my forte." Mom sighed. "I'll talk to your daddy, and between the two of us, maybe we can think of something. But don't you dare let him give up without a fight! Flagstaff needs Froyo."

"Strawberries, please."

I shrieked and literally jumped a mile into the air. My phone slipped through my fingers, bouncing off the tips like a volleyball as I scrambled to grab it before it hit the floor.

"Mom? I gotta go. I'll talk to you later," I said in a rush, not waiting for her reply before ending the call. I faced Tanner. "You scared the chlorine out of me. What the heck are you doing?"

He ran his free hand through his hobbit hair. "Sorry about that."

"How long have you been standing there?" I said, hoping it was not long enough to hear me telling my mom about him.

"Not long." He glanced at my paper and then quickly flicked his gaze away.

I refrained from rolling my eyes, but just barely. "You can read it. I'm making a to-do list. Froyo's in trouble." I held the pad so he could see it. "I was just talking to my mom about it. What do you think? Do you have any other ideas for how we can save it?"

"Uh." He cleared his throat, taking the list from my hand. "I'm just a math teacher, not a...not a businessman."

"Sure, sure," I said, waving my arm, "but you're no dummy, right? How many guys teach college in their early twenties? I'm sure you have ideas in that big brain of yours that could help me improve this business." I tapped the pen against my closed lips. "Oh! What about a date auction? We could hold it here, so people will buy yogurt as refreshments, and then all the money could go to Froyo!"

"A date auction?" Tanner wrinkled his forehead. "What would that look like, exactly?"

I stared at him. "Have you never seen a date auction? Not even on TV?"

"Yes," Tanner said, patiently, "but I don't know what *you* think a date auction is. Walk me through the details."

"Oh, you know." I waved my hands again. "People get auctioned off to the highest bidder. In this case, it would be for a date." I wrote 'date auction' down after the mascot idea.

"And Keith would get all the money," I said, staring off into space, picturing myself in a Miss America gown walking through the tables of Froyo.

"You don't think that's a little..."

"What?" I blinked, coming back from the glitter and rhinestones.

"Never mind." Tanner pulled a pencil from his flannel shirt pocket and crossed off the date auction. "Don't do that one. I might be able to help you." He sighed heavily. "But first, I need strawberries."

I stared at Tanner's ugly gray scribble on the paper, feeling annoyed as my dreams of glitter and tuxedos disintegrated into lead scratches. A date auction sounded fun, and I hated it when people say no before they gave a fair amount of thought to one of my spectacular ideas.

"What's wrong with the date auction?" I said as I reached for the spoon to scoop his strawberries. "Five dollars."

Tanner handed me a twenty. "Keep the change." He pulled his yogurt to a bar stool instead of walking to the corner table.

I stared at the money on the counter. "That's way too much, Tanner."

"No, it's not," he said through a mouthful of yogurt and strawberries.

I picked up the twenty and waved it in the air before his eyes. "Your yogurt costs five dollars. This is a twenty."

"A plus." He looked amused.

"Well, Mr. Math Professor, in case you didn't realize, even your standard ten dollars is a really generous tip. Twenty is way too much." I slapped the bill back on the counter.

He ignored it. "May I use that pad?"

I slid it towards him and tapped my foot as he began to write. He hunched over the pad of paper and scribbled with horrendous handwriting that I couldn't decipher while he completely ignored the money on the counter.

I tried to ignore it, too. I like to be stubborn as much as the next person. I just kept thinking that Froyo really could use the extra money, and it was obvious that Tanner wasn't going to take it back. With a sigh, I opened the register and put the whole amount inside instead of pulling out the customary five-dollar bill for my tip jar.

"You never answered my question about the date auction. Why not do that one?"

Tanner still didn't say anything.

"What? You got something better? Prove it, smarty pants. What could you possibly come up with that's better than a date auction?" I leaned on the counter with elbows.

Tanner straightened and moved the pad so I could see. I had to squint and turn my head in all different directions to make out his handwriting.

Advertise: Radio, Local TV news, Newspaper
Discounts: Two for Tuesday, Dollar-off date night, Family Friday
Product: New toppings, Swag
Contests: New flavor suggestions, unveiling of new products

"Wow," I said, reeling back. I couldn't help but be impressed. "Who says you're not a business guy? That's a ton of stuff right off the top of your head. All I could come up with was a mascot and date auction."

Tanner shrugged but didn't comment.

"Swag is a great idea," I said, pointing to it on the list. "It would be fun to have stuffed animals wearing Froyo accessories, like caps and shirts and pennants. Oh! Those plastic cups with straws—those are awesome. Or insulated water bottles. We could put Froyo's logo on the side!"

"Great ideas." Tanner wrote as quickly as I could say words. "See, you've got this. You just needed to get started."

"This could be really fun!" I said. "What about punch cards? Buy ten, get the eleventh free or something?"

While Tanner wrote this down, I let my mind go wild with all the possibilities. Then I watched as it all came tumbling down. Keith wasn't going to go for any of it. He would want to see more customers before he invested money in a dying business. But I didn't know how we would get more customers without spending money. And around and around and around we go. I had no idea what to do about that.

I should have majored in business.

Except that it was super boring.

I huffed and let my cheek sink to my palm.

"What?" Tanner set the pencil down.

"It's no good. We need more customers first," I said, speaking as though I was continuing a conversation with Tanner, even though he hadn't been privy to what I was thinking.

Tanner jumped right in like he knew exactly what I meant. "I know a guy who does a podcast out of the broadcasting building at NAU. It's really popular on campus. I'm sure he'd do a free interview promo for us. It won't cost us anything. We can start there and see what happens."

"We?"

Tanner jotted down a few more things I couldn't read. I'd have to have him translate his handwriting for me later.

"We?" I tried again.

"Yes, well," Tanner finally looked up from the pad of paper, "where am I going to go all day if Froyo goes out of business?"

I laughed. "Good point. You'd be forced to set up camp in a coffee shop with all the hipsters."

Tanner suppressed a shutter. I honestly couldn't tell if it was a real one, or if he was pretending.

"I'll call Dan right now."

"Dan?"

"The podcast."

"Oh, right."

While Tanner made his phone call, I refilled the toppings, even though they didn't need it, and shamelessly eavesdropped on Tanner's conversation. It was interesting to listen to him shoot the breeze, casually bring up Froyo, and make the request for free advertising in a much smoother way than I could have. I was impressed. He was really good. I think I would have been tempted to do anything he asked me to do if he used that earnest, velvety tone of voice and looked at me all sincere with his chocolatey brown eyes—

Wait, what?

He was good with people. That was all I meant. It was just unexpected. I wonder why I didn't notice that about him before?

Oh yeah. That's because up until yesterday, I thought he was a dirty hobbit impersonating a homeless person with a laptop.

Or something like that.

"Sounds great. Thanks, Dan." Tanner put his phone down with a grin. "Dan will do it. A thirty-minute interview on Monday."

"Wow," I said. "That's amazing. Thanks, Tanner!"

Tanner ducked his head like he was trying to get away from my compliments and wrote on the pad. "Can you meet me at NAU Monday morning at seven?"

"Yeah. I mean, no problem. I'll do whatever I need to do."

"You will?" Tanner stopped writing but kept his eyes purposefully glued to the notebook.

"Yeah, why?" It was mildly offensive that he looked so surprised. I was a super helpful person. I helped people all the time. I was the helping-est person who ever helped.

He lifted one shoulder. "I didn't think you cared about this place all that much."

My brain went nuts trying to justify and explain, but I ignored it and leaned forward. "That's the whole idea." I whispered without thinking. "I act like I don't, but I do. I really care a lot about Keith. I kind of love that guy."

Tanner opened his mouth, but I put up a hand before he could say anything, unintentionally grazing his lips with my fingers. I pulled my hand back and stuck it in one of my pockets. "Just don't tell him or anyone else because I will deny, deny, deny, and you will look like a big, fat liar."

Tanner pulled at the collar of his t-shirt and cleared his throat.

"What?" I asked.

"What?" Tanner's eyes shifted away from me.

"You cleared your throat."

"So?"

"You only do that when you're uncomfortable or you don't know what to say." I pointed my finger at him. "Which is it?"

Tanner shrugged. "I don't know."

"Yes, you do," I said impatiently. "Just say what you're thinking."

Tanner's eyebrows went up. "I will," he said. Then, he rushed the words like he needed to get them all out before he changed his mind. "You are so different from every girl I've known before. Frankly, it makes me uncomfortable. I'm never quite sure what you're going to do or say."

I burst out laughing.

"What's so funny?"

"I'm totally normal. You're the weird one around here. You either say nothing or weird things." I rinsed a rag and wiped along the toppings bar until the metal glistened. "Why are you so reserved?"

"Why are you so blunt?" Tanner shot back with a grin.

I laughed, "Why not?"

"It's funny—" Tanner hesitated.

"Yeah?"

"Well, I've been here a lot the last year, and up until last week, I had a completely different opinion of you. Maybe that's why I feel so surprised with everything you say, now that I'm getting to know you better. You are not who I thought you were."

Yeah, I knew that feeling; but I wasn't about to tell Tanner that up until yesterday I thought he was an underpaid Lord of the Rings extra.

"Who did you think I was?" I asked, shaking out the rag and rinsing it again.

Tanned deflated. It was almost like I could see him thinking he had said too much. "Just...just different."

"Yeah, like how?"

Tanner cleared his throat.

"Nuh-uh!" I stopped and pointed at him. "None of that! You aren't allowed to clear your throat around me anymore."

"I don't do it on purpose," Tanner smiled. "It's a habit, I guess."

"Well, pay attention and stop it," I said. "Clearing your throat means you are choosing your words carefully, and if we are ever going to be real friends, you have to stop choosing your words carefully. Right?"

"Is that how that works?" Tanner twirled the pencil through his fingers.

"Yes," I slapped the rag on the counter. "Yes, it is. Friends don't pick and choose words to sound better or hide their meaning. Friends let it all spew out like a fire hose and love each other anyway." I looked up, catching Tanner's eye. His neck went splotchy red before he covered it with his hand. As he rubbed his skin back to a normal color, I concentrated on rinsing my rag again. When I turned back to him, he could meet my eyes without shifting away.

"So, no more throat-clearing." I pointed at him until he nodded meekly. "Good. Now tell me who you thought I was."

A long silence followed. I let it be long. Obviously, it was going to take Tanner some time to get used to sharing his thoughts. He clearly didn't tell people what he was really thinking very often.

"Fake." He said it so quietly I almost couldn't hear the word. Then it reverberated through my head like he'd yelled it at the top of his lungs.

Fake.

"Oh," I said.

He thought I was fake.

"I don't think that you are fake now that I know you. I was obviously wrong."

Was he?

I hated to admit it. I hated to think about it. Shame twisted around the inside of my belly. It was too noisy to ignore. Tanner was totally right about me.

I was fake.

Before I made that stupid promise to Dayton, I would lie my tongue out all day long if it got me whatever I wanted at that particular moment. For the last week or so, I'd been forced to be totally truthful with everything I said. If I was going to be brutally honest with everyone else, it was only fair that I should take this moment of self-reflection and let it tell me something important about myself.

I quieted all my judgy thoughts so that I could concentrate. Tanner faded, and the world blurred slightly at the edges. I took a solid look at the depths of me and what I saw was...

Nothing.

I breathed in sharply.

"Bailey?"

A feather-light touch grazed the back of my hand. It was gone so fast, I wasn't sure if I'd imagined it.

"Are you okay? I'm really sorry. I shouldn't have said that."

I blinked a couple of times, and the world came back into focus. "I made you say it," I whispered. "I practically forced you to say it. And actually, I'm glad you did. You don't talk enough. And I...I talk too much. Stick us together, and we would be the perfect person."

Something flickered in Tanner's eyes. I couldn't identify what he was thinking, and it troubled me. It really shouldn't matter. I don't care what people think about me.

I don't.

Was it getting warm? I felt warm. I needed to check the heater. It would melt the chocolate if it kept running this high. Not to mention, it was going to cost Keith a boatload of money he didn't have.

Tanner said my name softly.

I stepped away, looking around for something that needed to be done. There had to be something; there was always something. My eyes flicked to the pot of fudge resting in place on the warmer. Just the other day, Keith had mentioned that the fudge pot needed a deep cleaning. I could do that.

Without giving Tanner another fleck of my attention, I turned my back and got busy. I unplugged the warmer and filled the sink with warm, soapy water. Then I found a container to put the remaining fudge in and pulled out two hot pads. I was so caught up in what I was doing that I didn't notice Tanner come around the counter until I nearly knocked into him.

"What are you doing?" I said more harshly than the situation called for. "No customers behind the counter. It's like a health code violation or something."

"Let me help. That looks heavy." Tanner ignored my sputtering and reached around me for the stainless steel pot.

I pushed him away. "No, seriously. You can't be back here. I got this. I do it all the time."

That was an absolute truth—as long as a person defined "all the time" as whenever I chose not to ignore Keith. I heaved the pot off the warmer with both hands. The thing needed to go on a diet.

Tanner watched as I tipped the pot and poured the leftover fudge into a new container. He reached out his hands, as though to take the pot from me, but he stopped himself before he went through with it.

I blew a stray hair out of my eyes and dropped the pot into the sink to wash. In the few seconds it took me to put the hot pads back where they belonged, Tanner had once again violated the codes. He was behind the counter, up to his elbows in chocolate-colored soap suds.

"Tanner!" I grabbed the back of his shirt, pulling him away from the sink. "Seriously, go back to your corner!"

He stumbled over his own feet. My tugging turned him around, knocking him into me. Water flew from the sink and into the air as his arms flailed. It all came raining down on the two of us. I slid into Tanner's chest, then pushed myself away and knocked over a container of pretzels. They rained onto the tile, breaking into tiny pieces.

What a disaster.

I had to get this mess cleaned up before Keith got back and freaked out.

"Forget what I said about violations," I pointed at Tanner. "You finish scrubbing that pot, and I'll go get the mop." I slid toward the stockroom, moving across the floor like an ice skater.

Once the stock room door was between us, I leaned against it to breathe for a second.

But just a second. Any longer than that and I'd start thinking, and that was the last thing I wanted to do right now.

I grabbed the mop and pulled it away from the other stuff without bringing anything else with it. This was a first for me. Usually, I knocked everything over, making a bigger mess than the one that needed to be cleaned up. Then, Keith would tell me to go away so he could clean it up himself while I ate Starbursts from the toppings bar and told him where he missed a spot.

When I went back into the store area, Keith stumbled through the door with his arms fully loaded. I held my breath, waiting for the tirade about the mess. Then I realized there was no mess. Tanner had wiped up the floor in the super short time I'd been gone and was hard at work on the pot.

He caught my eye for a brief second, then ran to grab the door for Keith. While I stood there like a dummy with a useless mop, Tanner disappeared to finish unloading Keith's sedan.

"Here." I reached for one of the boxes in Keith's arms.

"No, no. I have this perfectly balanced. If you take something, I'll drop it all," Keith said.

"Okay, fine." I'd had enough of bossy boys for one day. "Then load everything onto that table, and I'll start putting it away."

Keith did as I said, sat at the table, and wiped his forehead dramatically. "That Sam's Club is a zoo, I tell you. This town could stand to have another one. I got everything on the list except chocolate chips. They only sell the big baking wafers right now. We'd have to chop them up."

"That's okay. We can order chocolate chips in bulk online."

Tanner brought in the last of the groceries. Now three tables were piled with supplies. "Where do these go?" he asked.

"Oh, I'm so glad you asked." I bossed Tanner around, which felt pretty dang good, while Keith sipped a glass of water.

"Good. Now that that's done," I said once the last thing was put away, "we need to have a family meeting."

Keith raised his eyebrows.

"You know what I mean. A company and loyal customer meeting. Tanner and I have been brainstorming while you were gone."

Keith pushed his glasses down his nose to peer at the notepad as I slid it across the table to him. I waited impatiently for him to read through it.

"Hm," he grunted as he looked up.

"What do you think?" It took him forever to read. No one should have to wait that long for anything.

Keith rubbed his eyes. "I don't know, sis. This seems like a lot of work. I don't want anyone wasting their time or money on something that's about to kick the bucket."

I shook my head. "It's not too much, really." I pointed to the list. "Tanner already got us a podcast interview on Monday. That's huge! Then—"

Keith held up his hand. "I'm not denying you have some good ideas. Let me think this over. You can go do that radio thing for now."

"Podcast, grandpa." I rolled my eyes.

Keith let out a long breath, and I decided to shut my mouth before I irritated him enough to change his mind. It was miraculous that he agreed at all. I shouldn't press my luck, but really? Who even listened to the radio anymore? Maybe, I should just be grateful he didn't make a reference to carrier pigeons.

Keith rubbed his eyes. "If you don't mind, I'm going to go take a snooze on the couch in my office. I have a headache that's threatening to be a doozy."

I waved him away. "Don't worry. I got this."

"I know you do, sis."

I watched him go, feeling a strange pang of worry at the shuffle of Keith's feet and the slump of his shoulders as he disappeared through the door. Had he always looked that frail?

"Alrighty, then." I spun around, looking for Tanner. He must have been standing right behind me that whole time without me knowing because when I turned, we were suddenly face to face, in a count-the-freckles-on-your-nose kind of way.

"Steady." Tanner gripped my elbow.

"I'm fine," I said, pulling my hands away from his biceps.

No, I did not notice that, for a flannel-clad hobbit, he had surprisingly toned arms. It was impossible to imagine him at the gym in his baggy jeans doing arm curls.

I shook my head and stepped away from Tanner so that I was no longer breathing his air. "Well, that was encouraging," I said in my most business-like voice. "I thought we'd have a way bigger fight getting Keith to agree to anything on that list."

Tanner nodded but didn't say anything.

"Thanks again for your help, by the way," I said lightly. "We'll have to get you a cape."

"A cape?"

"Yes," I huffed. "Because you saved the day again. Work with me here."

Tanner smiled. "I didn't do anything, not really."

"I disagree." I walked back behind the counter. He followed me, taking his seat on the opposite side. "You remember those bygone days when you used to stay in your corner all day long with your nose pressed against your computer screen?"

Tanner laughed. "You mean two days ago?"

"Yeah."

Was that only two days ago? It felt like a lifetime.

"What did you do on your computer all day, anyway?"

Tanner shifted. "Oh, you know, this and that." He picked up the pencil and made a couple of notes on the pad. I waited, but it became very obvious very quickly that I wasn't going to get any more information out of him.

"Well, anyway, thanks for your help today." I flicked a marshmallow at his beard to get his attention.

Tanner lifted his head just in time to see it miss his face and fall to the counter. When he looked at me, my breath caught in my throat.

What was going on with me? Maybe I was getting sick or something. That had to be it. Hot and cold flashes, stuff in my throat. I should have listened to Dayton and gotten that flu shot in the fall.

Ways to Improve Bailey #6

Just leave the fence alone

I felt fine when I woke up the next morning and was totally good all day. It must have been some random, short-lived bug because when Monday morning dawned, bright and early, I was totally ready to take on the world. Or at least that podcast interview with Dan.

Dayton had to run a bunch of errands for one of his engineering classes, so he dropped me off at NAU before the sun had even come up. I checked my watch as I climbed out of the car. I was fifteen minutes early.

"Have fun! Don't do anything I wouldn't do," Dayton called as he drove away. He was going to come pick me up when the interview was over unless I caught a ride with Tanner.

I picked a fuzzy off my jeans and turned towards the broadcasting building. I wore my favorite pair of dark blue skinny jeans, a flowy white top with embroidery around the neck, and brown boots with enough of a heel to help me reach adult height.

In other words, I looked amazing.

I carefully stacked a couple of boxes of muffins in my arms. I made Dayton take me to the store before dropping me off. It couldn't hurt to bribe Dan a little bit with some fresh baked goodness.

An arctic blast whirled around me, seeping through my light cardigan like it was nothing. I wished I'd brought my ski coat. It was down-filled and warmer than Aruba. Obviously, our so-called heat wave had come to a crashing halt.

I missed my coat even more when I realized the door to the broadcasting building was locked. Why didn't Dayton wait for me to get inside before he drove off? He just doomed me to become a popsicle.

With a sigh, I shifted my stack of boxes to the other arm and pulled out my phone to call Tanner. Hopefully he was already inside and could just come open the door for me. He picked up in the middle of the first ring.

"Bailey?"

He sounded awful.

"Tanner? What the heck is wrong with your voice?"

"I woke up with a cold." He sneezed.

"Really? That's weird. I totally thought I was coming down with a cold or something, too, but I was fine." I stopped myself because I was babbling. "Tanner?"

I heard a thump and a groan.

"I'm fine. I'm still coming to the interview. Don't start without me."

"No way." I shook my head, even though he couldn't see me. "No stinking way. You go back to bed. I'll call you when it's over."

"No, really. I'm fine. I'll be right there."

I stomped my feet, not because I was upset, but because I was losing feeling in my toes. My adorable boots were not actually that warm. "Tanner, go to bed. That's an order."

He hacked and then wheezed. "I thought it was supposed to be the oldest child who ended up with the bossiness gene."

"Well, you know me, the expectation blower. Here are the facts: you're sick, and it's freezing out here."

Tanner's voice wavered. "I set this up for you. I don't want you to have to do it alone."

I was close to winning this argument, I could tell. Tanner didn't sound at all certain anymore. I decided to seal the deal with a southern drawl. "Please, Tanner. If you won't do it for yourself, do it for me." I stretched my words out and added a choke at the end. It was a Golden Globe performance. Too bad everyone but Tanner missed it.

"Okay," Tanner sighed in defeat. "I'll stay home, but only because your accent is awful."

"Mean!" I said. "Do you need anything?"

A tall, red-haired guy chose that moment to walk out of the broadcasting building. I grabbed the door before it could close again, almost dumping my phone and the muffins all over the concrete.

"No, thank you. If you're making me stay home—"

"I am."

"—then I'm going back to bed."

"I'll let you get to it," I said, my phone slipping down my cheek. I nudged it back up with my shoulder.

"Call me when you're done?" Tanner asked. "I'd like to hear how it goes."

"Nope," I said, taking a deep breath. In front of me stretched a staircase that looked like it reached the sky. I looked around.

No elevator.

Boo.

I should have worn sneakers. And yoga pants, come to think of it. It was silly to dress up for a podcast interview.

"That's okay." Tanner sounded embarrassed. "I—"

"I meant—" I huffed and puffed, wishing I'd climbed stairs more often, so I didn't feel like my lungs were going to explode— "I'm not going to call you. I'm going to come over. In about two hours. I'll bring you juice and soup or something."

"You don't have to."

"See ya soon," I said with a sudden burst of breath. I didn't mean to be so abrupt, but I really didn't have air for more words. I turned off my phone.

And climbed.

And climbed.

And climbed.

When I finally reached the top of the stairs, my legs felt like jelly, and I was noticeably less excited about the interview. I paused to give myself a stern pep talk outside the studio door. Froyo was my priority right now. Froyo needed all of my attention.

Froyo, Froyo, Froyo.

I pushed the door open, ready to take on the world. Or, at least, Dan's podcast.

Two hours later, I stood in the hall outside Tanner's room, completely exhausted and totally hyped up.

Yeah, it's possible.

I knocked a second time, listening for sound on the other side of the door. I didn't want to wake Tanner up if he was resting.

Maybe I should just go.

There was a faint shuffle, then the clank of a lock being turned. I went to the window and waved to let Dayton know I was good. He gave me a stupid grin and sped off. I was going to have to do something nefarious to get back at him. He had been the biggest stinker during the drive. Both because I wanted him to drop me off at Tanner's house and because I made him stop at Safeway on the way to pick up soup, juice, and rolls.

Tanner pulled the door open just a crack.

"Holy cow. You look terrible."

He ran his hand over his matted beard, pulling at the ends. His head looked like he'd been playing with a hair dryer in the bathtub. His t-shirt and flannel pajama pants were wrinkled.

"When was the last time you showered?" I wrinkled my nose.

"Hey!" Tanner croaked. "You insisted on coming over, remember? I tried to stop you." His words were tempered with a lopsided smile.

"I know." I stepped forward, forcing Tanner to get out of my way or be mowed down with my heeled boots. But then I had to stop, in shock or awe—I'm not sure which—at the sight of his room. It was a tiny space with a card table in the corner, a mini fridge next to it, and a bed crammed into the other corner.

I opened my mouth to comment.

"Don't say anything. I know it's a disaster. I was going to pick up before you got here, but I fell asleep."

I took a long look at his rumpled self and bloodshot eyes. "Go lay down, Tanner. You look like death married Frankenstein."

Tanner laughed as he plodded back to the bed. He dropped, face down on the covers and groaned.

"Are you in pain?" I asked. "Or do your sheets stink as bad as the rest of this place? When was the last time you cleaned?"

"I clean." Tanner's voice was muffled. He turned his head so I could hear him better. "I do laundry." His voice trailed off. I assume because that was the end of his cleaning repertoire and not because he was starting to get hoarse. I mean, seriously, the room looked like it had not seen a vacuum, a duster, or disinfectant wipes.

Like, ever.

"Good thing I brought utensils," I said mostly to myself as I unpacked the Safeway bag. "I didn't bring a bowl, though. I guess you can just eat out of the container." I opened the lid of the soup and stuck a spoon inside. While I was rummaging through the bag for rolls, I heard Tanner's cackle.

"What?"

Tanner flopped over onto his back. "I have never heard anyone make so much noise in my life."

I took the plastic bag and crinkled it back and forth in my hands. "I don't know what you're talking about!" I yelled. "I'm not making that much noise. Can you drag your sick self over here to eat, or do you want me to bring it to you like a pathetic invalid?"

Tanner groaned and covered his ears.

"Table it is then." I pulled out one of the metal folding chairs, clanked it open, and pointed to it.

Tanner rolled onto his feet. "What kind of soup is this?" he asked, leaning over the plastic container so that the steam fogged his glasses.

"Tomato basil."

"It smells like summer."

"You're welcome. It also makes good leftovers, so feel free to drop as much as you want into your beard for later."

Tanner dropped into a chair with a thump. "I take it you don't like my beard?" The corner of his mouth quirked up slightly.

"Whatever. It's your face. If you want to look like an extra on *Duck Dynasty*, that's your business. Personally, I think beards are weird," I said, and laughed. "Look at that, the start of the next 'Great American Poem'."

"Entitled 'Weird Beard?'" Tanner raised an eyebrow, reaching for the spoon.

"It's amazing. Now, eat. I'm going to clean up this pigsty. I mean room."

"Don't clean. Eat with me. Have you had lunch?" Tanner kicked out the other folding chair, making it screech away from the table.

"I brought this for you." I rested my fingertips on the back of the chair.

Tanner gestured to the small folding table loaded with food. "There's plenty for two. Oh, and a small army."

"Tanner!"

"What?" His eyes widened as he looked around.

I shook my head. "You sound like me. I think I'm a bad influence on you!"

Tanner grunted and brought a spoonful of soup to his mouth. He wiggled the spoon to cool it off before putting it into his mouth. "You're right."

"Duh."

"You don't want to know what you're right about?" He raised an eyebrow.

"We don't have that much time."

Tanner's shoulders shook. "I was going to say you're right about the soup being amazing," he said, taking another bite. "The rest remains to be seen."

I rolled my eyes. "I don't want to sit and watch you eat. That's as weird as your beard."

Tanner swallowed, wiping his face with a paper towel. "Why are you so mean to my beard, Bailey? Beards have feelings, too."

I didn't think that statement deserved a response. At least, not a vocal response. I had plenty of commentary going on in my head. Like, because Tanner was sick and hadn't trimmed his beard in a few days, it looked like a small animal was burrowing into his chin for winter.

"No comment?" Tanner looked up from blowing on his soup.

"Nope." I tossed my head. "But if you want to keep talking about it, you can tell me why you don't shave that thing off. I've never understood facial hair. A mustache alone makes a guy look like a creeper. A mustache with a full beard is the opposite of attractive. Thank you, Santa Claus. A beard alone is an abomination. I guess a goatee can be hot, depending on who's wearing it..." I trailed off. There were a couple of country music singers who pulled that off quite nicely.

Tanner studied my face. "You know what? I don't want to talk about it anymore. You can hate my beard all you want."

"Why, thank you." I nodded once. "How about this: I will sit with you while you eat, and then I will clean." I spun the chair around on one leg and sat in it backwards with my chin resting on the back rail.

"You're not hungry?"

I shook my head. "I ate, like, a billion muffins."

"What muffins?"

"Blueberry and poppy seed."

"Homemade?"

"Ain't nobody got time for that."

Tanner shook his head. "I meant to ask, did you take muffins for the interview, or were they already there?"

I wrinkled my forehead. "Not that it matters one iota, but I picked them up at the store on the way there."

"And why did you do that?" Tanner swirled his spoon through the soup.

"Again, weird question. I was trying to suck up to Dan."

"And did it work?"

I leaned back, rubbing my hands up and down my legs to give myself something to do besides feel interrogated. "No. Dan is gluten-free, sugar-free, vegan, and something-everything intolerant."

"I didn't know that."

"Did you also not know that Dan does yoga, has three dogs, and takes monthly sabbaticals to Sedona's vortex?"

"I did not."

I shrugged. "Not like it's a shocker. This is Flagstaff. Anyway, more muffins for me, so it's all good."

Tanner finally looked up. "Did you eat the entire box of muffins in front of Dan? No shame?"

I tossed my head. "Actually, I ate two whole boxes of muffins after the interview while I waited for Dayton to pick me up. Stop laughing! I was hungry. Saving Froyo takes a lot of calories."

"Indeed."

"Indeed," I mocked him with a snooty tone and reached over to dip a piece of bread in his soup.

"So, you found out quite a bit about Dan. Did the two of you talk about Froyo at all?" He tore off a bite-sized hunk of roll and set the rest on the table.

"Yes," I sniffed. "For like an hour and a half. You can hear it for yourself tomorrow. Well, you can hear the parts he doesn't edit out for yourself tomorrow."

"Tomorrow? That's fast."

"I guess," I tossed my head. "Dan said he would expedite our podcast for Froyo's sake."

"That was nice of him." Tanner tore a roll into small pieces. Some he ate slowly, the others he spread around on the table.

"Sure, whatever. I don't think he had anything else going on. He said he's running out of people to interview." I flipped my hair over my shoulder. "Anyways, I'm pretty sure I was amazing, so it won't be any work at all to edit our talk. Except for maybe the part where he asked me to dinner. That would be super weird to broadcast." I set the piece of soup-soaked bread on my tongue, savoring the spicy blend of basil and tomatoes.

It was heavenly.

Tanner coughed, spurting bread goobers all over the floor. I flicked a napkin at him. There was no way I was cleaning the floor. There wasn't a mop in sight, I'd have to Cinderella it up in here on my hands and knees.

Uh, no thank you.

After more deep coughs, Tanner took a sip of water.

"Sorry. Went down the wrong tube."

"No problem." I pushed more napkins towards him.

"So, you're going out with Dan?" His voice cracked, and he hurriedly took a long swig of water, watching me out of the corner of his eye.

"I'm going out to dinner with Dan." I corrected. "We're going to go to that pho place that just opened downtown."

Tanner didn't say anything, and the silence weighed on me. I felt the uncontrollable urge to keep talking, even though there wasn't much more to say about it.

"I've been dying to go there. I read reviews right after it opened, and everyone loved it. Even the critics that don't love anything raved about the Vietnamese crepe. It's made with coconut milk and rice flour but stuffed with cilantro, mint, sprouts, whatever meat you want, and a peanut sauce. It sounds so amazing! I'm super excited to try it, finally."

Tanner kept staring at me, so I kept talking. I was like a runaway train or something. I don't think I could have stopped myself if I wanted to.

"Get this! They have oxtail soup. Isn't that so cool?"

Finally, he spoke. "Oxtail soup? Is it really made from an oxtail?"

"I hope so." I reached to dip another bite of bread into the soup. Tanner pushed the container closer to me. "I've never eaten the tail of anything. I'm super curious if it's good."

He cleared his throat. "You like Dan, then?"

"Sure, he's great," I shrugged. "Do you think I should get the banh mi with the oxtail soup, or try the crepe thing? I've been thinking about it off and on since I left NAU, and I really can't decide. If I get the crepe, I'll miss out on the banh mi, but if I get that, there's a chance Dan will get the vegetarian crepe and let me try it. I don't think he'll get the soup, though."

"Personally, I wouldn't eat anything that was ever that close to an animal's behind." Tanner set his spoon on the table. "Bailey…"

"Yeah?" I looked up from the roll I was dividing into pieces. I guess I was hungrier than I thought. Tanner had stopped eating, so I didn't feel bad stealing it from him.

"Never mind."

I held up a finger. "Uh-uh. None of that. Finish your thought."

Tanner scooted the container of soup to the side, and then moved it back to the original spot. "What if you don't like what I want to say?"

I put the roll down and looked at Tanner until he would meet my eyes. "Then we'll talk through it. It's not like you say something that I don't like and that's that, right? We just figure it out until we both feel okay again. That's how friendship works. So, you can stop hesitating, and you can stop clearing your dang throat." I pulled the soup the rest of the way across the table and had already started eating before I realized I was using Tanner's spoon.

And he was sick.

Lovely.

Oh, well. Too late now.

"Okay, then. What I was going to say was you seem more excited about the food you're going to eat than you do about spending time with Dan."

I put my spoon down with a sigh. I had a feeling I knew what was coming. There was something eerily familiar about Tanner's tone of voice and the way he was looking at me.

He'd been spending too much time with Dayton, I think.

"I was...just wondering. Do you think... Is it—"

"Spit it out, Tanner."

"Are you being fair to those guys if you only go out with them for the food?"

I stared at him. "Really?"

"I'm not trying to attack you," Tanner continued. "I know it might look like I am. It just got me thinking, that's all. So, I asked. You don't have to answer." Tanner was suddenly super interested in picking at the puffy green material that covered his card table.

"I'll answer."

But what would I say? I picked the spoon back up and ate some more soup to give myself time to think.

Tanner glanced at me once, then again when I still hadn't said anything after a few minutes.

"Okay." I twirled the spoon. "Dayton and I had this exact conversation. It's not that I'm only interested in the food. I still talk to most of the guys I've been out with; we're friends. Most of them are in my classes and stuff. I just don't do the second date thing because I don't want to lead them on and make them think there's a chance for something more, you know? I think that's a good thing in the long run."

"Sure," Tanner nodded. "Except, he has to be at least a little interested in you if he asks you out. So, in that case, saying yes is leading him on. He's not going to spend money on a date unless he has some thoughts about being more than friends."

"What are you talking about? You did."

"I did?" Tanner flinched, even though I hadn't even raised my voice. "I did what?"

"You took me out to dinner as friends without expecting it to be more. Right?"

Tanner looked down at his hands. "Is that what I did?"

"I don't know, you tell me." I narrowed my eyes. Why did you ask me out, anyway?"

"Technically, I didn't." Tanner looked up with an ironic smile. "That date was a return favor for saving your phone, remember?"

"Oh, I remember," I snapped, then stopped myself to take several deep breaths.

This conversation was cuckoo.

The silence across the table drew my eyes to Tanner. He was tracing his finger over the table, purposefully not looking at me. I took a deep breath. Grandpa Hendrix always used to tell me not to take offense or give offense. Just leave the fence alone.

It was a whole lot easier said than done.

"What's the real problem here, Tanner?"

Tanner looked up, caught my eye, and looked away. "Dan. He's... I mean, the guy is great." He cleared his throat three times.

"Yes?"

"I may not know about the yoga and the vegan thing, but I do know that Dan would not have asked you out if he was not interested in you."

"Okay?" I still didn't get what the big deal was. I couldn't be the only person in the world who dated just for fun. I'm sure there were tons of people not interested in relationships.

I sat back, dipping the spoon in and out of the soup but not eating anymore. It was totally and completely Tanner's turn to do some talking.

Finally, he looked up. His eyes were serious. "Dan is focused. He doesn't do anything without a reason. He asked you out because he's interested in you. I'm concerned he might—"

"What?" I burst out laughing. I felt so wound up with tension that I couldn't help but laugh. "He might what? Come on, Tanner. I've been dating for, like, years. I'm a big, tough girl. I can handle it."

"Famous last words," Tanner muttered.

"Okay, seriously." I held out a hand to him, trying to restore peace. "In all seriousness, what do you think will happen if Dan is suuuuuuper interested in me. What will he do? Open the door for me, hold my hand? No! Try to kiss me? Gasp! Come on, Tanner. What kind of danger am I in here?"

Tanner's head snapped up. "No danger. That's not what I meant. Dan's a good guy."

"So, he's not a creeper or a predator or a bully." I interrupted. "Then what's the problem?"

Tanner's eyebrows met to form a V shape crease.

"Tanner." I ducked my head to meet his eyes. He flicked them away. I huffed and slapped my palms onto the table. Tanner still didn't look at me, so I pushed myself out of the chair, walked around the table and leaned down to stare creepily at his ear until he turned my way. He held out for longer than I thought, but I knew I was winning when the tip of his ear turned red.

He slowly turned to look at me. Because of where I stood, his forehead gently brushed against mine. Tanner went still, like he had been turned to stone. Not a muscle in his face flickered. He hardly seemed like he was breathing.

I moved back until we were far enough apart that I could look at him without going all cross-eyed. "Tanner, come on. Lighten up. I already have one idiot brother all up in my life; I don't need another one. Truce?"

His breath came out slowly, tickling my chin. "Truce."

I moved to the other side of the table again. "Good. There's nothing to worry about." I picked up an empty grocery bag and stuffed trash inside.

Tanner watched as I put the soup into his mini fridge, closed off the bag of rolls, and wiped the table down. I looked around for cups and saw a package of plastic ones sticking out from under the bed. I retrieved one and poured Tanner a glass of juice.

"Drink this. You need vitamin C."

"I need something," Tanner mumbled and took the cup. He drained it in about two seconds. When he was done, he thumped it on the table and dragged himself toward the bed. "I feel like garbage."

That might explain a few things. "Right, well, get some rest. I'm going to clean. Where's the trash can?"

"In the alley, around back." Tanner's voice muffled into his pillow.

The walk was exactly what I needed. I tossed the bag into the trash can and took a deep breath. Cool, mountain air filled my lungs until I could think straight again.

When I got back to Tanner's room, I didn't get a chance to say a word before I was greeted by a loud snore. Tanner was totally out.

There wasn't a kitchen or a sink or anything, but after some looking, I found a container of disinfectant wipes tucked in the corner under the table. I mentally apologized for my mean and hurtful thoughts about Tanner not cleaning.

It took about twenty minutes to scrub down the table, the chairs, the doorknob, and some scuff marks on the wall that didn't come off—but at least they were now germ-free.

I gathered all the laundry that was randomly thrown everywhere and made a pile next to the door. I didn't know where he did laundry, but at least it was all in one place now.

I looked around. What else could I do while I waited for Tanner to wake up? I didn't want to just leave without saying good-bye.

The tiny room was already spotless.

I leaned against the wall and slid to the floor. My phone was in my back pocket, so I pulled it out to check texts. There weren't any, but I did have a calendar notification about my swim lessons that night. I quickly texted Dayton to pick me up in thirty minutes. I needed to get ready for work and do my own laundry. Hopefully Tanner would wake up by then.

Tanner's light snores had long since erupted into sawing logs. It was difficult to ignore the noise, which meant it was difficult to ignore him.

There was so much about him that I didn't know, and what I knew didn't make sense. He came from big money, but he lived in a tiny, dirty hostel room by himself.

And if I was hoping to get clues about him from his natural habitat, I was disappointed. His room had nothing in it except furniture. No mementos, no pictures, nothing on the walls. His clothes were the only other identifying things in the room, and instead of in a dresser, they were heaped in a suitcase that was shoved under the bed.

No wonder they always looked rumpled.

Wait a sec.

I set my phone to the side and turned my face to see better under the bed. Next to his suitcase was a shallow plastic box filled with what looked like papers and pictures. My fingers itched to pull it closer. I wanted to see if there was anything in there that would solve the mystery that was Tanner. He would never know. He was dead to the world, sawing logs up there.

Should I?

No.

I should not.

But I wanted to. It would help me understand him better.

It would also be a huge invasion of his privacy.

I wasn't going to do it.

Tanner was my friend. Friends don't do stuff like that. If I wanted to know about him that badly, I should just ask him, not snoop in his business.

I sighed and kicked the box further away, then moved some blankets so I couldn't see it anymore. "Out of sight, out of mind" is a big, fat lie. That stupid little box filled my mind like noxious gas. But at least it was now far out of reach. If I wanted to get it now, I'd have to crawl under his bed with my booty in the air to pull it back out.

I wasn't going to do that.

For multiple reasons.

I made the right decision. I knew I did. But the temptation to invade his privacy was still strong. I recited the alphabet backwards and then started counting to a billion. By the time I got to one hundred and fifty-six, I was almost cured.

I played a word game on my phone until Tanner's irregular snuffles told me he was waking up. I stretched my stiff knees while he rubbed his eyes, and then I climbed up to sit on the edge of his bed.

"Good morning, sunshine."

"Hey." His voice was low and thick with sleep. "You're still here."

"Yep, for about three more minutes. Dayton's picking me up soon. Good news. You have edible food, and your room is clean. You don't need me anymore." I swept my hand across the room.

"You didn't have to clean my place." He arched his back and stuck a pillow behind him.

"Someone had to do it. It was about to be condemned." I stood up and looped my purse over my shoulder.

"Don't go yet. You haven't told me what Dan said about Froyo. I really hate that I missed that interview."

I paused. Didn't he remember our whole conversation from before? The one where he went weird on me about going out with Dan? I looked at his bloodshot eyes and decided the answer was no. Colds make you all fuzzy. He probably didn't remember a thing, which was good news. It was like a conversation redo.

"Dan was really nice and he really talked Froyo up. In fact, I think his exact words were, 'Only a moron would stay away from this frozen yogurt place.'"

"That sounds like Dan," Tanner grinned. "I'm glad it went well."

"Thanks to you. Keith is going to be thrilled. I really hope it brings in enough business to convince him not to close."

Tanner nodded. "So do I."

A long, awkward silence followed where I examined my nails. Finally, Tanner cleared his throat. I refrained, but just barely, from rolling my eyes.

"Thanks again for cleaning up. I've been meaning to hire a housekeeper."

I stopped picking at my nails to look at him. "What for, you bum. Why don't you clean it yourself? This place is tiny. It would take, like, five seconds. You can handle it."

Tanner laughed, his shoulders shaking.

"Why do you always laugh at me?" I wondered. "Seriously, like, everything I say makes your belly shake like a bowl full of jelly."

Tanner coughed into his sleeve. I went to get some more juice and stood over him while he took a sip. He looked up with a small smile. "You're so blunt. It catches me off guard. If you said things like that in front of my parents or my sisters, their heads might actually explode."

I wondered if Tanner's amusement at my bluntness would hold up if I asked him more about his family. He seemed to be an expert at avoiding that subject. But then, this time he was the one who brought it up.

I opened my mouth, but Tanner was quicker. "So, I take it you and Dayton don't have a housekeeper?"

"No!" I scoffed, even though I totally wished we did. "Dayton and I rotate the chores."

"I thought Dayton mentioned a housekeeper once." Tanner adjusted his pillow.

"Maybe he was talking about our parents? Mom and Dad have a company that comes in and cleans twice a week." I took the juice from him and put it back on the table. "Mom offered to find one in Flagstaff for us, but Dayton decided it would build character to clean our own space for once. He read somewhere on the internet that the most successful adults had to do chores around the house when they were young. And Dayton *loves* anything that he thinks will improve me." I couldn't quite manage to keep the bitterness out of my voice.

"I noticed that."

I crossed my arms, leaning against the card table. "You did?"

Tanner nodded. "He talks about you a lot."

"Oh, fabulous." I could only imagine what he said about me to his friends.

"He means well," Tanner added.

"Does he, though?" I flicked a rogue crumb from the table with the nail of my index finger. I must have missed it when I wiped the table earlier. "I think he just loves to torture me."

"I think he's worried about you."

"What? Why?" I narrowed my eyes. "Why do you think he would be worried about me? I'm fine. I'm great, even."

Tanner took a long time to answer. "Not too long ago he was worried about some of things you were doing."

I took a step closer to the bed. "Like what?"

"He said...something about...you not being...always...very truthful."

I flung my arms up in the air. "Really? He told you that? Why doesn't he mind his own beeswax?"

"That upsets you? You told me yourself you were a liar."

I gaped, because seriously? He had to know saying something about yourself and then hearing someone else say it were two very different things. My heart pounded in my ears. It was like we'd never had the break in our conversation while Tanner slept. We just jumped right back into an argument.

So much for the do-over.

"That's another thing. If you are such share-all buddies with Dayton, why didn't you ever mention that you knew my brother? You came into Froyo, like, every day, and you never said a word to me except for, 'Strawberries, please'." I lowered my voice to sound like him.

Tanner sat up all the way, swinging his legs to the floor. He hugged a pillow to his belly the way I'd hugged my purse the other day in his truck. Did he feel as upset as I did? "Bailey."

"What?"

Tanner sighed and racked both hands through his hair, making it stand completely on end. "Thanks for all your help. I'll see you at Froyo later today."

What?

I stared at him, but he wouldn't meet my eyes. Everything from his words to his mannerisms was a blatant kiss-off. Tanner really wasn't going to answer my questions. He really wasn't going to explain anything about anything. I couldn't believe it! He was too frustrating for words.

"Don't bother," I snapped, yanking the door open. I didn't even look back as I slammed it shut behind me.

Ways to Improve Bailey #4

Trust people

I sat on the edge of the pool with my feet dangling in the water. Despite the temperature outside, or maybe because of it, the aquatic center was boiling hot. The water felt more akin to a hot tub than a swimming pool, but I wasn't complaining. I thought it felt fantastic.

I had just finished my last swim lesson of the day with a little girl named Payton who was either nine, thirty, or twenty-three. She told me a different age every time I asked her. Normally, I would be in the locker room, moments away from going home for the day to nurse a half gallon of ice cream. But halfway through my lesson with Payton, my boss, Jordan, came out of his office to voluntell me to take a third lesson tonight. He didn't even give me a chance to say no.

Now I'm stuck here for who knows how much longer, bone tired with my stomach growling like a starving rhinoceros. I wish I'd taken Marnie up on her offer to cover the lesson for me. It had been a mondo long day. I wasn't in the mood for a last-minute sign up.

I splashed my toes in the water and dreamed about cheeseburgers. I didn't care how much Jordan yelled; I already decided that I wasn't staying one minute past seven. If Last-Minute Larry was late, he was out of luck. Though, I guess, it could have just as easily been a Last-Minute Lucy.

I didn't think to ask who the lesson was for.

"Hey, Bailey." Marnie waved to catch my attention. She came out of the locker room wearing street clothes with her full, brown curls shoved inside a huge knit cap. Blow drying her hair was out of the question, and it was way too cold to go outside with wet hair. Instead of a head full of gorgeous, thick curls, she would have had curl-sicles. "See you in class tomorrow?"

I lifted my hand and turned my head, so she could see my overstretched, cheesy grin.

Marnie puffed out her lower lip, walking closer so she could whisper. "I really wish Jordan would let me teach this lesson for you. You look so wiped out."

"I'll be fine. It's only thirty-one more minutes and twenty-seven seconds."

"Aw, Bailey," Marnie patted my head. "I'll come by Froyo tomorrow, okay?"

"Sure." I squinted at the clock over the lifeguard stand. "That sounds great. I'll make sure we have the good chocolate for fudge."

"Love it." Marnie kissed two fingers and waved good-bye.

Mystery student had exactly fifteen seconds before I was out of there. The swim team and lap swimmers had long since gone. The only people left were Jordan, who was in his office, and a mom tugging her son into a thick coat at the doorway.

Five more seconds.

"Hey."

I turned my head slowly.

No stinking way.

Tanner cleared his throat. "Am I late?"

I craned my neck to look up at him. "For what?"

He pointed to the clock. "Lesson at seven?"

I pulled my legs out of the water and stood so I could see Tanner without giving myself whiplash. "*You* are the last-minute lesson?"

"Yes."

"Tanner," I said with all the exasperation I could summon, "what are you doing here?"

"Learning to swim." He said it like it was obvious.

That wasn't what I meant, and he knew it.

"Right," I rolled my eyes. "You grew up in San Diego. I'm willing to bet my passport that you've been swimming since you were a baby."

"Do you have a passport?" Tanner leaned forward, his eyes dancing.

I crossed my arms. "That is beside the point. You know how to swim, *and* you are sick. What are you really doing here?"

"Not everyone in San Diego swims. Just because someone lives next to the ocean doesn't necessarily mean they know how to use it. You shouldn't categorize people," he said, sidestepping my question. "Also, I drank a bunch of cough syrup. I feel great." Another lopsided grin had me thinking he was possibly slightly intoxicated on said cough syrup.

"I'm going to go home. This is ridiculous." I moved to step around him, but Tanner grabbed my arm, gently tugging me closer. As I tried to pull away, my feet tangled over his. Before I knew what happened, I was leaning against Tanner's bare chest, listening to his heart pound. I jumped back as soon as I got my feet under me.

"Sorry." Tanner's cheeks were bright red. "I'm sorry, Bailey. Maybe this was stupid, but I had to do something. You ignored my texts and spent your whole shift at Froyo hiding in the stockroom to avoid me."

"I was not hiding. I was staying out of Marnie's way so she could focus on her weird frozen yogurt matchmaking." I rubbed my arms to get rid of the goosebumps. "How did that go, by the way?"

"Seemed good from where I sat. She convinced a couple to hang out together because they both put Sour Patch Kids on their strawberry yogurt."

"Well, good. I'm sure that made her happy."

"It seemed to." Tanner took a deep breath. "Look, Bailey, I know I'm frustrating—"

"Yeah, you are. And?"

"And I wanted to say I'm sorry. About what I said, or what I didn't say. I'm sorry I didn't answer your questions or explain myself very well."

"Don't, and at all."

"What?" He blinked.

"You don't explain yourself at all."

"Then I'm sorry I didn't explain myself at all." Tanner shifted from foot to foot. "Will you please give me a swim lesson? Your boss has been staring at us for the last five minutes, and it's giving me the willies."

I burst out laughing. "Did you just say 'willies'?"

"Is that wrong? What would you say?"

I glanced at Jordan's office while I considered my options. He was, indeed, standing in front of the glass with his face pressed up against it, staring at us.

"No, you're right. 'Willies' covers it."

Tanner grinned. "So...?"

I heaved a great sigh. "Okay, fine. I will give you a swim lesson. As long as you are fully aware that I think this is ridiculous, and you are a nerd."

"Noted."

I tossed my whistle to the ground and launched a perfect cannonball into the pool. When I came up, Tanner was wiping water from his eyes.

"Get in the water, already," I yelled.

Tanner's face lit up. He skipped back a few steps, his gaze fixed on a point to my left.

"Uh-uh." I swam to the side to retrieve my whistle and smiled up at him. "You can't do a cannonball. It wouldn't be safe for a beginner like you. You have to get used to the water first. Why don't you walk—never, ever run—to the shallow, baby end and ease into the water one toe at a time. Like a good boy."

Tanner's eyes narrowed. "I think this was a bad idea."

"You think?"

For the next thirty minutes, I put Tanner through the most idiotic swim lesson of all time. After I made him ease into the pool up to his waist one baby step at a time, I had him practice sitting on the step for five minutes to get used to how water feels. Next, he had to move his arms from front to back, underwater, fifty times to increase muscle memory for swimming. Then I had him kick his legs, also completely underwater, fifty times, then do the two together.

Then, he had to hold onto the side of the pool and pull himself around the pool, hand over hand, twenty times. Why? Because it was funny.

No, none of that is a thing. I made it all up to be a brat.

I wish I had a waterproof camera.

When the lesson was over, I gave him a chart with a red, shiny star sticker and suggested he practice at home with push-ups and squats to build good swimming muscles.

"See you next Monday," I smiled cheekily as I handed him a towel. I wrapped my towel around me and walked on tiptoe toward the women's locker room.

"Wait, Bailey."

"Yeah?" I stopped walking but didn't turn around.

"What are you doing after this? I mean, right now?"

I glared at him over my shoulder. "Going home, duh. I'm starving." My stomach responded immediately to confirm my words.

Tanner toweled off his hair, making it stick up all around his head like a furry helmet. "You don't have a date?"

"Not tonight," I said, slowly.

I actually kind of forgot about that. Between the podcast, being irritated at Tanner, and avoiding him all day, I forgot to find a date. That was a gross oversight.

I turned around and glanced towards the locker room where my phone was waiting. Who could I call this short notice to take me to dinner?

"You're shivering." Tanner's eyebrows dropped in concern.

"I'm good." That might, technically, have been a lie. But not close enough to worry about. I didn't say I was warm. I said I was good. Actually, I was freezing my whistle off. How had the temperature dropped that much in thirty minutes?

Tanner moved closer and wrapped the towel I'd given him around my back, He tucked the edges into my crossed arms with a small smile. The towel was damp, but it was warm and smelled really, really good.

"Anyway," Tanner looked at the puddle gathering around our feet. "I was thinking, I haven't eaten either. We could..."

I was already shaking my head.

In a rush that almost made his words indistinguishable, Tanner said, "A new sushi place just opened around the corner from Froyo. I remember you saying you really like sushi but haven't found a good place. One of the reviewers is from Hawaii and said this is the best sushi he's had in the mainland. You know you want to go."

Tanner was a sinister fiend. He blatantly exploited my only weakness. I really did love sushi; I craved it all the time, which was why I checked out that library book to try and make it at home.

Now I had to go there. Not even exhaustion could stand in my way. But I wasn't about to let Tanner see how interested I was. I sighed deeply, like I was making the biggest concession of all time. "Yeah, I guess I'll go, or whatever. I'll meet you back out here in ten minutes."

Tanner wasn't as skilled as I was at hiding his enthusiasm. "Bet you can't do it in eight," he said with a grin.

I narrowed my eyes. "I'll be ready in seven."

"We'll see."

I was going to wipe that smirky smirk right off Tanner's face with my mad skills. Without another word, I speed walked to the dressing room, something I'd mastered when I was four and took my own swim lessons. I hopped in the shower with my suit on, was out in a blink, and got dressed as fast as I could. I blow dried my hair just until it was almost dry and then twirled it up into a bun. I covered my head with the hood of my jacket and finished by putting on a warmer coat.

Six minutes.

Beat that, Tanner.

When I strolled out of the locker room, Tanner was nowhere to be seen. I checked my watch. Why wasn't Tanner there to witness my triumphant six-minute record? No one was there to witness me gloat.

I wrinkled my nose and plopped onto the bleachers to text Dayton that I wouldn't need a ride home. Then, I waited.

And waited.

And waited.

Ten minutes later, Tanner emerged from the men's room looking flustered.

"That was almost twenty minutes!" I stood up, pulling my purse onto my shoulder. "That's, like, an eternity in waiting time."

"I know," Tanner breathed. "I'm sorry. The shower wouldn't work, then it got really cold and wouldn't heat up. I tried every single one, but they were all the same. I couldn't remember what locker I used; the numbers were blurry. When I finally found it, the combination wouldn't open—"

I held up a hand. This was going to take all night. "All I hear are excuses."

Tanner laughed. "So, what do you want to hear? I lost? You won?"

"That works, for starters." I grabbed his wrist. "Now come on. Let's go find your dilapidated vehicle and get some food. I'm dying here." I tugged Tanner all the way to the door of the aquatic center before I realized somewhere along the way that my wrist wrap had morphed into holding his hand.

I quickly pulled my hand away and stuck it in my pocket. "So cold." I pulled my hood close with my other hand to keep the air from getting to the wet parts of my hair. "Where are you parked?"

Tanner cleared his throat. "Over there."

I followed him to his truck, hopping from foot to foot while he opened my door for me. It was a little warmer inside, but it was much better when he started the truck and the heater came on.

Even though it sounded like a rampaging bull elephant.

We drove in silence. Well, Tanner did. I jabbered on and on about sushi rolls, and the pros and cons of wasabi. I don't even know what I said, but the silence was intolerable. I felt so relieved when we stepped inside the noisy restaurant.

An older woman seated us at the bar, which were the only seats left in the restaurant. I didn't usually sit at bars, but I kind of loved the twirling barstools.

"One more, and then I'm done." I whirled around, stopping the spin against Tanner's stool with my toes.

Tanner just shook his head.

Instead of freezing, I was now roasting. I peeled off my coat and hoodie. Now that I was out and about, I wished I hadn't changed out of the cute outfit that I had put on for the interview that morning, but after trekking those boots up and down all those flights of stairs, I was so over them. They would be lucky if I ever wore them again. The clothes I had on now were super boring and totally not date worthy, but then again, this wasn't a date. It was just Tanner.

"Check your menu. I want to see what you think," Tanner said, watching me.

I picked up the menu, and my jaw dropped. It was totally ginormous. There were at least five pages of sushi roll options. My eyes bugged as I read through them all. There were a few words I didn't recognize, like "iki". It made me so excited I almost fell off the barstool.

Twice.

"What do you think?" Tanner asked. I could tell he'd been holding the question back for a while. It burst forth like a puff of air.

I slapped the menu down and looked at him with huge eyes. "This. Is. Amazing! Also, what is sashimi?"

Tanner grinned. "Where?"

I leaned over to point it out on his menu.

"Oh, that's raw salmon with sauce and rice."

"Like sushi without the roll?"

"Basically."

A young waiter interrupted us. "Ready to order?"

"Yes!" I exclaimed. I ordered one thing from each category on the menu, including the iki thing I didn't recognize.

"For two?" the waiter asked, looking from me to Tanner. Understandable. I'd just ordered an insane amount of sushi, but it wasn't the same as Basil's; sushi doesn't fill me up at all.

I nodded. "Unless, was there anything else you wanted to try?" I asked Tanner.

"Did you get a dragon roll?"

I couldn't remember. I looked at the waiter, who nodded.

"We'll take two of those. Thanks," Tanner said. "And that will be all."

The waiter smiled and turned away.

"He didn't write anything down," I whispered to Tanner.

"Watch." He flicked his eyes to the right until I turned my head.

The chef made everything right there in front of us. And he was wicked fast! My mouth dropped open again as I watched. My eyes couldn't keep up. I was never eating sushi at a back table ever again!

Tanner's breath tickled the side of my face. "You look like you're at Disneyland."

"No way," I murmured. "This is way cooler."

Something about the experience of watching the chef work, made the sushi taste so much more amazing. Everything I ate was an explosion of flavor. I savored each bite, so I could remember what it was like when I wrote down all the details in my food journal. I didn't want to forget even the smallest thing.

Tanner ate a little and watched me a lot.

An hour later, we walked out into the cold, but I didn't feel it. I was so jazzed. I talked Tanner's ear off, comparing this restaurant to other sushi restaurants I'd been to. I told him the history of sushi and how it is different in all parts of Asia. Even though I'd never told anyone before, not even Dayton, I revealed my travel itinerary for a trip I'd planned to Japan.

I was so involved in everything I was saying that I didn't notice we had pulled into the parking lot of an old movie theater. The city had shut it down to expand the MVD, but they hadn't actually done it yet. The empty lanes looked lonely in the moonlight.

I shivered. "What are we doing here?"

Tanner left the car running but leaned back in his seat. "You have so much to say. I parked to let you finish talking."

I tipped my head to the side. "You could have just told me to shut up!"

"That would be rude," Tanner grinned. "Did you know that your whole face lights up when you talk about traveling?"

"How would I know that? I can't see myself when I talk. Don't park here; it's super creepy."

Tanner raised an eyebrow. "Where should I park?"

I bit my lip to help me think. "Let's go to the duck pond. It's too cold to walk around, but you can park right next to it and gaze at water. I know how much you love the water."

"That I do." Tanner moved the truck into drive and headed back to the main road. "Where am I going?

I directed him to the duck pond that was tucked behind the ball fields off Country Club Dr., and I gave him a plethora of useful pointers while he tried to back into the dirt parking lot.

He didn't even say thank you.

But he did keep the truck running, so we didn't freeze our buttooschkas off. So, that was something.

Tanner shifted in his seat to face me. "Tell me about somewhere you've been."

"Oh," I zipped the zipper of my jacket up and down. "I haven't really been anywhere."

"You haven't?" Tanner lifted an eyebrow. "Your travel plan to Japan is elaborate; it sounds like you travel all the time."

"Only in my mind," I laughed, but cut it short.

What I said wasn't actually that funny.

"You haven't been anywhere?"

"I've been to Arizona, obviously. All over Arizona. My family went to the Grand Canyon for spring break every year, even though we live right next to it. My daddy was all, 'People travel from China to see this, so we are not going to take it for granted.' We went to Lake Powell a lot; my mom has friends that have a house boat we borrowed. My dad has family in the White Mountains, so I've fished every lake at least once. I've seen the Painted Desert and Antelope Canyon, hiked Havasupai three times, and I've got tons of petrified wood on my bookshelf at home. Oh, and obviously I've been to Phoenix."

Tanner waited.

"That's it," I said, opening my hands and staring at them.

That was it.

"Why?"

"Why not? Arizona is pretty cool. There's lots of things to explore. It doesn't make any sense to venture outside the state I live in until I've explored all of it, does it?"

Tanner's eyebrows drew together like someone scribbled with black crayon over his eyes.

"What?" I asked. "Why are you all tense?"

"I think," the words came out clipped and sharp as nails, "that it's interesting you get after me for holding back, and then you do the same thing."

"Who says I'm holding back?"

Tanner raised one of his scribbly eyebrows. "Are you holding back?"

I found it much harder to meet his eyes now. "Maybe."

"Look at me, Bailey."

I did for a second. Then my gaze flickered around the truck, out the windows, and anywhere except his face.

"What aren't you telling me?"

"Why does it matter?"

Tanner let out a long breath. "It just does."

"Why?"

He kneaded his hands over the steering wheel. "I see now why you're so frustrated when I give you half answers."

"Boom," I dropped the mike on the seat between us with exaggerated motions. "Thank you."

Tanner's mouth quirked into a half-smile. "And yet, I still want to know what you aren't telling me."

"Maybe I want to know what you aren't telling me."

We stared at each other in a complete stand-off. I wasn't about to give in, and I had no idea how stubborn Tanner was.

"Bailey?"

"What?"

"Please tell me why you haven't traveled anywhere."

I didn't want to. I thought it was stupid that he would ask me that and refuse to volunteer any information about himself. I told myself he was out of luck if he thought I would answer that question. But even as I thought that, the words started to leak out of my mouth like water dripping from a faucet. It appeared I didn't get to make the decision to say them. They had a mind of their own.

"I'm afraid." My stomach clenched, trying to hold me together. I never said those words out loud. I hated those words.

"Bailey."

I slowly looked up, not wanting to see pity in Tanner's face. I also hated pity. It felt like garbage when people were all sympathetic and sorry for you. I prepared myself with a flippant comment to change the subject but stopped before I could pull it off.

Tanner's eyes locked onto mine and filled the whole truck. There was nothing else in the world besides the chocolate brown color of his eyes. But what really got to me was the feeling behind his look. What I saw in his eyes wasn't pity, it was understanding.

And radical acceptance.

"Everyone is afraid," he said softly.

A huge, hot tear rolled down my cheek, followed closely by another and another. My other eye followed the same pattern, leaking tears without any sign of stopping. And suddenly there I was, sitting in Tanner's truck, looking at the empathy in his face with streams of tears falling into my palms.

It was so not normal.

Tanner didn't say a word. He reached his arm around my shoulders and gently pressed until I scooted closer to him. I rested my head on his shoulder and leaked tears down the side of his ugly flannel shirt. He rubbed my arm in a soothing motion, up and down, until I finally stopped crying.

I closed my eyes, feeling the tightness in my chest ease as the tears finished rolling down my cheeks. Tanner reached over and wiped my face with the sleeve of his free arm. The flannel was surprisingly soft, not gross and scratchy like I had imagined. I took a deep, shivery breath, and leaned into Tanner's shoulder.

"I have no idea what just happened."

"You cried."

"Well, yeah." I rolled my eyes.

"And snorted."

"What? I did not!" I pushed him away, scooting back to my side of the truck. "I don't know why I told you that stuff about being afraid. I don't know where that came from. I don't—"

"Bailey, stop. It's fine."

"It is not fine!" I routed through my purse for a tissue; I seriously needed to blow my nose. "This open and honest stuff is crap." I gave up, dropping my purse at my feet. "I get why you avoid it."

Tanner reached to open the glove compartment. He tossed a small package of tissues into my lap. Without qualms, I pulled one out and trumpeted into it. No point in holding anything back now.

"You know," the corner of Tanner's mouth quirked up slightly, "it's okay to be human and have feelings."

"You should talk!" I pointed the icky tissue at him. "You don't tell anyone anything."

Tanner's smile disappeared.

I could hear my words echo over and over in my mind in the snarky voice that rakes on Dayton's nerves. There was only one thing to do. It was something I rarely did, but it needed to be done.

"I'm sorry," I whispered.

Tanner held his hand to his ear. "What did you say?"

"I said I'm sorry, you brat!" I huffed. "I was rude. Obviously, you have your reasons for not talking about yourself. I shouldn't have said what I said the way I said it."

"Wow." Tanner put his hand over his chest, his eyes dancing. "That was so heartfelt."

"Yeah, well," I waved my hand, "take it or leave it. I really am sorry."

"I know. Thank you."

I leaned forward, crossed my arms, and rested them on the dashboard. "I wish it wasn't so cold. It's such a clear night and perfect for a walk; you can see all the stars. You'd be able to get a better look at the pond if we could walk around it."

Tanner leaned forward to look out the windshield. "There's the Big Dipper."

"That's my favorite."

"Why?" He turned his head to me.

"Because it's so obvious. I think you could probably find it anywhere in the world."

Tanner stared at me.

"What? Quit looking at me like that. You're creeping me out."

Tanner laughed and leaned back against the seat. "I was just thinking."

"Yeah?"

"I bet we could figure out a way for you to travel. What are you afraid of, exactly?"

The way he asked the question made it sound so logical. What are you afraid of? Let's just solve the problem. I'd never looked at it that way before. Actually, my fear had sort of become a monster in the closet. I hated thinking about it, and I never wanted to open the door. But now, because I did open up, it was like I discovered that the monster was actually just a pile of stinky laundry.

"I'm not sure," I said, willing to go along with it.

"Are you afraid of being far from home?"
"No."
"Flying?"
"Nuh-uh."
"Foreign diseases?"
"Gross, but no."
"Language barriers?"
"Noppers. I'm amazing at languages."
"Really?" He paused. "How many do you speak?"
I shrugged. "I'm not fluent in any except English."
"Okay. How many are you passable in?"
I counted silently. "Eight."
Tanner's eyes flew wide open. "Are you serious? Which?"
I ticked them off on my fingers. "Spanish, French, Italian, Portuguese, German, Hawaiian, Swedish, and some Russian."
Tanner whistled long and slow. "Hawaiian is endangered. Did you know that?"
I nodded. "That's why I learned it."
"That is impressive."
"I told you, it's my dream to go everywhere."
"So, what is holding you back?"
I chewed my bottom lip, not sure how to put it into words. My fear was starting to look like a monster again.
"Just say it; don't think about it," Tanner said. "The more you think, the less you're likely to say."
That sounded familiar. I took a deep breath and closed my eyes, leaning back into the seat.
"Alone."
"Alone?" he repeated.
I nodded. "I'm afraid of being alone."
"Hm." Tanner leaned his head back until he was staring at the ceiling of his truck.
I waited. If anyone could figure me out, it was Tanner and his big genius brain. Heaven knows I couldn't figure myself out.
"You're afraid of traveling alone? Tell me some more about that."

I leaned my chin on my knuckles and thought hard. "What if I get lost? I am terrible with directions. What if I have trouble and get thrown into jail? Uniforms make me nervous. I always say the dumbest things. I don't want to be an idiot all over the world. I'd feel better if I have someone with me; it would make me feel more confident or something."

"Okay," Tanner nodded. I thought it was nice of him not to mock me. I probably would have mocked myself if I were in his shoes. "Could you take your parents? Or Dayton?"

I shook my head. "No way. All three of them are the most unadventurous people on the planet. They are totally content to stay home. We'd go to Paris and spend the whole time watching TV in a hotel room."

Tanner laughed. "Okay, what about friends?"

This part made me squirm. "I don't really have any friends. I mean, I have lots of friends, but none that are close enough to travel with like that."

"Marnie?"

I shook my head. "She's definitely my closest friend, but even she doesn't totally get me. She'd probably want to sit in the hotel room and watch TV, too."

"Okay," Tanner leaned back again. "Then there's only one more solution I can think of."

"What's that?" I asked, hope bubbling up like carbonation.

Tanner paused to let the suspense build. "Get over it, and go alone."

"What?"

"Seriously. If you want something, *really* want something, you have to just do it. Because it's important to you and because you are important enough to do it for."

"You should put that on a bumper sticker." I crossed my arms and slumped forward.

"I'm serious. Just do it, Bailey."

"Okay, Nike."

"Hey." He waited for me to look at his face. "Do it for you."

"So, I just get over my fear? Just like that?" I snapped my fingers.

"Yes," he shifted. "Just like that. Nothing is really stopping you except for you, and this is obviously important to you. So, plan a trip. Set up all the details, and then just go do it. Don't wait for the fear to go away; take it with you."

I squeezed my palms together. "I don't think it's that easy, Tanner."

"No, it's not." He looked at the ceiling. "But it is that simple."

I stared out the window and let Tanner's words wiggle around in my brain. I wanted to travel; that was the truth. He made it sound so easy: just plan and go. Thinking about actually doing those things made the tingles and the nausea come back all over again. I couldn't do it.

Could I?

When I turned my head, Tanner was watching me, taking me in thoughtfully. His hand moved from his lap to the seat between us.

We both stared at it.

It was like this moment hinged on his stationary hand. What would happen if he moved it? He could reach over and intertwine his fingers with mine.

Or, he could rest it on the back of my neck and tug me closer.

What would happen if we—

"I should get you home; it's late." Tanner faced forward, and his jaw clenched tight enough to change his profile. He put his foot on the brake and glanced over his shoulder. His hand between us was the last thing to move, sliding into position on the steering wheel with white, splotchy knuckles.

Ways to Improve Bailey #17

Stop the Sassafras (Unless the person is a pimple and totally deserves it)

I slept like a proverbial rock and woke up wide awake and hyper at ten the next morning—which was exactly halfway through my first class. If I didn't get a move on, I was going to miss my second one, too. I didn't want to do that. Marnie and I had that class together, and I needed to talk to her about promoting Froyo.

Dayton was noticeably absent as I moved around the house to get ready for the day. A bright orange sticky note on the fridge explained that Dayton went for a run and would be back around eleven. I stuck a yellow note over his to let him know I was going to class and work, and I would see him that night. Then, I texted Marnie to see if she'd left yet and could give me a ride.

She responded instantly. *Love to!*

I grabbed two leftover bagels and nibbled one on my way to Marnie's house. She was just stepping out of the cute little duplex she shared with a couple other girls when I walked up her driveway.

"Good morning!" Marnie beamed, putting our Arizona sun to shame. "It's so beautiful today. Isn't it beautiful today?"

"It's the most beautifulest day in the whole entire world." I tossed her a bagel, which she caught with one hand. "Why are you so peppy?"

"I don't know." She grinned before she stuck the bagel in her mouth to free up a hand and open the car door. She didn't speak again until we were both inside and buckled. "Maybe I'm just a peppy person."

"Yeah, duh."

"Okay, I'll tell you." She gripped the steering wheel and wiggled it. The car wasn't even on yet, so I didn't fear for my life. "I met up with some people at Froyo last night."

"Why were you at Froyo?"

"I went there after lessons to practice my matchmaking."

I took a big bite of my bagel, so I wouldn't have to respond.

"Anyway, Dayton was there. Did you know he puts cinnamon bears on his frozen yogurt?"

He probably put something different on his yogurt every time he made one, he was that random. I swallowed before I'd chewed my bagel well enough and had to swig a bunch of water to get the lump of bread out of my throat. "I had no idea."

"So, his date—"

"Wait!" I held up my palm. "He was on a date? Who was his date?"

Marnie was probably the only person on the planet who didn't mind interruptions. "A girl named Tammy. Don't you know her? She said they've been together for a couple weeks."

I shook my head. Why was it that Dayton knew everything about my life, and I knew nothing about his? I was beginning to think he bugged my room.

Or maybe my purse.

I eyed it suspiciously.

"Anyway, Tammy put pineapple and coconut on her frozen yogurt. That is the *worst* combination with cinnamon bears."

I actually agreed with that statement. "So, what did you do about it?"

I pictured several scenarios. My favorite was Marnie standing on the table, dumping the cup of frozen yogurt over Dayton's head.

A girl can dream.

"I didn't do anything. How can I? No one asked my opinion."

"Marnie." I was in an exceptionally good mood and could be generous with Marnie's dilemma, even though I thought she was borderline cracked. "People give unsolicited advice all the time. It's practically a national sport. If you believe you have a gift, then you have a responsibility to share it with others."

"Maybe." She started the car and slowly backed down the driveway. "I don't know. I don't want to push my matchmaking on people if they aren't interested."

"But how will you ever know if they're interested if you don't let people know what you can do?"

"That is a very good point." Marnie said slowly.

I chewed the last of my bagel and brushed the crumbs from my hands. "So, you had to watch my big brother schmooze his girly-pie all night? That sounds atrocious."

"No, not really. They got in a huge fight halfway through their yogurt, and Tammy left with Harvey, who puts cherries on his yogurt." She widened her eyes. "Cherries with pineapple and coconut. I knew they were a better match."

Marnie hadn't sold me yet. It wasn't matchmaking if she decided people were meant to be together based on their yogurt preferences but never told them about it. To matchmake, she had to figure that stuff out ahead of time and *then* get people together to see if it worked. Not decide they were going to work or not after they already hooked up.

I explained all of this to her as we waited for a train to cross the tracks near campus. It helped that the train was really long, both because we could blame our tardiness on that and because I took the extra time to explain my point in great detail. I finished the same time the train did. Marnie put the car into drive and chewed on her lip.

"I see what you mean."

"Right? So, what you need to do is..." I stopped talking as the best idea in the entire world landed fully formed in my brain.

"What?" Marnie glanced at me. "What? Why did you stop talking? Bailey? Are you alright?"

"Marnie!"

"What?" Her head whipped back and forth as she tried to give me and the road the same amount of attention. "Should I pull over?"

"No, just park up here. We can walk. It's not that far."

Marnie followed the direction of my finger, then turned off the car and pressed her hand on my forehead.

"What are you doing?" I squirmed away.

"Something must be wrong. You never want to walk farther than we have to."

I unclicked my seatbelt and swung the door open. "That's because I don't always have the most amazing idea in the world. Come on!" I jumped out and hip checked the door closed.

Marnie moved quickly, but she couldn't ditch the worried look that stuck to her face. "What's going on?"

"Okay, check this." I looped my arm through hers and steered us towards the English building. "I was going to pick your brain for ideas on how to save Froyo—"

Marnie stopped walking so suddenly that I almost kissed the concrete. "What's wrong with Froyo?"

"It's going out of business," I said, waving my hand like that wasn't the point, even though it was the point. I couldn't waste time talking about that when my super idea was still unspoken. "Anyway, Tanner and I came up with a list of things we can do to help get some more business."

"You and Tanner?"

"Focustrate, Marnie." I tugged her arm to get her walking again. "What if we advertise your yogurt matchmaking as, like, a publicity stunt? You can set hours to be there and try matching people based on their yogurt preferences. No one else does something like that, and it would be super fun! Come on. Best idea ever, or what?"

Marnie walked steadily, chewing on her lip. I didn't need her to confirm that my plan was brilliant; I just wanted her to say the words. I hopped every other step to get the extra energy out of my system.

She still hadn't said anything by the time we got to class. I gave her an exasperated look before I took my seat.

Our professor—I forgot his name, but he's the one that looks like Andy Serkis—had already started class with his usual lecture. I was sorry that train hadn't made us miss it. He droned on for way too long, then gave us the last half hour of class to work on stuff while he texted his girlfriend.

Don't ask me how I know that.

Marnie nudged her desk closer to mine, and I leaned in as far as I could without falling on the ground.

"I thought you didn't believe in my matchmaking?"

I actually didn't. But that doesn't mean it wouldn't be a fantastic marketing ploy for Froyo. I arranged my face to look as innocent as I could.

"I believe that you believe in it."

Marnie pursed her lips. "What if I mess it up? Would that be worse for Froyo?"

"You're not going to mess anything up, Marnie." I all but rolled my eyes. "You're pretty much perfect. What about the guy and the chick, and the compatible toppings you were telling me about? Wasabi never jived with pink lemonade."

"That is not what I said," Marnie giggled.

"You know what I mean." I tossed my head. "Believe in yourself. This will be so good! Hey!" I turned around to whisper at Clay, who sits two seats behind me. "What do you think about finding your perfect match based on your favorite frozen yogurt toppings?"

He looked up, "Are you talking to me?"

"I'm looking at you."

"Oh, that's interesting." He put his pencil down. "Maybe I should ignore you like you ignored my texts after we went out."

"That's a stupid idea," I scoffed. "Then you would miss out on the amazing opportunity to find the perfect girl at Froyo."

"I thought I already found the perfect girl at Froyo," Clay narrowed his eyes. "And she didn't return my texts."

I tipped my head to the side. "You are being a big baby about that, you know? It was obvious we weren't going to work, Clay." He took everything I said literally and put ketchup on his tacos.

Dealbreakers.

He rapidly tapped the top of his pencil on the desk. "It wasn't obvious to me."

"Here, I'll show you." I gestured to Marnie. "Ask him the question."

"I don't know." Marnie looked from Clay to me. "I feel like I'm getting in the middle of something here."

"Whatever. I'll do it, then." I whipped back around. "Clay, what is your favorite frozen yogurt flavor?"

Clay stared at me, then sighed. "You're not going to leave me alone until I do this, are you?"

"Nope."

"Fine. I like root beer."

"And what toppings?"

He set his pencil on the desk and flicked it with his finger, watching it roll instead of looking at me. "Marshmallows."

That was perfect. Now, all I had to do was think of a combination of flavors that would be horrible with his choices.

"So, Marnie, do you think root beer and marshmallows go with peppermint and blueberries?"

"That sounds disgusting," Clay said.

"Exactly!" I jabbed my finger in his direction. "That's exactly what I'm talking about. We are disgusting together. Marnie, what do you think? What would go well with Clay's root beer and marshmallows?"

Marnie's narrowed eyes surveyed me for way longer than they should have if she was thinking about the perfect combination for Clay. Finally, she turned to him. "Vanilla yogurt with black licorice."

Clay nodded. "Thank you for confirming that I am going to die alone."

"That's not what I said!" Marnie's eyes widened. "I'm sure there's someone out there who likes vanilla and licorice."

"Black licorice," Clay grumbled. "There's no one who likes black licorice."

"Hey," I leaned forward. "There is only one way to find out. Would you come to Froyo to let Marnie work her magic and find your match?"

Clay bunched his lips up to his nose.

"It might be interesting," I said, trying to appeal to his nerdy science side. Heaven knows I saw enough of it on our one date. "It's like an experiment. Don't you feel like you have to know if it's possible now?"

His mouth worked like he wanted to say no, but I knew he couldn't. He slapped his hand on the desk. "Fine. I'm in. What do I have to do?"

I hadn't really thought that far ahead, but I didn't let a silly thing like that stop me. "You pay ten dollars to get through the door, and then pay for whatever you swirl and top. The matchmaking is free."

"Make it five, and we have a deal."

I slapped Clay's hand, feeling pretty dang good about myself. So good, in fact, that it was easy to ignore the niggling part of my brain that worried about silly stuff, like the fact that I hadn't mentioned this to Keith.

It was too good of an idea to bog down with negativity.

Clay went back to whatever he was doing, and I pulled a bunch of paper out of my bag. "Do you have any markers?" I asked Marnie.

"Of course." She rummaged for a minute and held out a large package of scented markers.

This is why we are friends.

"Thanks." I took them and pulled out the light green just so I could sniff the artificial lime. Then I grabbed the cherry red and got to work.

"What are you doing?"

"Huh?"

Marnie glanced at the professor, who was grinning to himself in the corner, and then back at me. "Is this school work?"

I gave a short laugh. "I wish. This is how we are going to save Froyo."

"Coloring?" She looked honestly confused, so I took pity on her.

"I'm making flyers to advertise your matchmaking thing at Froyo this Saturday. We can hand them out after class. I think this is going to be big," I said honestly.

Marnie reached for some of the paper I'd pushed to the side and grabbed the blueberry marker. "I love making flyers! Let's do this!"

"What are we doing?" Clay's friend Niko scooted his seat closer to Marnie and me.

Clay let out a long, loud breath.

Which we all ignored.

"Making flyers to save Froyo," Marnie said, picking up a bright pink marker—cotton candy, of course.

"What's Froyo?"

"Exactly!" Marnie pointed her marker at him.

Niko gave her a weird look and turned to me. "Have you never heard of a computer? You could make flyers and print off an infinity of them in about two seconds."

"Did I ask you?" I still hadn't gotten over my date with Niko. We went to his apartment and ate marshmallow cereal while his roommates serenaded us by burping catchy pop songs.

"You should have," he said, tossing the last of a packaged pastry into his mouth.

I wrinkled my nose. Considering Niko's taste in food and entertainment, I shouldn't have been surprised that he was eating garbage and spouting off.

Niko turned back to Marnie, effectively dismissing me.

"What's this Froyo?"

"It's a frozen yogurt shop, and it's adorable. You get to swirl your own yogurt and then top it with whatever you want. There are so many fun choices."

I wanted to put her words into a jingle that would get stuck in everyone's head for the rest of their life. Marnie was a walking Froyo advertisement.

"Bailey works there," Marnie added.

"You do?"

I just rolled my eyes.

The reason he didn't know that is because on our date, when he asked me about work, he was playing Xbox with one of his gassy roommates.

I knew he wasn't listening to anything I said, so I tested it out by yelling weird things at the top of my lungs. Stuff like, 'Look, aliens' and 'I love it when the bananas start a conga line on the counter'. Not a single thing I said got a reaction until I announced that Scarlett Johansen just dropped off their mail. All four of them ran to the door to check, and I took that opportunity to shut off their game without saving it, then dart out the back door and hoof it home.

I could hear the cries of anguish two blocks away.

"Here," I shoved my finished flyer into his hands. "Take this and show it to everyone you pass on your way to your next class."

"I don't have a class after this one."

I took a deep breath and grabbed the banana yellow marker to keep myself from kicking Niko's chair out from under him. "Then show it to the people you pass on your way to wherever you go after this."

Niko studied the paper for a minute, then looked up. "You're a matchmaker now?"

"Not me. Marnie." I jabbed my marker in her direction.

Niko shifted towards her. "Did you hook up Todd and the chick he's dating, because she is h-oy-t."

Marnie's face scrunched in confusion. "What are you talking about?"

"On my way here, I saw Todd making out with some blond girl in the commons," Niko explained.

"Oh, gross." I puffed out my cheeks. "It's only, like, eleven in the morning!"

Niko smirked. "Kissing isn't the same as eating dessert, Bailey. I'm pretty sure people can do it whenever they want to."

Joke's on him; I ate dessert whenever I felt like it.

Well, if Dayton wasn't watching.

I stopped my witty retort because Marnie put her hand on my arm.

"Are you sure it was him?"

"Yeah. Did you hook them up?" He looked hopeful.

"That was fast," Marnie said thoughtfully. "I guess I was right about him and me."

I took that opportunity to jump in. "Of course you were. You have amazing intuition." I checked to make sure Niko was paying attention. "Marnie would love to tell you more about her matchmaking at Froyo on Saturday. Will you be there?"

"Maybe."

That wasn't very enthusiastic, but I didn't let that dampen my spirits. The only thing Niko got excited about was video games, so obviously he wasn't our target audience.

Plus, unlike Clay, who really was a pretty nice guy, Niko was an idiot, and finding a match for him really would have been impossible and would therefore ruin our event. It was better he stayed away.

Professor what's-his-name stood up to dismiss us and threw an essay assignment our way. Clay held out his hand as I walked by.

"What?"

He heaved a great sigh. "Give me a flyer. I'll tell people about it."

"Yeah?" I smiled.

"Yeah," he shrugged, tucking the paper into his folder. "Like you said, it will be an interesting experiment."

"Thanks, Clay." I pursed my lips. "I'm sorry about...you know."

"No," he shook his head. "You're right. Peppermint and root beer would never work."

I followed him out of the classroom with a bounce in my step. If I wasn't a believer in Marnie's powers before, I was now.

I wished I had believed her sooner. That would have been the easiest way to get out of repeat dates ever.

There was a fifteen-minute window before I had to get to work, so Marnie and I spent the time driving around campus to post our flyers. We went to dorm bulletin boards and the food court, then we ran out. Marnie came to the rescue when she took a photo of the last flyer and posted it on her social media accounts. Since she was friends with everyone, she had about a billion likes by the time we jingled into Froyo.

"That was seriously awesome." I handed Marnie her phone back. "Good thinking."

"What was awesome?" Keith looked up from the cash register. "Also, you're late."

I checked my watch. "It's, like, three minutes after."

"Three minutes today, thirty tomorrow," Keith said, waving his hand.

I leaned on the counter. "Did you just make that up?"

"Apron," he pointed.

I rolled my eyes but went and pulled the apron over my jacket. It was still too chilly to take it off.

"Keith!" Marnie spun on the bar stool she'd claimed. "We just put up a bunch of flyers for Froyo! You are going to be so busy this week!"

Keith pursed his lips at me. "You got her in on this nonsense, too?"

"It isn't nonsense!" Marnie protested. "Flagstaff needs Froyo!"

"It does, huh?" Keith looked around the empty room. His eyes looked wistful.

"It does," Marnie nodded firmly. "And Bailey came up with the best idea to promote business. You're going to love it! I mean, you're... I, um..."

Marnie looked down, so she could no longer see me waving my hands like a crazed football fan behind Keith's back. At least she quit talking. I wasn't totally sure how Keith was going to take my awesome idea. I wanted some more time to think about how to bring it up.

Marnie shot a sideways glance at me that was too suspicious to ignore. Keith folded his arms and turned to give me the 'spill your guts' look.

My arms dropped to my sides. "So...about that."

For the first time in my life, Dayton had good timing. He chose that moment to burst into Froyo with a gaggle of guys I didn't know.

"Heya!" Dayton said with his big booming voice. "We saw a couple of sweet flyers that smelled like fruit salad and decided to come try out this yogurt place."

Marnie clapped and turned to me with shining eyes. "Our flyers worked!"

"Of course they worked." I scooted behind Keith to get to the register, but he followed me with his grumpy eyes. While I watched Dayton and his friends put together the biggest cups imaginable, I racked my brain to think of a way to sell this matchmaking event to Keith. He was going to think it was hooey, but he was also a savvy business guy and could spot a good idea when he came across one.

This was a good idea. I could feel it in my pinky toes, but I wasn't so sure Keith would see it the way my pinky toes did.

Dayton and his bros bought the biggest cups with as much yogurt and toppings as they could fit without spilling onto the counter. After I rang the first one up, I saw Keith's eyes widen. The second one made his lips curl upwards, the third unscrunched his shoulders, and so on until Keith looked like the happiest guy in the world.

Each guy paid over twenty dollars for his yogurt. Then Dayton threw an extra twenty into the tip jar on his way to the booth where his friends were. They made as much noise as a football stadium of people, but Keith was in such a good mood from the sales that he didn't glare once.

"Your brother is *nice*." Marnie leaned over to whisper. "He teases you so much that he seems mean, but he really is a nice guy."

I decided not to comment. Both because I didn't want to burst her bubble and because this was the perfect time to talk to Keith. He hadn't looked this happy, well, ever.

"Hey, why don't you go practice your matchmaking with Dayton and his friends?" The conversation with Keith would be easier if it was just the two of us.

"There aren't any girls," Marnie said as she looked at the table full of guys.

I lifted one shoulder. "No worries. You can make a list of their favorite yogurt combinations, then encourage them to come back Saturday. It will give you a head start."

"What's on Saturday?" Keith asked without turning around. He was filling the caramel bottle, which was a job that needed full, undivided attention, or it became a tragedy.

Marnie nodded. "That's a really good idea."

"I'm full of good ideas." I slapped a pen into her hands and shooed her away. I could feel the clock ticking on Keith's good mood.

"So, speaking of good ideas..."

Keith turned around, twisting the lid on the caramel bottle. "Do I finally get to hear what you girls are plotting?"

"Plotting?" I gasped. "That sounds so harsh. This is the opposite. It's the best idea in the world."

Keith wiped his hands with a damp towel, his eyes never leaving my face. I'm not going to lie; it was kind of freaking me out.

"Marnie," I began because I knew Keith's soft spot for her would keep him from shutting me down right away, "and I had a great idea."

Keith grunted.

"Marnie," I tried again, "has this crazy awesome ability to matchmake people depending on their favorite frozen yogurt flavor and toppings. It totally works."

This was not a lie. Maybe I didn't actually know that it worked other than Marnie telling me it did, but her word was good, so I felt confident promoting her.

Keith's eyebrows disappeared into his hairline. "Are you pulling my leg?"

"Ew, no."

"It's a saying." Keith pushed his glasses up his nose. "It means, are you fooling around?"

"Oh, no to that, too," I said. "It really is a thing."

Keith skeptical eyebrows lowered enough for me to see them.

"Okay, even if it's bogus, who cares? It's fun! Marnie can use her skills, we can sell a butt ton of yogurt, and everyone is happy."

Keith chewed on this logic for a long time. So long that I started snitching gumdrops to give myself something to do while I waited.

Finally, Keith sighed.

"Alright."

What? Just like that? It worked?

"For reals?"

"Yes, for reals." He matched my voice, sounding so much like me it gave me the willies. "You can have your matchmaking thing, and we can see what happens. I don't buy into this type of thing, but I see that it's unique enough to get some attention. In the future," he said, his index finger stopping right between my eyes, "I want to know about these great ideas before you start advertising."

"Sure. Yeah. Got it. No problem," I nodded.

The bell jangled again. This was the busiest we'd been in a long time. Before I could turn to see who it was, Dayton bellowed.

"Hey, Tanner! Come sit with us, man!"

Tanner waved to him but stopped at the counter first. "I saw your flyers. Nicely done."

"Right? I'm pretty much brilliant."

Tanner shook his head and called over his shoulder, "I'll be right there," in answer to the second round of bellows from Dayton. Keith gave me a look and strolled away whistling.

Whatever.

I reached for the strawberry spoon. "Where's your cup? You're slowing down, old man."

Tanner's eyes flicked across my face, but I was as expressionless as concrete. He glanced over at the spoon in my hand and shook his head. "I think I'll try something different today. What do you recommend?"

My mouth dropped like I was in a cartoon, leaving a large, gaping cavern from my nose to my chest.

"Oh, come on," Tanner shifted. "It's not that big a deal."

I pulled my jaw up with great effort. "Is so. You come in here almost every day for a year, and all you ever get is vanilla and strawberries. I don't even know who you are anymore."

"Whatever," Tanner said, mimicking me even better than Keith did. It was uncanny. "I'm interested in a matchmaking preview. What do you recommend?"

"I'm not the matchmaker. Marnie!" I yelled, almost as obnoxiously as Dayton, then waved her over to us. "Marnie is the expert. And that's not how it works. She'll find your match based on what you already like."

Marnie was by my side before I finished talking, and she picked right up where I left off. "That's right. But there aren't any girls here to interview, so you'll have to wait until Saturday."

Tanner put his knee on a stool and turned from the left to the right while he considered Marnie and I. "Start at the beginning. Tell me how this works."

I nodded to Marnie who said, "It works because your frozen yogurt flavor and topping choices tell something about your soul. So, it has to be your absolutely most favorite things, not just cravings or whims. Then I find your soulmate based on their favorites."

Tanner's face softened into a smile. "I wish I'd known you sooner, Marnie. You would have saved me some heartache, I think."

Marnie blushed.

"Tell me about the matches you have already made." Tanner said.

While Marnie launched into a description of all of the happy frozen-yogurt-compatible people she'd met, I noticed the strawberry spoon had made a puddle of juice on the counter. I dropped it back into the container and looked under the counter for a rag.

Dayton let out a wall-shaking belch just as I snatched the rag and stood back up. Marnie and Tanner watched him in horror and humor, respectfully, while he shook his clasped hands in the air like he'd just won something.

"That's how it's done, boys."

They tossed napkins at his back as he made his way over to us.

"Whatcha doing?"

I wiped the counter. "Cleaning," I said.

Dayton scooted closer to Marnie and Tanner, who were not as boring as me, apparently. "What about you two? Did Marnie tell you about her superpowers?"

Marnie giggled and pushed Dayton's arm.

His ears turned pink.

He was staring at her like a love-sick walrus.

What the heck?

I didn't need frozen yogurt to tell me that Dayton was crushing on Marnie, but it did pose an interesting thought. Since I already knew he liked her and it wouldn't take much for her to like him, I wondered if they were frozen-yogurt compatible.

"Dayton, what's your favorite frozen yogurt flavor?" I asked.

"What?" He interrupted himself mid-laugh to look at me.

I repeated my question slowly.

"Why? You think you can matchmake, too?" he snorted.

Marnie gave him a disappointed face that was so poignant he moved to the other side of Tanner to get away from it.

"Vanilla yogurt and cinnamon bears," he said meekly.

"That's your favorite?"

He rolled his eyes, then coughed when Marnie made scolding noises. "Yes. That is my very most favoritest in the whole widest world."

Marnie's mouth dropped while my brain went into overtime, putting it all together. Marnie liked chocolate everything. Chocolate and cinnamon bears were amazing together. I caught her eye and totally knew she was thinking the same thing.

"Hm," I said as I folded my arms across my chest.

Marnie put her hands over her flaming cheeks. Tanner watched all of this with a half-smile, then spoke up.

"And what about you, Bailey?"

"What about me?" I was still reveling in a match well made. Okay, well made for Dayton. I wasn't sure it was a great deal for Marnie, but Dayton was certainly better than Todd. And, okay, Dayton wasn't a total goober. He would treat her a million times better than most of the guys she dated.

"What's your—how did you say it?" he asked Dayton.

"Very, most bestest, favoritest in the whole wide universe," Dayton supplied.

"Yes, that."

"My favorite frozen yogurt? Are you kidding me? I sit around this stuff all day. I can't stand frozen yogurt."

Marnie tipped her head to the side. "But you told Clay you like peppermint and blueberries."

Dayton barked a laugh. "Bailey hates blueberries. She thinks they squish like black widow spiders."

"They do," I agreed.

"Which means, you lied." Dayton's playfulness fell away like he was dropping his winter coat on the floor for someone else—me—to pick up.

"No, I didn't!" I held up both hands so he wouldn't shoot. "I didn't lie. I just asked Marnie if she thought Clay's favorites would go with peppermint and blueberry. I never said I liked them."

Marnie squinted into the distance. "That's true. You never did say you liked those flavors. I just assumed."

"See?"

Dayton surveyed me for a few more seconds. "That is toeing the line, Bailey, and you know it."

"Give me a break." I rolled my eyes and dampened the rag I was holding to finish wiping the counter.

"You didn't answer the question," Tanner said. "What is your favorite frozen yogurt?"

"No lyin'." Dayton growled.

"Why does it matter?" I flicked the rag against the trash to get out the loose crumbs. "I'm not looking for a match, so who cares?"

"Curiosity," Tanner said.

"I'm curious, too." Marnie leaned forward. "You always sidestep the question."

"Like I said, I'm not interested in matching."

"But do you really hate frozen yogurt?" Tanner wondered.

I wanted to say yes. It would be an easy lie to pull off. Everyone detested the food they were forced to work with every day. I had a friend who worked at a donut shop and never touched them because he was so grossed out by them. Same for Dayton and pizza after his two-year stint at Dominos in high school. I could pull this lie off; I knew I could.

Except I couldn't.

"No, I don't really hate it."

Marnie stood up, her excitement propelling her right off the barstool. "Then, what's your favorite combination?"

I glanced at Tanner just enough to see if he was paying attention. I wished he wasn't. I wished he got one of his phone calls and had to leave the store while I said my favorite. I knew what everyone was going to think, and I wasn't ready for any piece of that business.

"Bailey?"

"Fine, whatever. Not like it matters. I like cheesecake yogurt with chocolate-covered strawberries."

Marnie's lips pursed while she mulled this over. I knew it wouldn't take her long to come to a conclusion.

"Do you have chocolate-covered strawberries on the toppings bar?" Tanner's forehead disappeared into wrinkles.

"Nope." I slapped the rag into the trash again.

"Bailey," Dayton dragged out my name, so it sounded super busted.

"It's not a lie, stink brain. It's off the menu."

"Do you cover the strawberries yourself?" Tanner asked.

"Duh. Watch." I tossed the rag and reached into the mini fridge under the counter for the container of whole, fresh strawberries. I took out four, washed them, and patted them dry. Then removed the stems and ran them through a skewer.

"So violent," Dayton shuddered.

"Don't tell Keith I do this part," I said, dipping the skewer all the way into the pot of hot fudge. When I pulled the skewer out, I set it on wax paper and stuck it into the fridge to harden.

I skipped around the counter to snag a small cup, and I filled it with cheesecake yogurt. It was a flavor we always had on hand.

I made sure of that.

Marnie put her hand on the lever, scaring the snot out of me. "What are you doing?" I yelped.

"Fill it the rest of the way with vanilla."

I narrowed my eyes.

"Do it. Trust me."

I did. But I didn't have to like it.

Marnie followed me to the toppings bar, took the cup from me, and scooped a spoonful of strawberries from the toppings bar. "Go get your chocolate strawberries."

I did. But, again, I didn't have to like it.

Because we used fudge that hardens quickly to make a shell over the frozen yogurt, the strawberries were perfect. I carefully sliced them into blite size pieces dumped them into the cup Marnie held.

She grabbed a spoon and stuck it in the cup, then handed it to Tanner. "Try it. Tell me what you think."

"Wait," I saw my salvation in the form of a whipped cream can. I reached for it and sprayed a huge mound on top of the frozen yogurt. "There. Perfect."

Marnie pressed her lips together at the look on Tanner's face.

Uh..." He cleared his throat.

I batted my eyelashes. "What is it?"

"I don't like whipped cream very much."

Dayton stared at him. "You have got to be kidding me? Who doesn't like whipped cream?"

Tanner raised his hand with a smile.

Dayton snatched a clean spoon and scooped the huge mound off Tanner's yogurt. "There is something wrong with you," he said as he opened his mouth wide and ate the whole scoop.

I busted up laughing.

"You stole Tanner's whipped cream!" Marnie gasped.

"He didn't want it."

"And now you have whipped cream all over your face." Marnie pulled a napkin from the dispenser and reached over to dab Dayton's lips.

He went completely still, watching her as she worked.

Yeah, he was totally crushing on her.

Before I could point it out in the most obnoxious, little-sisterly way, the door to Froyo jingled. Marnie snapped away from Dayton and stuffed the gross napkin in her pocket. Then her face went as pale as paste.

I moved to the side because Dayton's big head was blocking my view, and there was Todd.

"Marnie!" He came straight to the counter. "I've been looking all over for you. Why didn't you answer your phone?"

"I—" She looked at me like I was the one who had it. I took pity on her and mouthed, 'On silent', which was true. She never turned the ringer back on after class.

"I guess it was-" Marnie started.

"Doesn't matter." Todd elbowed himself between Tanner and Dayton without looking at either of them. "Can I speak with you? Alone?"

That was the dumbest idea in the world. I linked my arm through Marnie's and shook my head. "She's working."

Todd sniffed. "You work here?"

The disdain snapped Marnie out of her foggy state. "Well, I'm starting to. I do yogurt—"

I raised my voice so there was no way Todd could pretend not to hear me. "So, Todd, who's this girl you were making out with this morning?"

Except for the barking laugh Dayton struggled to cover with his hand, the room was silent.

Todd's shocked face morphed into an easy smile. "You shouldn't believe everything you hear, Bailey."

I raised an eyebrow. "You're assuming I heard it? What if I saw it?"

"That would be impossible, since it didn't happen."

I knew in my soul Todd was lying through his ears.

Or nose.

Or whatever.

I stared him into the ground. His fingers twitched against the side of his legs.

With an exaggerated breath, Todd gave Marnie a wounded look. "I was looking for you to tell you I was wrong about not seeing each other. I miss you, Marnie. I want to get back together."

"Did blondie dump you already?" I pretended to look sympathetic.

Todd pressed his lips together so hard they turned white. It took more effort for him to smile this time. "There's no blondie. Niko is an idiot."

While I agreed with that whole-heartedly, I couldn't stop the smirk. "No one said anything about Niko, Todd."

His smile dropped. "She's just an old friend from high school. We've known each other since we were kids."

"Aw, that's so sweet. Childhood friends reunited and making out."

"Before lunch?" Dayton craned his neck up at Todd. "That's indecent."

Marnie laughed a real laugh that made her eyes dance. Todd opened his mouth to say something awesome—I'm sure that's what he thought, anyway—but I beat him to it.

"So, would you, like, call that friends with benefits?"

"Yes." Todd stopped, his face reddening. "I mean, no." He heaved a big sigh again. "It was just a quick peck good-bye. Not even a big deal. Like the kind you give relatives and close friends."

I wrinkled my nose the same time I heard Dayton say, "Dude, that's weird."

"Seriously," I agreed.

"I kiss my little cousin," Marnie offered.

"He's four." I clasped my hand so Marnie couldn't escape my arm lock even if she wanted to, and I gazed into the distance as though contemplating to myself. "I wonder how Niko got a small, friendly kiss and making out so confused. I mean, I know he's not the brightest fish in the school, but I'm pretty sure those things look totally different."

Todd's face flushed vivid red.

"Do you want to retract your statement?" Maybe I should be the one to consider law school. I was kind of amazing at interrogation.

"I'm not in court," Todd snapped. "I'm going to go get a yogurt."

"Good idea."

We were all silent as Todd picked his flavor and moved to the toppings bar. I let go of Marnie to help him.

"What will it be, Todd? Red hots? Chocolate kisses?"

Dayton snorted.

Todd slammed his cup on the counter. "You know what? Fine. I kissed her on the lips. A lot. It was totally hot. Happy?"

"Thrilled."

Todd followed my eyes to Marnie. He fumbled with his hands as he tried to get a complete sentence to come out. When he couldn't get her to look at him, Todd jabbed his finger at me.

"This is your fault. You just can't leave things alone. It's dinner at Momo's all over again."

I blinked. "What?"

"You don't even remember? Classic."

"Remember what?"

Todd flung his arms, knocking his cup to the floor. "I took you to dinner over a year ago. I wanted burgers, but you were so set on a new, weird place called Momo's. You kept bringing it up until I finally gave in. It was the worst dinner I ever had."

Ah! That's right! I remembered now. Momo's. I loved Momo's. Dumplings with a thick curry sauce that was so good it made me want to lick the plate. Todd was a bigger idiot than I thought. Worst dinner he ever had? Seriously? I knew there was a reason I couldn't stand Todd.

Marnie finally met his eyes. "You never told me you went out with Bailey."

"It was just that one dinner. It didn't mean anything." Todd gave her his smolder. "Come on, baby. Let's get out of here so we can talk about this."

Marnie shook her head. "No, thank you. Have a nice day, Todd."

He worked his mouth like he was about to say something, but before he said a word, he stomped out of the store, banging the door behind him.

"Well done," I nodded to Marnie.

"I should have listened to you," she said, letting out a long breath. "You were right. Todd is swell, but not the good kind."

That was the closest I had ever heard Marnie come to insulting someone. It made me so proud.

While Marnie filled in the blanks for the Dayton and Todd so they could be less confused, I went to the stock room for the mop to clean up Todd's mess.

"Hey," I called to Keith.

"How's it going out there?" He poked his head out of the office.

"Oh, you know." I yanked the mop cart. "Just another day in paradise."

Ways to Improve Bailey #18

Everything is not about Bailey

I didn't have any classes on Wednesday mornings, so Jordan usually scheduled me for swim lessons, depending on how many instructors called in sick that day. I typically ended up teaching three or four. With this in mind, I decided to go to the pool an hour early to swim laps.

Marnie was the one who gave me the idea to swim for fun. She said if I only used the pool for work, it would get old fast. It was totally true. When the smell of chlorine started to make me feel horrendous, I knew it was time to swim just for me.

The aquatic center was packed—as it usually was on Wednesday—but after some sassy smooth-talking, I managed to claim a lane of the lap pool for myself. I practiced every stroke known to man and got out of the pool ready to take on the world.

"Tanner?" I blinked the chlorine away and grabbed a towel from the shelf to wrap around myself.

"I signed up for lessons twice a week. Didn't Jordan tell you?" Tanner kept his eyes trained on my face. "Mondays at seven, Wednesdays at ten."

I glanced at the office window where Jordan was hunched in front of the computer, no doubt playing solitaire. "He didn't tell me."

"It's ten." Tanner turned his watch slightly so I could see, but I didn't look at it. "Should we, uh, get started?"

"For reals?" I crossed my arms. "How long are you going to keep this going? I know you know how to swim."

Tanner's face cleared of all expression. "How can you be sure? What if I can't? What if you refuse to teach me, and I fall into the water and drown? How are you going to feel then?"

"Whatever," I smoothed my hair back from my face. "I just want to know how you, with your high-and-mighty honesty, think it's all okay to pretend you can't swim?"

Tanner's eyes flicked away and back again so quickly that I almost didn't notice. "I'm not pretending."

I crossed my arms and stared at him, waiting for an eyelash flicker or a mouth twitch. Nothing. "Fine. We'll play your stupid game."

"Okay," Tanner nodded. "Glad we have that settled. Before we get started, though, I have something for you."

I teetered between excitement and suspicion before committing to excitement. "Yay! Gimme!" I grinned, holding out my hands.

Tanner laughed. "Are you three? I don't have it with me. I will give it to you after lessons."

"That is just mean."

"Trust me. When you see it, you'll understand. Your present and water do not mix."

I narrowed my eyes. "Fine. Into the pool." Then I put my whistle to my mouth and blew.

Tanner backed away, his arms raised. "I'm going, I'm going."

We reviewed everything from his first lesson, complete with sitting on the stairs for five minutes, before I had him put his face underwater without plugging his nose. Despite all my 'whatevers' from before, I really couldn't be sure if he knew how to swim. Everything he did was just on the border, making it hard to tell if he didn't know how to swim, or if he did and was pretending like he didn't.

I was just going to go with it. I would do my best to treat him like a real student that didn't know how to swim.

I got paid either way.

But I was going to miss making him do stupid things, like going around the whole pool while holding to the side. That was super funny!

Oh well.

When Tanner's time was over, my next lesson was already in the pool waiting: ten-year-old home-schooled twins named Hailey and Kailey. I don't even want to talk about how confusing that was. I didn't get a chance to say anything to Tanner, but I figured we would meet up at Froyo later, and then I'd get my present.

To my surprise, he got changed and sat on the bleachers to wait for me. He sat there through two lessons and a stern lecture from Jordan. At least, I think it was stern. I chose not to pay attention to every little thing Jordan sniped about.

When Jordan finally finished talking, I hurried to the locker room. I quickly showered and dressed into jeans and a yellow hooded sweatshirt that said, 'Swimmer's ear, Can't hear'. Tanner stood up as I came out to meet him.

"Sorry that took so long. You didn't have to wait for me," I said.

Tanner shrugged. "Why are you carrying your shoes?" he asked.

I sat on the lowest bleacher bench. "It's less slippery. Where's my present?" I used a towel to wipe my feet off, so I could get my socks and shoes on.

Tanner sat next to me. "I should make you wait until you learn how to ask nicely."

"Here's the funny thing about that. The longer I have to wait, the more annoying I get. Just ask Dayton. You really don't want to risk it," I said.

"Maybe you're right. Never mind. There's no present."

"That is not what I meant!" I punched his shoulder. "Come on, seriously! I haven't been able to think about anything else since you told me you have a present for me."

"It's not a big thing." Tanner's forehead wrinkled. "I think you might be disappointed after all this build up."

I caught the partial throat clear he was trying to cover up and the way he kept shifting on the bench. Maybe it was time to stop teasing him. Or at least tone it down. I finished tying my shoelaces and brought both feet up so I could rest my chin on my knees.

"It was really nice of you to get me something. You didn't have to. I mean, it's not even my birthday. I'm just so thrilled that you would think of me," I said, batting my eyelashes.

Tanner laughed. "Okay, you can stop. Here." He thrust a wide envelope into my hand.

"What is it?"

"Open it." Tanner rolled his eyes.

I rolled mine right back, doing a much better job, and carefully ripped into the envelope. "Wow," I said with a grimace. "A whole bunch of paperwork. You shouldn't have."

Tanner sighed, pulling the papers from my hand. He turned the first page around so that I could see it, and he pointed to the title.

"Passport Application," I read slowly.

"Yeah. I know you can just fill these things out online now, but I wanted to print it and give it to you so you can see it as a visual reminder for your goal," he said, his voice suddenly taking on a self-conscious note.

I ripped the papers out of his hands. "This is the coolest thing ever!" I jumped to my feet and twirled around the bleachers squealing until Jordan came out of his office and blew the whistle at me. I stopped, resting one hand on the top of Tanner's head while I waited for the world to stop spinning. "I can't wait to get started! Do you have a pen?"

Tanner laughed, removing my hand so he could stand up. "You like it?"

"Yes!" I giggled like an idiot and threw my arms around him, squeezing until he cried uncle.

Literally.

"Thank you, Tanner! This is super awesome! I'm going to have a passport!" My mind was already envisioning it coming in the mail with my name and picture on it! I could set it on my dresser as a reminder of all the trips I was planning. I could look at it every day and...

My shoulders drooped.

And watch it gather dust.

Who was I kidding? I wasn't ever going to go anywhere.

I pasted a smile back on my face for Tanner's sake. This was an incredibly thoughtful thing for him to do. I didn't want him to think I wasn't grateful.

"Thanks, pal! You're the best." I punched his arm before turning to walk out of the aquatic center.

I went as fast as I could without making Jordan blow the whistle again, focusing all my energy on what I needed to do next.

My shift at Froyo.

I usually walked to Froyo, but with Tanner here, I could bum a ride and save myself the freeze fest. Once I got there, I needed to restock the napkin dispensers on each table. I also needed to refill the sprinkles. Those never seemed to last long. I was pretty convinced Keith ate them when I wasn't looking.

I also wanted to review our plan and check in with Marnie about the social media response.

Marnie was going to be there today, right?

I couldn't remember if we set that up officially or not. I pulled my phone out of my pocket and sent her a quick text.

What else did I need to do?

"Bailey," Tanner caught up to me just as we stepped outside.

"Yeah?"

"What's going on?"

"I have to go to work."

"Yes, but—"

"What?" I snapped. "I said thank you. What else do you want?"

That was probably not the best way to ask for a ride.

"I mean, I have a lot to do today. If we're going to be ready to start the matchmaking thing, I need to get to Froyo. It's probably super busy after all the advertising we've done. So, thanks for the thing. Can you give me a ride?"

Tanner blinked a couple times. "Of course." His voice was light and totally uninquisitive, which was my favorite way for a voice to be.

I shoved the passport papers into my purse and zipped it up so that I could pretend they didn't exist while Tanner unlocked the passenger door for me.

I made no effort to break the silence. Instead, I leaned my head against the cool glass of the window and watched my breath make puffs of fog. Tanner didn't try to talk either.

When we pulled into the parking lot of Froyo, there wasn't a single parking spot.

"Wow," Tanner breathed as he turned the truck down another row.

I craned my neck to see how far the line stretched outside the door. It went all the way to the corner. Never had I ever seen a line outside of Froyo. It was like Black Friday at Bath and Body Works.

As soon as Tanner stopped the car, I flung the car door open and jetted across the parking lot. Since I was his only employee, Keith was all alone with that merciless mob.

I squeezed through the crowd and took a second to survey the damage before plunging in. Keith was all over the place, ringing up yogurts and scooping toppings. He looked like a hurricane.

I pulled my apron on without tying it and took the register. We were so busy for the next thirty minutes that I forgot all about Tanner. Keith and I twirled around the small space; scooping, squirting, and refilling like we'd rehearsed every step. When the last person had been taken care of and every single one of Froyo's tables was occupied, I leaned against the counter and let out a long breath.

"Hopping hyacinth! How long has it been like this?"

Keith took off his glasses, held them to the light, then rubbed them on his shirt. Since he was covered in sugar substances, I didn't see how his glasses got clean, but he put them on again like they were. "There was a line when I opened the door at ten."

"You should have called me. Maybe I could have come in a little earlier." Even as I said the words, I remembered that I had a swim lesson at ten. So, that wouldn't have worked. But I could have had Marnie or Dayton come in for me. Keith shouldn't have to work that mess all by himself.

"I didn't get a chance to call anyone." Instead of languishing on the counter like I was, Keith hopped on the balls of his feet and laughed.

I had never heard him laugh like that. The sound made me feel like everything was right in the world.

Keith saw the look on my face and put up a finger, his face going back to the stern lines I was very familiar with. "Now don't be jumping to conclusions yet, sis. This is just one day. We'll need a lot more days like this to make a difference. I can't see it staying busy like this for much longer. So, you just keep your head until we see where this is going."

Whatever. I already knew where this was going, and I was right. Keith and I were busy all day. So busy that I recruited Marnie to keep napkins filled, and she called in Dayton to wipe down tables. Tanner kept the yogurt machines clean, clear, and under control instead of hiding in his beloved corner.

There was not a single solitary second to do anything extra during my entire shift. I spent the whole time topping, weighing, and collecting sweet, sweet moola.

For four whole hours.

Two minutes before my shift ended, we finally caught a break.

"This is bananas!" Marnie squealed.

I stuck my finger at Keith. "Now can I say I told you so?"

Keith shook his head but smiled.

"You're going to need to hire more people," Tanner said. "You two can't keep up with this on your own every day."

"Seriously," I slipped off my apron. "I don't feel like I can leave this place right now. Even though I totally don't want to work anymore. What if we get another rush like that?"

"Nice honesty, Bay," Dayton rolled his eyes.

"No, no. You go ahead," said Keith. "If I run into trouble, I'll call Janelle."

His wife.

"Or one of the many bums in this city that owes me a favor."

"You're sure?" I placed my hands on my hips and looked around at the crowded store. "I have a date, but I can bring him to work with me. Nothing says hot date like frozen yogurt."

"Oh no, that's okay," Keith said, but his words were drown out.

"What do you mean, 'hot date'?" said Dayton.

At the same time, Tanner said, "That's a good idea."

"I already told you about this." I gave a loud sigh. Seriously though, did anybody listen to anything I said? Ever? "It's my date with Dan, the guy who did the podcast. I didn't even coerce him for dinner. He asked me all on his own."

"Yeah, I got that part." Dayton crossed his arms. "I didn't get the part where this date was hot."

"Oh please," I rolled my eyes. "It's just an expression. It doesn't mean anything."

"Really?" Dayton shook his head at me then appealed to Marnie. "What do you think of when I say 'hot date'?"

Marnie's cheeks flushed, and she busied herself with reorganizing the cup that held all the sample spoons. "Um, I guess it means that the date is, um, not a friend thing?"

"Right!" Dayton turned to Tanner. "and what do you think of?"

He shook his head. "I plead the fifth."

"See?" Dayton waved his hand in my face. "My point exactly."

"Whatever." I pulled my phone out of my pocket; it was jiggling like it was hopped up on Sour Patch Kids. "Hey, Dan!"

"Bailey! How are you, girl?"

"Exhausted! And it is totally your fault!" I turned my back on everyone, so I wouldn't have to see them eavesdropping on my conversation.

"How's that?" He sounded amused.

I explained in a few short sentences how busy Froyo had been all day, thanks to his podcast and the shoutouts he gave on social media.

"It is my pleasure. About our date tonight..."

That almost sounded like he was preparing to cancel on me. Even more surprising, I kind of hoped that's what he was doing.

I didn't get a chance to analyze why.

Dan broke his pause. "Can I pick you up early? I can't wait to see you."

Guilt followed right on the tail of disappointment. This was so weird. I had never felt like I didn't want to go out with someone before. I was just tired, that's all. It had been a busy day, so bunny slippers mixed with Netflix sounded amazing.

"I'm good to go now if you want to meet me at Froyo."

"I'd love to!" His enthusiasm boosted mine. That Vietnamese crepe really did sound amazing, and I was super hungry.

"Awesome!" I said. "While you're here, let's boost business even more and get some frozen yogurt." The idea occurred to me out of nowhere, but I knew in an instant that it was fabulous. I was curious to see what Dan put on his yogurt.

"You want frozen yogurt before dinner?"

"Yeah. It will be super fun. Eating dessert first is, like, the best part about being an adult. Anyways, you should probably taste our froyo since you're practically endorsing it every day."

"You're cute," Dan laughed. "Be there in five minutes."

Five minutes? I hung up, my mind racing. I whipped around in time to see Dayton, Tanner, and Marnie jerk away like they hadn't been listening.

They were terrible actors.

Keith watched me with his disapproving face, the one where he pursed his lips like a prune.

Whatever.

"How do I look? Do I look like I taught swimming lessons and came straight here?"

No one answered, so I stood on my tiptoes to catch my reflection in the mirror above our apron hooks. I was too short to see anything except the top of my hair, which looked frizzy.

I started towards the bathroom, but I had to stop when the bell jangled. Dan strolled into Froyo a whole three minutes sooner than he said. Now that was provoking. How's a girl supposed to get ready in that amount of time?

He stopped in the doorway and looked around. His gaze moved past me twice, so I raised my hand to let him know I was there. When his eyes stopped on me, his face creased.

"Bailey?" He moved toward me, his voice uncertain.

"Hey! Are you ready for Froyo appetizers?"

He looked around the room for a long time before he came back to me. "What do you recommend?" He didn't quite meet my eyes.

I squeezed by the eavesdroppers and grabbed Dan's arm. "Don't ask me for recommendations. I'm off duty. Let's just see what sounds good."

Dan stood like a statue in front of the yogurt machines. He didn't make any move to take the cup I handed him.

"What sounds good to you?" I read off a couple of the flavors. "Anything?"

Dan looked down at the cup I offered. "That's way too big."

"It's the regular."

"Is there a kid size?"

"Nope."

Dan sighed and took it.

"Well," I swung my arms, "I think the cheesecake sounds amazing, so—"

"Cheesecake is really high cal," Dan said, looking at the labels. "Is there anything here that's sugar-free, low fat..."

I barely refrained from saying "ew" and managed a "no" instead.

"No?" Dan looked at me. "But at the interview you said froyo is healthy. No sugar, no fat, no calories."

"I was totally joking. I didn't realize you thought I was serious."

"I did." Dan's eyebrows formed a straight, black line above his eyes.

"Dan," I tipped my head to the side, "I told you the calories stay at the store. You seriously believed that?"

He didn't answer.

"Okay, for real? That's ridiculous. You have to put fat and sugar into things. That's what makes it taste good."

"No, the fat is also what makes you fat," Dan said, his eyes resting on my waistline.

What the heck?

Was he implying that I was fat?

People shouldn't say things like that to other people. It's one of those unspoken rules of humanity, like washing your hands after using the bathroom.

For a second, I thought he might be joking, but his face was as smooth as stone. There wasn't a twinkle in his eyes. He just kept looking at my body in a knowing way, like I was going to burst into Fat Albert any minute.

"Get whatever you want," I said, pushing past him. "I'm getting cheesecake."

Dan put out his arm to block me. "Why don't you get the vanilla. That's probably less fattening than cheesecake."

I ducked under Dan's arm and, just to prove a point, exchanged my regular cup for the super-sized one. Then I went back to the cheesecake and pulled the lever. I swirled and swirled and swirled until the frozen yogurt was a few inches over the top of my enormous cup. I shot Dan a sassy smile before walking to the toppings bar.

I didn't bother to see if he followed me.

"What will it be, sis?" Keith gave me a rare smile, his hand hovering over the fudge.

He knew me well.

"I don't see anything but candy. Do you have fruit, by chance?" Dan stood next to be, holding a regular-sized cup with a tiny squirt of yogurt in the bottom. His eyes roamed up and down the toppings bar.

"Down at the end," Keith pointed.

Dan hesitated, looking at my cup. "Come with me, Bailey."

"Right behind you." I nodded at Keith, who poured fudge over my yogurt. I kept nodding until the cup was almost overflowing. Dan watched with gritted teeth.

I joined him at the fruit and waited for Keith to meet us there.

"I'll have some blueberries. A small scoop–no, a *small* scoop!" Dan sighed. "Forget it. That's fine." He eyeballed the six blueberries at the bottom of his cup.

"And you?" Keith winked at me. His hand already hovered over the strawberry spoon.

"That'll do." I pursed my lips. "A nice big, *fat*, scoop of strawberries."

Dan grunted.

"Thanks, that's perfect." I smiled at Keith and carefully carried my cup to the scale.

I happened to glance over at Dayton and Co, then wished I hadn't. Dayton couldn't look at me because his face was hidden in his armpit while his shoulders shook. Marnie examined the wallpaper, and Tanner watched me with his usual intensity, like he was trying to solve a puzzle that I had the answer to.

My cup, after being weighed, rang up to a whopping seventeen dollars and sixty-seven cents. I'd never swirled a cup that cost that much.

I was so proud.

This moment made me realize we needed a wall of fame with pictures of people who swirled the biggest cups. And another wall for those who finished all of it. Today, I planned to get my picture on both walls.

As soon as I set them up.

I waited for Dan to weigh his cup so we could go sit down. His yogurt cost two dollars and thirty-five cents. That was pretty much the cost of weighing the cup and sneezing into it.

Keith announced the total.

Dan made him repeat it three times. He grumbled as he pulled out his wallet. "I can't believe this costs so much," he said, but he paid it to the exact penny. I looked for an empty table while he meticulously counted.

"Do you want to eat here, or on the way to dinner?" I said when he finally finished paying and shoved the receipt in his pocket.

"Food isn't allowed in my car."

"Here then. There's a table in the corner," I pointed.

It was, in fact, Tanner's table. I took the chair Tanner usually sat in and waved my hand regally for Dan to sit across from me. He did, but he didn't look happy.

I dipped my spoon into my cup, cracking the shell of fudge. The sound was so satisfying, I began to feel an itsy bit better. My first bite of cheesecakey goodness banished the remainder of my irritation.

Dan looked around the room, now and then making comments about dust or knicks in the paint. I shoveled spoonfuls into my mouth as fast as I could, so I wouldn't lose that lovely yogurt-induced feeling of contentment. If it disappeared, I couldn't be held responsible for what I did, or said, to Dan.

"You shouldn't eat so fast; it isn't good for your system."

That was the same thing that Dayton said to me on a regular basis. It was annoying coming from my brother, but unbearable from Dan. He made the words sound even more condescending. Lava moved up my throat. I took another huge bite to cool it down.

Dan sighed the martyr sigh and leaned back in his chair, crossing his arms.

"Is there a problem?" I asked after being the recipient of several more deeply disappointed looks.

Dan pursed his lips, calculating, then leaned forward and clasped his hands on the table. "Can I be honest with you, Bailey?"

"Oh, please do." I wiped my face with a napkin.

"I don't think this is a good idea."

"You don't think what is a good idea?" I asked, even though I knew what he meant. I wasn't about to make the conversation easier for him.

"This." He moved his hand between the two of us. "You and I."

He stopped and stared at me, waiting for a response. I blinked stupidly and took another bite of chocolate-covered goodness.

Dan heaved another huge sigh. "This is what I mean. When we visited on Monday, you were gorgeous and glowing, fun and vivacious. Today you are..."

"Uh-huh," I said, like he was making perfect sense. The truth was, I couldn't take anyone seriously who used the word "vivacious" in real-life conversation.

"I thought we had so much in common then. But now," he waved his hand again, "I can see that you're not the girl I thought you were."

My brain erupted with thoughts.

Lots and lots of thoughts.

Who did he think I was, exactly?

When I was dressed up and cute, he liked me. When I was semi-grungy and tired, he didn't.

Dan was a superficial ding-dong.

It was not my problem that he thought I was someone different. I hadn't changed that much in a few days.

Dan was a jerk.

I was a jerk.

That last thought surprised me, pushing to the top of all the others. It waved back and forth to get my attention.

I was wrong about dating.

Very, very wrong.

I never should have gone on dates with people I wasn't interested in. It wasn't fair to them.

Dan might be a ding-a-ling, but he was absolutely right.

This wasn't going to work.

I put my spoon down. "I'm really sorry, Dan. I shouldn't have said yes when you asked me out."

He blinked, his head rocking back like I'd punched him. "What? Why?"

"Because I am not interested in you. I never was. It was wrong for me to lead you on." I pushed my chair back and stood up. "I really am sorry."

Dan grabbed my wrist. "Wait, wait, wait, wait, wait, wait." He shook his head, over and over. "You can't just leave like that. Don't you want to know why *I* think it's not going to work?"

"Nope." I wiggled out of his grasp. "Thanks for the yogurt. It was amazing." I turned and walked away.

"For the record, I was the one who knew it wasn't going to work first!" Dan called.

I didn't bother turning around. I went behind the counter and put my apron back on. Four pairs of eyeballs bored into my back. "Looks like I have some free time to help you out tonight," I said to Keith. "So, you're welcome."

Dayton applauded as I turned around.

"What?" I said as Keith put his arm across my shoulders.

Keith squeezed me close to his side. "That was great fun to watch. Much better than them reality TV shows. Thanks, sis."

"Yeah, well, now you're going to have to pay me more because I'm working overtime."

"You're worth it," he said in the brief moment of stillness before the bell over the door started up again.

Ways to Improve Bailey #8

Listen to other people

"I hate frozen yogurt," I said as I dropped into a chair. I had just kicked the last of the customers out the door and locked it in the face of a crowd of teenagers. "Whose idea was it to save this place? I say we let it go."

Keith flicked water at my face as he walked by. I was so glad to see him closing out the register. I didn't have the brain cells left to do it, even with a calculator to help me.

I leaned my forehead on the table and groaned.

"What are you talking about, Bailey? This was so fun!" Marnie patted my hair. "Dayton and I are going for tacos. Come with us?"

"Pass." I groaned again, leaving my head right where it was.

"Come on." Dayton punched my shoulder. Even though I couldn't see that it was him, I knew that punch anywhere. "Come with us. How else will you get home?"

"I'll take her," Tanner said.

I lifted my head slowly and looked at Tanner. His face was void of expression, but there was something in his eyes that made my heart speed up.

I should go get tacos with Dayton and Marnie. That was infinitely better than trying to figure out my feelings right now. I could rally enough energy to go with them.

Maybe.

My neck ached in protest when I tried to lift it, but that was way easier to deal with than the thought of being alone with Tanner.

"Cool." Dayton's stool scraped across the tile as he stood up. "That's settled. See you at home."

"Wai—"

He was already out the door. Curse his long legs.

Keith stretched his arms over his head. "Good work today, sis. You go have fun. You deserve it." Then he disappeared into the back room.

"Ready?" Tanner stood and waited.

Was I?

I gathered my things slowly and tried to wrangle my thoughts. They were as slippery as jellybeans after you suck off the candy coating.

It was just a ride home. No big deal. If Tanner asked about the passport, I would say thank you and change the subject. I can always talk about the weather. This wasn't a big deal.

Tanner and I were friends.

I followed him to his truck, shivering. Even with the truck started and the heater raging, my insides quaked and quivered. Neither of us said a word until Tanner pulled into the driveway of my house.

"Thanks for the ride."

Tanner nodded.

I reached for the door handle but couldn't bring myself to pull on it.

I'd just had that mind bomb today about dating, and as I sat in Tanner's truck with country music filling the silence, I had another one. For sure, it was wrong to lead people on and let them think I was interested when I really wasn't. But this was wrong, too. I was doing the same thing to Tanner, just in a different way. It obviously wasn't a datey way, since we were just friends, but I was letting him think I didn't care when I really did.

I mean, I cared about him the way I cared about Dayton. I didn't like to see that slump in his shoulders, and part of me knew I had something to do with it.

So, I couldn't pull the handle. I couldn't leave like that.

"Tanner?"

"Yes?"

"Have you been to the Frances Short Pond?"

"Excuse me?"

I let go of the handle and turned to face him. "Frances Short Pond. It's pretty cute. It's also not far." I paused, realizing he probably had other stuff to do. "But—"

"I'd love to see it."

"Yeah?"

He nodded, putting the truck in reverse. "Where do I go?"

I gave him directions; it took, like, fifteen words. The pond was just around the corner and down the street from my house. When Tanner came to a stop in the teeny parking lot, he looked around. "I haven't been here before."

"Thorpe Park is right over there," I pointed as I stepped out of the car, then I swung my arm another way. "And this is Marshall Elementary School."

"I see." Tanner nodded and followed me toward the path that wound around the lake. I pulled out my phone to turn on the flashlight, since it didn't look like the moon was going to light our way tonight.

I pulled my jacket tighter and tucked my free arm into my armpit. It was cold. Hopefully it would warm up as we walked.

Tanner broke the silence with a clearing of his throat. "Froyo was busy all day."

"It was."

"Does that make you happy?"

"Of course it does." I picked my way slowly down the path. Even with my flashlight phone, it was difficult to see the bumps and ruts. "Does it make you happy? Now you don't have to be a hipster at a coffee shop."

Tanner chuckled. "Well, thank goodness for that."

"You didn't answer the question."

"It does make me happy." Tanner shook a pebble out of his shoe. "For Keith's sake, and for yours."

"Thanks for your help."

"Of course."

The moment we stepped into the opening by the pond, the clouds shifted. The moon was there, shining into the water. Tanner's breath caught.

"Better than the ocean?" I teased.

Tanner cleared his throat. "It's a different kind of beautiful."

We strolled to the edge of the water. I was glad it was too dark for him to see how murky and gross the water actually was. In the dark, it looks magical.

Romantic.

Wait.

I opened my mouth and words spewed out in one breath. "There's a bench over here. We can sit down if you want. Or we can walk around the pond. It's not very big, but we could walk around it. Or we could sit."

"Let's walk," Tanner said, his eyes glued to the water.

The silence settled into a cozy space as we slowly circled the pond. On our third lap, Tanner cleared his throat again.

"Are you...are you...upset about Dan?"

I'd already forgotten about Dan. That felt like a hundred and fifty thousand years ago.

I tossed my head. "Whatever."

Tanner peeked at me through his wavy bangs. He reminded me of an animal hiding in the bushes. "No?"

"Nope."

"You seemed...upset."

"Well, I was. But not about that mess of a date."

Tanner kicked a rock off the path. "What upset you?"

"I just—" I sighed. "I hate it when Dayton is right."

A smile curled around the corner of Tanner's mouth, moving his beard up with it. "And what was Dayton right about?"

I narrowed my eyes. "Oh, please. Don't act all innocent. You were right, too. It's so annoying."

Tanner leaned forward. "I was right, too? Please, tell me more. I love being right."

I rolled my eyes, but I gave in and explained the realization I had about dating. "So, congratulations. You and Dayton were right. I was wrong."

Tanner looked at me for a long time before replying. "So, you're done dating?"

"I am," I said. "I'm done dating. So, you better prepare yourself."

"For what?"

"For going with me to try new restaurants, duh. Since I'm done with dates, I need a restaurant buddy. I will go bananas if I have to eat at B-Dubs with Dayton every weekend."

"And you want me to go with you?"

I shrugged. "Dayton's obviously out. Marnie would go only out of pity; she won't really enjoy it. But you would have fun trying weird stuff with me, right?"

He ate eel; he would try anything.

But then, Tanner didn't answer right away and the awkward started to set in.

"Obviously, you don't have to-" I said, trying to undo the silence.

"I want to." Tanner said, cutting me off. "No, I want to. That sounds great. I'll go with you anytime. Just let me know when and where."

"Yeah?"

"Yes."

"How about right now?" My sleepiness was gone from all the walking, and now I was hungry. Other than that mammoth yogurt I swirled to tick Dan off, I hadn't eaten anything since breakfast. "I'm starving. Let's go see if we can find Juanicita's."

"What-a-cita's?"

I tugged on his arm to get him to turn around. "*Juan*icita's."

"And what is that?"

"A food truck. They have the best carnitas in the world! But they are never in the same place, and they don't keep their Facebook page updated, so we have to search for it."

"Is it worth the search?" Tanner unlocked my door and waited for me to slide into the truck before closing it.

"So worth it," I assured him.

We drove through downtown, then out to the fairgrounds, but Juanicita's bright red truck was nowhere to be seen.

"Bailey?"

"Yeah?" I turned away from the window.

"I can hear your stomach growling, and it's starting to freak me out."

I burst out laughing. "Okay, let's try the CCC parking lot on Fourth. If it's not there, we can go to Basil's. Deal?"

"Deal."

Ten minutes later we pulled into the parking lot, and fifteen minutes after that, I sat in Tanner's truck with half of my face covered with a carnitas burrito.

Tanner shoveled carne asada fries into his mouth so quickly it was like he'd never eaten food before.

"What do you think?" I asked him the next time he came up for air.

"These are the best fries I've ever eaten. And the carne asada is..." There were no words.

I laughed. "See? This is why I want to write a food blog. Food is so fun, right?"

"I do see what you mean."

We ate in happy silence for a moment longer, then Tanner rested the container of fries in his lap. "Can I ask you a question?"

"No," I said. "I'm eating."

"I can wait." He stared at me.

"Okay, fine. Ask your question." I couldn't eat with someone staring at me like that.

Tanner twirled the plastic fork through his fingers before he looked up. "Are you upset about the passport paperwork I gave you?"

I floundered for a moment, trying to collect my thoughts. "Not at you. At me. I want to do it, but I'm chicken. I'm not upset you gave it to me. I'm upset I won't ever use it."

"I see." Tanner caught my eye and held it. "Are you sure you won't ever use it?"

"I know I don't make any sense. I want to leave here, but I've never left here before, so I'm scared to. I want to travel, but not alone. It's like a huge cyclone in my brain. Around and around and around we go. I have no idea how to break out of it." I dropped my head until it rested on the back of the seat. "You're a math whiz. Solve this for me."

"Numbers are my thing, not concepts," Tanner said.

I picked a tomato from what was left of my burrito and sucked it off my finger. "Can I tell you a story?"

"Please do."

"It's super embarrassing, so you have to promise you will never repeat it to another living soul."

"I promise."

I held up my pinkie, but Tanner just looked at me. "Have you never done a pinkie swear?" I asked.

He shook his head.

"There is something wrong with your childhood." I hooked his pinkie with mine and squeezed. "Now promise."

Tanner squeezed back. "I promise."

"Okay." I took a deep breath and launched into the story of my most embarrassing moment ever. It was a horrific tale. The first time I drove alone after I got my driver's license, I got pulled over for speeding. The police officer stood patiently outside my window while I fumbled with the window buttons. I rolled down every other window in the car before I finally got to the driver's side. He asked for my license and registration; I gave him my purse. He asked if I'd been drinking—because I was acting like a flustered loon—and I told him how many water bottles I'd finished that week. He let me off with a warning, and then three seconds later, I got a text from my dad, my mom, and Dayton. Apparently, Officer Langley used to be our paperboy and went to Coconino when Dad was principal. I guess I should have been grateful no one filmed the encounter and put it on YouTube.

"So, that's why I can't. I'm a disaster on my own. I'd probably end up rotting in a foreign prison for the rest of my life. I just don't handle things well."

Tanner squinted at the ceiling. "You actually handled it just fine."

I snorted.

"No, really," he said. "It was awkward, but you got through it. The officer was understanding. I think you'd be surprised what you can do when you really decide to just do it."

"That sounds like a motivational poster."

Tanner laughed. "It might be. Henry Ford said something similar: One of the greatest things to happen to a man is to realize he can do something he thought was impossible."

"And that sounds like paraphrasing."

"Well, that's because it was. Are you done?"

I nodded and handed Tanner the leftovers of my burrito. I couldn't fit it all into my stomach. Believe me, I tried.

Tanner left the truck to throw our trash away. I shrugged out of my jacket because that little vehicle could really crank up the heat. When Tanner got back in the truck, he looked at me.

"You know what I think, Bailey Hendrix?"

"Do tell," I said, rolling my eyes. I was getting major Dayton vibes from the look on his face. Any second now, he was going to tell me to eat more vegetables and always cross the street at crosswalks.

Tanner shook his head. "You make it really hard to tell you things sometimes, you know that?"

"No," I said. "I am the most open-minded person in the world. What are you talking about?"

He shook his head some more and started to back out of the parking lot. Wait, that was it? Now that it seemed like he wasn't going to say what he was going to say, I realized I really wanted to know what it was.

"You're right. I'm a pain in the butt. What were you going to say?"

Tanner pulled up to a stop sign and, thankfully, took that opportunity to answer me. "I was going to say that I think you don't know everything about yourself. And what you do know isn't the whole truth."

"Okay," I raised an eyebrow. "I'm so glad I asked you to share that thought because it totally makes sense."

"You asked for it."

I shook my head. "I asked for an answer, not a riddle."

Tanner smiled. "Alright then. All I'm saying is I think you are stronger than you think. And once you figure that out, you will be able to do whatever you want. Nothing will stand in your way."

Something stuck in my throat as Tanner's words replayed themselves over and over in my mind during the drive home, while I talked to Dayton, and as I got ready for bed.

Was Tanner right?

Was what he said true?

Could I do it?

Ways to Improve Bailey #19

Surly No More

With zeal that would have made the most zealous zealot jealous, I threw myself into saving Froyo. Whenever my mind drifted to anything else, I whipped it back to Froyo with the flick of my head. I was so full of ideas—and nervous energy—that I was literally on the move from sunup to sundown every day.

I made more flyers for the public libraries. I ordered t-shirts with the Froyo logo that Marnie designed for us: a cute swirled cone with a smiley face. I priced out artists to redo the window display and finally gave the job to Marnie so that the display matched the shirts. Dayton and his team of boys helped me repaint the awning and buff the knicks out of the tables.

The yogurt matchmaking was such a hit that we hired Marnie as resident matchmaker every Monday, Wednesday, and Friday afternoon. She even found a girl who loved black licorice. Clay's chances of not dying alone were looking up.

All this went down despite Dan the troll and his fifteen-minute podcast rants about how fat Americans are and how places like Froyo are contributing to the epidemic. None of his diatribes made any difference. Froyo stayed packed every day.

Personally, I thought Dan was the reason we stayed so busy; he was making people curious.

On the Monday of spring break, I came out of swim lessons feeling like I was carrying the weight of the world. I was so seriously tired.

Dayton was waiting for me at the curb. I hopped in the car, and off we went.

"How were your lessons?"

"Fine."

Dayton's stupid sing-song tone dropped. "What's up with you lately?"

"What are you talking about?"

Dayton tapped the steering wheel with his thumbs. "You're surly, Bay. Surly."

I glared at the side of his head. So what if I was. I have the right to be surly every once in a while.

Thankfully, Dayton didn't push it. But when he pulled into the driveway of home, he stopped me from getting out of the car.

"It's going on the list, Bay. Surly is no good."

I didn't respond to that, either. Okay, I did. Just not in words. The gigantic slam of the passenger door made my point for me.

I dropped my stuff in the entry way—even though that most likely meant Dayton would add another thing to his list—and went straight to my room. When I opened the door, I froze.

Was I in the right place?

Of course I was. This was my house. My key worked in the front door. The bathroom was to the right. There was a dent in the wall.

So, then, who filled my room with helium balloons?

And just as important, why?

"Something wrong?" Dayton leaned against the wall with a smirk.

"No." I pushed my way into my room and slammed that door too.

Except, now I couldn't see a blasted thing.

There must have been a billion balloons in my room. It was a new experience to swim through balloons. They clung to my face and hair as I moved slowly across the carpet. I tripped over a shoe on my way to my desk, where I searched for some scissors and hoped that whoever did this wasn't hiding somewhere in the sea of color. I might freak out and jab them.

With scissors in hand, I began popping the balloons that stuck to my shirt. At first, the noise made me jump out of my skin, but I quickly got used to it. To tell the truth, it was kind of satisfying.

Fifteen minutes later, balloon debris covered my feet and the floor. I had finally popped enough balloons to see my bed.

It was covered in candy.

Not lame candy, either. It was fancy candy from all over the world. The labels were even in different languages. I couldn't read what they said, but they looked good, so I decided to eat them anyway.

This was perfect. I could fill my starving belly without going to the kitchen where I would have to talk to Dayton. I reached for the closest candy—something soft in a bright yellow wrapper—opened it and popped it into my mouth.

Oh, yummy!

It tasted like sunshine feels. I reached across the bed for another one and savored it. When I finished all those candies, my hand hovered over the mess, trying to decide what to try next.

"Bailey!" Dayton hollered through my door.

"What?" I slurred through my mouthful of candy.

He opened the door and pushed through balloons to get to my bed. "What are you doing?" He crossed his arms and glared down at me.

"What are *you* doing in my room?"

Dayton shook his head like that wasn't important, even though we had super strict privacy rules. He wasn't supposed to enter my domain unless I actually said the word "enter".

"You wrecked it," he said.

I finished chewing and swallowed hard. "What?"

He waved his hand over the mass of candies. "Did you read this before you decimated it?"

"The wrappers aren't in English."

Dayton squeezed the crease between his eyebrows. "The candy spelled out words, Bailey."

I stood up on my tiptoes and turned my head from side to side. "It just looks like a pile of candy to me."

"Yeah, because you already wrecked it."

"Whatever. Just tell me what's going on and get out of here."

"Surly." Dayton pressed his lips together.

I shifted to my weight all the way to one side and waited.

"I can't even with you right now." Dayton turned around and walked out of my room.

I shoved balloons out of the way so I could slam my door again. Then I slumped on my bed, scattering candy everywhere and wondering what just happened. And what was the deal with the candy and balloons?

A lovely throbbing started in my temples. I laid on my back and kicked balloons as they shifted in the air above me. My phone vibrated in my back pocket, but I didn't pull it out. I rolled over, hugged my pillow to my chest, and willed myself to sleep.

When I woke up an hour later, my headache was gone, and I felt way better. Even the balloons weren't quite as annoying. I waved them away as I changed for work and then went to the living room for my shoes.

"Dayton?"

He didn't answer.

I tried to call him, but he didn't answer his phone, either. Then I tried to call Marnie for a ride to Froyo. When she didn't answer, I started to wonder if I'd stumbled into a *Twilight Zone* episode, like the one where the guy wakes up and he is the only person left on the planet.

I started to work myself up pretty good when a knock sounded on the door.

Okay, so, I wasn't left alone in the world.

I swung the door open and shaded my eyes against the bright afternoon sun.

"Tanner?"

"Hi, Bailey."

"What are you doing here?" I did sound surly. I hate it when Dayton is right. I softened my voice and tried again. "I mean, hello, how are you? What are you doing here?"

Tanner shifted. "I thought you might need a ride to work."

"I do."

"Great." Tanner turned on his heel and walked toward his truck, which was parked on the curb.

I grabbed my purse, shrugged on my jacket, locked the door behind me, and scrambled after Tanner.

"So," Tanner cleared his throat as he pulled onto the main road, "Dayton told me something unusual happened today."

"Yeah?" I clasped my hands in my lap.

There was silence for a moment while Tanner regrouped. "Did something unusual happen today?"

"I guess that depends on what you consider unusual."

Tanner's eyes shifted over to me.

"Spit it out, Tanner."

His profile showed half of a huge grin. "I had an idea."

"Congratulations."

"I planned a surprise for you."

I held out my hand, palm up.

Tanner laughed. "It's not that kind of surprise. If it works for you, I'd like to pick you up after work tonight. It will take maybe three hours."

"What are you planning?"

"Seriously?" Tanner shook his head. "You know how surprises work. I'm not going to tell you until tonight."

"Fine." I dropped my hand. "Wait, are you the one who vandalized my bedroom?"

Tanner opened his mouth, then closed it. "If by 'vandalized' you mean 'decorated', then yes."

"Why?"

We pulled into the only empty parking spot in front of Froyo. "Have you ever been to prom?"

I blinked. "Yes."

"I was going for that. I thought you'd like it if I asked you out creatively."

I guess I should be grateful he didn't send me on a scavenger hunt around the city or freeze all my underwear into ice blocks—even though it was going to take me a thousand years to clean up all those balloons.

"What did the candy say?"

Tanner shook his head again. "I can't tell you that. If you didn't see it, I don't think you were meant to."

Really?

"Whatever." I opened the door and slid to the ground. "See you tonight."

"You will," Tanner nodded. "I'll pick you up around five. Be hungry."

"I'm always hungry," I muttered as I made my way through the crowd of customers to my apron hook.

Keith and I hardly had a chance to breathe much less talk during my entire shift. I knew we had done a good thing saving Froyo, but as much as I hated to admit it, there was part of me that missed those quiet days of daydreaming at the counter while Tanner sat in the corner and clicked away on his laptop.

At ten minutes to five, I hung up my apron. Last week Keith hired Clay, so he no longer needed me to stay late. I wanted a couple of minutes to collect myself before Tanner showed up. The last few weeks had been a flurry of classes, homework, swim lessons, and yogurt toppings. Time moved so quickly that I began to feel like all I did was whirl from place to place, then sleep, then wake up and do it all again.

"Hang on there, Bailey," Keith said, following me into the back room.

"What's up?"

Keith rubbed his forehead with one hand resting at his waist. "I didn't think it was possible, but we're going to make it, kid." He closed the distance between us, hugging me tightly to his side. "Thanks to you and—."

"No," I wiggled out of his grasp. "It's the window display."

"Well, now, be that as it may, you can stop all this running around like a chicken. Froyo is safe."

"Okay." I didn't understand why he followed me into the back room to tell me that.

Keith's face was completely void of stress wrinkles. Even that worry line between his eyebrows was gone, which was weird because I actually thought it was part of his face.

"I'm trying to tell you everything is taken care of."

"Okay." I crossed my arms and waited. Keith needed to work on his communication skills. Or have a setting where I could move him to 2x speed.

"Froyo is safe. We don't have to worry about it and whatnot, even if business slows down again. The property owner sold out—"

"Wait, what?" I interrupted.

"That's right," Keith smiled. "The new owner lowered the rent. They might as well be giving us the place for free."

"That's...that's great, Keith." My mind reeled. Froyo was safe? Just like that? I barely knew what to do with this information.

Keith squeezed me again. "Get out of here, girlie. You deserve a break."

Tanner was waiting for me in the parking lot when I stepped outside. When he saw me, he opened his door and started to get out. I waved him back into place. There was no point in him coming out in the blistering cold just to be gentlemanly.

I really wished spring would make up its mind.

"Hey. How was work today?" Tanner rested back in his seat. He was wearing his usual flannel uniform. I swear, if he didn't wear flannel and jeans, I wouldn't recognize him.

I climbed into the truck. "Busy."

"That's good?"

I squinted at him. "Are you asking me or telling me?"

Tanner laughed. "Actually, I was trying to figure out what you think about it."

"Then just ask." I buckled up buttercup and set my purse at my feet.

"Are you glad it's busy at work?" Tanner's voice was carried a smile.

I almost answered something flippant like 'ecstatic', but I changed my mind at the last minute. "I am glad. I'm especially glad Keith doesn't have to worry about Froyo anymore. I didn't realize how much that was stressing him out."

"Yes, I noticed that, too."

"And he told me just now that there's a new landlord for the shopping center, so he doesn't have to worry about rent either. So, it looks like we did it!"

"That's—" Tanner cleared his throat. "That's great."

"Yep," I nodded for way longer than was normal. "So, uh, are we just going to sit in the parking lot? Is this your big date?"

The word "date" did weird things to my insides. I had to start babbling to cover it up.

"You put an awful lot of effort into asking me out. It would have taken me hours to clean up my room if I hadn't made Dayton do it while I was at work. So, that can mean one of two things: either you used up all your imagination energy and we're going to Taco Bell, or you have a whole, elaborate plan."

"Which do you think it is?" Tanner reached under his seat and came back up with a hat, which he placed on his head at a jaunty angle.

I blinked. "Are you Magic School Bussing this date?"

Tanner then proceeded to quote, word for word, the flight attendant spiel they give before taking flight. I tried to interrupt or derail him, but he was vigilant, never wavering until he had finished the whole thing and tossed a bag of peanuts into my lap.

"Okay." I opened the bag and poured some peanuts into my palm. "Apparently, we're flying somewhere. Where are we going exactly?"

Tanner didn't answer. The truck was quiet except for the sounds of me chewing.

That was lovely.

Tanner handed me an envelope. I opened it and lifted one eyebrow.

"A passport?"

Tanner reached over to point. "Tonight, we'll be taking a self-guided tour of the Hawaiian Islands, Thailand, India, and Haiti. You will earn three stamps on your passport—since Hawaii isn't a passport stamp, sorry—but only after you try the cuisine and write a critique here." He turned the page to show me a large box with lines inside, blank and ready to fill.

I stared at it for a long time, my mouth working without words coming out. "I don't know what to say."

"Are you ready for takeoff?"

"Tanner, this is cool. I mean, it sounds pretty cool, if you can pull it off."

Tanner grinned back at my sassy smile and tipped his dorky hat. "I can pull it off."

Something twisted in my belly, and I had to look away. Why couldn't he be a tasteless moron who only ate at restaurants with drive-thrus? My life would be so much easier if he was.

The first place we went was a tiny, hole-in-the-wall Hawaiian restaurant stuffed between two tourist traps.

"I know this isn't exactly foreign, but it is authentic," Tanner explained as we stepped inside. My eyes widened when I saw poi on the menu board. I'd been to a lot of Hawaiian places, but none of them had ever offered poi. I couldn't wait to try it.

We ordered a small portion of poi, the roasted pork, and spam rolls to share, since we still had three other places to visit.

"Before we leave, write your thoughts in your passport, but don't tell me yet. I want to hear all about it at the end."

I did what he said, using my best food blog lingo. Then I followed Tanner back to the truck, where he donned his pilot hat and drove to Pato Thai. This one had been on my restaurant bucket list for a long time. I wondered if Tanner knew that.

And how.

We ordered red curry, pad thai, pad woon sen, and an eggplant dish that rocked my world. And I don't even like eggplant. I had to keep stopping to critique as we ate because everything tasted so unique, and I wanted to remember all the details.

At Delhi Palace, I enjoyed gazing at a mural of the Taj Mahal almost as much as I enjoyed the butter chicken, vegetable korma, and ridiculous amounts of garlic naan. I had to restrain myself from licking the plate.

When we got back in the truck, I looked at the empty square for Haiti. Tanner had just stamped India for me with one of those smiley face stamps that elementary school teachers use.

"Tanner, are you sure there's a Haiti restaurant here? I'm pretty sure I would know about it, and I don't know about it."

He just smiled and backed the truck out of the parking lot. After several turns that took us farther away from the commercial part of Flagstaff and deep into the residential, I couldn't hold my tongue anymore.

"Where are we going?"

"Here." Tanner pulled into the drive-way of a cute yellow house with a large front porch.

"And where is here?"

"You'll see."

That's all he would say as he opened my door, took my hand, and led me up the front walk. My hand instantly started to sweat, so I slipped it out of Tanner's grip and hid it in my pocket.

"Tanner!" A nice-looking guy opened the door. He was maybe six years older than me and carrying a baby. He reached out to slap Tanner on the back. "Come in, come in. You must be Bailey." He hugged me tight as I tried to slip by him.

I am not a hugger.

But something about his solid grin and the bundle of drool in his arms made me stay where I was and let him squeeze my guts out.

The guy hurried into the other room, calling that the guests had arrived. The house smelled more amazing with each step we took toward the kitchen. I turned to Tanner for an explanation.

"This is Josef's house. He's a professor at NAU in the science department. He and his wife moved here three years ago from Haiti."

Now I got it.

We sat down at a table filled with so many different foods that I felt like my eyes turned into ping pong balls while I tried to take it all in. Josef and his wife, Sia, treated us like royalty, serving us first and making sure we had everything we could ever need or want.

And the food!

I contented myself with eating way more than I should have. That was probably the greatest compliment I could give them, judging by the way they watched the food on my plate disappear with pleased faces.

We lingered around the table in that cozy little room with candles flickering shadows on the walls and listened to Josef and Sia talk about growing up in Haiti. My eyes grew bigger with each new story. It was so different from everything I was used to. I ached to go there.

"Josef, Sia, thank you so much for dinner," Tanner said after a while. His words brought the room back into focus. Just like that, I was transported from laying in a hammock next to the ocean and back to a little room filled with shining eyes.

"Yes! Thank you. Thank you," I said, unable to think of any other words that would convey what I was feeling. When they hugged me good-bye, I squeezed them back.

"That was so nice," I said to Tanner once we were driving again. "They just gave up their night for us."

"Well, they are the nicest people on the planet," Tanner said.

"Except for Marnie," I smiled.

"Yeah, except for her," Tanner agreed.

My mind wandered as we drove. Being with Sia and Josef made me realize just how little I knew about anywhere outside of my hometown and home state. My experience was so limited. My world was so small.

"That was your last stamp," Tanner said, interrupting my thoughts. "Tell me what you thought."

He didn't need to ask me twice. "So, Hawaii. I loved the pork! It had such a different flavor than any other I've tried. It's like I could taste the dirt! I loved it! The poi, however, might be something you have to get used to."

Tanner laughed. "Not a fan, huh?"

"Not so much," I shook my head. "I could do without the spam roll, too."

"Fair." Tanner glanced at me as we stopped for a red light. "And Thailand?"

"The curry was delectable. I loved the noodles, and I could eat the eggplant every day for the rest of my life."

"As could I."

"I loved everything about Delhi Palace." I leaned back in the seat, remembering the garlic naan.

"Wholeheartedly agree."

"And Haiti? I just want to live with the Hermanes. Tanner, that was the best date I have ever had. Thank you so much."

Tanner swallowed. "You're welcome."

I opened my passport, even though I'd done that so many times already. I loved the row of smiley face stamps. It was like I'd actually been to each of those places tonight. "What's next?" I asked.

"Dessert." Tanner wouldn't say any more, no matter how hard I tried to make him elaborate. I was as obnoxious as I could possibly be, but he held out strong until we pulled into the parking lot in front of an old strip mall. I looked from the game store to the Chinese restaurant, trying to figure out what we were doing there.

"Are we signed up for a Dungeons and Dragons tournament?" I asked as Tanner got out of the truck. I had to wait until he walked around to open my door for the answer.

"Not tonight." He swept his arm out so I would walk ahead.

I stepped onto the sidewalk and waited for Tanner's lead since I had no idea where we were going. As he walked by me, he grabbed my elbow and tugged. I followed instead of asking all the questions that were bouncing around in my brain.

He led me to a small side door that was partially hidden by the wide awning of the Chinese restaurant. The door had fluorescent yellow vinyl lettering, informing me that it was a marketplace. I'd lived in Flagstaff for, like, a hundred years, but had no idea this place was here. For a moment, I had a strange sensation, like I was in another city or country.

I kind of liked it.

The door made no sound when we pushed it open, and there was no one to be seen inside. Tanner turned to me and rubbed his hands together like the evil mastermind he was.

"Here's what we are doing for dessert. You are going to shop for three dessert items in this store. Here's the rules: The name of the item can't be in English, you can't ask anyone to translate it for you, and you have five minutes. Ready?"

"Wait! What? Dessert? English—."

"Set!"

My eyes darted to the shelves. The only thing I recognized on the one closest to us was ramen, but it wasn't the brand I was familiar with, and it definitely wasn't dessert.

"Go!" Tanner pushed my back to get me moving.

That's all it took, and then I was all over the place. I grabbed a package that looked like it might have cookies, but I couldn't tell because it was in another language that didn't even use the English alphabet.

I scanned the next shelf for something that looked like it could be a dessert, but I wasn't sure enough to pick anything up. The shelf next to that one had a spherical container full of wafer-looking sticks that were dipped in what could possibly be chocolate. I decided to risk it.

There was a long, lift-top freezer in the center of the store. I barely heard Tanner announce one minute as I shimmied around it. There was something that looked like a carton of ice cream. I reached inside and added it to my collection right as Tanner started counting down the last thirty seconds.

"Done and done!" I announced, bringing my armload back to him. "Check this out."

He did.

And he laughed a lot.

"Why are you laughing? These are chocolate-covered cookie sticks, right?" I held up one of the packages. "That's dessert."

"Pocky, yes. They could count as dessert, except you got the wasabi flavored."

I gave him a stink eye. "What about these? They are cookies or something." Suddenly I wasn't sure about anything.

"Buttering biscuits. It's kind of like a shortbread cookie."

That was definitely dessert, so why, then, was he still laughing? I lifted the ice cream and turned it all around. There wasn't anything on it to identify what it was. I shrugged and held it out to him. "Ice cream?"

"Pig fat," he snorted.

Well, that's gross.

"Two out of three isn't bad," I said, tossing the lard back into the freezer.

"Not bad at all," Tanner said, his face so smooth it was obvious he was trying not to show his smile. "I just keep wondering what would have happened if I didn't tell you what that was, and you took a big spoonful expecting it to be ice cream."

I mimed barfing into my purse, just as an old man walked into the market from the restaurant next door.

"I can help you?" he asked in a thick Asian accent. I tried to guess what country. Korea?

"Yes." Tanner set the Pocky, buttering biscuits, and a mysterious container he chose to replace my pig fat next to the cash register. "We'll take these, please."

"Good, good," the man nodded.

While Tanner paid, I took time to look around the store without a timer stressing me out. It was really awesome. I wondered how Tanner found it.

"Have good day," the man called. I turned to wave before I followed Tanner outside.

Once we were back in the truck, Tanner set each item on the seat between us. I opened the Pocky first, since I was pretty sure I knew how chocolate would taste. I was wrong. It was more bitter than I was expecting, and the wasabi set my tongue on fire.

The biscuit things were not my favorite. They were like a cross between a cracker and a cookie, but the one I ate left a weird aftertaste.

Tanner's mystery item ended up being jelly cups, sort of like the Jell-o my mom used to pack in my elementary school lunches. I couldn't decide if I liked them or not.

"The problem is, these desserts aren't that sweet," I announced, setting the jelly cup down. "I keep expecting this burst of sweetness, and my taste buds feel gypped."

Tanner laughed.

I chewed on my lip while Tanner took another jelly cup shot. We didn't have spoons, so he had to squeeze the container and use momentum to toss it into his mouth. "Have you traveled to a lot of places?"

Tanner stopped with another jelly cup halfway to his mouth. Looking at me that way, out of the corner of his eye, made him look shifty. "You don't want to know."

"Yes, I do. I asked, didn't I?"

Tanner swallowed his jelly, set the cup aside, and started listing all the places he had been around the world in his short and obviously over-privileged lifetime.

He was right.

I didn't want to know. I didn't have enough fingers or toes to keep up with him.

"Is there anywhere you haven't been?" I asked, annoyed for reasons I didn't want to analyze.

"Hawaii, actually," Tanner said. "It's funny. That's the one place I actually want to go, and I haven't been there. You know, that would be a great one for you to start with because it seems exotic, but you don't have to worry about passports and language barriers or foreign prison."

"Haha." I rolled my eyes and flicked biscuit crumbs off my shirt. Secretly, I considered what he said. Maybe I could go to Hawaii.

Tanner went on, "Guam or Costa Rica would be good, too. Your first passport country could be Canada, eh? It could help you get used to a foreign country without going too far from the States."

That was a good point. Maybe I *could* go to one of those places.

"And traveling alone is not a big deal at all. It's actually really fun to talk to other people at the places you visit. I still keep in touch with some of the people I've met on planes and boats."

My spirits dropped again. Never mind; I totally couldn't do that.

"Bailey, can I ask you a question?"

"You already did," I murmured, gathering the wrappers and empty jelly cups to throw in the trash later. "In fact, you do that allllll the time. It's getting annoying."

"Funny." He stacked the jelly cup he just emptied onto my pile. "I want to know something; will you answer honestly?"

"I'm always honest."

Tanner raised an eyebrow.

"I am! Well, now I am."

He leaned back in his seat. "Have you given any thought to traveling alone, like we talked about?"

"You know what? I think *you* have given way too much thought to this. Why does it matter if I go anywhere or not? Why do you care?"

Tanner watched me for a while, his face thoughtful. "I care about you."

I couldn't look at him. My hands in my lap were fascinating.

"And this is important to you," Tanner went on. "I just think that sometimes things sound impossible when we think about them, but if we try, we realize we can do more than we think we can."

"Maybe," I mimicked his solemn tone and waggled my head all sassafras. "I'm just waiting for the American flag to pop up behind you and start waving."

Tanner shook his head and reached for another jelly cup.

"Do you even like those things, or are you just eating to eat? Also, you have, like, a boatload of crumbs in your beard." I resisted the temptation to brush his face. "Are you saving those for later?"

Tanner shook his head like a dog trying to get dry. I covered my face to protect against the rain of cookie crumbs.

"You are always hating on my beard." He stroked his beard like a cartoon villain. "Maybe you would like beards better if you grew one."

"Did you just say that out loud?"

"Yes, I did."

"You are such a weirdo." I silently added, "with a beardo". Then I said, "To be honest, the beard is growing on me."

He stopped stroking, his eyebrows jumping to his hairline. "Really?"

"Maybe." I shrugged as I stirred the Pocky around in their container; they made a cool tinkling sound. "Don't let it go to your head."

"I won't," he said solemnly.

"So, is this finished? Or do you have more up your sleeve?" I waved my pretend passport in the air.

"This is all I got." He snatched the passport to stamp Haiti, since he hadn't done it at the Hermanes' house. He checked his watch as he handed it back. "It's almost ten. What do you have going on tomorrow? Do you want to go home now?"

"I just need to be at Froyo by one."

"Do you want me to take you home?" Tanner asked again.

"Do you *want* to take me home?" I narrowed my eyes.

"I asked you first."

I slapped his arm. "Okay, I see we're back in kindergarten. Sure, take me home."

Tanner grinned and headed toward home. Halfway there, I was struck with inspiration. "On second thought, have you been to Lowell?"

"The observatory? No."

"Want to? There's a bunch of pullouts on the way up Mars Hill. We can park on one and check out the city. The view is spectacular."

Tanner pursed his lips.

"What?"

"Mars Hill sounds like a make-out spot."

"Oh my gosh!" I slapped his arm again, harder this time. "You have such a gutter brain. It's a city lookout, sheesh."

I left off the part where Mars Hill actually was a pretty well-known make out spot. That was not lying. It was withholding information that had nothing to do with what we were doing. I really did want him to see the view of Flagstaff from the hill.

No ulterior motives.

I directed Tanner to the right road and watched the city unfold until we reached the perfect spot. "Pull over here."

When Tanner looked up, his breath caught the way it had at the pond. I wasn't lying about the view. The lights of the city spread out as far as we could see, twinkling like stars. It was breathtaking.

"Was I wrong?" I asked, rubbing it in just a little.

"No," Tanner said. "You were not wrong. Thank you for bringing me here. I would be sad to miss this sight."

"You're welcome." I smiled, feeling like I'd just won a gold medal in the Olympics. "I'm glad you like it."

We enjoyed the view in relative silence. I lost track of time as I gazed at the blinking lights of the city I called home. With my head leaning against the plush seat and my belly full of yummy food, my eyelids were growing heavy.

"Bailey?"

My eyes fluttered. "I'm awake."

Tanner laughed. "Come here." He slipped his arm behind my shoulders and scooted over until I was leaning against him. "Now you can sleep."

Yeah, except, now I was totally wide awake. I was hyper aware of the feel of his flannel shirt against my cheek, the spicy smell that was just him, the way his fingers moved along the top of my arm.

Fall asleep?

Yeah, right!

I couldn't stay where I was, but I didn't want to hurt his feelings. I pulled away so we weren't touching quite so much. Tanner's arm stretched like a neck pillow behind me. "I'm not sleepy anymore. Let's talk. Tell me a story."

"About what?" Tanner sounded amused.

"About you. Tell me about you."

Tanner stopped moving; he even held his breath. After a moment, he spoke so quietly I had to lean closer to hear him. "I don't like to talk about myself."

"I noticed. Why?"

Tanner sighed. "I don't like my story."

As much as I wanted to know what he was hiding, to know if it was really that bad, I wasn't going to make him talk about it.

"It's okay, Tanner. You don't have to tell me anything."

He rubbed the back of his neck. "No, I will. I will tell you. I...want you to know. Remember when I told you guys about my family?"

I nodded.

"They are...wealthy. My life was very different before I moved here."

"Before Arizona? That sounds like a country song."

"Haha." Tanner ran his hand through his curls. "Bailey, money sucks. It changes people. It makes them care more about things than people. I...I hate it so much."

"It doesn't have to be that way," I said, thinking of my family. We were pretty well off. I mean, we weren't mansion rich, but we always had enough for needs and wants, and then plenty to share. My parents were the most generous people I had ever seen. Money didn't make them selfish; it made them kind.

"It doesn't have to, but it is that way with almost everyone," Tanner laughed, bitterly. "I was... I mean, well, my life looked perfect. I had a college degree, a successful job, a beautiful girlfriend who I was about to ask to be my wife..." Tanner trailed off.

My heart sped up in the silence. I waited for him to go on.

"Mitzi knew I was going to propose."

"Wait," I interrupted. I couldn't help it. "Her name is really Mitzi? You are kidding me, right?"

"No joke. Her name is Mitzi."

"But," I breathed, "Mitzi is, like, what you name a purse dog!"

Tanner burst out with an amazing laugh that made goosebumps appear on my arms. And, just like that, I was the funniest person in the world.

"I'm sorry," I said. "That was super rude. I'm sure she is a very nice girl, despite her name."

"You tell me if you think so by the end of the story. Our families threw a big party, so I could propose and announce our engagement to all fifty thousand of their closest friends."

"Did she turn you down?" I whispered. My mind swept into his story like I was an eyewitness to the whole thing. I could picture a Cinderella ballroom with everyone dressed in tuxedos and glimmering gowns.

Except for Tanner; he was still wearing flannel.

"No." Tanner shook, then wrapped his arms around himself. "I mean, I don't know. I never asked her. The night before the party, I overheard her talking on the phone to someone. About me. It was a total fluke. I wasn't supposed to be there; I'd come back early to surprise her. I was going to take her out to dinner and shopping for a new dress to wear to the party. She loved to do things like that."

"Who was she talking to?"

"I never found out. It doesn't matter." He took a deep breath. "She was only marrying me for the money."

"Nuh-uh!" I gasped. "How do you know that?"

"She said those exact words."

"That is so messed up! What did you do? Did you just leave?"

Tanner sighed. "I waited until she was done talking and walked into the room. I figured she would act ashamed and sorry, but she didn't. She gave me an air kiss over one shoulder and walked by me to the car, talking about dinner and the dress she was going to buy. She didn't notice anything was wrong. She didn't notice me."

"Tanner, I'm so sorry."

"It's for the best." His voice rose, gaining strength. "I confronted her and told her what I heard. She shrugged it all off, saying no one gets married for love anymore. That's why there are so many prenups and divorce lawyers." He gave a short laugh. "I think, in a way, she was right."

"No way." I sat up, turning to face him. "No stinking way. That is a load of garbage. Tons of people get married for love. She's messed up."

Tanner didn't answer, which was more of an answer than if he'd said actual words.

"Love is real." I raised my voice so it wouldn't get lost in the silence.

"Is it?" Tanner turned his eyes on me. They were bright and pained. "Is it really? I don't know, Bailey. I don't even know what it is. Explain it to me. Tell me what love is."

I blinked.

Define love? How do you do that? It was like trying to explain what salt tasted like.

Love is a feeling. It feels like love.

I had to do better than that.

My silence took too long. Tanner's eyes dimmed until they were just pain. He looked away.

I grabbed his face with both of my hands and turned it until he couldn't do anything except look at me. Our faces were so close together I could see faint freckles on his nose that I had never noticed before. "You listen to me, Tanner Banner." I choked out a laugh and then swallowed it. I couldn't help it; his name was ridiculous. I worked extra hard to get my face stern.

"Love isn't a problem you solve. There's no equation that adds up. You can't really grasp or calculate it. I can't explain it to you. But, somewhere deep inside of you, you know it exists; you know what it is. I know you do. Maybe it's buried under all the junk from your past, but it's in there somewhere. You just have to let yourself feel it."

I gasped as realization settled into place.

"Tanner! You are exactly like me! You're afraid! We're the same, just different. So, what you told me applies to you. All you have to do is decide that something—in this case, love—is worth it, and then you just do it. Or, I guess, in your case, you just let it in."

I stared into his eyes, willing him to believe and feel what I believed and felt. I held his face there for so long that I didn't notice when things shifted. Tanner's eyes dropped to my lips. I could feel the heat of his exhale. If I moved the tiniest bit forward, I could kiss him.

He could kiss me.

We could kiss.

I reeled back as that thought took full form. I scrambled to the other side of the car, my breath coming out in gasps. Though I stared intently at the steering wheel, I didn't see it. All I could see, all I could think, was the word "kiss".

Kiss.

Kiss.

We couldn't kiss!

Something would happen if we kissed. Something would change. It couldn't stay the same after that, and I didn't want things to change. I was just getting used to Tanner as a friend. I didn't know what to do with him as something else.

I buckled the seatbelt over my middle and hugged myself tight. "Dayton is probably flipping out right now. It's super late."

"I'll take you home," Tanner said, turning the key in the ignition.

Ways to Improve Bailey #20

Dethrone the Queen of Denial

I woke up to silence.

No sounds of Dayton banging around in the kitchen, no smell of bacon or pancakes. It was so eerily quiet. I laid in bed longer than I should have, wondering if I was still asleep.

I wasn't. My itchy eyes and raw throat could attest to me being fully conscious. I got up and walked to the kitchen slowly.

Dayton was gone somewhere and hadn't even left a note. That wasn't like him. It went against our house rules, but I couldn't muster enough indignation to feel angry.

I padded around the house in a stupor, pretending to clean and be busy, but in reality, I was moving to keep my thoughts from catching up to me.

I flung a dirty t-shirt across the room. I'd been using it as a makeshift duster, and since Dayton never dusted and I rarely did, it left a trail of dirt in its wake. With a noise that resembled the incredible hulk, I stomped to my room for my gym bag. I had to get out of this place.

A short bus ride later, I let myself into the aquatic center. I could see Jordan shuffling around his office. He was the only one there. I couldn't remember the last time the place was this quiet. The water was still, reflecting the ceiling like an enormous mirror. I stepped to the edge and looked down at my reflection.

The lines that defined me were a little fuzzy and melded into the water, the way an image distorts when you see it through tears. I backed away quickly. Instead of inviting me in like it usually did, the water was giving me the creeps.

Maybe this wasn't such a good idea.

I turned to leave.

"Hey, Bailey!"

I disappeared into a hug that mostly consisted of Marnie's long, wild curls.

"What are you doing here so early? You don't have lessons today, do you?" She pulled back to search my face.

I shook my head. "I just wanted to swim laps."

"Awesome! Me too! I'll race you to the locker room!" Marnie twirled around me and took off.

I followed, but slowly.

"You totally lost!" Her voice echoed off the walls when I got into the locker room.

It was all I could do to force out a half-hearted, "Aw, rats."

Marnie clanged and chattered as she changed, but I didn't register any of it. My thoughts felt so heavy; I was tired from thinking them.

I entered a stall and changed into my swimming suit, then stuffed everything else into the locker. Before I locked my phone away, I checked to see if anyone called. My heart gave a flip when I saw that I had a missed call from Tanner and two new texts.

One from Dayton.

And one from Tanner.

I sat down on the small bench before I opened the one from Tanner.

> I tried to call. I wish I could tell you this to your face, but I don't have time, and it's a bit of a story. Even a phone call would be better than a text. Since this is my only option, it will have to do. I didn't feel right leaving without telling you.

I rolled my eyes. I couldn't help it. Even in his text, I could hear him clearing his throat and stuttering.

> *I have to go back to California. I'm leaving first thing this morning, and I can't come back. I don't know any words that could describe how much I've enjoyed getting to know you, Bailey Hendrix. I wish things hadn't ended this way. I'll miss you.*

And that was it.

I read the text three times, but there was nothing more. I was used to him and his mysteriousness by now, but this was a whole new level of ridiculous.

He couldn't just be gone.

I opened Dayton's text, wondering if he might fill the gaps.

> *Where the heck are you? I went to the store to get stuff for French toast, but when I got home you were gone.*

I wondered if Dayton had talked to Tanner. Maybe he knew something I didn't. Actually, that was silly. I could just call Tanner myself. I didn't need Dayton to be my go-between. My finger hovered over the call button.

"Hey!" Marnie thumped the door of my stall with her knuckles. "Are you in there?"

"Yeah, sorry. What did you say?" I shoved my phone into the locker and closed the door with a clang.

"Just wondering if you're ready. I can't wait to get into the pool today!"

"Ready." I pinned the locker key to my swimsuit strap so I wouldn't lose it. I should have told that trick to Tanner; he was always forgetting where his locker was and losing the key.

But I guess that wasn't going to be a problem anymore. Tanner was gone.

I opened the stall door to find Marnie arranging her hair into a huge messy bun on top of her head. She looked at me curiously. "Are you okay?"

I opened my mouth, racking my brain for something to say that had just the right amount of flippancy and carelessness, but I had nothing. Finally, I sighed and leaned against the door. "No."

Marnie's hands dropped to her side. "What's going on?"

"I—"

I was interrupted by the sound of my phone vibrating on the locker shelf. I didn't waste time unpinning my key; instead, I stretched my swimsuit strap to reach the lock.

While Marnie watched, I grabbed my phone and tried to unlock it. In my rush, I typed my password incorrectly three times. The call went to voicemail before I got it right.

"Oh," I said. "It was just Dayton."

A text chimed up instantly.

> *Call me. Call me. Call me.*

I glared at the screen, focusing all of my disappointment on the poor, innocent phone. I don't know why I thought it would be Tanner. His text had been pretty final.

It didn't make any sense, though. He had almost kissed me last night, and now he was running away to California and never coming back? He didn't have to do that; he could have just told me he didn't want to be anything other than friends.

A jolt of anger went through me. Stupid Tanner and his stupid secrets. How could he leave after our date last night?

I squared my shoulders and shoved my phone back into the locker. I wasn't going to be that girl that jumped at every phone chime. It didn't matter one iota to me what Tanner did with his stupid life.

It didn't.

"Bailey?" Marnie asked gently. "Everything okay?"

"That was just Dayton."

Marnie chewed her lip. "What did he say?"

"He told me to call him. Three times."

"Are you going to?"

I shrugged, "Later, maybe."

Marnie shook her head. "You should call him now."

"Why?" I looked up in surprise.

Her cheeks went pink. "It's rude to ignore phone calls."

I put my hand on my hip. "Everybody ignores phone calls. It's, like, survival. If we answered our phones every time someone called or texted, we would never get anything else done."

Marnie thought for a minute. "True."

"Why do you care if I call my brother back?"

Her face was usually so transparent. It was taking a lot out of her to try to hide what she was thinking.

"I don't!" Marnie said, blinking rapidly for a few moments before she heaved a great sigh. "Okay, I do. I think Dayton is..." She stopped and smiled to herself.

I stared at her until she came back to reality, blushing furiously.

"We, uh, we went on a date last night." She paused. "We went out for ice cream. That's probably what Dayton wants to tell you. We wanted to make sure—. Is this okay with you?"

It took me a minute to realize what she was asking. Marnie and Dayton?

It was about flipping time!

"Of course it's okay with me. It's not like you need my permission."

"You're sure?"

"Yes," I assured her. "Dayton is my brother; therefore, I think he's half idiot, but he is a million times better than Todd."

"Aha!" Marnie pointed at me. "I knew it! I knew you didn't like Todd!"

I grabbed her finger and lightly shook it. "Duh!"

"Why didn't you just say so instead of resurrecting the word 'swell'? It took me a week to figure out whether you meant that as a good thing or a bad thing."

"That was the point," I said. "I didn't want to hurt your feelings. You were so excited to date him."

"Yeah," Marnie scrunched her eyes thoughtfully. "Although, I wish you had told me what you really thought. It's better to know the truth than to wonder."

I nodded, picking up speed as her words rang truer and truer. It was better to know then to wonder. She was totally right!

"Yeah! Hold on a sec; I need to call my brother." I got my phone back out of the locker and pushed on Dayton's number, bouncing impatiently on the balls of my feet as I waited.

"Hey, Bay."

"Hey, Day," I said. "You rang?"

Dayton sighed, "I messed up, Bailey."

Okay, so not expecting that. "What are you talking about?"

"Bailey," Dayton said, "I love you. I was tired of watching you coerce weirdos, creepers, and deadbeats to take you out to dinner."

"Um…"

"I was trying to help, but I went about it the way wrong way. I realize that now. I messed up with you. I guess I've gotten into a habit of looking at you with a critical eye. It's like what Mom used to say when we were little: when you look for something, you'll find it. There are a lot of things that you need to improve, sure, but that's the same for me and everyone."

"Dayton, where the heck is this coming from?"

"I told you. I was thinking about it last night. After my date with Marnie. She told you about that?"

"Yeah."

"Yeah, well, I had a moment where I saw myself, and what I saw was not good. I've been a beast. You're right about me. I'm an idiot."

"Dayton—"

"No, it's true. I'm sorry I made that list. I'm sorry I've been a pain. I'm sorry I forced you into going out with Tanner."

I cleared my throat. "Why are you sorry about that?"

"Did you know he's gone?" Dayton asked slowly.

"He texted me this morning."

"Did he tell you he's not coming back?"

"That's what he said. So what?"

Dayton spoke intentionally. "You don't care?"

"Why should I?" I forced the words past the blasted lump in my throat.

"Bailey," Dayton said, his voice full of sympathy, "it's okay for you to feel something about it. I know you like him."

"Whatever."

"Where are you?" Dayton asked.

"At the pool. I was going to swim laps."

"Are you there alone?" His voice took on that stern tone he always used. Then he laughed. "Sorry, this is going to take some getting used to."

"It's okay, and no, I'm not alone. Marnie's here."

"Oh?" Dayton's voice perked up. "I'm going to come over."

That sounded like the same old Dayton, except he added, "Is that okay?"

"Yes, you weirdo, come over."

"Awesome! See you soon."

I said good-bye and hung up, locking my phone back in the locker before turning to Marnie. "Dayton's coming over to hang out with us."

Marnie's smile lit up the room and the hall and the pool area as we walked through each one. I wanted her to have that moment of excitement and giddiness all to herself, so I assured her that I was totally fine.

I was fine.

It wasn't a big deal that Tanner left. People leave all the time. So what? I had plenty to think about without Tanner taking up space in my head. Classes, lessons, work—tons of stuff. So, he was gone. So, what?

I dived right into the pool and started laps, pushing myself harder than I usually did. The burn in my legs and lungs felt so good that I kept going, even when I realized Marnie wasn't in the pool with me. She was probably waiting for Dayton to show up before she swam so she could talk to him.

I swam five more laps and turned to start another when I saw Dayton waving me down from the side of the pool. I kicked over to the side and held on with one hand while I pulled out my ear plugs.

"What?" I called.

Dayton pointed. "Jordan wants to talk to you."

I reluctantly climbed out of the water. I wrapped three towels around myself and walked to his office.

"You're not working this morning," he said without turning from his computer screen.

"Nope, just swimming," I said.

"And," he continued, his fingers clicking the keyboards like he was playing the notes of a song, "what about this afternoon?

"I have a lesson—" I stopped. No, I guess I didn't now that Tanner was gone.

Jordan turned around slowly, his feet moving over each other like a complicated dance move. He started talking and waving his hands, but I couldn't hear a word he said.

Tanner was gone.

He wasn't coming back.

I wasn't sure why it took so long for that to really sink in, but there we were, reality and me.

And if that wasn't enough, reality hit me with one more thing. It knocked me upside the head, actually.

I gasped.

"What?" Jordan interrupted himself, looking irritated. I'm sure he was giving me a really well-planned lecture about drumming up more business or losing my job. I totally hadn't heard a word.

"I love him," I whispered.

"Come again?" Jordan leaned forward.

"Oh my gosh!" I put both of my hands on my flushed cheeks. I was emitting enough heat to bake a casserole. Why had I not seen this before?

I was in love with Tanner.

I tried to argue that I hadn't even known him that long. He was scruffy and a horrible dresser and way too reserved. In fact, if there was a picture and description posted somewhere of my type, he would be the exact opposite. But I couldn't convince my heart that any of that mattered.

I turned on my heel and sprinted from Jordan's office without looking back. "Dayton!" I shrieked as I skipped over puddles.

"What?"

I slipped across a small patch of water that I probably made when I got out of the pool. I flailed for a moment I, then I grabbed Dayton's arms to steady myself.

"What's wrong?" he asked, his eyes full of concern.

Marnie stood up next to him, her hands reaching for me like she wanted to do something but didn't know what I needed.

I shook my head, trying to put together words that made sense, but my thoughts were too scattered.

"Bailey?" Dayton shook me slightly. He wasn't very patient.

"Tanner," I gasped, choking on the word. "I am totally in love with Tanner!"

Dayton and Marnie's arms dropped to their sides, as though they were attached to strings and the marionette suddenly let them go.

"That's adorable!" Marnie clasped her hands under her chin. "I knew it the minute Tanner tried your cheesecake, vanilla, chocolate, and strawberry concoction. It was a perfect match!"

I decided to let her have it. If it meant that Tanner and I would end up living happily ever after, I would attribute our forever love to our yogurt tastes.

Dayton just looked at me. I searched all over his face for some expression that would tell me what he was thinking, and finally I caught it: that tiny dimple in the corner of his mouth. He nodded as a full smile broke out over his face.

"I knew it!" he said, crossing his arms.

I think it says a lot about how much I've improved, that I didn't take that moment to argue the fact. He could think he knew it all along if he wanted. I didn't care. I just needed to find Tanner and tell him I loved him. Now that I realized the truth, the words refused to stay inside of me. Tanner needed to know. I had to talk to him right away.

"What do I do?" I asked, slightly desperate. Tanner was gone, and he wasn't coming back.

Dayton tapped his top lip. I waited impatiently while he considered, wishing I could see his thoughts. The easiest thing to do would be to simply call Tanner on the phone, but that seemed so lame. Plus, I wanted to see him. I wanted to see his face when I told him. Maybe he would smile, crinkling his eyes with those wrinkles I totally loved. Maybe he would close the space between us and—

"I got it!" Dayton lifted a finger into the air.

"What?" Marnie clung to his arm, digging her fingers into his skin in anticipation. It must not have hurt, though, because Dayton didn't flinch as he made his grand announcement.

"You gotta go to California, girl!"

Ways to Improve Bailey #21

Face the Fear

"It's perfect!" Dayton went on, not noticing the look on my face. If he had, it would have totally burst his grand-idea bubble. I couldn't go to California; I'd never been there before. I didn't know my way around at all. I couldn't drive there alone.

There had to be other options.

Maybe Dayton could go with me? Or Marnie? Even as I thought it, I knew there was no way Dayton could take time off, and I couldn't ask Marnie. She would drop everything to go with me; I knew she would, but then she'd be way behind when we got back.

My parents?

No. They would ask so many questions. And it seemed weird to show up to declare my love for Tanner with my mommy and daddy in the car.

Who else?

Keith needed to be at Froyo.

And just like that, I was out of options.

I had to drive to California alone.

How could I do that? Not only was I terrible with maps and directions, but suddenly my brain was flooded with all the stories I had ever heard about California traffic. In my frantic state of mind, the stories sounded like the types of tales people tell around campfires with flashlights illuminating their freaky faces.

I tuned back in just in time to hear Dayton say, "I'm sure Tanner feels the same way."

Wait what? I blinked as his words sunk it. It hadn't occurred to me until that moment that Tanner might not feel the same way about me. I sat heavily on the bottom bleacher. All my light and giddiness transformed into darkness and despair, just like that.

This wasn't going to work.

Tanner left me behind without even saying good-bye. Texting did not count. He must not feel the same way about me. I couldn't drive there alone just to have him reject me. It was way too risky. There were so many ways for this to go wrong.

Tanner chose to leave. It's not like he would come back just because I said I loved him. Even Disney movies couldn't convince me that that was possible. There was no point in telling Tanner anything; he left without even trying to see me. That was a pretty good sign that I didn't mean anything to him.

I groaned and folded over, resting my forehead in my palms.

Marnie sat next to me, rubbing my back in circles.

"What's the problem?" Dayton stood in front of me. All I could see were his dorky, laceless tennis shoes. "There's tons to do; come on! Get up! We have to get you ready to go!"

I shook my head.

"Why not?" He crouched down until his face was level with mine. "What's going on, Bay?"

I flopped my hands down so I could look Dayton in the eye. "I can't."

"What?" Dayton asked. Judging by the shape of his eyebrows, he was honestly confused.

I sighed. "I can't go to California."

"Why not?"

I should have been flattered that Dayton didn't get it. Maybe I came off a whole lot more confident and capable than I felt.

"Dayton, I am totally scared. What if he doesn't love me back? What if I take a wrong turn, end up in Mexico, offend some authority figure, and rot in jail? I can't do it." I said all this in a rush, and then held my breath.

"Pfffft!" Dayton flung his hand like he was swatting a fly.

I'd just confessed my soul's deepest secret, my source of shame and patheticness, and he'd just blown it to smithereens with a well-placed raspberry.

"Listen to me." Dayton sat on his rear end, shifting around while he crossed his legs. He took my dangling hands in his and looked deep into my eyes, completely still. "Get over yourself."

Marnie squeaked.

"Excuse me?" I blustered. I tried to pull my hands out of his, but he held them in a firm grip.

"I'm serious, Bailey." He tugged me closer until I would look him in the eyes again. "You make all these excuses for why you can't do this or that. You never try anything that scares you because you give up before you start. I've been waiting almost nineteen years for you to realize what I've known since mom and dad brought you home from the hospital."

"What?" I barely breathed.

"That you were the ugliest baby I had ever seen."

"Dayton!" I freed one hand to smack him across the shoulder.

Marnie tsked, shaking her curls at us.

"No, really; you were disgusting. I had no hope for you until you were about five."

I rolled my eyes, done with this conversation. Dayton captured my hands again and held them both tightly.

"Aren't you even going to ask what happened next?"

"No," I said.

At the same time, Marnie said, "What happened?"

Dayton smiled at Marnie, then turned his lowered eyebrows on me and my bad attitude. "When you were five, you wanted to ride a big bike like I did, but dad thought you were too little. So, when no one was looking, you sneaked—is it sneaked or snuck?"

"Sneaked," Marnie said.

At the same time, I said, "Snuck."

"Anyway," Dayton continued, "you went outside when no one was paying attention, rolled my bike out of the garage, and taught yourself to ride it. Like an hour later, mom realized you weren't in your room napping, and we all freaked out trying to find you. Then came Baybee, strolling through the front door, covered in scrapes and blood, with the biggest grin ever. The only thing that would have made that moment cooler would have been if there were fireworks and a marching band wearing those really groovy hats following behind you."

"Shut up," I laughed.

Dayton tugged until I looked at him again. "The point is, Bailey, at that moment I knew something that made me super proud and scared the socks off me."

I took pity on him and his dramatic pauses this time. "What was that, Dayton?"

"You can do anything you put your mind to. Bailey, I messed up *hard* if by trying to improve you I made you think there's something wrong with you. There's not. You are fearless."

He finally let my hands go. I stared into my palms, feeling prickles behind my eyes.

Was that true?

"So," Dayton said, lowering his voice, "what you need to decide is, how important is Tanner to you? Is he worth driving to California? Even if he doesn't want you back? Even if the whole thing blows up in your face? Even. If?"

"This is completely crazy," I murmured to myself as I pulled onto I-17. Headed South. To Phoenix. To loop 303, and then I-10 to the 85 to I-8. To San Diego.

By myself.

Butterflies had long since given up fluttering like ballet dancers in my stomach; they were rocking out to heavy metal in there. I kept telling them they'd get arthritis from all that head banging, but they couldn't hear me over the music.

I glanced at the passenger seat where I'd set the notebook Dayton helped me prepare. It had a hand-drawn map that I'd labeled after studying

Google maps for a solid twenty minutes. It also had a list of phone numbers, possible phrases if I took a wrong turn and was stopped by border patrol for some reason, and a dorky drawing of Dayton and Marnie smiling at me with their thumbs in the air.

It was all ridiculous, but it made me feel so much better.

"This is for Tanner," I whispered one last time, then I put on an audio book with the hopes that my mind would become so absorbed in Jane Austen, I would forget to be afraid.

I can't say the drive was completely fearless. For the sake of my pride, I'll just admit to losing whatever it was I ate for lunch in the ditch at a semi-truck pull off. But when the highway divided into five lanes to prepare for California traffic, I did feel more confident.

A few miles later, when the ocean came into view for the first time, my insides filled up with excitement like an overinflated bullfrog.

I just drove to California all by myself!

What-what!

If I didn't have such an important mission, I would have gone straight to the ocean. It winked at me between buildings, teasing me into wanting to see more. Bigger than my desire to see the ocean in real life for the first time, however, was my desire to see Tanner.

So, I kept driving.

For probably the first time in recorded history, I was glad for heavy traffic. The stop-and-go gave me lots of opportunities to review the directions to Tanner's house that Dayton got from a buddy of his. I knew exactly where I was going, and I knew exactly what I was going to do. I'd been imagining it the entire drive.

Now, I just had to find Tanner.

I took the next exit and turned right. I recognized landmarks from Google maps, which made me feel better; it was like I'd already been there. At the next left, I paused and pulled over.

This couldn't be right.

I pulled out my phone to call Dayton.

"Where are you?" he immediately asked when he answered his phone.

"I'm in San Diego, but there's something wrong with the address you gave me. Are you sure it's Tanner's house?"

"Pretty sure." Dayton sounded confused. "Read it off to me again."
I did.

"Weird, that's the one I have."

"Where did you get it, though?" I'd been too buzzy and fuzzy to wonder about this before. Now it was an increasingly humongous deal.

"One of my buddies works with Tanner in the math department. He's his emergency contact. Or, the other way around, anyway. That's the address he has for Tanner."

"Yeah, but why did he give his California address instead of his Flagstaff address?" Especially since Tanner didn't seem all that keen about remembering his life in California.

"I don't know." Dayton sounded worried. "Why? Is the address wrong?"

"No," I looked at the address painted on the building. "Unless his family home is an In-N-Out Burger."

Dayton groaned. "A burger sounds amazing right now."

"Dayton, focus!"

"Sorry, okay. Um, I could call Tanner?"

I shook my head even though Dayton couldn't see me. "I don't want him to know I'm here, or even get suspicious. I want it to be a complete surprise."

Dayton mumbled to himself for a minute, then came back to me. "I'm gonna call my buddy and sort this out. Lock your doors and stay wherever you are until you hear from me." He paused. "I mean, if you want to."

I hung up and tossed my phone into my purse with a groan. This amazing surprise I concocted was actually kind of stupid and not well-planned. Which was exactly why I didn't do stuff like this.

Despair and fear tried to gather for a fiesta, but I wasn't having it. I straightened my shoulders and gave myself a hard look in the mirror. I was going to see this through. I could figure it out. I'd come all this way; I was not about to give up now.

I racked my brain for people who might know something. Oh! The Hermanes! Tanner said he was really good friends with them. I pulled up the white pages on my phone and looked for Josef Hermane. I could have cried when his name came right up with the correct address and a phone number. I was so relieved that something was working. I had to dial three times; my fingers felt like bratwurst sausages.

"Hello?" Josef's voice was like music.

"Josef!" I gasped, stopping to steady my voice. "This is Bailey. Remember? I came to dinner at your house? I'm looking for Tanner. Do you know his address in California?"

"He is from California?" Josef said. "I had no idea!"

My heart very quickly went from stuck in my throat to stuck in my stomach. "I guess- I thought maybe—"

"He did call me this morning to say good-bye. A family emergency, I think he said. I don't know anything else. You cannot call him to find out his address?" Josef sounded so concerned that I wanted to put him at ease, even though I was the one who called him for help.

"I was trying to surprise him," I said, feeling like a little kid caught snitching cookies. "I'm in California now, but the address I have is no good. I'll figure it out, though."

"I am so sorry. I wish I could help. You will let me know when you find him? So I know it is all okay?"

"Of course. Sorry to bother you."

"You are never a bother," Josef said.

"Thanks, Josef. Take care."

I hung up and rolled my phone around my hands. There had to be someone who knew something about Tanner. Someone I could call. While I was thinking, I checked my voicemail. When I'd stopped for gas in Yuma, I noticed a missed call, but I'd forgotten to check it.

It was Keith. I listened to his message while I waited for Dayton to call me back.

"Hey, sis. Just wondering if you're coming in today."

Oh, swim laps! I'd completely forgotten to tell Keith what was going on! Feeling like an idiot, I called him.

"Bailey? Is everything alright? Where are you?"

I rubbed my forehead, trying to ward off a headache that had been threatening to take over for the last ten minutes. "I'm sorry, Keith. I meant to call you, but everything was all zooey. I'm in San Diego."

"What?" Keith barked.

I couldn't really blame him. There were a lot of reasons why that statement was surprising.

"Yeah, I- it's a long story. I'm trying to find Tanner." I hurriedly summarized the last few hours to bring Keith up to speed. "So, I probably won't be in tomorrow, either."

"Bailey," Keith sounded like he was still trying to catch his breath. "Well, don't you worry. Clay and I have things covered here. You just take care of yourself, okay?"

The concern in his voice tugged at my heart, still swimming somewhere in my stomach. "I will." Maybe I didn't sound all that confident because Keith's voice flipped to stern.

"What's wrong?"

I sighed deeply. There was no point in sugarcoating it. "I drove all this way to find Tanner, but the address I have is for a restaurant. Dayton's asking around, but I'm not sure what to do now."

I heard tapping on the line; I could almost see Keith with his glasses moving rhythmically against the countertop at Froyo. It made me slightly homesick, but not enough to turn around and go home.

"I guess I could try calling country clubs." I said. "Tanner said his family is rich. There can't be that many, I'll just call them all. Someone might be able to tell me something,"

Keith still didn't answer. He just continued with the tapping, so I kept babbling. It made me feel better to believe I had options.

"I could also go to the beach. Tanner loves the ocean. He might be there."

"Okay, sis," Keith said in a rush. "I don't know if I'm doing right here, but I can't let you wander around San Diego looking for Tanner when you obviously have no common sense."

"What?"

"Walk all the beaches? Honestly," he mumbled to himself.

"What else am I supposed to do, Keith? I'm not coming back until I find him."

"Yes, yes," Keith said, taking a deep breath. "I can help you."

"What?" The word came out very differently this time. "How?"

Keith took a deep breath. "I know how to find Tanner."

"What?" Again, very different in tone and pitch than the other two times I said the word. "I'm in California, Keith. You know how to find him in California?"

How was that possible?

Another deep breath. "Remember when I was about to close Froyo?"

"Duh, Keith."

He was silent.

I sighed. "I'm sorry. Yes, I remember."

"Well, do you remember how it was resolved?"

"Yes," I tried to keep my voice level. Why was Keith dragging this out? It had nothing to do with anything. I needed information about Tanner, not Froyo. "The landlord sold, and the new owners lowered the rent."

"Exactly," Keith said, sounding satisfied. I, however, was not.

"Exactly what?"

"Haven't you been listening? Tanner bought Froyo. I have his information because he owns the store." Keith chuckled. "Actually, the whole shopping center."

I blinked, realizing that my mouth was hanging open. Tanner bought Froyo?

"How is that possible?"

"Well, now, his company bought it." Keith said. "You sound confused. Weren't you listening when I told you all this?"

"I don't know." I blinked slowly. Was this real life? Everything that had happened in the last twelve hours felt like a weird dream. "How could he buy Froyo? Why?"

Keith chuckled. "I should think that was obvious. But since it isn't to you, I'll ask you the same question. Why do you think he did?"

"I don't know? Because he has a crush on vanilla yogurt with strawberries?"

"Ah, now, you can do better than that."

I blew out a puff of air. "Because nowhere else in Flagstaff would let him sit in a corner booth all day?"

Keith grunted.

"Because saving Froyo was important to us?"

"To you," Keith said. "Because saving Froyo was important to you. I would be just fine if this place closed. We've had a good run, but there will come a time when it's over, and I'm just fine with that. You, on the other hand, put so much into keeping us open. I don't know if I'm right in saying so, but I think that boy would do just about anything to make you happy."

"Can I have his address, please?" I had to concentrate to keep my voice steady.

I could hear Keith shuffling around. "It's uh...hang on." The phone tapped as though it had been set down. I tried not to bite my nails to nubbins while I waited. I grabbed a pen and the notebook from its place in the passenger seat, so I was ready when Keith was.

"Here it is. It doesn't look like a residence though. This must be his company address." He rattled off the address, repeating it once and then commanding me to repeat it back to him. When he was satisfied that I had it correctly, his voice grew tender. "Go get him, sis. This one is worth fighting for."

I thanked him and hung up. Then I pulled the address up on the map app. It wasn't far but it was now past office hours. Tanner wouldn't be there.

What should I do?

My eyes lingered on the phone number for Tanner's office. I didn't have a lot of confidence that Dayton would be able to track down Tanner's home address in Cali considering how Tanner didn't tell anyone anything.

I could just call the office and see what happened. Maybe they had a receptionist there that could help me.

An irrational part of me hoped Tanner would pick up the phone. I know it was silly, but it would sure make this whole tracking him down thing infinitely easier. I pressed the number and held my phone to my ear.

"Banner Enterprises. How may I direct your call?"

Wait – they were open?

Okay, so I didn't actually think anyone would answer. Words gathered in my throat, making me choke on them instead of saying them.

"Hello?"

"Um, hi!" I said, and then my mind went blank.

"Yes? Are you there?" The voice kept the same perky tone that could only be achieved by someone who was getting paid a butt ton to be friendly.

"Yes, I'm sorry." I stammered. "I know this is a weird request. I'm a friend of the Banners and I want to surprise them. Is there any way I could get their home address?" I cringed. There was no way this was going to work.

"Oh, I'm so sorry. I can't give out that information."

My heart sloshed into my belly. "I guess I knew that. It's just, I'm in love with Tanner Banner, and he left so fast that I didn't get a chance to tell him how I feel, and I drove all the way here." I was just babbling now, surely making it worse. My pathetic meter was off the charts. "Anyways, I'm really sorry I bothered you."

"Wait! Don't hang up!"

"I'm here," I said.

"Okay, I really can't give out their home address, but I will tell you that the Banners use the Merry Maids home cleaning service. They have for years. The owner is a friend of the family. She might be able to help you."

Something like hope swept through me. "Oh, my gosh. Thank you so much!"

"Good luck. Her name is Nancy."

I said thank you and hung up. With trembling fingers, I searched for Merry Maids on my phone and found a phone number. This time, when someone answered, I was ready.

"Hi, I'm looking for Nancy."

"This is."

I took a deep breath. "Hi, Nancy. Do you have a minute?"

"Depends. Is this a telemarketer?"

I laughed and shook my head. "No, but it's kind of a story. I don't want to take a bunch of your time."

"Intrigued."

That sounded like a go-ahead if I ever hear one. "My name is Bailey Hendrix. I met Tanner Banner…"

"Now, hold on. Did you say Tanner?"

"Yes, I met him when he was living in Flagstaff- "

"Is that where he's been?"

"Yes," I swallowed. "He's my friend. I mean, I love him, and he left this morning before I could tell him that. I need to find him. His company said they couldn't give me their home address, which I totally understand, but they said you might."

There was a long, excruciating silence. After the interruptions, it was kind of hard to handle.

"I *am* a friend of the family," Nancy said, almost to herself. "I've known Tanner since he was in my daughter's preschool class. I love that boy."

"So do I." My voice cracked.

I could feel Nancy's smile through the phone. "I believe you do. I think you're alright, Ms. Bailey Hendrix. I'll help you out."

I almost cried.

Like, almost burst into tears, ugly cried, right there in the In-N-Out parking lot.

"Thank you," I said. "Thank you so much."

Nancy rattled off an address, and I wrote it down, not trusting my memory. I read it back to her, and she confirmed it was right.

"You let me know what happens, will you? That boy is like my son."

"I will."

I said good-bye and hung up, then texted Dayton that I had an address. He tried to call me right away, but I let it go to voice mail. My emotions were way too close to the surface to talk to him right now.

I took a deep breath and entered the address Nancy gave me into the map app. I wanted to give someone a really big high five when I saw how close I was. Literally a few blocks away, right on the coast. I didn't even have to get back on the freeway.

I merged back into the flow of traffic and glanced at my phone in my lap to make sure the moving dot that was me still went in the right direction. When I pulled up to the gate at Tanner's house, I was ready.

Except, I didn't know how to get through the gate.

I idled in front of it, debating what to do next. Rich people with their gates. Seriously! How is someone supposed to surprise them with a visit if they have to announce themselves?

After hemming and hawing for no small amount of time, I finally decided that the best thing to do would be to park outside the gate and walk up the driveway to his house. There was a stretch of curb behind me. I pushed the gas to park my car there, thinking I was in reverse.

But I wasn't.

I lurched forward, hitting the brakes as soon as I realized my mistake. It was then that I discovered that everything really, truly happens for a reason—even dorky things like this—because my lurch forward activated the gate. It swung open to welcome me.

Before me was the longest driveway in the history of all driveways. Right when I thought I would spend the rest of my life following this path of concrete, I came to a fountain in the center of a round-about. I parked close enough to the house to walk comfortably, but far enough away that Tanner wouldn't see Dayton's car, just in case Tanner happened to be sitting at a window pining for me.

I got out of the car and closed the door firmly. I had to stay focused on moving forward and not think about anything or I was going to lose my nerve. I could feel it. Everything about this place was intimidating. It was like it was built to repel people with its sharp corners and spiky turrets.

I rounded a corner of the walkway, almost smacking into someone.

"Excuse me," I said, backing away a few steps. I looked up from the suit to the face of a clean-cut guy with slicked-back hair. In his hand, he held a briefcase, which he promptly dropped when we crashed into each other.

"Sorry." I reached for the briefcase, but he got the handle first. I swung my arms like that's what I meant to do all along. The guy was standing right in the middle of the walkway. I'd have to push him into the shrubbery to get to the front door. I considered it, but if this was Tanner's brother or something, I didn't want to make the wrong first impression. He just kept standing there, staring at me. I glanced at the door. So close. I took a step to the side.

"Well, sorry to run into you and run, but I'm in kind of a hurry. Excuse me." I squeezed past the guy to the front door.

In just a few seconds, I would finally be able to tell Tanner how I felt. I rang the doorbell, listening to the loud chimes. They played out a song that went on for what felt like forever. I guess in a house that size, a person needed time to get places.

A short, elderly woman opened the door.

"Yes?" she said in a heavy accent. I didn't recognize it. Maybe Russian?

"Hi!" I said a little too loudly. I lowered my voice as I clasped my hands together in front of me. In a vague way, I thought this made me seem more demure. "Is Tanner at home?

"Tanner?" Her face wrinkled in confusion.

"Is this..." I looked around for house numbers but didn't see any. The address outside the gate had matched what Nancy gave me, but maybe I got it wrong. Or maybe she gave me a dummy address. "This is the Banner's house, isn't it?"

"Ah, yes." The woman's face brightened.

"Um," I chewed on my bottom lip. "I'm looking for Tanner Banner. I think this is the right house. He just got here today from Flagstaff, Arizona?"

The woman nodded. "Mr. Maxwell."

"No, um, Tanner?"

"You look for Mr. Maxwell."

"So..." I tried to pull it all together. "Tanner's name is Maxwell? Maxwell Tanner Banner?"

"Maxwell Tannen Banner."

Tannen? Did he change his name? I really hoped I had the right house and the right guy. My knees started to twitch.

"Okay, then. Is Maxwell home?" I asked. The name felt weird, like I was asking for someone I didn't know.

"He left now." She pointed down the walkway. I turned around but didn't see anyone.

My sluggish, overstimulated brain lit up with realization. It all clicked into place. Tanner didn't have any brothers. That guy I ran into just now was Tanner! Why didn't he say anything?

I turned and jogged away without another word. Only a few steps into my sprint, I realized how rude that was. I waved and called, "Thank you!"

She waved back and closed the door.

I rounded the corner, hoping with all my heart that Tanner was waiting. Relief like I'd never known before filled my soul when I saw Tanner leaning against my car, his briefcase resting on the concrete at his feet.

"Bailey," he said as I ran up to him.

During the whole drive to California, I had imagined what I would do when I finally saw Tanner again. I imagined that I would throw myself into his arms and kiss him until we both couldn't breathe.

It didn't feel like that kind of moment now that I was here. I slowed and stopped in front of him. He looked so different, like a stranger. His suit was expensive; it was well-cut and fit him perfectly. I'd never noticed that he had a body under all that flannel and denim, but now it was hard to notice anything else.

He was pretty dang hot.

But that wasn't all. For the first time ever, I could see his face without his beard in the way. His curls were all slicked back and trimmed. He was totally and completely gorgeous. I couldn't do much else but gawk at him. Marnie would flip when she saw him this way. He really did look like Zac Efron under all that facial hair.

"Tanner?" I gasped. It felt wrong to call him Tanner when he didn't look a thing like the Tanner I knew. "I mean, um, Maxwell?"

Tanner flinched, his face clouding over.

"You look so different," I went on. "I didn't recognize you."

"I noticed." His words were clipped. Even his voice sounded different. The whole experience was beginning to feel surreal. "How did you get here?"

"I drove." I gestured to the car in his driveway.

"Alone?"

I nodded.

"And how did you get *here?* I believe our house is unlisted."

"I have my sources," I said with a grin.

Tanner sighed and ran his hand through his hair. "What are you doing here, Bailey?"

My grin disappeared like someone erased it. Those were not the most welcoming words in the world.

"Where are you going?" I said, trying to regroup with my courage.

"To the office," Tanner grunted.

"This late?"

Tanner's laugh was sardonic as best. "There is no off time at Banner Enterprises."

This felt all wrong, he was all wrong, I was all wrong. But I had to do what I came here to do, despite the wrongness. I steeled myself and held out one hand, offering it to him if he wanted it.

"I drove here because I had to talk to you. I want to tell you something important." I paused for courage. "I love you."

In that moment, I realized movies were the biggest crock in the world. Here we were with the perfect setup: the sunset making the world glow pink around us, a gorgeous guy and a beautiful-if-not-slightly-rumpled girl, and a declaration of love. If we were in the movies, Tanner would have wrapped me up in his arms, gazed lovingly into my eyes, told me he loved me too, and kissed me until the sun went down.

Instead, Tanner scoffed.

The dude scoffed in my face and shook his head. "No, you don't."

That really ticked me off. Who was he to tell me who I did or did not love? He might look like a studly underworld spy, but he was still the Tanner who spilled stuff on his beard and cleared his throat when he was nervous. He had no right to act like I was ridiculous.

"Yes, I do," I said, my hands on my hips.

"No, you don't," he insisted.

"I do, too." I took a step forward.

Tanner held out both hands to stop me from coming any closer. "You don't. You love this." He waved his hands up and down his suit. My eyes followed the movement, lingering on his broad shoulders and chiseled jawline like I'd never seen them before.

Which I hadn't.

I shook myself abruptly to snap out of it. Was it suddenly kind of warm?

Tanner glared like I'd proven his point.

"No," I said. "You don't understand. I drove all the way here *by myself* to tell you I love you before I knew you looked like this."

Tanner shook his head.

"Stop telling me what I know, you butthead!" I yelled, taking another step forward. His hands shot back up, hovering in front of my shoulders.

I had reverted to potty names again. It wasn't my proudest moment, but I was seriously coerced.

Tanner swooped to pick up his briefcase and strolled by me to some kind of fancy convertible parked in the driveway. I'd been so focused on finding him that I hadn't noticed it when I drove up. It was black and sleek and dangerous looking.

I missed his beat-up, old truck.

And the flannel.

But, if anyone asked, there was no way I was going to admit that part about the flannel.

Tanner eased into the driver's seat and flipped on some sunglasses. He started the car and backed up to where I stood.

"Go home, Bailey," he said to the rearview mirror. At least, I think that's what he was talking to since he sure as sneakers wasn't looking at me. Without another word, he turned the wheel and roared away.

Literally leaving me in the dust.

Or exhaust.

Or whatever.

I coughed.

What the heck was I supposed to do now?

Ways to Improve Bailey #10

Do one thing at a time

I resisted the urge to throw an egg at Tanner's house.

I didn't do it for two reasons. One, I obviously had zero eggs with me. And, two, throwing one would have been the equivalent of throwing a tantrum.

And I didn't do that anymore.

I also resisted the urge to collapse in my car and bawl, call Dayton and rant, and stick my tongue out at Tanner's taillights.

Because I was better than that.

I shifted my weight to one leg and rested my hand on my hip to help me think.

There was no denying that Tanner was acting like a stink brain, but I sort of got why. It must have been difficult for him to come home and jump back into the world he avoided when he'd transformed into a flannel-clad hobbit. So, I wasn't going to let my first incredibly sad and pathetic attempt at declaring my love for him stop me from doing it again. I was not going to give up on us before we even got started.

There was a way to make this work; I just had to find it.

I walked to the fountain and sat on the edge, looking into the water. It was hard to see in the dusky light, but I thought there were coins in the bottom. I fished through my pockets until I found a penny. I kissed it and threw it into the water.

There.

Now what?

I trailed my fingers through the water while I considered my choices. As much as I hated to admit it, Dayton was right when he insisted that I book a hotel. Back at home, I was having trouble thinking past the moment when I would see Tanner and declared my love for him. But now, after seeing how that turned out, I was grateful to have somewhere I could go and regroup.

That was probably the best thing to do.

Just go to the hotel and regroup.

And eat.

Eating was a good idea. With the adrenaline wearing off, I was starving. I'd go to the hotel, order room service, get a good night's sleep, and come up with a brilliant plan that would hammer through Tanner's big, stupid, hard head.

I flicked droplets of water from my fingers and stood up just as the headlights of an approaching vehicle caught me.

For half a second, I thought it was Tanner coming back to apologize.

Then, this bright pink convertible with a license plate that said 'hot-mama' pulled into the driveway. I waited for the car to park and for the world to get dark again before I unfroze. Trying to be stealthy, I tiptoed to my car, hoping to escape unnoticed.

No such luck.

"Well, hello." A gorgeous woman with long auburn hair and high heels that made my feet hurt just looking at them glided out of the car. "Are you the new sous chef?"

It sounded to me like she'd just sneezed. Even though I didn't catch her words, I instinctively knew that the best response to her question was probably no. I let the word slide out as I opened my door to leave.

"Wait." She held out her hand.

I paused.

"If you're not busy," she gestured to the trunk of her car, which had just eased open with the click of the button on her keys, "could you bring those in for me? Thanks." She kissed her fingers and flipped her hair over her shoulder as she walked away. Her perfectly curled locks hovered in the breeze, mocking me. I looked down at myself. Okay fine, I did look like the hired help, but still, she was making some serious assumptions here.

With a sigh, I slammed my door shut and emptied her trunk of designer shopping bags. I didn't bother closing it. My hands were full, and she had a magic button. I figured she could at least do that part herself.

I trudged back to the front door. It was ajar, so I left the three-string orchestra bell alone and pushed my way inside with the toe of my shoe. Even though I was tempted to, I refused to gawk at the entryway. I trained my eyes on a side table in the foyer and dumped all the shopping bags on it.

Without further ado, I turned and was about to leave when the girl caught my hand in a swirl of perfume and Prada. She slipped a twenty in my palm with a smile.

I looked at it. "I'm not going to take your money."

Her face widened in surprise.

"I'm not, like, a servant," I said. "I came here to see Tanner and was just leaving."

"Who, now?" Her perfect face wrinkled in ways she would probably Botox later.

I pursed my lips. "Maxwell. I came to see Maxwell. I did, and now I'm going."

"Oh, dear." Her tinkling laugh echoed from the hardwood floors to the crystal chandelier above our heads. "That is funny. Well, thank you for your help." She tried to give me the twenty again.

"I don't want your money." I held up one hand to stop her.

"You don't want the money?" She stared at me like I was a foreign thing she couldn't figure out.

"Nope." I turned to leave again.

Again, she stopped me. "Wait. You came to see who?"

"Maxwell," I sighed without turning around. The long drive and all that uncertainty were starting to catch up with me. I tried to remember his fancy name. "Maxwell something Banner." I looked over my shoulder. "I'm going to go now. It's been a really long day."

She shook her head, hair swinging like a shampoo commercial. "No, no, no! I sniff a story." She grabbed my hand and tugged me away from the door, leaving it wide open. "You come right in here and tell me everything." She let me go in front of a series of pure white couches. She sat, crossing her impossibly long legs. The anklet she wore glimmered enough to make me squint. I looked again at my rumpled jeans. I couldn't possibly sit on those couches. What if I got something on them? There could be melted chocolate stuck to my butt for all I knew.

She reached over and rang a bell that sat on the table next to the couch. A tall, uniformed man stepped into the room.

"Yes, please bring us two Evians and something to snack on. I'm famished. You?" She turned to me. My stomach grumbled in reply, causing her to smile. The man nodded and walked away without ever having said a word.

"Now," she said, patting the seat next to her, "come sit, and tell me everything."

How could I get out of this? I entertained myself with thoughts of running out of the room, but those ended with the uniformed guy dragging me back in for a chat. Whatever. It would be easier to just talk to her for a minute, then go. I dragged myself to the couch and sat primly on the edge, only after I'd swiped at my bum a couple of times.

"Start with your name," she said imperiously.

"You first," I smiled. Her commands and demands were starting to get on my nerves.

She pulled her chin inward, then laughed again. "I'm Vanessa." She held out her hand, limp at the wrist. I took it in a firm handshake and pumped it twice.

"Bailey. Nice to meet you."

Vanessa pulled her hand away, wiping it discreetly on a handkerchief she pulled from her pocket. "Bailey. So, tell me. How do you know Maxwell?"

I challenged her with my eyes. "You first."

Her smile grew tight. I don't think she liked being opposed. "He is my brother."

Ah. So this was one of his sisters. I was going to make a wild guess and assume it was the sister that was married and just had a baby, even though she totally didn't look like she'd just had a baby. The other sister was living in Hawaii, though, so that made the most sense.

"I met Tanner in Flagstaff," I said.

"Flagstaff!" She leaned against the back of the couch and crossed one leg over the other. Her bedazzled flip flop hung by a toe as she swung her top leg. "Such a quaint little town. I had no idea Tanner cared for it."

I ignored the way she made my hometown sound like a cute little puppy." "You mean, you didn't know where he was?"

She shook her head.

"But," I paused, trying to make sense, "but, my brother said Tanner got an urgent call. He came home—"

"Yes, well," Vanessa shrugged one shoulder, "Daddy hired an investigator. Maxwell wasn't easy to find. It took some time. We may not have found him at all if he hadn't purchased that shopping center. That was a bit too large to cover up," she laughed lightly.

It didn't sound funny to me. It sounded sinister.

And creepy.

Vanessa leaned forward, touching my arm. "But you haven't told me why you came all the way here. It is a bit of a drive, no?"

I wasn't about to tell her anything. Right when I'd given up on movies being reality, I found myself caught in a thriller of some kind, full of intrigue and espionage. There was no way I was sticking around until I knew what part I played in this whole mess.

Or what part Tanner was playing.

I stood up. "I'm going to go now."

"Oh?" Vanessa lounged back on the couch. "But we were just beginning."

I shook my head. "Good night."

As I turned to walk away, Vanessa's tinkling laugh made me look over my shoulder. Her eyes were on her perfect manicure, but it was obvious her words were for me.

"You know, I'd hate for you to have come all this way with unrealistic expectations. I assume you know who Mitzi is? Well, her divorce was finalized last week. She was here waiting the moment she heard Maxwell was back in town.

"How special." I made it out of the door and into the fresh air without anything more from Vanessa. I took a deep breath, tasting the salt in the breeze. It felt fantastically cool, which was a switch from the freezing temperatures I left behind in Flagstaff. As I walked to my car, I let my mind go blank. I was done analyzing; I just wanted to sleep.

I woke up the next morning bright, shiny, and starving. I flung back the covers and jumped out of bed, snagging my phone on the way to the desk. I immediately started texting like my life depended on it.

Because it did.

My love life, that is.

> *Dayton, are you up?*

> *Marnie, I need advice!*

> *Mom, how do you make friends and influence people again?*

> *Dad, what does it mean to be a multi-international hospitality company?*

> *Keith, how did Tanner buy Froyo?*

There.

Now I could sit back and drum my fingers until someone responded. I rested my cheek in my palm, resembling a toddler in time-out more than a competent adult who, if not an experienced world traveler, definitely qualified as a fear-conquering superstar.

My phone had barely finished chiming when I snatched it close to my face. Marnie was the first to respond. Just another reason why she was my very favorite person.

> *Oh good! I've been waiting for you to text. What's happening with Tanner?*

I was going to assume Marnie was all up to speed. I'm sure Dayton filled her in at some point last night. Not that he knew much; I only had the energy to text him I was at the hotel and that Tanner was a punk before I fell into bed for, like, ten hours.

> *He's all ticked at me.*

I sent the message and then pulled up the internet browser. The only other thing I had done since checking into the hotel was Google Tanner's family company. The Banners owned a huge hotel empire, apparently. Tanner, all snazzy in his suit, was featured on one of the pages. I found the page, took a screenshot, and sent it to Marnie.

> *Who's that?*

> *Tanner.*

> *Wow! He's really handsome.*

Dayton chimed in next, followed immediately by Dad.

> *Yeah, yeah, I'm up. What's going on?*

> *Interesting question, Baybee. That would be a hotel company that is all over the world.*

Okay, so maybe sending a bunch of texts rapid fire wasn't the best idea. I was going to get super confused if this kept up.

One conversation at a time. Since Marnie was first, I answered her.

> *So, here's the thing. He thinks I like him because of the way he looks.*

> But you liked him before you knew he looked this way.

> *Exactly! He doesn't believe me.*

> But you never lie anymore.

> *Could you call him and tell him all of this? :) He wouldn't listen to me.*

> Text me his number.

> *I was kidding, Marnie. I think it would just tick him off. What would you do? What should I do to convince him?*

I figured that loaded question would take her some time to think about, so I started responding to the other texts. I started with Mom this time, since she'd just barely texted, and she often got antsy waiting. If I didn't respond immediately, she would probably book a flight here.

> Oh sweetie, you don't need to influence people. Just be you!

> *Is that enough, though?*

> *Absolutely, angel. Otherwise, it's not meant to be.*

I tapped my phone against my bottom lip to help me think. What could I do that would be me, that would convince Tanner that I meant what I said? I refused to think about the alternative, the 'not meant to be' part. I was not ready to accept that yet.

I went to Dayton's text next, reread it and responded.

> *You know Tanner probably better than anyone else. How do I get through to him? He wouldn't hear a word I said last night. He just kept thinking I liked him for his moola.*

> *Does he have moola?*

> *Apparently, his family is super rich. This is the link to the article I sent Marnie.*

> *Who's the guy?*

> *Tanner.*

> *What the what?*

> *Right?*

> *What are you going to do?*

> *I don't know, Dayton! That's why I'm talking to you!*

> *Right, okay. I got it! What if you found out where he's working, barged into his office dressed like a thrift store gone bad, and smother him in kisses? Think he would believe that you don't care about looks then?*

> *Sure, we can be together after I've served my term in prison.*

> *Is it against the law in Cali if your clothes don't match?*

> *It might be.*

> *Okay, so minus the weird clothes, what if you did the rest of it?*

> *You don't think that's a little creepy? And a lot invasive?*

> *Maybe...*

My phone rang then. It was Keith.

I answered it. "Hey. Good morning."

"I hate texting on these confounded devices. It takes three times as long to have an actual conversation with someone. In my day, a phone call was considered impersonal. Now a phone call is as rare as someone showing up on your doorstep just to shoot the breeze."

"You know what else takes three times as long?" I laughed.

Keith grunted.

"Ranting about technology!"

"Yeah, yeah. So, you asked about Tanner? I don't know the answer, exactly. What I do know is that the shopping center was purchased by something called Banner Enterprises United."

So he had used his company. Did he know that buying Froyo would make it possible for his family to track him? And did he do it anyway? That had to mean something. Either he ridiculously loved frozen yogurt, or he was willing to make sacrifices to help people he cared about. I was staking my life on the second one.

My love life, that is.

"Thanks, Keith. I just wanted to check."

"Sure thing. Don't you give up on that boy. Some people are worth fighting for, even if you have to fight them. For them."

I wasn't even going to try to puzzle that out. "Okay, I will. Talk to you soon."

When I hung up, there were a bunch of new text messages. Dayton's was ginormous, so I decided to answer everyone else before I dove into his. Mom first this time.

> *You are amazing. I love you.*

> *Thanks, Mommy. Love you, too.*

Then, Dad.

> *May I ask why you asked?*

> *Dayton filled you guys in, right? I was researching Tanner's company. Thanks for clarifying.*

Then, Marnie.

> *This is tough, Bailey. I don't know what I would do. But I do know that you and Tanner are the perfect match. I saw his face when he ate that froyo I made with both your toppings. He loves you.*

A tear slid down the side of my face and dripped off my chin. Marnie was a goof, but she was my best goof. I loved her to the moon and back for telling me that.

> *Thanks, Marnie. I needed to that!*

And now, Dayton.

> *If I were you, I would do what I said and show up at his work. You don't really have to dress like a weirdo, but I think it would make a statement. Like you don't care what people think. He doesn't trust that you mean what you say. Show him that you do. You're willing to risk total humiliation for him. Think about it.*

I did and while I understood what Dayton was saying and even thought he was a little right, I didn't want to make things worse. This Tanner was different. The last thing I wanted to do was embarrass him in front of all his people.

But I could do the other thing, the showing up at his work part. Now that he knew I was here and had all night to ruminate on it, maybe he would listen better today.

I had to try.

Memories flowed through my mind like waves in the ocean. The way Tanner would look at me, how he honestly waited to hear what I would say, the way he laughed with his crinkled eyes, the times he'd held me or reached for my hand.

I was positive he loved me. I think that after what happened with Mitzi, he was scared he wasn't enough. Like, without the money, and the name, and the looks, and the suit no one could love just him. He was scared.

Well, I knew all about that feeling.

Something like hope flickered inside me. I could totally help him. I had totally just done scared, like, for seven hours in a car by myself. It wasn't easy, but I knew now that it was doable. No one else was going to be able to hurt him as much as his own thoughts.

So, my next step: Banner Enterprises.

Ways to Improve Bailey #19

Be brave

Three hours later, I stood outside the gazillion-story building that was Banner Enterprises, staring up at the glittering chrome. Even though the spotless glass on the front of the building was doing its very best to make me feel inferior, I was so not having it.

I pulled my shoulders back, tossed my head, and stepped through the revolving door.

I walked into an enormous waiting room that expanded over the entire bottom floor. There was a reception desk, those sneaky chairs that tried to trick you into thinking they were comfortable when they actually feel like you're sitting on concrete, and a whole wall dedicated to pastries and beverages.

Fancy.

As I walked across the enormous lobby to the reception desk, I caught a glimpse of myself in one of the gargantuan windows to my right. Curling my hair was a great idea. High-heeled, strappy sandals with my coral pencil skirt was an even better idea. My white t-shirt understated everything else, but it still worked.

The receptionist raised her head slowly as I approached her desk. Her dark hair was short, framing her adorable, heart-shaped face. Blunt-cut bangs gave her a look that was exotic and elegant at the same time. She quickly tucked a book under the desk and out of sight, but not before I caught the title.

"Hi!" I said with a smile that few can resist. Not because it's mine, but because smiling that big is totally irresistible. It makes people feel like the two of you are about to embark on something super awesome together, even if it's just a conversation.

"Hi," she smiled back. "How can I help you?"

"I'm looking for Tan— I mean, Maxwell Banner."

She glanced down at her lap where the book was still hidden under the desk. "Do you have an appointment?"

"No. I was hoping—"

"I'm sorry," she said, cutting me off. "Executives are available through appointment only."

The power of smiling was wearing off; I could tell by the way she avoided my eyes and droned her words like a robot.

A bored robot.

I had to do something to bring the humanity back.

"Do you like that book?" I asked, nodded to the desk.

Her eyes widened. "What book?"

I leaned forward to whisper. "The one in your lap."

Not only were her eyes huge, but they were now resigned to the inevitable. She glanced to the side. When I followed her gaze, I saw a security man leaning against the wall with his arms folded. "We're not supposed to read at the front desk," she whispered back. "But, like a dummy, I started a new book this morning, and now I can't put it down."

"Oh, I won't tell anyone," I assured her. "It's a great book. I loved it, especially the ending."

She glanced to the side again and leaned forward, her full attention glued to my face. "Don't tell me details, but I have to know: does it end happily?"

"It is completely perfect."

She sighed and pulled the book out, putting a piece of paper in to mark her place. "I can wait, then. As long as I know it all ends up okay, I can wait to read it. Thank you so much! It's so stressful trying to read at work, but I was completely sucked in." She put the book in her purse.

"I get it."

She folded her hands, one over the other on the desk and smiled at me. "What did you need again?"

"To see Maxwell Banner," I repeated.

Her face fell, truly sad for me. "I can't—"

I held up one hand. "I know. I totally know, but is there any way around it? I really need to see him as soon as possible."

I could tell by the look in her eyes that there wasn't. But she didn't want to have to tell me no again.

"What's your name?" I asked.

"Sabrina."

"Sabrina, I'm Bailey. Here's the thing. I'm not here for business, to talk about hotels or whatever. I am totally over my head, crazy in love with Maxwell. But something happened; we had a misunderstanding, and now he won't talk to me. I have to see him as soon as possible so I can explain. I drove all the way from Arizona." I clasped my hands together. "Please, is there any way at all that I can see him without an appointment?"

Sabrina's eyes were full of stars. "That is sooooooo romantic," she sighed, leaning back into her chair.

I desperately hoped that her silence meant she was trying to think of a way to help me out. Slowly, she sat up straight. With another glance at the security guard, she began writing feverishly on the notepad in front of her.

"I wish I could help you, but you can't see an executive without an appointment," she said loudly, ripping the page off and handing it to me. "Have a nice day." Her eyes widened again, looking from me to the paper in her hand. I took it, glancing at it briefly.

'Go outside before you read this' was written in big letters.

"Oh. Well, okay. I understand. Thanks anyway." I said, turning to go. I hurried back across the lobby and out the doors. I walked all the way around the corner before reading the rest of Sabrina's note.

On the south side of the building is a bakery. The executives have bagels and donuts delivered every morning. Go tell Becky that Sabrina asked you to make the deliveries, then come back. NOT THROUGH THE LOBBY, but through the south entrance. Tell the security guard what you told the bakery. Mr. Banner is on the tenth floor, office number 1007. Good luck. Text me how it goes.

And then she listed her phone number.

I tucked Sabrina's note into my purse and looked around. I've never been that great with directions, but the fates had pity on me that day. When I turned to the right, I could see the bright awning that advertised Becky's Bakery. There was no way I could have missed it.

I hurried across the street, checking for traffic, and walked inside. A bell jangled as I opened the door, reminding me of Froyo. For some strange reason, this gave me courage.

"Hi!" A young girl, probably around my age, with freckles greeted me as I stepped inside. It smelled so good, and the bright array of treats and goodies caught my eyes before I reminded myself why I was there.

"Hi! Are you Becky? Sabrina sent me from Banner Enterprises." I tried not to fidget or look like I had never done something like this before.

I could do this. I would make it work. I was determined.

"I'm Ray, but I have the order ready right here." She turned around to pick up four pale pink boxes each about the size of a cookie sheet. I stepped forward to take them from her.

"Have a nice day!" she smiled.

"You, too. Thanks so much."

That was so easy. I started to wonder if something was going to go wrong at the south entrance. But no. I got through without incident and found myself riding the elevator to the tenth floor, trying to resist the temptation to snitch a bagel. The boxes were still warm, and the smell was delectable. I knew it wasn't just me thinking that because the other people in the elevator kept looking at me enviously.

The elevator doors opened, and I walked onto the tenth floor. It was deserted except for another receptionist. This one was blond and maybe ten years my senior. She was hurriedly stamping papers with so much efficiency that I hated to disrupt her.

"Excuse me. I have the delivery from Becky's Bakery."

She looked up, but her hands didn't stop moving. It was so impressive that I would have given her an ovation if I wasn't holding a bunch of boxes. "You're new." Her tone made that sound like that was a personality defect.

I nodded, trying out that smiling thing again. "Just helping out for today."

She pursed her lips like I had mortally offended her family and her dog. "Everyone is in a board meeting. You can leave the delivery here." She gestured with her head to the edge of her desk.

No, I could not leave it right there!

I flipped through my thoughts, quickly trying to find a reason to deliver the boxes personally. "Oh, I don't mind taking them to the boardroom myself."

The woman stopped stamping to glower at me. "We do not interrupt board meetings."

I searched her eyes. Now that I had her attention, it was obvious that my romantic tale of woe was not going to make any difference to her like it had to Sabrina. She was too busy to feel it.

"Look," I said, slightly leaning against the desk, "you're busy, and these are fresh from the oven. We all know bread doesn't improve with time. Let me save you the time and the headache. I'll be in and out, so fast. I think the executives will be grateful to have warm bagels. It might even make them more productive." I winked like a goon.

Her hands had long since gone back to stamping. She eyed me thoughtfully. From the look on her face, I couldn't tell what she was going to say. It made me so nervous. As she opened her mouth to reply, the phone rang. I seized my opportunity while she was distracted.

"I'll just scooch back and drop these off, then be out of your hair," I said in a rush, taking off down the hall before she could respond. I didn't even risk a glance back over my shoulder. She wouldn't be on the phone long; an escort down the stairs with two uniformed security guys was a real possibility for me in the very near future.

Okay, now, where was I? It shouldn't be hard to find a boardroom. I passed empty offices with gorgeous views of the ocean on my way down the hall, but I barely took the time to enjoy them. At the end of the hall was a large room. As I got closer, I was relieved to see it full of people.

Without giving myself a chance to chicken out, I balanced the boxes in my hands and knocked lightly before barging in on the board meeting.

Forty eyeballs turned to stare, but I only noticed two.

Tanner was at the head of the table, standing in front of a screen with flow charts. His words choked in his throat when he saw me. As he reached for a glass of water on the table in front of him, I stepped forward, handing the bakery boxes to whomever was closest. I didn't even look to see who it was.

"Tanner." I stopped, not wanting to get too close to him.

He swallowed, setting the glass back down on the table.

"What is this all about?" A stern-looking man at the other end of the table stood up, resting his knuckles on the table. It made my hand hurt just looking at him. "Maxwell?" The steel in his eyes matched his graying sideburns perfectly.

Tanner looked from me to the man, obviously in deep dilemma.

This made me more determined. I ignored everyone else in the room, locking in on Tanner's eyes. I had come all this way and gone to all this trouble. I was going to say what I came to say. It might be my last chance to talk to him, so no holding back.

"I'm sorry to interrupt, but this is important. More important than your meeting." I ignored the gasping protests, keeping Tanner locked in my gaze. "Hear me out for just a second, Tanner. Please."

He looked down, but didn't object, so I kept talking.

"It took me way too long to realize how much you mean to me. I've been a snarky brat. I guess I thought you would always be around to patch things up, but then you were gone, and I realized how much I love you. I can't give you any proof that I won't do stupid things or be stubborn and selfish and sarcastic ever again, but I can tell you this: I love you. I fell in love with you before I knew this part of your life, when you looked like a hobo from the Shire. I love you because you are thoughtful. You're kind to everyone, no matter what they look like, what they do for a job, or how old they are. How I feel has nothing to do with the suit, the car, or the money." I scoffed. "Dude, my family has tons of money. I don't need yours. I'm not asking you for anything except a chance to show you that I'm telling you the truth."

I stopped then. There was so much more I wanted to say, but I had a vague sense of people stirring around the room and the word "security" was being tossed around. My time was rapidly running out.

Tanner's red-rimmed eyes rose to mine.

"Maxwell!" the older man barked. "This is completely unprofessional! We are in the middle of a meeting."

Tanner blinked, breaking his connection with me. He moved slowly, like he was just waking up from a dream. He looked at the man, but he spoke to me.

"Miss, I am going to have to ask you to leave."

My heart sank.

That was all he was going to say after I laid my heart on his flawless boardroom table? If only I knew for sure what was going on in his head. I mean, his words were against me, but the look in his eyes... It was pain in the rawest form. He looked like a trapped animal.

Tanner needed me.

I knew he did even if he didn't know he did. I had to do something to get him out of this room, away from these people.

I rummaged through my purse. "I apologize. I must have walked into the wrong room," I laughed, airily. "I'm such a ditz sometimes. Do you validate?" I pulled out the parking receipt I'd gotten from the parking garage.

My heart lifted when a ghost of a smile tickled the corner of Tanner's lips. "We do. If you'll come with me, I'll get the stamp from my office."

The older man, whom I assumed was Tanner's father, blustered from his place at the end of the table. "Surely Ms. Burns can take care of a validation!"

Tanner shook his head. "I'm sorry. This one needs my attention. Please excuse me," he said to the board. He and his power suit walked around the table, passed me, and went out the door like he couldn't wait another second to be free.

I gestured to the bagels that were still sitting in some woman's lap, where I'd set them earlier. "You might want to dig into those while they're fresh." I closed the door behind us.

I followed Tanner down the hall and around a corner to office number 1007. He stood in the doorway until I walked through, and then he closed the door behind us. Because I wasn't quite ready to look in Tanner's face, I moved to the ginormous window to gawk at the view. The ocean stretched as far as I could see. It was completely breathtaking.

"Bailey," Tanner said softly, almost like he was talking to himself. I turned around, he was still standing in front of his office door with his back to me and his hand on the knob.

I heaved a dramatic sigh. So, it was up to me. Again. Why was I always the one who had to be the grown-up? I wasn't mature enough for this much drama.

I covered the distance between Tanner and me in just a few steps, reaching out a hand to touch his shoulder. I could see the muscles tense as I made contact. With no warning, Tanner turned around and wrapped his arms around me, crushing me into his chest.

I leaned into him, listening to his heart pound for a moment before his hands were all tangled up in my hair. He tilted my face upward until he could see me fully. His eyes locked in on mine as he lowered his head. I closed my eyes at the exact moment his lips met mine.

There was no more Tanner, and there was no more Bailey. Somehow, in the few seconds that had passed since I touched his shoulder, we had molded into the same person. I could feel all of Tanner's conflict, his regret, his uncertainty, and, was that hope?

It was the hope that got to me. Tears made their way down my cheeks until I could taste the saltiness on our lips. He filled my heart so thoroughly that I thought it would burst.

Tanner pulled away first, resting his forehead against mine.

"I am such an idiot," he said, his breath tickling the top of my nose.

"Uh, yeah you are."

Tanner's laugh felt like I was wrapped up in a warm blanket next to a fire. He pulled me closer, even though I wouldn't have thought that was possible. His chin grazed the top of my head. "Will you forgive me?"

As much as I hated to do it, I leaned away from him so that I could see into his eyes. "There is nothing to forgive. We've both done and said stupid things. I meant it a few weeks ago when I told you it's not a big deal when we mess up, Tanner. But—and this is a big but—you have to talk to me, dude, so we can figure things out together. Right?"

He blew out a large puff of air. "Right."

I smiled, snuggling back under his chin. The sound of his heartbeat was like home.

"So, talk." I leaned into him as he rubbed my back. "Tell me everything that happened since I saw you last. Don't leave anything out."

Tanner chuckled, but he followed my instructions exactly.

He told me about the phone call he got from his dad, insisting he come home. When he refused, his father threatened to turn Froyo and the shopping center into a hotel. Tanner knew then that he was trapped; he couldn't stay and let that happen. He had to go. So, he drove home, and from the moment he walked through the door of his childhood home, he said he was like a puppet on a string.

His mother took him to the salon for a shave and a style that cost more than the monthly rent on his room in Flagstaff. His father had a closet full of new suits waiting. His sister filled him in on all the family gossip and told him everything he never wanted to know about all their friends and neighbors.

Tanner told me that it felt like his will was being drained away with each minute that passed. He was stuck; he had to do what they wanted. He realized that he could assume another identity and go hide out in another city, but he couldn't bring himself to do it. He just wanted to go back to Flagstaff, sit in the corner at Froyo, and watch me all day long.

I smiled at this.

And then I frowned when Tanner told me that his mother, not twenty minutes after he arrived home, had informed him that Mitzi married a stock trader three months after he disappeared. But, good news, she was recently divorced. It was obviously meant to be.

I scowled into his shoulder. "Yeah, your sister told me the same thing."

"Vanessa? When did you talk to her?"

I groaned. "Last night, after you left me in the dust. She totally made it sound like you and Ditzy were going to give it another shot."

"Mitzi." Tanner chuckled, pulling me even tighter to him. "Don't you know, I was obsessed with you from the moment I walked into Froyo and saw you duking it out with Keith about something he wanted you to do. You were so real. As much as I tried to keep it from happening, my world has revolved around you for almost a year."

"Hey," I said, leaning back to look at him, "how did you stay off your family's radar for that long? Vanessa said they hired a P.I. and everything."

"Oh, you know." Tanner waved his hand.

I gave him a look. As if I was going to be satisfied with just a hand wave.

"Okay, okay. One of the guys on the sales team is a buddy of mine. I helped him out in a tough spot a few years ago. Anyway, when I left, I set it up to fulfill my responsibilities to the family business through him. I couldn't stay, but I didn't want to leave them in a tight spot, either. I'd send my work to him, and he'd send it to my father. That's why I was always at Froyo, using the Wi-Fi. I thought I'd be less traceable."

"Then you bought Froyo."

"How'd you find out about that?" Tanner's eyes widened in genuine surprise.

I smiled and tossed my head. "I told you I have my sources."

"Keith caved, didn't he?"

"Yeah. He took pity on me. The address Dayton found was an In-N-Out. What's that about?"

"Just...covering my tracks," he sighed heavily. "It doesn't matter now. They found me, and I had to leave."

"Without talking to me, other than that lame text? Why didn't you say good-bye?" I whispered into his chest.

"Bailey." He tipped my chin to look at him. "I couldn't. I couldn't stand the thought of never seeing you again. I had to get out of Flagstaff before I changed my mind. You and I would never work. It's a different world in Flagstaff. You know. You met my family, my father and Vanessa..." Tanner sighed. "We can never make this work."

I didn't miss his switch from past to present tense, and it seriously ticked me off. I took his face between the palms of my hands. "We're not trying to make anything work with *them*!" I said, bumping his forehead with mine a couple of times to make my point. "This is between me and you. So, tell me. What does Tanner Banner want?"

"You." He didn't even hesitate. "But it isn't going to work, Bailey."

"It has to." I said.

Tanner's voice shifted like he was talking to a toddler. "That's not how real life goes."

I tossed my head. "You said you believe in Marnie's froyo matchmaking skills. She told me we are the perfect match."

A smile wiggled through Tanner's lips before it disappeared into a frown. "I really wish it were that easy."

"Well, maybe it could be if you weren't giving up before you even try."

Tanner blinked. Very slowly, I saw something spark in his eyes, like the sun rising over the San Francisco peaks.

I let go of his face and stepped back so I could see him all the way. "I know we can figure this out, you goober, but before we go any further down this road, I have to know if I'm what you really want. I don't think this is going to be easy, and I don't want to constantly wonder if you're going to disappear on me."

"Why would you think that?" Tanner asked, hurt punctuating his words.

I paused, feeling all the emotions from the last couple days gathering in my throat. "I went through crap to get here, and when I saw you last night, you acted like you hated me."

"Bailey." Tanner tugged the ends of my hair gently. "It wasn't you. Well, not really. I mean—"

"If you clear your throat, I'm going to slap you."

"I'll try to refrain."

I touched the smile wrinkles that gathered around his eyes.

"It threw me off, you being there and calling me Maxwell the way you did."

"Speaking of getting thrown off!" I protested. "You didn't look a thing like Tanner. Where did Tanner come from anyway? It's not your name at all."

"Nancy. She's like a second mom to me- "

"I met her, actually. That's how I found your address."

Tanner's eyes widened. "You're going to have to explain that later. I can't fathom how you connected all those dots."

"Later. Go on."

"Nancy used to call me Tanner when I was little. I always liked it."

That made sense. Nancy was getting a big high five from me as soon as we were done here. "I like it, too."

"But," Tanner pressed his lips together, "last night you made such a big deal about how different I look. You should have seen your face. It was like a kid in a candy store."

"Very cliché," I said.

"Yes, but true." His voice was edged with uncertainty. "I think being around my family brings out the cynic in me. It starts to feel like people only want me for how I look and what I can do for them. For that one minute last night when you first saw me, it seemed like you were only interested in me because of the way I looked."

"Well, yeah," I said, "you're totally hot."

Tanner pulled back to see my face. When I gave him a sassy grin, he relaxed into me. "Was I hot as a hobo hobbit?" He asked, his voice lighter. "You said the beard was growing on you."

"It was. I kind of miss it, actually."

His arms came around me again. I could have stayed there forever, and probably would have if not for the knock on the door. It opened slowly.

"Mr. Banner? Your father requests your presence in the boardroom."

When I looked up, the receptionist eyed me with disgust. She seemed to have enough respect for the suit to not rip my hair out.

Tanner stepped back and took my hand. "Thank you, Ms. Burns. You may tell my father I'll be with him shortly."

She left the room, shooting me one last glare. I was beginning to understand where she got her name from. There were surely burn marks on my arms and neck.

When the door was closed once again, Tanner lost some of his confidence. "What do we do now? If I go back in there, I'm a puppet. If I don't, it's the end of Froyo."

"Tanner." I spoke carefully so he would listen carefully to what I said. "If you want to stay here and work for your family, we will make that work for us. If you want to leave and go back to Flagstaff, we will work things out for Froyo. You don't have to carry the weight of the world by yourself anymore. We can figure all this out together. You just have to stop overthinking every dang thing."

His brow furrowed.

"No!" I smacked his arm. "No thinking. What do you want to do right now?"

"Take you to the ocean," he blurted.

"I love it!" I smiled. "Then what?"

"Then go with you somewhere that will stamp your real passport?"

"Was that a question?"

"Well, what do you want to do next?"

I shook my head. "I don't even care. I just want to be where you are." I placed my palm on his chest. "Now go tell your dad to take a chill pill, and let's hit the beach. I've been dying to play in the waves since I got here, and this office building smells like sweaty gym socks."

Tanner laughed. He wrapped me all up in his arms, breathing deeply into my hair. "Okay," he said, finally pulling away. "I'm going to go quit. If you can drive here all alone, I can do this."

"Darn right you can," I said. "Do you want me to come with you?"

"Yes, but no." He squeezed my hand tightly before he let go. "Wait for me here. I don't want my dad to blame you for my decision any more than he already will."

"Then go get 'em, tiger." I slapped his butt with a hearty smack.

Tanner jumped. "What the—. I can't believe you just did that!" He laughed deep from his belly. "What am I going to do with you?"

"I have so many ideas!" I flung my hands in the air. "Now, go quit your job so we can get on with life!"

Tanner shook his head as he closed the door behind him. Before it shut all the way, he stuck his head back inside and grinned at me.

"In case you were wondering, I love you, too."

Ways Bailey Has Improved

Yeah, It Happened

While Tanner quit his job, I went to the window again to stare at the ocean of possibilities spread out in front of me. This was the beginning of a new beginning, and the perfect time to make my own list.

But first, I whipped out my phone to text Josef and Nancy so they would know I found Tanner and everything was alright. Then I texted the same thing, with romantic embellishments, to Sabrina and my family–including Marnie and Keith.

The fact that I so thoughtfully remembered to text everyone would definitely end up on the new list. Not number one though, that spot was reserved for conquering my fear and coming after Tanner.

Number two was for sure the part of the story where I didn't give up, even when Tanner gave me every reason in the world to go home crying.

Number three was my favorite one so far because I planned on gloating until the end of time that I was the one who said 'I love you' first.

And that's the truth.

Acknowledgments

Oh wow, this book was such a blast to write! I loved every single minute with Bailey's sass and Tanner's dry sense of humor. I am so thankful to Staci Olsen and Holli Anderson for loving it as much as I do and accepting it for publication!

Yay, Publishing Team!

I can't express enough appreciation to my editor, Bridget, for her constant care and feeding of this novel! Without all the fabulous suggestions and thought-provoking questions, this novel would be a very different beast. Bridget - you're the bestest editor in the world!

Even though this is the middle of my appreciation list, it is not a reflection of where my family fits on the gratitude scale. Very top, y'all! For putting up with me monologuing about plot for HOURS, for debating the hows and what fors, for listening to me read excerpts out loud and cracking up like I am seriously funny, for helping with chores and making meals - Chad and Kids, you are fantasticalsome and I love you the mostest of anybody!

It's always a little intimidating to bounce into a new genre; middle grade/young adult to rom-com is nothing to sneeze at. I'm so grateful for all the Alpha and Beta readers who gave me that extra confidence boost I needed. And especially for my parents who constantly convince me that I can do anything!

And to you, dear readers, for showing up - two gold stars! I'll give you another one if you can tell me what fairy tale Bailey's story hails from. :) Thank you, thank you, thank you!

About the Author

Cori Cooper always wanted an older brother, so maybe this story is her way of making herself feel better about that! (She has three little brothers, who aren't so little anymore. Big Fry, Medium Fry and Small Fry. They are adorable!)

Cori went to high school in the town this story is set in. It's kind of super fun to write about her hometown. (Some names of places were changed to respect the businesses.) It's also interesting to note how much a city can change. Just in the years it took this book to go from written to published, a lot of places are different. For example – "Juanicitas" isn't a food truck anymore. They have two brick and mortar locations now. Just some random facts, I'm sure you've waited your whole life to know this!

Besides cataloging the evolution of her hometown, Cori loves hanging out with her family. She's also a sucker for Jane Austen remakes, Musicals and 90's Romcoms. Try and guess how many of those the boys in the house will watch with her. If you said zero, you are just about right! Except for her puppers, Bandit. He'll watch anything for a belly scratch.

And to be fair, the other guys have been known to sit through Fiddler on the Roof. Tevya is just that good. :)

Cori loves writing stories. it is pretty muchthe funnest thing. Which makes you like a fairy godmother for reading and reviewing so that she has a reason to keep doing this.

THANK YOU!

Connect with Cori

Instagram, Bookbub, Goodreads, and her website www.coristories.com

If you liked this book, be sure to check out the others!

The Bake Believe Trilogy
Bake Believe – Bake Off – Bake Happy

The Senior Year at Cromer High Series
Sage Advice – The Importance of Being Roxie – The Perfect Girl for Kai – Gavin to the Rescue

Ways to Improve Baily
A Tale of Two Crushes
One Quarter Villain
Tears into Gold
Drama, Drama, Drama
Merry's Christmas

www.ingramcontent.com/pod-product-compliance
Lightning Source LLC
LaVergne TN
LVHW040040080526
838202LV00045B/3424